September

Jeanne!

Many blessings on your walk!

M. E. Peto

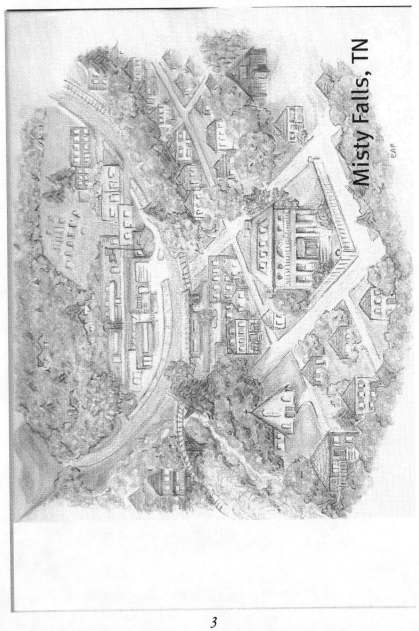

Misty Falls, TN

Winnie's Walk & Misty Falls: Journeys of Faith and Romance

By

M. E. Palmer

ISBN-13: 978-0615785714

I thank my editors, Stephen D. Palmer & MIchael Gilsdorf, my illus-
trators: Vivian Watson and Beth Ann Palmer, as well as my loving
husband, David Palmer, who was a great inspiration for me.
Thanks, also, to many friends and family members who have pre-
viewed Winnie's Walk and provided me wise feedback. Without this
team of helpers this book would be sadly lacking.

Winnie's Walk is dedicated to all who follow Jesus, past, present,
and those yet to hear the call. Disciples truly do comprise the great
cloud of witnesses that encourage us on our walk. I thank all Christ
followers who have crossed paths with me — teachers, neighbors,
family, church family — and helped me on my way. Blessings to all!

All Biblical quotes can be found in the NRSV, the NASB, or the NIV
Bible.

TABLE OF CONTENTS

List of Characters:

The Rev. Evangeline (Winnie) Taylor, pastor (former pastor) of Muddy Creek UMC

Winnie's Family
Claire (Taylor) O'Neill (married to Alex Kent O'Neill)
   Alexander (Derry) 5; Babsie 3
Paul Davis Taylor (Married Patricia (Tricia) Eleanor (Ellingsworth) Taylor
   Suzanna Marie, 8, (Suzzie)
   Paul Wesley, 5 (PW)
Jonathan C. Daniel, PHD (Professor of Philosophy at University of Chicago

Misty Falls citizens
Pearly Mae Moore (widow of Danny Moore) long time teacher/principal of David Crockett Elementary School
   Matt Moore, Dan Moore, sons
Tucker Joe Tennyson: owner of Friendlie's Foods, Misty Falls' grocery store
Nina Mattingly — RN, prize winning baker, widow; works for Dr. Sedgwick
Jillian Post: owner of Post's Antiques;
Mickey Allen Barrymore, sheriff; Jodi Lee, wife
Mayor Greeley

Muddy Creek United Methodist Church personalities
Clive Deborah and Weston, new pastor & wife
Gus (pharmacist) & Martha Reeves (works at Friendlie's Foods)
Tim & Mary Lou Owens
   Bubba (Thomas) — almost 8; Katelyn — 5; Andy 4; Carlie,
Sheryl Lynn and Kevin Thompson—
Matthew & Marva Lynn twins; 12 y.o.

Faith AME(African Methodist Episcopal) members
Tinsley Booker, pastor
Pearly Mae Moore
Miss Daisy (Gram) Livingston
   Keisha Livingston, daughter
   Trudy Livingston, granddaughter
      Kareem Lucas Livingston, Trudy's baby

Ebenezer Missionary Baptist Church in Kirby, TN

Pastor Henry & Sara Wilson
  Ned Wilson, cadet at USAF Academy
  Jason Wilson, Ned's younger brother

Oliver family
  George and Connie
        Samantha Rose & Shelby Ann, twin daughters
  Sallie, Connie's mother
  Tanya Oliver, George's ex-wife
  Missy Oliver Clancey, George & Tanya's youngest daughter

St. Luke's Presbyterian Church
  Rev. Allen Remington, pastor
  Theo and Mary Nell Smith
    Lucy Jane Smith-McPherson

First Baptist Church
  Pastor Kenneth Creighton & wife Janice
  Ruby Anders, owner of the Depot Diner
  Ms. Juanita Reynolds, owner of Countrified Cuisine

The Phineas Cobb Crusade team
    Rev. Phineas Cobb, evangelist
    Lydia and Malcolm James: musicians
    Jeremy Mc Kissen, business manager

Prologue

The news came fast. *Bad news does, doesn't it?* They say that bad news travels fast, and so it was for Winnie. Mark was gone. That was the reality of the news — he wouldn't return. He would never again sweep Winnie into his arms to hug and kiss her. She had just lost her dearest friend, and a great chapter of Winnie's life had snapped shut.

Shock was the word for such an event, yet shock was far too limited an expression to satisfactorily describe the pain, grief, and emptiness Winnie now knew. She would forever wonder how it was that the English language seemed quite unable to express the depth of her grief.

The first days, as the news rippled through the community that Lieutenant Colonel Mark Taylor had died in a training accident in the gulf, found Winnie and her kids surrounded by kind neighbors, Air Force friends, and, of course, their church friends. Everyone wanted to express the pain and sadness they felt for Winnie's loss. It was a tragedy for the whole community.

Whenever Mark had been deployed before, Winnie had assumed the head-of-house role and accomplished those necessary functions, but things were different this time — more permanent — with no hope of Mark's eventual return. Winnie was now the sole parent of her little family.

Winnie and Mark had shared the responsibility of raising Claire and Paul, their two teenagers. Mark had been especially wonderful as the strong, father figure for them. He was very clear about what his children needed to do to grow up, yet he was funny and lighthearted too with his beloved son and daughter. Winnie knew they would miss their daddy immensely; she also believed Mark had set some well-placed standards for them to strive for and to grow into.

Winnie's loss, like so many others who have lost someone really close, followed through the various steps of grief — denial, anger, some bargaining, depression, and finally accepting things as they now stood. Eventually Winnie's grief became less watery and more like a constant, nagging, shadowy companion that refused to leave.

Winnie found comfort in a number of sources, including her close neighbors, the Air Force community, and her church. Her church friends prayed with her and helped out however they could to make her way a little easier, even just lending a friendly, listening ear. Claire and Paul were grieving, too, and the three Taylors found some comfort just being together.

Initially Winnie felt as if the floor had fallen out from under her. She felt lost and alone, even when surrounded by others. She just wished someone would put a script in her hand, telling her what steps to take next. Without Mark to share confidences with, to discuss or even argue with everything seemed out of whack. Nothing about life felt the same anymore. The world for Winnie had changed the day Mark died, yet gradually she began to grope her way into a new life.

Winnie's day to day routine helped her, as she got up to see the kids off for school. Her usual activities were still there, and she should engage them. She accepted her piano students back. They came after school several days a week, so she had to be there for them. She still had church choir and Sunday school to prepare for; in fact she had been the lead teacher in Sunday school for several years.

The greatest solace Winnie realized came from her faith. She read Scripture daily and prayed and gradually found there was a difference between being "alone" and experiencing "solitude." Being alone was a horrifying feeling of lostness and being uncared for. This feeling of being totally alone was the first feeling Winnie knew as the reality as Mark's death began to sink into her consciousness. She felt being alone to a degree even when in the company of others, but it was especially evident when no one else was around.

Solitude became for Winnie a time she intentionally spent apart from others. This time grew in importance. It was a time of finding herself, again — that she, herself, was a whole person even without Mark. She could enjoy time in devotion — reading Christian books, Bible, prayer, and meditation. She even began writing her thoughts in a journal.

Slowly, Winnie began to find her footing. She missed Mark, of course, and she missed being married to him. She didn't consider herself not married, even though of course she was. It was more like Mark was away somewhere, and eventually he'd be coming back. She felt she should remain his exclusively as she had been over their seventeen years together.

One day it occurred to Winnie to go to seminary where she might seek a further degree that would lead to a position in the church, so she matriculated at seminary in Atlanta, not far from where they were living. Three weeks into the first semester, Winnie realized that seminary was more than she could have imagined — more enlightening, more interesting, more exciting, and much more demanding — and it was exactly what she could use to take her next step in her faith journey. She realized that she was being called into the pastoral ministry.

Prequel to Winnie's Walk: A Journey of Faith And Romance

A NEW APPOINTMENT

Rev. Evangeline "Winnie" Taylor first heard the name "Muddy Creek United Methodist Church" from her District Superintendent. He called to tell her that the cabinet had just met and determined that her next appointment would be at the United Methodist Church in Misty Falls, Tennessee not far from Knoxville.

Winnie had been expecting to hear from her superintendent after the unfortunate incident that had happened shortly after she had arrived at New Oaks UMC. That incident, and the vote by the Pastor Parish Relations Committee several months later to remove Winnie from her post, would add up to her moving to another church in June following annual conference.

"I think this is going to be a very good appointment for you, Winnie. Muddy Creek was planted just after the turn of the nineteenth century by one of our early, Methodist circuit riders, so it's one of Tennessee's oldest churches. There are several families who have been members of the church since it was planted; they are great-great grandchildren of the church founders," the D.S. told her.

"You'll like the parsonage, too," he continued. "It's located down the street from the church, so it's not on church property, *per se*. It has all the required amenities for a parsonage — four bedrooms, a study with an outside entrance, a kitchen, a family room, and a generous-sized living room/dining room. The backyard is fenced in, the garage has an electric door, and there is handicapped access to the house," the D.S. went on. "The church members have told me that they will be repainting the parsonage before you move in, and they are planning to have the linoleum flooring in the kitchen and bathrooms replaced soon.

"Pastor Neely has decided to retire this year at conference, so that is why this position is vacant. Neely has had a fine tenure at Muddy Creek, and I'm sure the members will miss him, but, from what I've been hearing, they are looking forward to having a new pastor come," the superintendent shared.

Winnie was listening with rapt attention, all the while trying to jot down details about her new appointment on an envelope as her superintendent spoke. She asked, "Have they ever had a woman pastor before?"

"No, you will be their first, but I have confidence that you can help the Muddy Creekers see that you have been called to preach the gospel to them. This church is a good church. They have a reputation in the conference for being mission oriented and supportive of their pastors, and they are generally considered a healthy, small church. They see some sixty worshipers on a Sunday, including every age from tiny to very senior," the D.S. reassured Winnie.

Winnie had been preaching and serving United Methodist Churches in and around Chattanooga, since she graduated from seminary, which was more than fifteen years, now. Most of the churches she served were small, country churches, except for the three years she had been appointed on staff at a big church in Chattanooga. So it wasn't exactly Winnie's first rodeo when trouble came in the form of an "angry man" — a misogynist with an axe to grind.

Winnie had been the first female preacher in churches twice before. In both of those cases she weathered any initial discomfort from some of her constituents and found that within a few months, everyone seemed to be pleased with her as their new woman pastor.

But New Oaks United Methodist Church was different. Adam, the angry man, was a music volunteer at church. He worked with the children, teaching them contemporary, Christian songs and accompanying them on his guitar. Adam was a self-taught musician, and he worked well with the children, but working with a woman pastor turned out to be something he didn't want to do.

Adam was a very large man, who prided himself in being able to get his way in certain situations by sheer force of will, temper, voice, and physique. He told Winnie that he had been able to influence people in significant positions of authority to see things his way several times in the past.

Winnie recalled one of Adam's anecdotes vividly.

"Boy you should have seen me!" Adam told Winnie. "I was up at the Boy Scout camp Saturday, to pick up Norman after his week at camp. He took me around the compound to show me the facility, and I was shocked at the rundown conditions! The camp must be a hundred years old!"

Winnie was amused at Adam's passionate description of the scout camp, but she listened to hear his story.

Fortunately I had my camera with me, and I got some good pictures of the place." Adam pulled out his camera and began to scroll through his recent pictures of the camp. "Look at this one!" Adam showed Winnie a picture of the showers built of corrugated fiber glass, which were partially falling apart. Winnie agreed that the showers were sadly in need of repair. "And look at the dining room," Adam insisted, showing more pictures of the room and the tables, which revealed heavy use.

Adam then related to Winnie how he had begun action against the Boy Scouts for allowing their camp to get into such a state. "How can they think our young boys should have to camp in such conditions?" Adam wanted to know. "I have already called Norman's scout master, and the man who is over him; I will keep calling people until I get someone who can do something about that camp!"

Adam was infuriated and implacable. His ire had been engaged, and he vowed he would not rest until someone on the top paid for the mistake.

When he returned home that day Adam called other people, and he didn't stop haranguing his invective until he had called the governor's office in Nashville.

Winnie never learned if Adam got the response he was looking for after his many calls, but she did remember later how Adam bragged, "I just wanted you to see how far I will go to make my point. I won't leave a stone unturned, if I think it might help my cause."

One day, about two months after Winnie had arrived at New Oaks Church, she opened her email to find a note from Adam saying, "Enough is enough is enough! I won't work with you anymore. I'm outta here! I quit all my jobs at the church. You can do it yourself — the children's choir, the new adult choir, the fish fry next month — all of it!"

Winnie immediately informed the chairperson of her PPRC about the email, and the chair responded by calling a committee meeting and inviting Adam to attend.

Everyone on the committee was eager to hear Adam's concern and to see how there could be some sort of resolution to it. After all, isn't that how Christians act? They work to resolve differences. Unfortunately, Adam wasn't interested in any sort of resolution. He stormed out of the meeting in a great huff telling everyone that he would not work with the woman pastor. Two of the committee members followed Adam out to the parking lot and pleaded with him to return and try to find a peaceful solution to his concerns, but his anger could not be assuaged.

So Adam was gone, but it was a very small town, and he was not really gone at all. After he marched away from the church, Adam began knocking on the doors of every home in the valley telling them how angry he was at the new Methodist pastor. He told a long story about how Winnie had thwarted his work at the church, and he tried to gain sympathy for his cause. But Adam didn't leave the matter at that; he called the superintendent and the bishop, to complain to them about the woman pastor they had sent to New Oaks.

Regardless of Adam's tantrums, the year went along quite well at the church without him, Winnie thought privately. Adam was gone, she thought, and so she turned her interests to being the best pastor she could be. The church held a four-day revival and a fish fry in September; both events were much fun. The new adult choir was well attended and added good energy to the worship service. The children's programs didn't suffer in Adam's absence. In fact, the kids worked on and presented two musical programs to the church that year under Winnie's direction.

The unfortunate incident with Adam inspired a second problem for Winnie, one which would leave her no tenure at New Oaks UMC.

Adam, who had left the church, was still very interested in seeing that Winnie lost her job there. He worked with a powerful family at church to see that she would not be around after conference. One of the family members, Patsy, happened to be a member of the PPRC, so it became her job to bring charges against their pastor.

The trumped up charges that Patsy leveled against the pastor included forcing Adam to leave the church, indiscriminately switching two children's solos for the Christmas play, and not keeping regular office hours. At the meeting a number of committee members spoke in defense of Pastor Winnie affirming that she excelled in preaching, teaching, and working with the community. She was a good pastor, and they were pleased to have her with them. Those voices seemed to be the saner, more thoughtful response, compared to the diatribe brought by Patsy against Pastor Taylor.

Two weeks later, before the next PPRC meeting came, Winnie was not concerned. She had complete confidence that this foolishness would be realized and that right would win out, so she was completely taken aback when the chair of the committee convened the meeting and announced that the PPR had only one purpose that evening — to determine Pastor Winnie's fate. Would she stay at New Oaks or be asked to leave? Only five people were in attendance the meeting, but their presence provided the necessary quorum. Winnie was in attendance, along with two of her strong advocates; the chair was also present, of course, as was Patsy.

Winnie's two friends voted that she remain at her post. Patsy voted for Winnie's removal, then the chair added, "I am abstaining, but I have the proxy votes of seven other committee members who are voting for Winnie's removal."

That was that. Winnie and Carolee, one of Pastor Winnie's strongest supporters, spoke in the parking lot after the meeting. "I can't believe what just happened in there!" Carolee admitted. "I had no idea this could happen!"

"I can't believe it either," Winnie agreed, "but maybe I had a foreshadowing of what was about to happen this morning when I was having devotions. I thought it was a bit coincidental when I read in 1 Corinthians. St. Paul wrote that he would be staying in Ephesus until Pentecost, because he was seeing effective ministry even in the face of difficult opposition."

Carolee, who was quite a Bible scholar herself, was intrigued with Winnie's reading that morning. "That is interesting, Pastor Winnie, because Pentecost comes right at annual conference this year, and that would be the time you will be leaving!"

Winnie nodded her head slowly and said, "Maybe that's a small prophesy from the Lord just for me today! I'll be here until Pentecost, and I'm doing effective ministry even in the face of serious opposition!"

Winnie sighed, "That was not a United Methodist action to vote on a pastor for dismissal. I've never heard of a UM pastor being 'let go' like that."

There it was; the vote had been cast; it was a *fait accompli*. Winnie would be moving in June to a new church.

While she remained incredulous at the events that would cause her to leave the church, Winnie didn't blame the general church community for what had happened, and she continued to serve them as their pastor until she moved in June.

It never occurred to Winnie that this strange turn of events was a sign for her to leave the ministry. Although some of her colleagues thought that she might leave, Winnie never entertained such a thought. As far as she was concerned, she was called to be Jesus' follower and to preach the good news of Jesus for all who would listen.

Winnie would put her finest efforts into her call, regardless of the circumstances, and she believed that when you set your course according to God's will, God will support you in that effort (cf, Ps. 37:4-6). So Winnie continued to serve her church to the best of her abilities, but she also looked forward to her new appointment and secretly believed it could be the best one yet; although the name seemed a bit wry. *Who really names a church Muddy Creek?*

Misty Falls

Misty Falls was not a thriving city or a sprawling metropolis. It was a small town — the sort of small town you wish you came from. Even if you don't come from the South and Southern is not your mother tongue, you'd like Misty Falls.

Misty Falls was a proud little town. At one point in her history she could claim to be one of the several key train stops in the entire south. Trains, coming from several directions, would pass through Misty Falls, leaving cargo and goods, picking up passengers on their way to the city, and returning others to their homes. The business was good, and Misty Falls grew strong.

By the time the Gold Rush invited hopeful pioneers to make a bid for Pike's Peak or the gold fields of California, Misty Falls was realizing her own gold in the railroad. Rails were constructed through the whole valley, connecting the Shenandoah Valley in Virginia all the way south to Mobile in Alabama.

In Misty Falls the train tracks hugged tight to Main Street, paralleling it through town. The rail business was responsible for nearly all the commerce in the town. It provided quick movement for cattle and other creatures destined for market and carried freight cars full of dry goods, mechanical products, mail, and produce coming from the great fruit basket of the South.

Many of the town residents found employment directly because of the railroad — traveling with and maintaining the trains back and forth along their routes. Many others made a living through the supporting businesses related to rails: craftsman who built the depot in 1850, workers and managers inside the depot once it was built, and employees of the hotel adjacent.

Passenger trains, too, joined the rail system. The day the first passenger train lumbered into Misty Falls and came to a lurching halt at the depot, it was welcomed by the entire, cheering community, including the mayor and an *ad hoc* town band. Parents dressed their children in their Sunday best and herded them to Main Street, as neighbors clamored for the best view through the gathering crowd to see the historic event of the first ever passenger train to arrive in Misty Falls.

In those days there was a general, almost palpable, feeling of electric optimism that buzzed around Misty Fallers as they seemed to be watching history unfold right before their very eyes. Already in their lifetime, they had seen the rise of steam powered boats and locomotives, the invention of the bicycle, the electric motor, photography, the refrigerator, the sewing machine, something called "rubber," the typewriter, and the safety match. There seemed to be a new contraption every time one opened the newspaper!

The passenger train was simply a spin-off from the other trains that the Misty Fallers had already come to count on to improve their lives, but passenger trains had something unique to offer as well: folks were now able to travel beyond their known, insular world and to venture into the unexplored realms of the world beyond — the infamous and enigmatic West!

Those were good times for Misty Falls, and it gained a longstanding, statewide reputation for being a good place to call home.

❊ ❊ ❊

Misty Falls' countryside was nothing short of beautiful and striking. It was graciously verdant and hilly, as you would expect the foothills of the Appalachians to be. It had been planted on the southeast side of McCurry Mountain, where the countryside was lush with life. The first white settlers arrived in the valley and identified plots of land at the base of the mountain, which was generously populated with live oak, evergreen, and a variety of deciduous trees. Every autumn the mountainside treated the townsfolk to a gorgeous display of color, as the trees turned gold, red, plum, and mauve, and the sight of McCurry's autumn hues inspired many an artist to strive to capture the autumn charm on canvas.

Main Street ran through the center of town, following the contour provided by McCurry Mountain — swooping along the mountain's southside then curving sharply northwest at the center of town. The train tracks paralleled Main Street until the road turned west, but the tracks continued south, describing a distinctive "Y" at the town centre and creating an ideal space for the train depot and hotel to be erected.

One of the most beloved spots in town was the cemetery. The first settlers to the area, who arrived about the time Jefferson was taking office for his second term as president, chose a fine location — carved from the forest of trees that stood at the base of the mountain — where they could put their dearly departed family members to rest.

The result, which took several generations to develop, was a place of spiritual peace and natural beauty. The forest had been cleared, and a circular track was drawn, describing the twenty-some acres of land. Grass carpeted the area, spanning the entire park, providing a lush underground for the ubiquitous, flowering bushes. The cemetery held the final memories of Misty Falls' citizenry symboled by grey-white granite markers of varying sizes. Sprinkled throughout the cemetery were several quite, substantial gravestones demarcating the "whose-who" of Misty Falls from various years.

As beautiful as it was, the cemetery had one vestige of old-time thinking — it was for white folks only. Gradually the community began to realize that cemeteries shouldn't be segregated, but that new enlightenment couldn't change the past, nor could it influence the places where Misty Fallers had come to rest. The past was past, and in this case, it was literally carved in stone.

McCurry Mountain stood north of town, and "Peace of Heaven Cemetery" nestled just south of the mountain, guarding the town's former residents. West of the cemetery, before one arrived at Main Street and the train tracks, was a swath of land, populated by the town's gentry. This section of Misty Falls described the upper end of town, the "right side" of the tracks, and the homes of the town's elite.

This area was generally understood as Northside Misty Falls, or simply Northside. It was the privileged portion of town, boasting paved sidewalks and street lamps. The homes had been built individually by their owner's forebears, and they were considerable. Each home was a classic, southern plantation home, complete with two-stories and an encircling veranda. Northside was planned well, made up of cul-de-sacs on which no more than a half-dozen homes stood, and the resulting, smaller communities, developed into cozy neighborhoods of good friends.

Several churches also stood in Northside. St. Luke's Cumberland Presbyterian Church, All Saints Lutheran, and Faith Baptist Church had each been planted on Northside. Muddy Creek Methodist Episcopal Church, too, had originally been built on Northside, but it was moved across the tracks to the newer section of town early in the twentieth century. Muddy Creek Church had been named for a young river that scurried down McCurry Mountain and flowed just at the edge of the land where the church was built. In the spring when the river ran its fastest the water would kick up the mud, lolling at the edges of the stream and folding them into the mix of tumbling rapids. The result, a muddy creek.

One of Muddy Creek's members, Mr. J. Herbert Reeves, owned all the land south of the tracks as far as the county road, several miles east. Reeves' grandparents were among the founding families in Misty Falls. They had farmed corn, beans, wheat, and hay for three generations. J. Herbert thought he would do business in a different manner, and he began to sell off his land to community developers.

J. Herbert's father, Jacob Alexander Reeves, had constructed his family's home close to the depot. It could have held its own among any of the homes on Northside, but Reeves had chosen to live on his land, so he built just south of the tracks. Around the turn of the twentieth century, as J. Herbert began selling his land to developers, he had his own house moved from the center of town to the center of his land.

Moving the two and a half-story, wooden mansion was a favorite legend in town. Everybody who could manage to get away from work, even for a short time, congregated around the workers to watch the slow process of transporting the mansion.

Many great trees had to be felled and moved to the house in order to roll the house inch by inch across the fields to its new location. Teams of horses had to be gathered and harnessed to be the engine that would move the house. After several days of hauling, the mansion came to rest at its current venue. It had made the journey intact, although it forever retained a slight list to the south.

It wasn't long after Reeves moved his mansion to its new location, that Muddy Creek Methodist Church also moved to Southside. No, the physical building was not transplanted, as Reeves' home had been, but when Reeves offered to donate five acres of land in the newly developing community to his church, the offer was considered too handsome to decline. Soon Muddy Creek Methodist Church had a new address in the town, but she retained the name of Muddy Creek as it would help carry her spirit with her as she now stood among the rapidly growing community on Southside. All the members worked together over several weeks before harvest one year to erect the new church building. This new edifice, made on an A-frame design and displaying a dozen stained-glass windows, quickly became one of the must-see sights when visiting town.

As time went on, the greater portion of the Misty Falls community occupied the southside of town. This new section of town was designed on a grid with numbered streets and avenues named after trees. Hundreds of homes — one story cottages and ranch style homes — were built as the development continued to grow.

When Winnie arrived, Misty Falls was still a good place to live and bring up a family. Its economy had managed to stay ahead of the troubles that plagued some communities. Surely the world of the railroad had morphed over the years, and the railway enterprise could no longer brag of having significant influence on the economy of Misty Falls; the hotel no longer existed, but still the depot functioned, albeit with a much smaller staff.

Several businesses provided good employment opportunities to many citizens — the paper mill, the rug mill, a uniform manufacturing shop, and a big utility company on the Tennessee River. Infrastructure businesses — the schools, stores, churches, and community officials filled out much of the rest of the economy.

The greatest employer, initially, had been the farms, but small farms were on the wane. There were yet several good-sized farms surrounding Misty Falls, but they were perennially struggling with the competition of the larger companies that could do business more efficiently.

One farm family, the Randalls, who were also members of Muddy Creek Church, had enjoyed a good-sized land grant during the Jackson era and had been farming their land for five generations. Eventually, they took up horse racing on the side. At first the horses were just a diversion from the more serious business of farming, but several of the family members enjoyed working with harness horses.

The Randalls managed to acquire a pair of promising standard bred mares and a stallion from good stock, and soon they began breeding their own harness horses. Walter and Eunice Randall worked with the horses, and within a dozen years they began to see encouraging results at the track. They trained the horses to be trotters and entered their fastest horses in the Louisville races. Racing meant traveling several hours with their horses in tow and setting aside a week of farming every time a race was held. The family treated these trips as holidays for the whole family, giving everyone a break from the normal, heavy work of the farm.

The Reeves and Randall families were members of Muddy Creek Church, and their extended kin populated a lion's portion of the church's membership. It was their church. Muddy Creek was where they had been baptized, married, and buried. Muddy Creek Church was where they enjoyed youth fellowship, celebrated Christmas and Easter, worked together in the Women's Society and the Men's Missionary Outreach. Needless to say, Muddy Creek was near and dear to many people in the Misty Falls community.

The Reeves and Randall families were among the first to hear that their beloved Pastor Neely had decided to retire from preaching. After eight good years, he would be leaving his post in June, and the very next week the bishop would be sending them a new pastor — a woman. A woman! The news was met with silence when the chair of the PPRC made the announcement. No one spoke until, finally, Homer Randall spoke up.

He cleared his voice and said, "Y'all ain't sure about this woman comin' to be our preacher, but I think we all need to give her a chance. I suggest we fig're how we c'n make her welcome in our community and here at Muddy Creek Church. If she's got the word of God to bring to us, wouldn't we be foolish if we chose not to hear her because of our particul'r, funny way of seeing things?!"

Homer's words set the mood for the church.

✳ ✳ ✳

After hearing about her new appointment, Winnie planned to make a "drive by" later in the week. It was a blustery Saturday in March when Winnie made her trip to Misty Falls. *Driving into town from the freeway is not as impressive as the superintendent suggested.* Winnie thought. The route into the town was lined by several blocks of empty stores. The parking lots were messy, and the fronts of the stores were boarded up and needed paint. *Not the greatest first impression.*

Of course the first thing Winnie wanted to see was the church, and she made a beeline right for it. The church stood on the corner of a large lot near the center of town, and was surrounded by several acres of green grass with a copse of pine trees on one corner of the lot. *The Sanctuary appears quite typical, a comfortable size. I wonder what it looks like inside? I bet that large, extension building is the fellowship hall or Sunday school wing.*

In front of the church, standing a dozen feet back from the sidewalk, was an old, rugged, wood cross with the traditional symbol of Lent on it — a purple drape that snapped back and forth in the chilly wind. Winnie wondered what sort of folks had put up the cross. Already she was looking forward to meeting them.

Winnie ducked her head down slightly and tried to maneuver her small, lime-green VW through the town as inconspicuously as possible. *I don't want to attract undue attention before my official introduction in June.* She noticed the rows of houses, most of which sported large gardens. *These people may have come into town from the farm, but they have not forgotten how to put out vegetables and flowers.* Winnie had been the beneficiary of other country gardening communities and hoped privately that she would again be recipient of garden delights in this new place. *One more reason to look forward to this new assignment.*

Winnie continued into the center of town where she parked her car. The old depot stood on Main Street, and from the looks of it, it had been there for a long time. There were two sets of train tracks that ran along the back side of the depot. As Winnie stood gazing at the train station she could hear the advance of a train. The whistle was already sounding, but the sound was so loud that she couldn't tell if the train was coming from her left or her right; all she was certain about was that it was definitely on its way! Within a minute the train appeared, and Winnie stood riveted to her spot on the boardwalk as it swooshed past her and on down the line.

"*Goodness,*" thought Winnie. *I wonder if anyone ever gets used to having such a calamitous noise in their backyard?* After the train had passed Winnie noticed the old hotel adjacent to the depot. Part of the hotel was now a museum for Misty Falls, and part of it was a diner. *History and lunch sounds like a great combination to me!*

Winnie spent the next few hours exploring the museum and enjoying lunch next door at the diner. She met a docent at the museum, who seemed to know everyone in town — at least she certainly gave that opinion to the visiting woman. Winnie thought she ought not drop her new appointment or her vocation on her helpful guide just now. After all, the appointment wasn't set in stone, and the bishop might change his mind about sending Winnie to pastor at Muddy Creek Church. No, Winnie would keep that bit of news to herself for the time being.

I think I'm going to like Misty Falls. Winnie could see the town and its community members would be like many other towns where she had pastored. The town's people would be similar: some good, some not so good, and all standing in the need of God's grace, just like we all are. She could feel herself beginning to grow hopeful about this new place to do ministry. *Surely the Lord has some ministry for me to do here! Maybe there's something special that He has in mind for me in this place.*

Chapter 1. Fall Festival

Two years later — September 2008.

Saturday will be a full day. Winnie mused as she prepared for Misty Falls' Fall Festival. There would be food, games, and artisans displaying their wares; there would be a cake walk and a pie baking contest, and there would be prizes and opportunities for every age visitor. Winnie was expecting to see all that the festival had to offer — meeting friends she would no doubt see and of course the pancakes. *I love pancakes!*

As she was about to leave her parsonage for the festival, Winnie's phone rang, snatching her from her reverie. The voice on the other end of the phone tickled her memory. Yes, there was something oddly familiar about the voice. It was deep and sonorous, obviously a man of maturity. It was a voice she didn't recognize immediately, but there was something pleasantly familiar about it. And then Winnie remembered. Yes! She knew the owner of the voice. It had belonged to one more youthful, but who had the same cadence of speech. It was John!

It seemed ages ago when Winnie and John were students at Mile High High School in Denver. They had shared a couple of the same classes, but they had not been friends back then. Nonetheless, Winnie had had a great crush on him! Surely he had been an impossible *objet d'amour.* It was a case of puppy love, of course, and at that time Winnie believed that John was completely "out of her league." He traveled in a different circle from hers, so she had to content herself with fascination of him from afar. She relished every detail about him — his blue-rimmed glasses, which matched the color of his eyes, his freckled face, his boyish grin, his intelligence.

"That first, impossible love is such a funny experience," Winnie thought, *"because, while it is a deeply personal and isolating experience, it seems, when I think of it now, to be a universal plight of teenagers. I imagine everyone falls in love, desperately in love, with someone who for the most part is out of reach when we're young."*

Winnie smiled as those silly thoughts rushed back — being so crazy for John the young man. *Boy, was that a long time ago!* She grinned and shook her head, even as she tried to concentrate on what John was saying on the phone.

"As I was saying," John continued, "I got your name and phone number from Roger Clemens. He's on Mile High's Fortieth Reunion

Committee and asked me to make a couple of calls inviting former graduates to join us at the party in October."

"Goodness! Can it be forty years since we graduated, already?" Winnie asked rhetorically. "I guess it has been. We graduated in '68, and it's well into 2008 now."

John and Winnie had had a couple of classes together — an honors English class, called The Essential Ideas Class, and several years of Latin, which included Junior Classical League.

"I do wonder, occasionally, what has happened to some of the people we knew back at Mile High High," Winnie responded. "Remember Mr. Gunther, our First Year Latin teacher?" "He was an odd fellow — probably pretty smart, although I don't think I thought so back then. I actually had him again for chemistry class my junior year! It didn't occur to me as such a strange thing back then, but isn't it a bit unusual for someone to teach both letters and science?" Winnie wondered aloud.

"You'd be surprised at how often that can occur, Winnie," John answered. "I have a couple of colleagues who are fluent in disparate disciplines. One fellow teaches Russian and philosophy here at University of Chicago, and another professor, a woman, whom I've not met, teaches anatomy at UC, but she is also a concert pianist, who travels around the world concertizing.

"I don't know if I was aware of old Gunther being that sort of multi-disciplined person back when we were in school," John admitted. "Of course, I didn't have him for chemistry."

"It's interesting to hear about those talented folks. Are you up in Chicago, yourself, now? Is that how you happen to know about University of Chicago personalities?" Winnie asked.

"Ah, I should have told you. "I'm a lecturer at Chicago — have been for nearly thirty years," John explained to Winnie.

"I shouldn't be surprised, John. You were certainly one of the notable scholars in our class back in Denver. What do you teach? Are you a professor now?" she wondered.

John was amused with Winnie's sudden queries. "Yes, I'm a professor; I teach philosophy at UC."

Winnie gulped and caught her breath. "Philosophy! Of course, philosophy! That was my favorite class of all back in school. Our Essential Ideas Class with Mr. Holder when we were seniors was totally awesome! It caused me to really think, maybe for the first time. It was also the hardest class I ever took, but it was clearly the best!

"Do you ever give our Essential Ideas Class credit for the direction you pursued?" Winnie suggested.

John laughed and said, "You could certainly be right about that. Before that class I was probably considering something in math or science for my future career, but that class was unique.I agree; it was hard, but it was the best!

"I remember you from those days. You sat over by the windows on the far side of the room, but I knew you were there!" John added.

"How do you like teaching today's young people?" Winnie asked. "Aren't they different from when we matriculated in school, especially with all the advantages of internet and computers and all?"

"The thinking is the same. Students still have to read and work with the material and develop their own understanding of the ideas, but they certainly do have a number of benefits from technology," John agreed.

Today's college students are much more technically savvy than we were in school, and it's odd for our older generation to have to look to the younger set to gain understanding in things technical. That's not supposed to happen. Young folks should learn from their elders, not the other way around! For today's young people the world is incredibly different from when we stepped onto our college campuses, or should I say "campi?" John teased.

"We'd have to admit there's been more than a generation change from the sixties to now. At least today's college kids aren't hippies! What a time that was!" Winnie added.

Their conversation continued on and on. No, John had not been caught up in the Viet Nam War himself. He had been in college when the draft lottery came up, but his number was 360! [Winnie remembered how the draft lottery worked, pulling birth dates out of a tumbling bin. The first birthdate selected was numbered "one;" the second date was numbered "two," etc. Apparently, John's birthdate was the 360th chosen.] He was never called to serve his country. "It would seem that I managed to skip that entire chapter in the American saga," John admitted.

John spoke about his work teaching philosophy to college students, or as he facetiously called it, "corrupting the youth" in reference to the indictment which killed Socrates.

Winnie was thinking it was about time to tell John that she was a United Methodist pastor herself, when something caused her to hold back.

John was talking about politics. He mentioned the upcoming elections and all the hype that was in the news regarding the state of the economy and how critical the elections were for the country.

"I heard some news reporters the other day speculating about the influence that the church might actually hold on Evangelical Christians voters. Could the church sway their vote?" Winnie asked.

"I really don't see right wing voters coming from any particular denomination, so I don't think church has any real authority. Of course, I don't believe in church," John admitted.

A red flag flew up in Winnie's mind when she heard those words, but she wasn't exactly sure how best to respond. Somehow, a straight-on, theologically-based apologetic was bound to get too far into the academic trenches and ruin what was otherwise a rather engaging phone call. Agreeing with him was certainly not an option for her. Instead she contemplated her response carefully and decided on a flanking maneuver — humor.

"What do you mean you don't believe in church? I've seen it, in fact there are several in our town!"

They both laughed, and Winnie's tension abated.

John changed the subject, "Have you heard about our high school's reunion coming up? Perhaps you'd like to attend; it will be the last weekend of October — the 24th and 25th."

"I hadn't heard about an official reunion," Winnie admitted, pleased that the subject had changed. "Although, it did occur to me a few months ago that we graduated in '68 — forty years ago — and that someone would probably organize something."

"Yes, there's a committee in Denver working on the details of the party. That's why Roger called and asked me to take a short list of names from our class to invite to the reunion."

"Hm. Let me guess," Winnie interjected, "Roger knew my whereabouts because of his sister Ivey. She and I have kept up with one another over the years, and she would know my phone number. Right?"

"See, it's not such a mystery, Winnie," John added. "I hope we will see you in Denver that weekend. Do you suppose you could make it?'

"You make it sound quite tempting," Winnie confessed. "I'll see what I can do about coming. Thanks for the invite!"

⁂ ⁂ ⁂

Well, that was pleasantly unexpected! After the phone call Winnie plunked down in her kitchen chair, stunned. She had not given John a thought in years, yet his voice had been good to hear; it seemed to linger on in her head.

John's phone call had pulled Winnie back to a time before Mark. *A thoroughly enjoyable call save that one odd comment about church. If I see him at the reunion I'll have to find a better way to deal with the subject."*

It was very out of character for Winnie not to tell the truth, and she was feeling a bit uneasy about it. But her little white lie seemed justified in light that it did avoid a possibly unfriendly disagreement about religion. *I'll tell him at a more opportune time.*

With that most interesting conversation still spinning in her head, Winnie left her house for the festival.

Misty Falls had been putting on a fall festival every year on the second Saturday of September since 1953. Winnie hadn't lived in the town back then, of course — she had only arrived in town two years before — but she was calling Misty Falls her home now, although she knew that as a newcomer she would always be an outsider, no matter how long she lived there.

One of the things that helped Winnie settle into new communities well was that she'd never met a stranger. Her mother had taught her that "people she didn't know were just friends she hadn't yet met." Keeping that in mind, Winnie met new people easily. She also had a knack for remembering names, which definitely helped her when meeting new folks. *It's always a compliment to others to be interested in them and to remember their names.*

She walked past Jodi Lee Barrymore's garden. She was an expert in roses and grew wonderful varieties and colors of roses in her garden. Jodi Lee had grown up on a farm outside town, and she knew gardening — when to plant, when to weed, what to fertilize with, when the rains would come, and, most importantly, how to diagnose and eliminate the dreaded Japanese Beetle. Jodi Lee often came to church Sundays bearing a bouquet of roses right from her yard. What a great way to share the wonderful garden God had given her!

The Fall Festival was known throughout the surrounding area as an event not to miss. The day's activities had begun with a five kilometer run or jog around town, ending back on Main Street. Following the jog would be a community pancake breakfast. Winnie wasn't happy about missing the pancakes — she was very fond of pancakes. She had looked forward to sinking her teeth into a small stack of light, towering, fluffy goodness, but her unexpected phone call had delayed her too long. *Oh well! Maybe I didn't really need those pancakes.*

As she sauntered toward Main Street, it was obvious that something was happening in town — cars were parked along every street — and scores of people were making their way toward the center of town.

Nina Mattingly stepped out of her family's well-loved Lincoln Town Car as Winnie passed by; she reached gingerly back inside her car to take out a special parcel — her effort for this year's pie baking contest.

Nina called out to Winnie when she saw her walking just ahead. "Winnie, wait up a minute!" she called out. Winnie turned around and walked over to see her friend. Nina set her pie carrier down, and the two women hugged. Then she picked up her pie in one hand and her bag in the other, and the two hooked arms as they strolled toward Main Street.

"Glad to see you this morning; actually I figured you'd be somewhere around today," Nina admitted.

"You can't live in Misty Falls and not attend the festival, can you? How long have you been coming to the festival? AND how many years have you won the grand prize for your pie?" Winnie asked pointing to the pie carrier.

"I haven't won first place <u>every</u> year! In fact I only took third place twice and runner-up another year, but I have been lucky to take the blue ribbon for my raspberry-apricot-walnut-crumb pie a number of times. Actually, I sometimes wonder if I shouldn't enter a different pie one year, just to see how I'd do."

"I don't know, Nina. Your raspberry-apricot-walnut-crumb pie is wonderful. Whoever said, 'If it's not broke, don't fix it?'" Winnie speculated.

Nina tilted her head, thought a moment, and then said, "That's good for a lot of things, but wouldn't it stifle creativity? Wouldn't we be boring if we never tried any new ways of doing things? I'll bet your God would say that, too. I'll bet your God would say He gave us a brain to use and be creative with." Nina winked at Winnie.

Winnie and Nina teased one another a lot. "That's one of the things I like about you, Nina. You keep me on my toes when it comes to things of faith," Winnie smiled back.

Actually, Winnie wasn't quite clear about where Nina stood when it came to matters of faith. Winnie had her suspicions about the source of Nina's resistance, but she was waiting for the right moment to explicitly address the issue. Nina always spoke, in this "left-handed" sort of way, as if she didn't believe, but then, she could surprise you by speaking about God when you didn't expect it. Winnie figured she should encourage Nina, however she could, about faith. The two women seemed to have an unspoken agreement that Nina could say whatever she wanted about things of faith, and Winnie would represent to the "party line."

The party line, of course, was the general understanding of "People Called Christian," which Winnie thoroughly espoused. She was known to share her convictions and her personal journey in faith, if anyone ever asked her, but that didn't seem to come up much outside of church.

The festival planners had invited dozens of vendors to come and share their crafts, hobbies, goodies, and treasures. A few blocks away, a very large, blue and white-striped tent had been erected just past Maple Street, for the community chicken and corn dinner, which would begin midday.

Nina was headed toward the pie-baking contest area to carry her (hoped-for) prize-winning pie; it would be judged later in the day. The two friends separated at the corner, and Winnie continued on her way up Main Street. Winnie stopped at Friendlie's Foods, the local grocery store. The store was open even during the festival. Tucker Joe (Tuck) Tennyson, the owner, looked up and greeted Winnie as she stepped inside. "Mornin' Miss Winnie," Tucker smiled.

"Good morning," Winnie responded. "Do you suppose you'll get much business today? With all the folks at the festival, you'll probably not have many serious shoppers."

Tuck chuckled and said, "Well, you may be right about me not gettin' serious shoppers, but I do 'speckt some folks 'll stop by, 'n this store c'n use all the traffic it c'n git. See! You came on in yerself! Would you like some coffee?"

Tuck had been hoping to develop a coffee house in his store. He fancied putting in something like a local Starbucks at Friendlie's Foods — a place for folks to congregate, enjoy a flavorful coffee and, maybe, add a sweet to accompany it.

"Sounds great! What do you have?" Winnie asked.

Tuck turned to a pot of freshly brewed coffee, poured a small Styrofoam cupful, and handed it to Winnie. "I'm fix'in' to add a new section over here (he motioned with his left hand in the direction of the front left corner of the store). I'm going to call it Friendlie's Foods' 'Koffee Klatch.' I'm puttin' in some tables to sit at, and a big ol' flat screen, m'be I'll add Wi-Fi. I fig'r I'll make this store into 'The Place To Be' in Misty Falls."

Winnie took the cup of coffee and tasted it. "Mmmmm! Nice. Sounds like you've been thinking about your Koffee Klatch for a while. That might be just what Misty Falls could use." She had another taste and then dropped her empty cup into a basket and exited the store. "Have a nice day, Tuck. Thanks for the coffee."

Winnie stepped out onto Main Street again and continued her walk through the festival. Main Street was four and a half blocks long with stores standing side by each on both sides of the street; the red brick shops looked as though they had conspired to look alike. Their large, square windows — two across each shop — were topped with blue awnings, which protected shoppers during inclement weather and today shaded the visitors from the sun. The businesses, including Friendlie's Foods grocery store, Hanson's Drug Emporium, Misty Falls' Library, Post's Antiques, Smith's Antique Parlor, Richard's Tools, Nell's Specialties, as well as the depot, Misty Falls' Museum, and the Depot Diner, were open and enjoying the extra traffic today. The place looked very different from Main Street's usual appearance; the many kiosks and tables, displaying various wares and appealing merchandise, invited people to stop, look, enjoy, and "take something home."

Winnie saw the face-painting table and recognized the McBride family there. Janie McBride, the eleven year old, was proudly showing off the large red and yellow butterflies that had been painted on each of her cheeks. Her younger sister, Dawn, a petite six year old, was struggling hard to sit still while her face was being painted. She had asked for a clown face, and it would take patient work by the artist to get the ever-widening lips drawn on her face. Already Dawn's entire face had been covered in white makeup. Her brother Michael was waiting for his turn next. Mom and Dad McBride stood beside the table watching their kids. They were glad to have a Saturday morning together that didn't involve the hassle of "house cleaning" — their usual family activity for Saturday.

The McBrides lived just across the street from Muddy Creek Church, and they occasionally attended worship there. Winnie exchanged pleasantries with the McBrides for several minutes before she continued on her way. As she walked down the road, she stopped and chatted to the vendors and took note of their enticing offerings.

A block further, taking up the whole width of the street, stood the chicken dinner tent. Winnie poked her head in and saw a busy crew of people moving around inside the tent, setting up for the meal. The sign outside the tent advertised that dinner would begin at 11. There were long rows of picnic benches and folding chairs for the festival goers to sit at. There was a makeshift kitchen at the end of the tent where the chicken and corn were cooking. The thick, aromatic cloud of roasted chicken spun Winnie back many years to the way her entire house smelled when her mother cooked a chicken all day in a pot. *Mother's chicken was always so well done, it fell completely off the bone, perfectly tender, saucy, and delicious.* Winnie savored that memory a few seconds before she let go the corner of the tent door and let it drop down. *Lunch will be worth the wait!*

As she stepped onto the street and looked back down Main Street, Winnie saw Kevin Thompson walking toward her. She knew Kevin from church. He and his family were also relatively new to Misty Falls and had joined Muddy Creek Church shortly before Winnie arrived. Kevin and Sheryl Lynn had twins, Matthew and Marva Lynn, who were twelve years old and just teetering on adolescence. Winnie was especially fond of the twins; they were gifted children. Matthew was a star at mathematics and baseball, making him very popular with the guys and a natural heart throb of the girls, and Marva Lynn had a wonderful talent for art and dance.

Kevin smiled at Miss Winnie and approached her. "Mornin', Pastor Winnie. How about this festival?"

"Wonderful! Are you here with your family?" Winnie asked.

"I am, though you can't tell. The rest of the family will be meeting me here for dinner in a few minutes." Kevin dropped his voice, "Say, since you're here, I'd like to ask you somethin'. Do you s'pose you could stop by my work about lunchtime sometime next week? I have something I need to talk to you about."

Winnie straightened up a bit at Kevin's request and said, "Of course. No problem. Is there a particular day that would be better for you?"

Kevin smiled and said, "Just any day this week, 'round noon. I c'n get off then, and we c'n talk."

Winnie assured Kevin she'd put it on her calendar — probably Tuesday or Wednesday.

Just then Sheryl Lynn and the twins arrived and the subject changed. They stood talking together as other folks began forming a line in front of the tent for dinner.

Winnie left the Thompsons in line; "See you in church tomorrow!" They agreed, "Tomorrow!"

Winnie left, wondering what Kevin might be up to. *Has something come up at home? I hope he and Sheryl Lynn are okay. Wonder what's on Kevin's mind? Hmmmm. Guess I'll just have to wait and see!*

✴ ✴ ✴

By four o'clock Winnie realized it was time for her to leave the festival and turn back home. It had been a good day, but there was more for her to do before it was over, and she needed to put her feet up before getting to work on her sermon. Unlike most people, who relax on Saturday nights, Winnie's Saturday evening was always dedicated to work.

As she opened her kitchen door, she was glad to be home, but she also felt the empty lifelessness of the house. Pansy, Winnie's dog, wasn't there to meet her as she always used to with her overly exuberant greeting. Winnie paused in the doorway and Pansy's absence just hung in the air — a big blank!

Pansy, Winnie's dog of fourteen years, had died suddenly a few months before. She had been alerted to a drama in her backyard, as the neighbor's portly, twenty-five pound Siamese cat streaked across the backyard in hot pursuit of a local, lawn bunny. Pansy was immediately at the ready to join the chase, but the elder dog within her was not. *"The spirit was willing but the flesh was weak"*, Winnie smiled at her misuse of that quote. Pansy ran full out after the two fleeting creatures, but by the time she had reached the end of the yard her heart had simply given out. It was sudden, unexpected, and sad, of course, for Winnie, yet she tried to see the best side of what had just happened — *at least Pansy had left this earth doing something she loved!* Pansy was gone, and Winnie realized she probably should look for a new dog for company.

An hour later, after she'd put her few dinner dishes back in their proper order and had sat her lap top on her lap, Winnie opened the document she'd been working on all week and began typing. She'd be ready, or as ready as she could be, by tomorrow morning. That's what happened every week, miracle of miracles! The endless treadmill of preparing a weekly sermon was both a joy and a stress as each and every sermon to be researched, prayed over, thought through, and readied for Sunday morning. *I'll come together; It always does.*

✳ ✳ ✳

It took Winnie several months to appreciate the fact that Muddy Creek Church was located "on the other side of the tracks." Yet it had been standing on that piece of land since the beginning of the twentieth century.

The church building was known for her exceptionally beautiful, stained glass windows of Christ. Twelve windows depicted the Lord from birth to ascension, including many, favorite scenes of miracles and wonders. Inside the sanctuary was covered in deep, rich, walnut-stained wood. The large, wooden beams shaped like the bottom of an upside down ship extended to a peak in the center of the ceiling.

Winnie had come to love the people of Muddy Creek United Methodist Church. It had been a nervous moment when she led her first worship service at the church. Being Muddy Creek's first woman preacher, Winnie understood there were some folks who were not convinced that a woman could be called to be a pastor. To their credit, there were a couple of "misleading" passages in the Bible that seemed to justify such a position. Winnie was sympathetic to her congregants' hesitation but warmed them slowly to the idea of a woman pastor by teaching, preaching, and leading the church faithfully.

33

That first Sunday in worship at Muddy Creek two years previous before her sermon Pastor Winnie called the children to come forward for a Children's Moment. She wanted them to understand that God wants us all to grow up. She started by asking the children if they remembered how babies act, and one little boy immediately responded with a loud "Waaaaaaa" sound. His pretend bawling surprised the congregation, and many parishioners laughed out loud. The child, realizing that he had just captured the floor, continued with his wailing to more and more chuckles from the audience. This continued on and on for several minutes, and Winnie wondered which was worse — the howling child or the hysterical adults? Finally Winnie gave up on ever actually finishing her "children's sermon" and put a stop to the scene by saying the magic church words that instantly hush any crowd — "Let us pray."

Everyone had had a good laugh, and somehow those chuckles seemed to act as a release of nervousness or anxiety that some in the congregation had been holding. They relaxed a bit and found themselves pleasantly absorbed in their new pastor's sermon and her distinctive, feminine perspective on things.

Chapter 2. Surprising Confessions

"Monday morning coffee — I love it!" Winnie declared audibly in the privacy of her own kitchen. *It's a very agreeable way to start the day.* Winnie recognized that she was among a small minority of people that actually *liked* Monday mornings, but ever since she had been preaching that's how it seemed to her.

Whereas most folks did not exactly rejoice on Monday mornings, Winnie relished them. After all, Monday morning was the farthest she could get from Sunday morning and her next sermon; she had a whole week to put together the new one. *Mondays are definitely good!*

The week ahead was filled with the things that regularly populated a pastor's days: some quick housekeeping, morning devotions, reading and studying, some administrative office work, making a few calls, the Tuesday Bible Study, Wednesday morning prayer meeting, and choir practice that evening. Additionally, she had two special events on the calendar — Kevin Thompson's requested meeting about a mysterious subject and the Misty Falls' pastors' meeting on Thursday evening

This week will move right along. There's plenty to give it shape! Winnie smiled.

✳ ✳ ✳

Winnie made sure to put her visit to Kevin early in the week. He hadn't mentioned it again, even though she saw the Thompsons at church Sunday, and Winnie was growing more and more curious to find out what he had in mind. She really couldn't imagine.

Might Kevin need to unload some burden he was carrying, some painful memory or some event he wasn't proud of? That certainly could be the case. Winnie had heard her share of such confessions over the years, and she recognized the position a pastor has to receive such disclosures and to help the owners realize the grace available through confession and acceptance of Christ's gift of forgiveness. When someone receives forgiveness for wrong actions or forgives others from hurting him or her, it is as if a fresh breeze has wafted into the room. Suddenly the burden is laid down, and there is a new, clean slate on which to write.

Winnie had seen this many times, and she had also experienced it in her own life. She knew the value of confession and forgiveness had for Christians, making it possible to follow Christ anew.

Just before noon on Tuesday Winnie appeared at the shop where Kevin worked. He was an electrical technician, and he worked on small appliances. He used to have his own shop repairing televisions, but with the new flat screen technology and the demise of the "tube television" he had to find a job where he could use his skill with electronics to make a living.

Kevin was already outside the shop waiting. They walked over to a bench on a side street and sat. After a couple of pleasantries, Kevin jumped into the issue. "Pastor Winnie, I need help, but I have to be sure that what I'm about to tell you will be held in the strictest of confidence. It's really important!"

"You can count on my discretion. If this is something you don't want talked about and it's not about you harming yourself, someone else, or breaking the law, then you don't have to worry about me telling a soul," Winnie assured Kevin.

Kevin chuckled aloud. "No, no, it's nothing like that. You see, Sheryl Lynn needs to get a divorce from her first husband." Kevin stopped to let his words sink in.

"Excuse me? Your wife needs a divorce? What...?" Winnie was incredulous.

"It was more n' fifteen years ago. Sheryl Lynn was young. She met this guy, this loser, at some dance, and they got high on some stuff. Next thing she knew she was married to him. She lived with the guy for a while, but he couldn't keep a job. Her folks were very upset. Eventually the two drifted apart, and Sheryl Lynn moved back home. There were no children.

"Then, a couple years later she and I met at a dance, and we hit it off — right from the start. Sheryl Lynn told me up front that she was married, but they were separated. That was fine with me. I really didn't think it was any big deal. That man wasn't part of her life anymore.

"Pastor Winnie, you have to understand that back then I was not a Christian, and it didn't occur to me that what we were doing wasn't right. I didn't figure that out until I became a believer in Christ a few years ago. By then we had moved to Misty Falls and joined Muddy Creek Church, and now we're part of the community. Everything is going good for us, and I don't want to mess any of that up. I don't know what to do, but I know we need to make things right somehow."

Winnie drank in every word, but she didn't say anything yet. She wanted to let Kevin tell his whole story.

"We're not rich people, and we don't have a lot of money to pay a lawyer. What can we do? I'm hoping you could find a lawyer and find out what it would cost for Sheryl Lynn to get a divorce, 'cause we'd like to git married right," Kevin finished his thought.

Winnie smiled comfortingly. "Goodness, Kevin! Who would have thought? I'll be glad to help. Being a pastor means I know lots of people!"

Winnie stood up and said, "Kevin, I'm glad you told me, you did the right thing."

Winnie was glad that Kevin had trusted this matter with her. No one at church had any idea that this family was anything but what they looked to be — a nice, intact family, complete with father, mother, and twins. There would be a terrible rumor loosed in the community if any of this matter leaked out — EVER!

***

Winnie tried to spend time every day in study and sermon prep. She knew herself well enough to realize that she was not the sort of person who could possibly put such preparation off to the last moment. It wasn't like when she was in school when she could cram the night before a test and come out pretty well. She did have a reasonably good memory for facts and numbers, but there was no way she could allow herself to wait until the eleventh hour to begin pulling a sermon together. She needed to have a considerable portion of her message well in mind BEFORE the weekend arrived. Then she could polish and practice delivering her message to her private, captive audience — a collection of stuffed sheep which she affectionally called her "flock."

***

Wednesday afternoon Winnie stopped by the library. As she approached the front door she saw her friend Nina arriving from the opposite way.

"I'm guessing you took top honors for your pie, again," Winnie said.

Nina grinned and admitted that her pie had been a success, but that she really did need to think about a different entry for next year. "I shall do some experimenting this year and see what I can come up with. Might you be interested in helping me with occasional taste-testing?"

Winnie's face lit up with smiles. "You know I would! I love pie! Just let me know when you're ready, and I'll bring my taste buds over. That's one test I won't mind at all!"

The two agreed, gave each other a hug, and Nina disappeared through the library doors.

As Nina entered the library, Pearly Mae Moore was exiting the building carrying a couple of volumes in her hand. Her appearance brought another big smile to Winnie.

"Afternoon, Miss Pearly Mae! Good to see you!"

Pearly Mae is one of the finest people in Misty Falls. She has a way of making everyone she meets welcome in her presence, and I always feel a bit better inside after having spent time with her. She truly has the gift of hospitality.

"Pleased to see you, too, Miss Winnie. Are you here at the library to research something, or maybe you're looking for something on the lighter side to read?" Pearly Mae asked.

"I suppose we both enjoy the library for a number of reasons, don't we?" Winnie agreed, noting the volumes tucked under Pearly Mae's arm. "Looks like you might be doing some research yourself today."

"Indeed I am, Miss Winnie. I like to keep up on a number of items, both past and present, and the library's a great place to do so." Pearly Mae nodded her head.

"When I was a younger woman, my Danny and I were very involved in civil rights activities, at least as much as we could from Misty Falls, and I still enjoy reading and learning about the personalities and the situations that populated our communities and made important changes for us black folks," Pearly Mae's eyes twinkled as she spoke. "Of course the story of civil rights hasn't seen the final chapter written yet, not by a long shot."

"Sounds like you and Danny were a part of history in the making! How remarkable!" Winnie answered. "Did you realize back then that you were actually walking into history? Did you ever meet anyone famous?"

"In most cases we did simple things around Misty Falls, but we also took the train up to D.C. late in August '63 and participated in that amazing gathering. The Southern Christian Leadership Conference was encouraging as many folks as possible attend the rally. They hoped it would be a peaceful means of promoting jobs and freedom. That sounded good to us, so we hopped on the train and joined the others up there.

"That Wednesday afternoon on the mall, downtown Washington D.C. we saw many people of note, and we were thrilled to see so many different people gathered, not just people of color, who were interested in equitable living for all. There were movie star, and politicians, and, of course, Dr. Martin Luther King, Jr," Pearly Mae remembered.

"I was personally touched by his speech that day, and I've tried to be a better person for it.

'You know, Miss Winnie, Dr. King inspired me to be known for the content of my character, more than the color of my skin. I loved his challenge to me; I think it's made me a better person." Pearly Mae smiled, remembering.

"Goodness, I think you've done that quite well," Winnie assured her friend. "Of course most people around here remember you for your work at school. I gather you taught fifth grade for some time. I'll bet you know a lot of folks here in this community for having been at the elementary school for so long." Winnie stated.

"I expect I do know a lot of Misty Fallers, maybe most of them. At least I knew them as they came through the school. I also spent my last years at David Crocket Elementary as the vice principal. I think I had nearly forty years, all told, in education. Getting educated and helping others go as far as they can in education has been my life-long fascination," Pearly Mae admitted.

After a few more minutes talking, the two friends wished one another well, and Winnie continued through the big library door.

Winnie stopped at the desk where Jodi Lee Barrymore was busy stacking books onto a cart. Jodi Lee, the head librarian, was the sheriff's wife and a longtime member of Muddy Creek Church.

Winnie lowered her voice and said to her, "Jodi Lee! Nice to see you!."

Jodi Lee looked up at Winnie and smiled. She was enjoying the first woman pastor at Muddy Creek Church. Before Winnie arrived Jodi Lee was not too sure what to think about a woman filling that position in the church. She had never met a woman who preached before. She'd heard there were such women, but she wasn't sure she liked the idea. "*Maybe women are not supposed to preach,*" Jodi Lee thought.

It had turned out to be a non-issue for her. Pastor Winnie was doing just fine. She was serious about her faith in Christ — in following the LORD — and she was serious about carrying out her duty as pastor of Muddy Creek Church. For Jodi Lee it was a "good match." Jodi Lee thought one of the reasons Pastor Winnie was doing so well was because she seemed genuinely interested in every person she met. She'd visited many of the church members, prayed with them, and she was slowly becoming part of the town "family."

"I ordered a book from the library system, and I wonder if it has arrived?" Winnie said. Winnie had good resources in her own library and online, but occasionally she found it helpful to read up on a subject that was coming up in her studies. The library was her resource for that.

Jodi Lee found the book had arrived and issued it to Winnie. "There you are; it will be due back here in two weeks."

Winnie thanked Jody Lee and exited the library. She drove around the corner and continued three blocks to the town center, which included the sheriff's office, the jail, the courthouse, and the volunteer fire department all housed together in a large, red brick building. Winnie stopped at the outer office where she found the sheriff's secretary working.

Janice Creighton was the wife of Ken Creighton, the pastor of First Baptist Church. Janice had been working for Sheriff Barrymore since James Roy, Creighton's youngest, had been in school full time — going on seven years now.

Winnie greeted Janice and asked if the sheriff was available to speak.

Janice pushed a button on her desk for the intercom and announced to the sheriff that Miss Winnie was in the front office.

"Have her come right in, Janice. The door is never closed to my pastor," the sheriff replied.

Winnie walked into the adjacent office and sat down in the chair opposite the sheriff's big desk. "I have a favor to ask of you." Winnie said.

"Sheriff Mickey Allen Bannister, at your service, Ma'am," he responded. "What might you need me to do?"

"Would that getting help is always so easy!" Winnie winked. "Actually I'm hoping you might be interested in helping out with games at the church family picnic end of next month. The ramada at the park has already been reserved for the church, and the food will come from the hospitality committee, but we need someone to honcho the games for the families. I know how well you work with our middle schoolers already, and I can't think of anyone who could better organize games for our picnic than you."

Mickey Allen, the tall, ruddy-complexioned sheriff, checked the date of the picnic on his calendar, and finding there was no conflict, said, "I think I can handle that, especially since I know I won't have to do it all by myself. I can get some of the other dads to lend a hand. I'll see who can bring what equipment — balls, horse shoes, that sort of stuff. Thanks for asking. Sounds like fun!"

Winnie knew that fellowship at Muddy Creek Church was an essential element of a faith community. *The family that plays together, stays together,* she said to herself. *Well, that's not really the saying, is it? It's really 'the family who prays together, stays together.' and that's, of course, true, but I think playing together as a church family is important, just the same.*

❋ ❋ ❋

Winnie finished her dinner Thursday, did a quick clean up of the dishes, jumped in her car and drove to First Baptist Church. She was meeting with several other pastors in town that evening to prepare for the upcoming community Thanksgiving service.

Winnie walked into the fellowship hall with Dwight Gantry, the pastor at Ebenezer Missionary Baptist Church, and Matthew Brand, the pastor at Grace Pentecostal Church.

The meeting proceeded quickly with Pastor Gantry reading the minutes from the last meeting. Then Pastor Allen Remington (from St. Luke's Cumberland Presbyterian Church) passed out a spreadsheet detailing the activity of the community Traveler's Aid Account. This fund was kept for the explicit purpose of aiding travelers who might find themselves stranded in Misty Falls. It was generated by gifts given at the semi-annual community-wide worship services. All the pastors in Misty Falls held vouchers that drew from this account, which were good for a tank of gas, a dinner, and/or an overnight stay at the local motel.

The main agenda item for this meeting was to set the date, time, location, and the preacher for the upcoming community-wide Thanksgiving service. Minister Tinsley Booker, of Faith African Methodist Episcopal (AME) Church , offered to host the celebration at his church. "We just completed the renovation of our fellowship hall, and we'd be so pleased to serve as host for the Thanksgiving community gathering," Booker offered.

Everyone in the room agreed and thanked Minister Tinsley for offering his church.

"I'm sure my people will be happy to hear that we'll be hosting the event end of November. Of course the host church isn't the one to provide the preacher, so I'd like to nominate Pastor Winnie Taylor to be our speaker," Tinsley suggested.

As Tinsley sat down Pastor Matthew Brand seconded the motion.

"Yes, we should hear Pastor Winnie, after all, she's our newest clergyperson here in Misty Falls, and she hasn't spoken at one of our community gatherings yet," Ken Creighton, the Baptist pastor, suggested.

It was decided by unanimous agreement that Pastor Taylor from Muddy Creek UMC would be the one to bring the message on the Sunday evening just before Thanksgiving.

So, Winnie was signed up to preach. *What an honor!* She thought privately, and then a moment later, *An extra sermon to prepare that week!* Her initial elation abated just a bit with the second realization.

Tinsley agreed to design the service and to prepare the bulletin for it. The music would be in the hands of music people from the various churches headed up by Joe Ed Rafferty, First Baptist's choir director.

A final prayer to close the meeting was in order when Pastor Allen Remington spoke up.

"I need to say something, but I'm not quite sure how to begin," he said. "I've been pondering this thing for a while. I made a mistake, and I need to tell y'all."

All eyes and ears were fixed on Brother Allen.

"Back in April our last community event was at St. Luke's, as you know. I had a good bit on my mind just then, and you could say I was distracted. Anyway, after the service everyone went over to Carter's Hall for fellowship. I remember talking to my trustee about the roof on our Sunday school building that was leaking. Another church member came over and the three of us talked in the corner for quite a while. By the time the ladies had cleaned up, and everyone else had taken off, I left for home.

"What I'm saying is that nobody picked up the offering that we took that night. It was still in the basket where it had been left in the sanctuary. The next morning I went to the sanctuary and looked for the basket with the collection, and the basket was there, but the money was gone. I thought, maybe, I'd put it somewhere different, but I couldn't remember if I had. I know I should have been more attentive about it, but obviously I wasn't."

Pastor Lorentzen asked, "So you think that someone else picked up the collection?"

"I thought something like that had happened. I know I would have been responsible for banking the collection the next day, but there wasn't anything to bank. I waited for a while, thinking something would show up, but nothing ever did. I waited and waited, and the money was just gone!"

"I know I should have said something about this before, but I didn't, and I owe y'all a great apology for that!"

A second later Tinsley chimed in, "I'm glad you shared this with us. It must have been a painful thing to have held it back for so long. I think we understand, and I for one accept your apology."

Everyone else in the room nodded or murmured a similar note of agreement to Pastor Remington. He smiled, weakly, and said, "Thank you Tinsley, for your kindness and the rest of you, too. I feel really foolish in all this, and the worst of it all is keeping it a secret for so long! How in the world did I ever think that was right? How in the world did I think I would be a good spiritual leader of my flock with that sort of thing hanging over my head?"

Dwight Gantry spoke up, "It sounds like someone helped his or herself to the offering that night. An opportunity arose; the money was lifted; a crime took place. I suppose we should bring this to Sheriff Barrymore's attention."

Matthew Brand said, "Brother Allen, we're all sinners. We all fail everyday, and we need the grace of God in Christ to pick us up, dust us off, and put us on the right path again. Thank you for sharing your pain with us, for trusting us with that. As far as I'm concerned, you are forgiven."

Again, nods were seen around the table. Allen Remington, whowas still standing, smiled and said, "This calls for prayer. Brother Kenneth, would you lead us?" At this the whole group bowed their heads while Kenneth prayed, thanking God for the gift of forgiveness and the wonder of the Holy Spirit, Who was working among them and in their community.

Winnie was full of deep thoughts on her way home that evening, but she felt good inside. She had been moved by Brother Allen's admission of failure, and she was pleased to see how well his story was received, accepted, and forgiven by his fellow pastors. *This is a good community to work and live in.*

* * *

Sunday began before dawn for Winnie as per usual since she began preaching. There was always much to do before people arrived at church, especially the final polishing of her sermon. Winnie liked to run through her message once in the sanctuary on Sunday morning, just to get a feel for the flow of her words, to secure within herself the direction she was going with it.

This morning she would be focusing on the times when people experience a "dark night of the soul" (as St. John of the Cross once put it) — a most painful time in life. Surely everyone has such an event at some time in their lives, and for some people, those dark times color much of what they live with every day.

It is Christ who brings healing and forgiveness, comfort and light, guidance and wisdom to us. When we look to Jesus, our Lord and Savior, for help, we find Him there for us, ready to reach into our world and make all things new again.

Winnie planned to use an example from her own childhood to help listeners identify with their own dark times. Her example was laughable now, fifty some years after the fact, but when she was in first grade the lie she told to her teacher and then to her mother was not funny. Winnie saw the lie expand and grow into a bigger and bigger monster with each retelling. By the end of the week Winnie was in a frightful place in her spirit. She was very confused and in pain until finally with great, heaving sobs she told her mother the truth. THEN! Suddenly the heavens seemed to open and the sun came out and shown down on her smiling. She was finally free of the lie, and all was once again well for her.

Winnie smiled and shook her head remembering that time, so very long ago, when she learned for the first time how painful sin can be and how wonderful the truth is, exposing the lie. It had been an important lesson to carry with her down the years, helping to remember the wisdom she learned at that tender age.

After church as Pastor Winnie stood at the entry of Muddy Creek's sanctuary shaking hands with her congregation, she heard several of her people whisper, "Thanks, I really needed to hear that." Winnie smiled and thanked her encouragers politely and sincerely. *The truth is I need to hear your words too.* She admitted to herself. In fact the occasional kind remark from a constituent went a long way to help Winnie when she struggled with her studies to find the right message for Sunday. Knowing that she had been helpful to others as they sought to follow the Lord provided Winnie reason to work hard each week.

Chapter 3. An Announcement

All the church had been abuzz with the news! Yesterday in Sunday School and at worship, Tim Owens made an announcement.

Tim and Mary Lou Owens had long been members at Muddy Creek Church — growing up in Misty Falls, going through school together, and being active in Muddy Creek's high school youth group. Tim continued on to state college, while Mary Lou joined her mother working at Misty Falls' Little Lambs Pre-School and Day Care. She married Tim when he returned to town and secured a position in management at a local factory. They had been married fifteen years and expected children. Goodness knows they were looking forward to having children, but none had come.

Winnie believed they had sought advice and help from several sources, but apparently to no avail. Winnie had met with the Owenses before, and she knew that having children had become a point of conflict for them. They had considered adoption, but that would be expensive, and they weren't sure it was right for them.

The announcement Tim made Sunday was about a cousin of his who lived down on the gulf. Tim's cousin and his wife had been in terrible automobile wreck the day before! The wife died instantly, and Tim's cousin wasn't expected to live. The whole church clutched as they absorbed the terrible news. Tim's announcement wasn't complete. It seems that Tim's cousin and his wife had four children, all under eight years old. The youngest was barely out of diapers. The children were with Tim's uncle and aunt, but they needed to be with their son who was lying in the Trauma ICU at the hospital.

Tim and Mary Lou would be driving to the gulf to pick up the kids and some of their belongings and carry them back to Misty Falls for the duration. They would be back in town in a couple of days as soon as they could get things arranged.

While Winnie was shocked and surprised along with everyone else that morning, she instinctively led the community in special prayers for Tim's cousin and his entire family as they struggled with this great trial. She asked God to give the Owens family strength, wisdom, and love as they picked up the responsibility of caring for the four young children. She also asked God's help for Muddy Creek as they sought ways to help Tim and Mary Lou respond to this unexpected challenge.

Please God, let Your joy win out in this season of sorrow!

❊ ❊ ❊

A couple days later Winnie stopped at Friendlie's Foods to pick up a couple items and saw Tuck gazing out the window. Winnie couldn't resist asking him, "Is there something out there that we all should be looking at?"

Tuck seemed not to hear her.

He's lost in thought, Winnie mused. She tried again. "Got something on your mind, Tucker Joe?"

Tuck turned around, saw Winnie standing there holding a small hand basket, and smiled. "I guess I was day dreaming," Tuck admitted.

"Sorry I woke you up" teased Winnie.

"No harm! I guess I was j'st thinkin'."

"It must have been deep thought. I've been standing here a couple of minutes, and you didn't see me. Was it a good dream?"

"It j'st might be the greatest dream," Tuck admitted.

"I won't be nosey, but you can tell me, if you'd like," Winnie offered.

"Can't say nothin' yet. Too many 'ifs' and 'ors' to say anything, but maybe things are gonna change," Tuck speculated.

"Sounds a bit mysterious," Winnie answered.

Tucker answered, "I was thinking about something I saw on my computer this morning. It may mean nothing, but, well, I'll have to see."

Winnie saw that Tucker Joe was back to thinking to himself. *Wonder what's got him dreaming?*

She turned back to her shopping, moving over to the vegetable section and spotted Miss Jillian Post, the owner of one of the antique shops in town. Jillian was coming toward her.

Jillian, who was an attractively dressed woman always fitted with the latest fashion and spiked heels, could be heard from across the apples saying, "Ms. Winnie, I see you over there pinching the tomatoes!"

I suppose she's jesting, Winnie thought. But just to be sure she said, "I'm not exactly pinching them; in fact I was just comparing this tomato (she held it up and turned it around) with a couple I was just given. I'm the thankful recipient of much produce — zucchinis, beans, corn, and tomatoes — from my church members. That's definitely one of the bennies I get for being a country pastor."

Jillian had stepped over to where Winnie was standing and picked up a beefsteak tomato herself. "I envy you for that!" Jillian admitted. "Whenever I can get homegrown veggies, especially tomatoes, it's a whole different taste experience than what we get from a store."

"I wonder what really makes the difference in the taste?" Winnie asked. "Sometimes really good-looking tomatoes have no taste at all! They're such a disappointment!"

"Miss Winnie, may I ask you a question?" Jillian ventured.

Winnie smiled, leaned a bit closer to Jillian, and said softly, "You can ask me anything you'd like."

"I just wondered if you'd ever had an email pen-pal — an ePal?" Jillian asked.

"I probably have a couple dozen friends that I might call ePen Pals these days. But maybe you're talking about someone outside the usual bunch of folks we regularly email, right?" Winnie asked.

Jillian dropped her voice a bit and said, "I'm talking about some-one I've never met in person."

Winnie had an idea where Jillian was headed with this thought. She said, "These days we have more ways of meeting people, what with all the fancy technology available, but I think you're asking me if I've ever 'met' someone online and begun a relationship there? Do you have someone specific in mind?" Winnie asked.

Jillian's enthusiasm was hard to squelch. She tried to hold in her news, but she realized that Winnie was intuiting her situation pretty well. "I don't think I'm at liberty to say much, just yet, but suffice it to say that, yes, I have met someone online, and I find myself spending more and more time thinking about him. I just wanted to know if you have ever known anyone like me, who has met a significant other that way?"

Winnie wanted to share Jillian's excitement, but she also thought she owed her a second opinion. "Sounds like you might be falling for this person!" (Jillian's eyes were opening widely, but she held her tongue.) "It might be pretty easy to fall for someone who sounds really interesting from afar, but how do you suppose you can really know such a person? We've both heard of situations when people have been duped by some-one presenting him or herself to be something he or she is not. I suppose you just have to be careful!"

Jillian smiled a bit mysteriously and said, "You're right, I do have someone in mind, but there's nothing specific to say yet. I met a man on-line in a chat room, and he does sound like a genuinely nice person. I think he has good values, and we have enjoyed emailing each other back and forth. I've never met him, and I don't know how we might ever meet. He lives quite a ways from here!"

Winnie lifted both her eyebrows and knitted them together. "Well, that does present several problems, beyond the usual boy meets girl sort of narrative. I do think, though, that you should ... just be careful!"

Afterward, Winnie was thoughtful about her conversation with Jillian. She hadn't known her very well before this encounter at Friendlie's

Winnie's Walk / Misty Falls: Journeys of Faith and Romance

Foods. Their exchange had shed light on the owner of Post's Antiques. Winnie wondered if Jillian was lonely. She certainly could be.

As Winnie stepped out of the store, she saw another woman walking toward her. She was tall and tanned, possibly from a trip to the beach. She was a strikingly pretty woman, obviously new to Misty Falls. She smiled down at Winnie as they passed.

She is definitely NOT from around here, Winnie thought.

✳ ✳ ✳

Two days later Winnie met Nina for lunch. They met at the diner next to the train depot. Nina was already waiting for Winnie, sitting in one of the side booths, sipping her iced tea.

"I see you've got a start on me, already," Winnie teased.

Ruby Anders, the diner owner, appeared and handed Winnie her menu. "Specials today are catfish fillets, meat loaf, and chicken fingers. Sides include fried okra, sliced tomatoes, smashed potatoes, collard greens, coleslaw, and pickled onions."

"Thanks, Miss Ruby. Sounds really good. I'll start with ice tea, unsweet, please," Winnie ordered.

Nina and Winnie met a couple years before, just after Winnie arrived in town. She had decided to take a walking tour of the town, which she had been told could be accomplished in about ninety minutes. Winnie took her dog, Pansy, with her on the walk. They found Nina sitting on a stone bench in the town cemetery.

"It's a pretty day to sit here," observed Winnie. Nina looked up and smiled at the newcomer. "Yes, I come here about once a week to spend time. It's very peaceful." Nina agreed.

Winnie said, "I suppose you live here in Misty Falls."

"Yes, I've been here for nearly a quarter century. I came here as a young wife and mother when my husband, Dan, was transferred here. We came from New Orleans, via Jackson."

"Do you still have family there?" Winnie asked.

"Not since Katrina. I do have a cousin over in Slidell and another by Lake Charles, but no one in New Orleans," Nina told her.

"This is the first time I've seen this cemetery. It's really peaceful," Winnie noted, pointing to the many beautiful azaleas and honeysuckles that were blooming.

"Yes, it belongs to the citizens of Misty Falls. It's been here since President Jackson's time, nestled up against Mc Curry Mountain. I guess you can learn a lot of Misty Falls' history just reading the headstones," Nina suggested.

"I'll have to do that. I want to learn all I can about Misty Falls. I'm new here," Winnie explained.

"I figured as much. I haven't seen you before. What brings you here?" Nina asked curiously.

"I'm the new pastor at Muddy Creek United Methodist Church," explained Winnie. I was just appointed to preach here in June. Are you a church person?"

"No. I don't do church." Nina admitted.

Winnie smiled and nodded her head. She intuited Nina's reasons and didn't want to force her new acquaintance to defend her position. Instead she decided to voice them for her. "I understand some people have been hurt by church people. That's very sad. I'm sorry if you've had a bad experience!"

Nina smiled in relief and changed the subject. "How do you like Misty Falls?"

"I do. This is a good town, and everyone seems to be friendly and welcoming. I do know, though, that I shall always be a newbie as far as the Misty Fallers are concerned," Winnie commented.

"Yes, me too. Just because I've been here more 'n two decades makes no difference to the natives here. I'm still 'new'; I'm still from somewhere else," agreed Nina. "But Dan is here," Nina explained, waving her hand toward a gray stone marker. "I didn't want to leave him here, and the kids were only half grown and in school when we lost him. So I stayed and raised them here."

"What do you do here." Winnie wanted to know.

"I'm a nurse, an RN. I work for Dr. Sedgwick over on First Avenue; I also work some weekends at the clinic in town."

Winnie smiled as she learned about this new acquaintance. She was a talented woman who had raised her family alone. "Are any of your kids still in the area?" she asked.

"Not in Misty Falls, but my son, Todd, lives within a couple of hours drive. So I see him pretty often. My daughter and her family are up in Illinois. I'd like to see them more often than I do. A grandmother needs to be able to see those grandchildren, don't you agree?"

"Yes! It's nice, if you can arrange it," Winnie said.

They talked on and on that afternoon. Nina joined Winnie and Pansy on their course around town pointing out landmarks and speaking of interesting personalities that Winnie, no doubt, would meet as she came to know Misty Falls better. The day closed with the two having dinner together at The Depot Diner next to the train station, and they had become fast friends.

They were back at the diner for lunch today and Winnie was pleased how their friendship had grown. She did wonder if there was a key to Nina's reluctance about things "spiritual," but she was determined to have patience and let Nina find her own way to tell her. *Maybe she will share her thoughts on spiritual matters with me one day,* Winnie hoped.

✳ ✳ ✳

Later at the office, Winnie found an attorney's website that looked promising, and she made a call. After explaining the situation to the lawyer, how she had a congregant who needed to find an inexpensive way to end a marriage, she heard the answer she was hoping to find. The lawyer would meet with the couple for half an hour for twenty-five dollars. They could explain the situation to him, and he would tell them what the cost would be to get the divorce. This would include the filing fees and whatever it took to get the agreement from the other spouse. This, of course, was all dependent on it being an uncontested divorce.

Winnie called Kevin with the news. He was pleased to hear about the attorney, and he promised his pastor that he and Sheryl Lynn would follow up on her work and see where it led them. They ended the conversation with much encouragement, hoping that there could be a wedding down the road after all had been said and done.

* * *

Church went well Sunday morning. Winnie seemed to re-discover each week that she really did like to preach! Despite being a normally gregarious person, Winnie had to consciously and physically fight her nervousness every Sunday prior to the moment she began to preach. After her first few sentences, however, she was completely engaged in the message, sharing with her community what she had been working on. She realized that when she found a message, and believed it was a good message, then it was a delight to share it with others. It was rather like a great story that she had come upon and now wanted to tell to everyone! It was fun, really; at least it was in hindsight.

Chapter 4. Trip Into Town

Sunday was exciting! Tim and Mary Lou Owens arrived at church with their four new charges in tow. The kids were, for the most part, quiet and shy, especially the two younger ones who clung to their aunt and uncle. Little Carlie, who was not yet three, held tightly to her Aunt Mary Lou with both hands. Mary Lou, as a brand new mother, could hardly move with this terrified three-year-old gripping her with such determination. She couldn't quite decide if it was better to simply carry the child on her hip or set her on the ground and hold her hand. Carlie had been crying, you could tell from the streaks of redness on her face, but she had settled down once she heard Tim starting the motor of his car for their ride to church.

Mary Lou also held the hand of Katelyn, Carlie's sister. Five year old Katelyn was also struggling with this new experience, but she was trying to be a big sister for her younger siblings. Katelyn carried a large, well-loved chocolate-colored teddy bear in her arms. She had been clinging to her bear since the accident, and Tim and Mary Lou recognized the wisdom of having her good friend bear close by.

Tim was leading the two brothers — Thomas and Andy. He had taken each boy by hand, affording himself nothing with which to operate doors. The boys were silent, trudging after their uncle like little sleep walkers.

The kids were dressed reasonably well, considering how this young family was new to Tim and Mary Lou. They had not been able to bring much of a wardrobe of clothes for the children, as they were limited by space in their car. The Owenses had been up for several hours working with the kids, getting them all ready for their first trip out, which would be to Muddy Creek Church. Having absolutely no experience in readying children for church, they felt rather proud of their managing all the details of dressing and fixing breakfast for the kids before they left the house.

Letitia Washington saw the new family approaching the Sunday school building and opened the door, welcoming them in. Letitia, being the mother of a four year old herself as well as a school teacher, responded immediately when she saw the need of settling these children into a Sunday school class and making them feel comfortable.

Letitia was an adult Sunday school teacher, so she sent word to her class to begin without her — that she would be coming before long. Then she led Mary Lou and the two younger kids — Andy and Carlie — to her son's class. Mary Lou stayed with them for the class.

Tim was able to find the primary class, which was the right group for Katelyn and Thomas. When they walked into their classroom and saw a dozen first and second grade children there, they seemed happy to join them.

The whole morning went well. The new Owens family stayed after worship for the fellowship dinner, and the kids played on the playground with some of their new friends from church. They were beginning to feel a bit less strange and different in this new world of theirs. Tim and Mary Lou had just leapt the first hurdle in the game of parenting, and they were pleased with themselves to see that they had managed so far with their new project.

❋ ❋ ❋

Tuesday afternoon Winnie saw the same pretty, tanned woman she had seen the week before outside Friendlie's Foods. She was exiting the post office and walking right toward her.

The two women stopped and spoke to each other for a few minutes.

"Are you new in town?" Winnie asked.

"Not really. I've been away for a while, but I grew up here," Lucy Jane answered.

Winnie smiled. "I'll bet your family is pleased that you're home. What brings you back here, if I may ask?"

Lucy explained, "My husband, Chet, was diagnosed with an aggressive form of cancer back in May, and in less than six weeks he was gone! It was the second marriage for both of us. Neither of us had any children, but we were hoping to start a family, and then this." Her voice trailed off.

Winnie listened to the young woman and silently heaved a sigh. "I know how painful it is to lose your husband. It hasn't been very long for you, and your grief is still very fresh. I know it doesn't help to hear this now, but in time it will hurt a little less. It's good that you came back to be with family."

After a short moment, Winnie changed the subject. "Are you working somewhere?"

Lucy looked up and said, "Yes, I was able to transfer my job with the Red Cross to their office over in the city. I have a twenty-five minute drive in the mornings, but it's not too bad. I'm glad to have the job, and I'm also glad to be here. I tell myself, 'It's gonna' be all right, Lucy Jane. This is just a really weird time in your life. You just have to hang in there.'"

Winnie picked up Lucy Jane's hand and gave it a squeeze. "You are a wise young woman, Miss Lucy Jane. I've known some widows who can't seem to get their heads around their loss, and they get stuck permanently in pain."

"Oh, I have my moments, sometimes days and days it seems, but I'm trying to see God's guiding me even in this time."

Winnie was pleased to hear these words of faith from Lucy. "You must be a woman of faith! Have you found a fellowship here in town?"

Lucy explained that she was attending church with her family — her father, her aunt, her brother and his family. They were long-time members of St. Luke's Cumberland Presbyterian Church.

The two new friends stood chatting for several minutes more before they went their separate ways.

What an interesting woman! A new widow, but so young. Poor dear! She was smart to come home and start over, Winnie mused. She knew she would have good emotional support with her family and her church family close by.

✳ ✳ ✳

Winnie decided to stop by St. Luke's to check up on her friend Pastor Allen Remington. After his surprising admission at the meeting a couple weeks ago, she expected he would have met with Sheriff Barrymore to start an investigation. She hoped things would get ironed out or settled without much ado.

Winnie rang the bell and opened the door when the buzzer indicated it was unlocking. The pastor's office was just down the hall. Winnie saw the door was ajar, and she peeked in.

"Hi Allen!" Winnie called.

Pastor Allen, looked up, saw it was Winnie, smiled broadly, and said, "Well! Good to see you, too, Winnie. Come on in!"

Winnie advanced to a chair in the office opposite the pastor's chair and sat down.

"What can I do for you this fine day?"

"That's what I came to ask you, Allen," Winnie explained. "Your quandary has been on my mind, and I wanted to know how things are going for you now?"

"Oh! Yes. Actually Ken and Tinsley went with me over to see Sheriff Barrymore the next day, and I put in a complaint about the missing funds. The sheriff agreed that the trail was pretty cold, but he logged the complaint and followed me back here. He looked all around the sanctuary to see how things are: where the collection plates were stored; where they had been placed after taking the offering that evening; where the side door to the chancel is located; if it had a lock on it; was there a separate door exiting the building that was not through the fellowship area, etc."

"He said he was afraid that the money might never be accounted for, especially given the tardiness of my reporting the crime. I think he's just going to let it go, and not pursue any legal claim against me," Pastor Allen explained.

Winnie's face showed relief, and she said, "I'm sure he's right about that. What good would that accomplish to indict you for forgetfulness? We know you didn't purposefully hide the money from yourself."

Winnie was pleased to learn that the matter had been noted officially with the sheriff. She said, "Sounds like y'all were able to set the record straight on the incident. Goodness knows if the thief can be caught, but at least you've done what you can for now."

Pastor Allen seemed much lighter of spirit today in contrast to his mood at the meeting. "Glad you stopped by, Winnie," he said as she turned to leave his office.

✳ ✳ ✳

Winnie drove into the city later that week. She took Trudy, a young, African American mother-to-be, to the free clinic for an appointment. Winnie dropped her off at the office while she made several stops she needed to make in town.

The mall was one of those stops. Winnie was on the second floor of the mall when she spotted Tucker Joe Tennyson in front of her, just coming out of a store.

"Well! For goodness sakes! Tucker Joe! Are you here, too? I didn't know you took time off!"

Tuck grinned at Winnie and said, "Yes! In fact I'm gettin' a regular day off nowadays. I can leave the store in Martha Reeves' care. She's been with Mother and me at the store for over twenty years. She knows the store inside and out. I've been taking Thursdays off, just for me, since ...."

Winnie caught the drift of what Tucker was saying, "Since we lost Mother?"

"Yes, since we lost Mother. It's not that I couldn't take time off before, I could. But it was more often an afternoon, or a couple hours here or there. When you own a store, it's hard to git time off. Mother and I worked the store together ever since Pappy passed. He and Mother built the store and put their blood, sweat, and tears in it. I always owed it to Mother to lean into the job and make it good for both of them."

"And now you can find a whole day to take off. Sounds good to me. We all need time off from work occasionally. Even on a regular basis. What's that saying, 'all work and no play makes Jack a dull boy?'" Winnie teased.

"There's wisdom in that saying, I'm sure," Tuck agreed. "Anyway I'm here, and it feels good."

"That sounds like a fun change for you," Winnie observed. She was about to say, "since you lost your mother," but she thought better of it and didn't.

Winnie was aware that there are some men who don't marry until their mothers had passed on. She couldn't quite figure out why a man would wait so long, sometimes even into his fifties or so, but she had heard it happens, and she wondered if that might be the case here.

Winnie said, "Your family's from Misty Falls, isn't it? How many years have the Tennyson's been here?"

"On my father's side my family goes back five generations. My great-great grandfather was the first Tennyson to settle in this area. On Mother's side we go back four generations in this area. Mother's folks came from North Carolina. Back then they were all farmers, of course. They had a land grant from Jackson, like several families around here," Tucker explained.

"Your roots really run deep! You must know absolutely everyone in Misty Falls," Winnie said.

"I guess I do know a lot of folks, 'specially the ones I knew growing up. We go back a long way. But there are new folks these days I don't know much at all. Course, I know you! You're an easy one to get to know, Miss Winnie," Tucker assured her.

The wheels in Winnie's mind spun, and she figured that Tucker might know something about the woman she'd met earlier at the post office, and she wondered how to ask him, without sounding like she was insinuating herself where she didn't belong. "You would know a family named Smith, then. I just heard about them the other day," said Winnie.

"Smith! I'll bet there are a dozen Smith families in just this county, maybe more!" Tucker laughed.

"I met a really sweet woman the other day who told me she had just returned from somewhere out of state to live here. She said that she'd grown up here. Her maiden name was Smith," Winnie explained.

"You met Lucy Jane, did you! I heard she was back in Misty Falls. I haven't seen her in years. We knew each other in school. She was a year ahead of me, but we both played in the band in high school. I haven't heard much about her since she left, but she sure was a cutie when I knew her!" Tucker laughed.

Winnie could see all sorts of possibilities for the two of them down the road. She thought, *Who knows what might come of this*!

✳ ✳ ✳

On her way back to the clinic to pick up Trudy, Winnie noticed several of the cars ahead of her were swerving as if to avoid something on the road. The car in front of Winnie moved aside, and suddenly Winnie saw a small, very furry dog running around in the middle of the street not knowing which way to go. Winnie was nearly at the corner, so she maneuvered her car around the bend, slowed to a stop, and opened her car door.

As she opened the door the small, furry creature jumped into her lap!

"Goodness! Who are you?" Winnie asked the pup. she closed the door, so the pup wouldn't jump out again into further danger on the road.

"You are nothing more than a bit!" Winnie told her. "What in the world am I supposed to do with you? You're not in the least like any dog I've ever seen before!" The puppy was sitting on Winnie's lap; she patted the pup's fly-away hair and noticed how very soft it was — like very fine, silky strands, thickly clumped together and sticking straight out from her body. The result of all this fine, thick mop of fur made the pup look about twice as big as she actually was.

"Goodness, Doggy, you've just begun in this life, and I'm sure there's a lot of work needed to properly care for you. Hmmmmm. I think maybe the LORD has answered my prayer about a companion in an unexpected way!"

Winnie talked to the pup all the way to the clinic, where she picked up Trudy. She told Trudy "I'll have to make some inquiries about this dog's ownership, but I have a feeling that my household has just increased by one!"

Trudy thanked Miss Winnie for driving her to the clinic and said something about coming to Muddy Creek for worship one of these days. Winnie always wondered what folks who say "I'll come [to church]" actually do when Sunday morning rolls around. "Do you suppose they are even aware that it's Sunday morning, and the thing to be doing is getting

yourself to worship?" she asked the little pup.

Chapter 5. An Unexpected Delivery

Life with the pup, who soon came to be known as Bitty, brought back memories of other dogs from other times for Winnie. She had not trained a puppy in years, but the pup's needs were pretty obvious. She needed to be fed, watered, exercised, and TRAINED for the house!

Bitty was a smart little pooch. She was friendly, as puppies are, and she very quickly became a great companion to Winnie. It wasn't long before Bitty was thoroughly familiar with her new home surroundings. She seemed to delight in racing full out through the parsonage, chasing after some unknown, illusive playmate. She would race in circles, round and round, in the open areas in the living room, and then she'd turn back to the bedrooms and zip around each room, as if she had a pre-planned par course she must accomplish in record time. Watching such activity in the new pup caused Winnie to shake her head and laugh, "Bitty you are a terrible scamp! Where do you get so much energy?"

Winnie realized that most of the dog paraphernalia she had on hand was too big for Bitty. Pansy hadn't been all that big a dog, but she was grown, and her accouterments were too big. Winnie made a quick stop at Friendlie's Foods' pet section and picked up a couple of items that would tide them over. "I don't know that I'm ready for you to be here. I didn't exactly choose you! But it seems, like it or not, I guess you're here to stay!" Winnie told to the little dog.

Winnie mused that the good Lord surely loved all His creatures. "He helped you find a place where you'll be cared for," she told the pup.

Bitty was not a very large dog, but her fur stuck straight out all over her, and it was especially thick around her neck and tail. "Wonder what sort of pooch you are? You look like you got into an altercation with an electrical outlet and lost the battle! Your hair is an absolute mess! No matter, it's nice to have you around," she assured the dog.

* * *

Sunday had gone well, thankfully. The Owens family was back in church. Tim told his Sunday school class about the adventures he and Mary Lou were having being parents so unexpectedly. He said he'd heard from his uncle, the children's grandfather, who reported that the children's father wasn't expected to live; he was still in a coma from the accident — there was no indication of brain activity. Tim thought he'd be hearing more news soon from his uncle and the family would need to make another trip to the gulf soon when the news came.

Tim said that the kids were doing pretty well, considering the great change in their lives. The older two were settling into school, and the two pre-schoolers were with Mary Lou at the day care where she worked. Tim thanked everyone for their prayers and encouragement and mentioned the sizes of the kids, in case anyone had any hand-me-downs. The Owenses had brought clothes from their home on the gulf, but these children were growing, and new clothes would be needed soon.

✳ ✳ ✳

Wednesday afternoon Winnie was just getting out of her car having been out most of the afternoon, when she noticed something sitting next to the front door, something apparently left by a delivery person. *Wonder what it could be?*

Winnie jumped out of her car and went over to retrieve the package. It had her name on it: "Ms. Winnie Taylor."

The return address had only a street, city, and zip code, no name. *How curious!* She wasted no time in tearing open the brown paper wrapping and pulling out a book.

Who's sending me a book? The volume was small, soft cover, with a blue-toned picture of a lake with a dock and a large bird winging its way over the water. The title was *Finding Your Moorings* by Jonathan C. Daniel, Ph.D.

"That's John!" Winnie exclaimed to the air. "This must be one of his books! He did say that he also wrote along with his teaching."

Winnie opened the book and saw an inscription on the inside cover:

"To find one true friend in a lifetime is good fortune; to keep him is a blessing." — Baltazar Gracian, 17 C Spanish philosopher. Here's to friendship! Yours, John."

Goodness! He just sent me a present — that's an intriguing move! Winnie flipped through the book. It was filled with one page thoughts, almost like those in her morning devotional books, but, of course, these thoughts were not based on holy scripture. The book did have wisdom from various sources that were highlighted a day at a time. *This is a sort of 'Devotional for the Armchair Philosopher,* thought Winnie. "This should be fun!" She chuckled out loud.

Although John and Winnie had attended the same high school and even been in a couple classes together, they had not been friends — not back then. John, Winnie remembered, had been part of a small group of young men at her school who were exceptionally gifted. The seven or eight of them started a very exclusive club they called The Oligarchy. It wasn't an official club on campus, but they were well known, nonetheless. They were the top students in the Class of 68, taking all the honors classes, and they would, no doubt, be among the leaders of tomorrow.

I haven't thought about those guys forever! Winnie smiled. *"Wonder what became of them? No doubt they have all gone their separate ways since graduation.*

Winnie had found the announcement of Mile High High School's Fortieth Year Reunion on Facebook, as John had told her. Winnie had attended the fifth and the tenth high school reunion. She missed the later ones — the twentieth and the thirtieth reunion — and she didn't realize it was time for the fortieth reunion until John called and mentioned it. *It would be fun to attend,* Winnie thought. *You never know who'll show up to those events, AND of course, I could use the opportunity to check up on my folks.*

Attending a reunion could coincide with a trip to see Mom and Dad. They were still living in their home in Denver, and Winnie looked for reasons to visit them. *Coupling such a visit with my high school reunion would make it a double blessing.* She decided to make arrangements to go. *I'll have to find a substitute preacher for that Sunday!*

❊ ❊ ❊

Thursday afternoon Winnie stopped at the bank and was greeted by Bradley Washington, the bank manager and a member at Muddy Creek Church.

"Afternoon, Pastor Winnie," he said. "Are you coming to see me today?"

"Good to see you, Bradley," Winnie answered. "Actually, I'm here to make a deposit. I don't have any pressing bank business today. How's your family?"

Letitia Washington, Bradley's wife, had a father who was a Baptist pastor in South Carolina. Letitia was a third grade teacher at the David Crockett Elementary School in town; she also taught the adult Sunday school class at church. Bradley and Letitia had a four year old son they called Little Brad.

"Little Brad comes home every day from his preschool with new questions. He's about to drive us crazy with his 'Why questions!' 'Why is the sky blue?' 'Why do I get thirsty?' 'Why do you go to work?' 'Why are there bugs in the garden?'" Bradley told Winnie.

Winnie laughed with Bradley at this long list of impossible questions Little Brad was plaguing his parents with. "Sounds like questions my own kids asked when they were about that age. The questions will change, of course, but the challenge continues: "How do I raise my child in the nurture and admonition of the LORD?"

Bradley winked at Winnie, nodded his head, and returned to his office.

As Winnie stepped in line to make her deposit, Vicky Jackson, who was standing two people in front of her, saw her pastor. She turned around and said, "Pastor Winnie, wait for me a minute when we're through here, would you?"

A few minutes later the two women met in the vestibule of the bank and spoke.

Vicky spoke first. "Pastor Winnie, I just got some news!"

Winnie noticed that Vicky was looking serious. She asked, "What sort of news?"

Vicky nodded and explained. "We just heard that our shop is about to be bought by another business, and most of us will lose our jobs! Things don't look very good at the moment."

"How long have you known about this? Who else knows?" Winnie asked.

"I told Tom, of course, and the boys. It's just speculation, but we need to be prepared for whatever" Vicky confided.

Winnie asked Vicky, "What, exactly, does your shop do?"

"We make custom draperies for retail stores, mostly, although we can do custom work for designers, too. Our shop is being bought out by a bigger business."

"Maybe your news will turn out not to be news, after all," Winnie suggested. "I'd like to know what will happen. Please keep me informed, and let me know if there is anything I or the church can do."

Winnie was thoughtful after her bank visit. *Sometimes it feels as if I'm living on the edge of life these days, like I'm watching everyone else living. The Washingtons and the Jacksons have their beautiful families to work with. Of course, I've already done all those parenting things, and Claire and Paul and their families are doing well on their own now. I wouldn't have it any other way. They are both off doing what they should be doing in their respective worlds.*

Winnie! Are you feeling sorry for yourself? Do you really think life is leaving you on the sidelines? You really do need to ask the Lord for forgiveness, if that's what you're carrying around with you! AND you also know that the He has great plans for you, even at your advanced age! You just need to be on the look out for them. Maybe that's what the Lord meant when he warned us to stay awake and watch!

* * *

The next day Winnie answered a phone call in her office from a woman in the city twenty minutes from Misty Falls.

The woman, who identified herself as Ms. Betty Hawkins from the mayor's office, asked to speak to the pastor in charge.

Winnie smiled to herself and told Ms. Hawkins that she, Pastor Winnie Taylor, was that person. "How can I help you?"

Ms. Hawkins explained that she was calling from the Public Relations Department of the mayor's office. She was looking for a church that would be willing to accommodate a group of peace walkers making a trek across America. The walkers were on a mission of peace, carrying a flame from the city of Hiroshima, Japan all the way to Ground Level Zero in New York City. They had begun their American trek in Seattle about eight months ago. Their route took them down the West Coast and then across the South before scooping back up the East Coast to New York.

The twenty-two walkers, who were led by six Japanese, Buddhist monks, needed to be able to lay their sleeping bags down somewhere for the night. They had been averaging between fifteen and twenty miles each day on their long trek and had been staying each night at various churches. (A truck would bringing the walkers' provisions to their new overnight location each day.)

Ms. Hawkins explained that Muddy Creek was the first church she had contacted in Misty Falls to ask for help. "Would your church allow these travelers to use Muddy Creek Church as a place to stop for the night?" she asked Winnie. "Oh! And they would appreciate having a nice breakfast made for them the next morning that would give them a good send off for their next day's walk." Ms. Hawkins added, "And they have a special request. They would really like to have grits on the menu; they've heard about grits and would like to experience the real thing, southern style!"

Winnie wondered as she put down her phone how her members would react to such a request. She had promised Ms. Hawkins that she would ask the people at Muddy Creek this coming Sunday if they thought this was something they could manage to do. She couldn't speak for them without asking first. She'd call Ms. Hawkins as soon as she knew how the Muddy Creekers would react to the request.

Winnie was intrigued with the idea of people from a very different faith coming to Muddy Creek and camping out in the church for a night. What should she think of that? What might she say to her folks about accepting or rejecting this proposal?

This would be a great opportunity for Muddy Creek to show compassion and hospitality to strangers. That sounds like something Jesus would approve of!" She smiled widely and thought, *"This is a fine opportunity for us to grow in our understanding of folks who are different from us, but whom God has created in God's image, nonetheless. I hope my people will agree.* Winnie began looking forward to Sunday, just to learn how they would respond.

Chapter 6. Sallie

Winnie was proud of her church members. She had spoken to the adult Sunday school class at church and explained to them about the peace walkers, telling them how the sojourners would be coming through Misty Falls at the end of October and were looking for a place to lay out their sleeping bags for the night. The walkers would prepare their own dinner, but they were hoping that the church members would make them a big, southern breakfast to gird them for their next day's trek. They would especially like to experience grits!

The request by the peace walkers was not met with open arms. Almost all of the fifteen Sunday school members had some objection. They speculated about what the walkers might do to their church property: "These people are not like us." "We don't know anything about them, except that their leaders are Japanese, Buddhist monks!" "What if they damage or steal something in the church." "We don't have any idea of what they might be bringing into our building; they might be carrying lice or fleas or worse!" "Who is going to be in charge of them while they are here?"

The concerns voiced by the Sunday school members gradually transitioned from worries about the physical logistics to what Winnie intuited was the deeper issue — that these travelers weren't Christians. They were Buddhists, and no one in the room really knew what that meant. "What do they believe? What does it mean to have non-Christians sleeping in our church?" "Might they influence our children in some way?"

Winnie understood that her people meant the best, but they were not thinking with very open minds about those who are a little different from themselves. She pointed out that the walkers hadn't received any bad press so far, and they had crossed a goodly portion of the country already, staying each night in places like Muddy Creek Church. "Bad news travels fast, doesn't it? We would have heard something about these folks if they had done anything newsworthy," Winnie pointed out.

"God tells us to be kind to the alien who is among us," Winnie added. "In Leviticus, Chapter Nineteen, we are told to treat aliens as if they were native-born. So if we need a scriptural reason for being kind to the walkers we have it right there."

Winnie further pointed out that there didn't seem to be too much required of Muddy Creek as far as accommodations were concerned. The travelers would be bringing their own sleeping gear, cook their own dinner, and clean up after themselves. The only real requirement seemed to be putting together a full-sized breakfast.

When Winnie reminded the class about the request for a big, southern breakfast, suddenly the mood of the group changed. Putting on a pot-luck meal was something this southern church knew it could do. Martha Reeves offered to make a couple of big pans of her famous, homemade biscuits. Her offer inspired Homer Randall to offer some sausage from his most recent load of pigs. He had just picked up the sausage from the meat packers. Bradley and Letitia Washington agreed to cook the scrambled eggs. Others chimed in with what they would like to include in the breakfast. In the end, not only did the idea of hosting the travelers pass, but everyone in class was excited about sharing their hospitality with these strangers.

Winnie chuckled to herself when she remembered how the class had navigated across a rather labored continuum from being greatly averse to hosting the peace walkers to making detailed plans for welcoming them! "Call Ms. Hawkins and tell her we'll do it!" There had been a couple of members who were still unsure about the project, but they agreed to not stand in the way of helping out the strangers.

✳ ✳ ✳

Monday morning, as Winnie walked over to the church, she saw a car parked in the church parking lot with a young woman sitting in the car.

Winnie approached the car, and the window came down.

"Good morning!'" Winnie said.

The driver of the car looked up at Winnie and smiled. Winnie noticed that the woman, who was not much more than eighteen or nineteen, was not alone in the car — there were a couple of car seats in the back of the car with two little children in them.

"Can I help you?" Winnie asked.

The young woman looked at Winnie and said, "I was hoping that y'all had food that I can git for my family."

Winnie nodded and told the young woman, "Yes, we have a food pantry here at the church. You're welcome to come in and take what you need."

The young woman opened her car door and got out. She waved at the back seat of her car and said, "My boys will be all right for a few minutes." She locked the car, leaving the window partly open and followed Winnie into the church.

Winnie introduced herself to the young woman and got her name, Linda Anderson.

Winnie learned that Linda was married to Josh. Their two little boys were a year apart, the older one being two and a half.

Winnie was pleased to meet this young woman — pleased that Muddy Creek could serve her in her family's need, and that, possibly, the church might help the family with more than just physical needs. Might it be that Muddy Creek could also help this young family understand Christian faith? Might the church become a church home for them?

Winnie was always pleased to meet new people, being a very extroverted person herself. In the course of a few minutes conversation, it was apparent to Winnie that Linda and her family were poor.

Linda was barely twenty, yet she and Josh already had two babies. She had dropped out of high school in the middle of ninth grade and married Josh. *Probably because child number one was on the way,* Winnie hypothesized. Josh tried to stay in school to get his diploma, but taking care of the family and learning a trade came first. He worked as a carpenter's apprentice, which led the young family down to Florida in search of jobs and more training. Josh never completed his high school education, and after a couple years they decided to move back closer to home — to Misty Falls.

Winnie helped Linda fill a couple bags of groceries from the church pantry, took Linda's address and cell phone number, and saw her back to her car. Winnie was sure to invite Linda and her family to join her in worship at Muddy Creek next Sunday.

❊ ❊ ❊

Tuesday Winnie walked over to the post office after Bible study. The day was a windy one, and the temperature had cooled down several degrees, reminding everyone that fall was on its way. As Winnie arrived at the post office she saw Pearly Mae also arriving.

"Morning, Miss Winnie!" She smiled

Winnie smiled back at Pearly Mae. "Isn't it a gorgeous day, even with the wind?" she answered.

"I don't mind the wind; I am mighty pleased to just get around, wind or not."

Winnie liked her friend's attitude and said, "Not everyone has your spunk! Wherever do you get it?"

"My Mama was a very strong woman! She could do the work of two men, I do believe. I think I git my strength from her."

Winnie wondered, "Is your mother still with us?"

"No, Ma'am. She was just short of a hundr'd years old when she passed back in '96." Pearly Mae answered.

"There's an age to aspire to!" Winnie winked at her friend.

"Sure it is!" agreed Pearly Mae, "But it's not so much the length of life that I deem important, as it is the kind of life I'm alivin'!"

"You're so right!" Winnie agreed.

"The kind of life we live is a great deal more important than the number of years we occupy this earth. When we follow Jesus we are called to be new creations, different from the people we were before," Pearly Mae declared.

"We are called to be the people that God wants us to be. I don't know that we really get a complete picture of what that means. We may have some surprises in the process," Winnie admitted.

"Most of the characters in the Bible were called to be something completely different than the world would have told them to be," Pearly Mae added.

Winnie enjoyed this little impromptu, theological exchange. She always enjoyed the quick conversations she had with Pearly Mae. Neither of them ever shied from speaking about their faith or the challenges they met along the way.

"That's one of the things I especially enjoy about you, Miss Pearly Mae! We don't just talk about the weather or things, we jump right into the good stuff, don't we?" Winnie teased her friend.

Pearly Mae smiled in assent. "Yes'M, We do. Since we're on the subject, I do have a request for a prayer from you," she continued, "My son, Dan, Jr., lives in Albuquerque, and he's coming out to see me."

Winnie's eyes sparkled. "How really special! You must be counting the days before he arrives!"

"I am, but I think there may be more to his agenda, and I'm not sure what to make of it," Pearly Mae confided.

"Hmm. Was it something he said?" Winnie asked.

"He did, and he didn't," Pearly Mae said. "He said something about hoping to 'close the loop' on something. He wasn't more specific than that. Maybe it was the way he said it, that made me uneasy."

Winnie nodded and said, "Maybe you're anxious about nothing. Anyway, it's not your business, you know. Your business is to support Dan Jr. and to be there for him. Trust the LORD to work the rest out in time."

Pearly Mae smiled. "I know you're right, Miss Winnie. I mustn't clutch or try to take over a problem that isn't mine. It's always good to remind ourselves that we must leave our trust where it belongs with the LORD and not run ahead of Him!"

Winnie said, "I'm here for you if you need someone to talk to. You know that!"

* * *

Sometime back last summer Winnie met Sallie. She was an odd-looking woman who was standing under the eaves outside of Friendlie's Foods one afternoon, trying to avoid a typical summer downpour.

Sallie was not well dressed. She had worn down sandals on her feet and a sleeveless dress that almost covered her very, very well endowed self. She was more than just a bit overweight; she was an extremely large woman.

Winnie couldn't quite remember how she and Sallie got into conversation, but the next thing Winnie knew she had agreed to help the woman make a phone call to some little town in South Carolina. Sallie was most anxious to make the call, but she didn't have a phone. She seemed desperate to talk to her daughter.

Winnie thought it would be kind to help her make such a call, so she drove Sallie over to Winnie's office at church.

That was her introduction to Sallie, and eventually Winnie also met Connie, Sallie's daughter. Connie lived in South Carolina, where Sallie had come from.

Winnie learned that Connie was expecting a baby and she and her husband had just discovered that Connie was actually carrying twin girls! Sallie was more than excited about the twins coming, as one might imagine, but there was more to the story, Winnie later discovered.

That was last summer. Sallie was living with her sister and brother-in-law in a small cottage in Misty Falls, but she didn't have a job. Winnie wondered what sort of work Sallie might have ever done. Gradually the story about Connie, her husband, George, and the soon-to-arrive twins came to light.

Thursday, about noon, Winnie received an animated phone call from Sallie. She was at the hospital in Knoxville and had called to say that the twin babies had arrived safely that morning — in a hospital in Knoxville, forty-five minutes from Misty Falls, not in South Carolina!

Sallie told Winnie that it was a long story, which she would explain to her very soon. Right now she needed Winnie to help her and her daughter with some paperwork.

Winnie's ears naturally perked up when she heard that she might be able to help. Sallie agreed to meet Winnie at her office later that afternoon.

About four that day Sallie appeared at the church. Her sister had driven her to the hospital when word came that the twins babies had just arrived. Later that day, Sallie's sister dropped her off at Muddy Creek, so she could talk to Pastor Winnie.

According to Sallie, Connie and George had decided that their babies should be born outside of South Carolina. They were afraid that they might lose the babies to the DHR if they were born there. So the Oliver's (Connie and George) had taken a Greyhound bus to some place in Connecticut to stay with a friend who lived there. *Could you make up a story so bizarre?* Winnie wondered privately. The babies were nearly due when the couple began their trip to Connecticut, but upon arriving at the friend's house they realized that their plan wouldn't work. Their friend may have been horrified to learn that her visitors, and their soon-to-be-born twins, were planning on moving in with her and staying for an indefinite period. That was much more than the friend had anticipated when she'd agreed to host them for a visit!

Where could they go, Connie and George wondered? They would go to Sallie's!

Sallie, of course, was not living in a home of her own, rather she was staying with Sallie's sister and brother-in-law in Misty Falls. Nonetheless, the Olivers jumped on the next Greyhound bus and began the journey south to where Sallie was.

And, as it happened, Connie went into labor on the bus. By the time the bus was in Knoxville, Connie knew the babies would be coming soon. Something needed to be done! The driver was informed of Connie's labor, so he drove to the nearest hospital and left the soon-to-be-parents at the hospital ER.

Shortly thereafter Sallie got a phone call from George saying that the babies were coming causing Sallie and her sister to leave immediately for the hospital.

Winnie couldn't imagine that this was really happening, but there was Sallie sitting in front of her, completely swept up in the whole affair.

"How can I help?" Winnie asked trying to figure out how she might weigh into this drama.

At this point Sallie related an even more bazaar tale.

"To begin with, Connie is my only child. I've raised her by myself, because her father has been in an insane asylum since she was small. It's not been easy; she's all I've got. Connie married George four years ago when she was still in school," Sallie told Winnie.

Winnie had her listening ears open, not wanting to interrupt Sallie's chain of thought, she simply nodded her head in understanding.

"They have had three babies before this, but they lost all three to the DHR." Sallie waited to see Winnie's reaction to that news.

Winnie's eyes opened wide and she asked, "The DHR, you mean the Department of Human Resources? They took the babies?"

"Yes, those guys. They took the children. All three are now in foster homes in South Carolina," Sallie stated flatly.

"Hm. "I can certainly see how your daughter and her husband could be worried about their twins!" Winnie added.

"Exactly! They were immediately excited when they learned that their new baby was not one but two, and at the same time they were terrified that they might lose those babies!" Sallie remembered. "They feared that as soon as the DHR learned about the twins' coming they would be on their case and that their new babies might be taken, too!

"Excuse me!" Winnie interjected. "I'm missing something here. What in the world happened to cause the DHR to seize the children?"

Sallie explained that there had been an incident with the first baby. An allegation had been made that the child was not being treated properly — maybe it was a case of baby shaking. Maybe there was more than one incident. Sallie wasn't very clear about the events, but the final word was that the Oliver's baby boy had been taken into protective services by the State of South Carolina.

The following year a second baby arrived. He had a slight case of cerebral palsy, and DHR was on the case quickly, due to the history Connie and George already had with them. The second child was taken from them for his own good.

The third child, a little girl, arrived the following year. Connie was nineteen by then. The baby didn't even come home with her parents from the hospital. She was put into DHR protection immediately.

When the Oliver's discovered that they were expecting again they had to do something to protect themselves from the DHR. Winnie could appreciate why they fled. *What does this woman want me to do?*

Sallie explained that the DHR in Knoxville had already been notified by the hospital staff about the baby girls' arrival. *Could it be the parents showing up in the last moments of labor, having been dropped off by the Greyhound bus driver, might have given the hospital employees a clue as to the unusual nature of these births!* The DHR was on the case, and they were going to be sure the babies had the best chance to thrive in their new world.

Sallie explained that her sister and brother-in-law had a little cottage in Misty Falls, actually in the country just outside of town, and that this new, little family would move in with them. The DHR wanted assurance about anyone who would have contact with the babies — anyone living in the home. "I need you, as the pastor of Muddy Creek United Methodist Church here in Misty Falls, to speak to the DHR woman and say you know me, that I'm a very concerned grandparent, and I wouldn't let anything happen to the babies. Could you put something like that in writing?" Sallie implored.

Winnie took a deep breath and looked at Sallie. "I want what you want. I want your little granddaughters to have the best chance they can get in life. They should be with their parents, of course, and right now that's what the DHR is willing to allow. I'll be happy to talk to the DHR woman and tell her what I know about you."

Winnie was beginning to think that there was a lot in life about which she was pretty naïve. *Maybe that's all right. I'm glad I don't know about those sorts of things and that they are not part of my history. Only God knows everyone's complete story, I just hope I can help these people find the right thing for them to do now.*

✳ ✳ ✳

That evening Winnie called her friend Nina and invited her to the church picnic, which would be taking place Sunday afternoon coming up in the big park on the mountain.

Yes, Nina was free that afternoon, and, yes, she thought she would enjoy coming with Winnie. In fact she promised to bring something to share for the picnic — her new creation, a sour cream, pumpkin, pound cake.

"Sounds like another winner!" Winnie exclaimed.

They agreed to meet at the church parking lot that afternoon to drive together up the mountain for the picnic.

You never know. There are many avenues into a faith community and fellowship is certainly a good one. Maybe Nina can grow a little more in faith as she gets to know more Muddy Creek members."

Chapter 7. A Short Week

The picnic had started out like any other Sunday afternoon getaway. Folks began arriving at the park on McCurry Mountain about two-ish and immediately began setting up for the events.

The women were at once focused on setting out all the many dishes as they arrived — casseroles, plates of veggies and salads, fruits, and more. A couple men put up folding tables for the goodies, while others built fires in the ramada's two, big fireplaces. The fires would need several hours to develop the smoldering required to cook really, tasty hotdogs. *Hotdogs are best when crisped over fire, burned down to glowing embers.* Even though the main course was simply hotdogs, the other dishes would provide gourmet flourishes to those humble wieners.

Mickey Allen Barrymore tapped Bradley Washington and Thom Jackson to help him set up the games. They set out a volleyball court, horse shoes, and the paraphernalia for a multi-generation relay game.

Meanwhile Matthew Jackson, Thom's oldest son, led the children in a game of Tag. The children's wild, joyous screaming could be heard across the entire area as they ran hither and yon trying to avoid being tagged.

Mary Lou and Tim Owens were especially pleased to see their new family so happily engaged in playing with their new friends from church. Carly, who was barely three, wasn't ready to let go of her Aunt Mary Lou, yet, but her siblings were happily scrambling around the hill with the others.

The children were playing Hide-and-Seek, scurrying off in every direction to find themselves a nook or niche in which to hide. The mountain, with all its many rocks, caves, trees and bushes, afforded many a good hiding place.

Little Brad Washington and Andy Owens, both four years old, had become fast friends and had run off together to find a hiding place. They ducked behind a large, colorful bush to wait, but then Andy saw a deep blue butterfly flitting around their bush. The butterfly moved past the boys around a high rock and onto some other bushes, enticing the two youngsters to follow. They scampered around the tall rock and down a hill following the little, flying object. They didn't realize that they might wander too far away from the rest of the children. They were immersed in a new game of trying to catch the elusive butterfly. The little, flying beast stayed just ahead of the two boys, who continued to scamper after their objective.

It wasn't until the Hide-and-Seek game was over that anyone realized the two boys weren't among the group. They hadn't been found.

"Olly-olly-oxen-free" Matthew Thompson hollered at the top of his lungs to let everyone know that the game was over, and that anyone who had not yet been found was free to return without being caught. All the children gathered in the middle of the large, open meadow laughing and looking at one another. Who would be declared "IT" for the next turn? Who had been caught first?

Bubba Owens, whose real name was Thomas, first noticed that his little brother wasn't among the group. "Where's Andy? Didn't Andy get caught? Has anyone seen my little brother, Andy?"

Several of the parents heard Bubba's plea, and rushed over to the meadow where all the children were and noticed that not only was Andy missing, so was Little Brad. Tim and Mary Lou were immediately on the scene.

It didn't take any time for all the adults and the older children to start scouting for the lost boys, calling their names, imploring them to answer.

It might have seemed like longer, but actually the boys were not lost for long. Matt and his brother Bobby had taken off toward the tall rock and wandered down the hill on the far side. They were calling for Little Brad and Andy all the while. They found the boys further down the mountainside watching their butterfly as it was sitting on a tree limb just beyond their reach.

The two older boys hoisted the four-year-olds on their shoulders and brought them back to the picnickers forthwith. As soon as they were close enough to be heard they called out that the boys had been found. All was well, again, and the rest of the picnic was all the merrier for that unexpected moment of panic.

The games had been set up, and everyone felt it wise to keep the generations mixed to stave off any further possibility of mishap. They would not lose anyone else! The picnic was a fine success, and the incident of the lost boys seemed to remind everyone how very tenuous life can be, and how very blessed they were. It was a good time to be thankful.

Before the afternoon was complete the families gathered around the fireplace and sang some old favorite songs. It was a moment right out the nineteenth century camp revival meetings, and it was wonderful. "Do Lord, oh, do Lord, oh do remember me!"

∗ ∗ ∗

Monday morning was not a lazy time for Winnie. Most Mondays she could tarry over her morning coffee and paper, and not get to work too early, because Mondays were the furthest away from the next Sunday, and the "countdown" to the next sermon hadn't yet begun in earnest yet.

This week was different because Winnie wouldn't be preaching on Sunday. She would be in Denver at her high school reunion. Nonetheless, she had plenty to do before she could leave: prepare her Tuesday Bible study lesson; catch up on her reading for her class on church leadership on Wednesday; write a light-hearted, yet somehow inspiring and insightful, blurb for the bi-weekly newsletter; pick out the hymns and readings for the Sunday worship service; produce the Sunday bulletin; and finally visit several of the community's elderly on Thursday.

Winnie planned to fly Friday morning to Denver; she also had to pack and get ready to leave before then. Her folks would pick her up from the airport, so she would have several hours to spend with them before getting ready for the reunion.

The reunion was to be held at a resort in town on Friday and Saturday nights. Friday night's reunion agenda was simple — meet and greet old friends in the ballroom at the resort. Winnie expected there might be several friends that would show up. *That's a funny thing about reunions; you don't have any control over who might attend. If I made a list of the people I would most like to see, it would probably be very different from the people who will actually come! But, then, there's John. I have to admit I'm very curious to see him after all these years!"*

Their phone call over a month ago was still fresh in her memory, and she had enjoyed reading the book that he had sent her. *"To find a true friend!" That's what John had inscribed in his book. I don't think I'm imagining anything. I think he's interested in me.*

She certainly had enjoyed their talk on the phone, but his dismissive comment about church had left her feeling cautious. Maybe she misunderstood John's comment. Maybe it was really nothing at all. It was hard to tell exactly, but if John didn't even believe in God, then that was a problem.

Winnie's life was already very complete, she reminded herself. She certainly had enough on her plate, what with all her responsibilities at church, not to mention trying to be a vital part of her children's lives. She really didn't need any personal entanglements now. *I'm really just looking for a fun weekend — seeing old friends from long ago and spending some time with Mom and Dad.*

* * *

Tuesday afternoon Winnie drove over to the address Sallie had given her. The Hardys (Sallie's sister and her husband) had a cottage in the country, so driving to their place was a matter of meticulously following the directions: *drive down country road 118 as far as the broken down old barn and take a right; drive a couple miles along that dirt road, (watch for the two flanking cow pastures), cross the small wooden bridge and turn left immediately. The cottage would be about a quarter mile further on the right side* of the road. It stood alone among the trees, except for several weatherworn trailers along the dirt road.

Winnie was pleased to find the cottage without difficulty. She walked up the wooden stairs to the porch and knocked on the door. Sallie opened the door and showed the pastor to a chair in the front room. She explained to Winnie that everyone was in the back and that they would be out soon. Sallie then disappeared behind another door.

Winnie had visited many people's homes over the years as pastor. She was aware that not everyone is comfortable with having relatively unknown visitors entering their private domain. In such cases Winnie always respected their wishes and didn't push for an invite.

On the other hand, Winnie had experienced many and sundry homes over the years — some being most inviting and comfortable and some missing even the least evidence of domestic pleasantry.

This little cottage didn't appear to be too grand or overly impoverished. It was a simple cottage built of wood with a stone fireplace at one end and a wood porch on the front.

While Winnie sat alone in the room waiting for someone else to appear she reviewed the room. *Pretty modest living,* she mused. There was a sofa, covered by a faded, blue chenille bedspread; Winnie thought it looked lumpy, but comfy. Two La-Z-Boy recliners looked to be favorite siesta spots and took up a significant portion of the available floor space. In the corner of the room stood a large, old television console. It was blaring into the room, even though no one, save Winnie, was present.

Sallie appeared with Connie and introduced her. She was friendly, young, and nice looking, being casually dressed in jeans and a sweatshirt. She was slimmer than Winnie expected. *Considering the great challenge she's given her waistline these past three or four years she looks great!* They spoke about the new babies — the big news for everyone. Connie produced pictures of the babies that someone had taken for her at the hospital.

George Oliver, Connie's husband, entered the room. He was also not what Winnie had expected, but then, she wasn't exactly sure what she expected the babies' father to be like. George was slight in stature and not a large person overall. He, too, was dressed in jeans and a sweatshirt, and he wore boots. He was somewhat reserved in his manner. Winnie realized that George didn't know who she was or why she might be interested in his little family. He nodded to the visitor when she was introduced. George was older than Connie, in fact, George was possibly twice Connie's age! Winnie judged. *There's more to this story than I've heard so far.*

Winnie would have liked to see the babies, but they were napping in the back; they couldn't be seen at this time. The women talked for several minutes about the babies — their size at birth, their eating schedule, their clothing needs,how well they slept. So far both babies seemed to sleep and be hungry at the same time, which was fortunate. There were a number of helpful hands available to take care of any needs. George didn't add to the conversation; he let the women speak.

The Hardys came into the room and met their visitor. They seemed to be nice people who must have been surprised by this new influx of family and personality that had just descended on them. Considering these refugees, as it was, Winnie thought they were trying to do the right thing for everyone.

Winnie sighed to herself as she drove away, *Lord! Help and guide that family! Help me know what is right for them and what I can do to help them.*

✳ ✳ ✳

The week had flown by, and Winnie had only one more day to get things together before her trip. She looked down and saw Bitty at her feet and suddenly realized that she hadn't made plans for the dog while she'd be in Denver. 'Bitty! I can't leave you alone for the weekend. What am I to do with you?"

Winnie mentally rifled through all the people she knew in town trying to think who she might call for help with her pup. Bitty really wasn't a great trouble, but she did need to be fed and walked a couple times a day. Finally Winnie decided to call Trudy, the young, expectant girl. Winnie thought it might be a good thing for Trudy to get in the mode of being responsible for another life.

She called Keisha Livingston, Trudy's mother, and asked if her daughter was home. Keisha handed the phone to Trudy, who answered, "Yes, Ma'am. This is Trudy." Winnie explained to Trudy, "I'm going to be out of town this weekend, and I need someone to watch my puppy,"

"I remember the puppy! How big is she now?" Trudy asked.

"Maybe a couple pounds bigger, but not much. She's so furry, though, she looks much bigger than she really is," Winnie explained.

"Do you suppose you could 'puppy watch' for me this weekend over at the parsonage?" Winnie asked her.

"I'd love to!" Trudy assured Winnie. "I think it would be fun to play with the puppy. What did you name her?"

"I call her Bitty. How about we meet at my house later today, and I can show you what she needs. You'll need to walk Bitty a couple times a day, too," Winnie added.

"That sounds like fun," Trudy giggled. "I'll be able to play baby dolls with 'Itty Bitty'!"

"It really does sound like just the thing for you – practicing caring for another little being!" Winnie answered. "She's a sweet little pup; you'll enjoy her. Thanks so much. Please thank your mother for lending you to me this weekend. I'll see you around 4:30, okay?" Winnie asked.

They agreed to meet then, and Winnie was pleased that she remembered Trudy to help her out. *She probably would like to have some time on her own, anyway, and this is a good place to play house.*

✳ ✳ ✳

Winnie was hoping that everything was now in order for her to leave the community for the three days. She had a substitute preacher — a lay speaker — who would fill in with the message for Sunday morning. She had asked Gus Reeves, Muddy Creek's Lay Leader, to preach for her. He was the great grandson of the man who moved his plantation house across the town a century earlier.

Gus was a pharmacist, who owned the local drug store on Main Street; he was also a volunteer fireman and active in community affairs like the fall festival. His wife, Martha, worked at Friendlie's Foods, so they sometimes teased one another about "being in competition" with one another — Gus' pharmacy vs. the grocery store.

Winnie had discovered over the last year that Gus was someone who could be called on in a pinch. Moreover, he was willing to try new things — like preaching!

The Reeves family had experienced a very difficult time, as Winnie learned when she first arrived at Muddy Creek. Martha had invited Winnie over for dinner one Sunday afternoon shortly after she had arrived in town, and she and Gus told her about an event, actually two events, that occurred in their family, which they wanted to share with their new pastor.

The events took place fifteen years earlier when the three Reeves kids were still all at home. Tina, 18, was a senior in high school, Tommy was 16, and Julie was 14. That summer Tina graduated from high school and moved out of the house. The Reeves weren't even quite sure where she was living, but they had heard that she was staying with friends and had started working at a factory over in Kirby, the town nearby.

Several months later Martha heard that Tina was expecting a baby in the spring. Tina was very independent about her life and what she was choosing to do, and she wanted nothing to do with her parents. Gus and Martha would have loved to be part of Tina's life in any way she would allow, but she would not have any of it. Occasionally she would call them, and when she called they hung on her every word. All they could do was to pray for Tina's safety and the safety of their unborn first grandchild.

Later, that same summer, something else was happening even closer to home. It seems their son Tommy had a couple of boyfriends over to the house one afternoon while his folks were away at work. Julie, his younger sister, was also at home.

Somehow one of Tommy's friends found an opportunity to get alone with Julie. One thing led to another, and before she knew what was happening, the boy had his way with her! A month later Julie realized that she was expecting a child! She was mortified at the discovery, but, nevertheless, Julie came tearfully to her mother and father and told them what had happened. They loved Julie, of course, and they could see that she had hardly been a willing party in this situation. They would support her and see that this new child would have a loving home to grow up in.

That's exactly what happened. The baby came late the following spring, and she was brought into the Reeves's home and cared for as a member of their family. They managed to figure how to support Julie's high school education by working out a tag team plan for raising little Emma.

Gus and Martha never made a secret of those painful situations at church. The church family gathered around them, prayed with them, and supported them emotionally. In every way they could, they helped to make sense out of this surprising turn of events.

Eventually the older daughter, Tina, and her little daughter, Sara Faye, began coming around. Ever so slowly at first, the Reeves were allowed to get to know their first granddaughter.

Both granddaughters, Sara Faye and Emma, were a delight. They were only two months apart in age, and they were devoted to one another, looking for opportunities to spend time together whenever they could.

Tina still lived away from town, but she was becoming more willing to share about her life with her parents. They could have hoped that things between them and their first child had not been so cool for so long, but they could see her hard work, providing for her little family. Tina continued to advance in the factory, and her income and position continued to increase. She was making a success of her life against all odds. Her life was not how her parents would have written it, but they were supportive and impressed with Tina's accomplishments, nonetheless.

Julie, also, was a hard worker and an exceptional student even with the added duties of motherhood. She won scholarships to The University of Tennessee in Knoxville, so the Reeves found a way to see that she could go. They continued with the tag team effort, to see that Emma was cared for, and it worked out well.

Julie's story was remarkable. She managed to carry a stiff load of classes at UTK and graduate with honors. She studied pharmacology, following in her father's footsteps, and after graduation she began working with her dad at his pharmacy in town.

Winnie was touched as she heard this saga from Gus and Martha. They told her how they had not kept their troubles from the world, but had shared their crazy pain with their fellow church members. They had been open to God's healing in all their troubles. It couldn't have been an easy a road to walk, but Winnie could see how richly the Reeves had been rewarded through their faithfulness and willingness to see the trouble through.

Gus would bring a great message to the church on Sunday, because he had the respect of the congregation and an ocean of deep experience from which to draw. Winnie had no worries as she packed and prepared to leave for her reunion over the weekend.

Chapter 8. The Reunion

The class reunion left Winnie with mixed thoughts, rather like her favorite author had phrased it: "It was the best of times, it was the worst of times ...."

Winnie was aware of a feeling in the pit of her stomach — a certain emptiness, accompanied by several score of butterflies. She did not experience this pit-of-the-stomach queasiness regularly, but only when her world was somehow out of kilter, or when she was about to deliver a sermon.

Winnie had become particularly aware of this 'pit' feeling when she began preaching on Sundays. The pit came upon Winnie just prior to her standing up to preach. *It's funny how quickly the pit abates once I actually get into the sermon, but the time leading up to delivery is a mess!*

The pit uneasiness was not just a prelude to sermon giving, it could come at other times, too, and it reminded Winnie that something was amiss, something was foreign or uncomfy for her. It usually indicated that she needed to find closure to some circumstance.

So it was with the reunion. Not all of the reunion was pit-making, but the initial hour, as Winnie stood outside the ballroom in a long line of what seemed to be hoards of unknown reunion attendees, was one of those times that invited the pit's arrival. Winnie noticed the pit was beginning to make itself known, yet it wasn't simply a large crowd of unknown people that was causing the pit's arrival, rather it was because she had to stand for the better part of an hour waiting in line with total strangers. She was beginning to think she might be at the wrong reunion. *Why did I bother coming here!* She asked herself.

The last high school reunion Winnie had attended with Mark. They stayed in the company of two other couples that Winnie had known from her high school days. The three couples stuck together, learning about their various families and business endeavors, enjoying their reacquaintancing. Tonight, though, Winnie was alone, and that made an enormous difference in the way she engaged the reunion.

It was not the fault of the reunion itself, which had all the expected decor, music, and taste-tempting finger foods that a reunion should boast.

After standing in line for over an hour, the attendees were finally admitted to the hall. They were given a name tag with their senior high picture affixed to it, making it a valuable tool for memory-jogging. *Goodness! Look at the changes we've had over the years. Our pictures are surely a far cry from what we look like today!*

Everyone had aged, of course, and the waistlines of most of the graduates had expanded, some to shocking measures! Many of the men were either bald or had facial hair, and Winnie had to work hard to recognize those sporting such facial additions. Nearly everyone had some gray hair, save those who had employed a rinse to masque what time would inevitably do to their locks.

Winnie noticed a distinguished-looking, silver-haired man walking toward her. He moved across the ballroom floor and right up to Winnie. *Can that be John?* He looked something like she remembered him, but his hair was no longer reddish-brown. Silver was his new shade, and it favored him. He wore a maroon sports jacket with a gray cravat, reminding Winnie of pictures of old Hollywood stars.

"I see we both managed to make it to the reunion!" John observed.

Winnie smiled and said, 'Yes, I'm so glad you called and told me about it. This is turning out to be better than I had expected!" (And the *pit* vanished!)

"Did you like my book?" John asked.

"Yes, I did! I've never had a book hot off the press, so to speak, and personally inscribed by the author too!" Winnie admitted. "You write so well!"

Winnie commented on several of the daily selections in John's new book, which evoked a quick repartee between them that they thoroughly enjoyed. The two soon found that they shared a fondness for such thoughtful conversation.

"Reunions are an interesting mix of past and present, aren't they?" John commented.

"We've certainly had some good examples of that this evening," Winnie nodded in agreement. "Reunions surely are a mix of now and then. Or maybe you could say we reunion celebrators are a layering of past and present. I would think, though, that people are still the same, beneath our aged exterior. Maybe we look different — grayer, wider, and more wrinkly than when we were in high school, but aren't we the same persons deep down?"

"I'm sure there are psychologists that would affirm your observation and cite a host of solid references for proof," John returned.

"I've heard that our personality is set by the time we are five years old, or that 90% of our personality is set by then. Would you agree?" Winnie asked.

"You're positing that one's personality is the basic structure of who a person is," John observed.

"Either that or personality certainly is a major factor in how one lives one's life," Winnie returned. "Although, surely, there have to be other, similarly important elements that make up who someone is — dreams, economic advantage or disadvantage, natural talent, education, faith — to mention a few," Winnie theorized.

So, you would say that the composite person, including the factors you've just mentioned (plus others), is what makes a person who he or she is today," John theorized.

Winnie was enjoying this tete-a'-tete with John and added, "I don't suppose the answer is that simple; people are complex entities, but are you suggesting that a person is basically the same person, no matter what he or she has experienced along the way?"

"Maybe. I suppose there could be some major incident that could alter a person's life forever — for good or for otherwise," John noted.

"I would agree with that, for sure, because I have to believe that no matter what a person starts with, there's plenty that can sway a person's thinking and doing, and, as a person of faith, I have to include the good things that God does for us, as a positive stimulus for choosing to do what is right," Winnie said.

"That's quite a mouthful. I see that you bring God into the mix," John observed.

Winnie held her breath a moment and then smiled and said, "Yes, I do. I have been a person of faith in Christ for almost as long as I can remember, so I guess I do bring God into the conversation occasionally."

John raised an eyebrow and nodded his head. "You mentioned something about church when we talked before on the phone. Maybe you are pretty involved with your church?"

Winnie squelched a grin at this point. She was enjoying John's company too much to mess things up now. She wanted to know more of this intriguing man, before she threw her profession at him. A little time couldn't be a problem, could it? Instead, Winnie winked at John and said, "In fact, I work at my church."

"So, you would have more than a passing acquaintance with church affairs," John concluded.

"Something like that. I do various things at different times. I do the bulletin each week and put together the newsletter and get it out to mail. I'm in charge of our prayer list, and I'm trying to learn how to put our church online. Come to think of it, I do quite a bit at church," Winnie smiled.

"Then I'd better watch my tongue, since I'm in the presence of a saint!" John teased.

"You're teasing me, but you're closer than you think about how we speak among ourselves at church," Winnie explained. "You see, everyone who follows Christ is a *saint in the making*. I certainly wouldn't go around calling myself a saint, but I do believe that, as we follow the Lord each day, we are growing closer to Him. We are a work in progress," Winnie added.

John smiled and might have commented further when Jenny walked up to them and began to talk. She had been moving from one group to the next on the ballroom floor, talking with former classmates. She saw John, probably because he stood out a bit taller in the crowd, and she maneuvered over to where he was.

Winnie had known Jenny when they were coeds at Mile High High School. Jenny had been a tall, slender girl with long, jet black ringlets, flowing down her back. The one thing that distinguished Jenny in high school was that she ranked at the top of the class — even out of a thousand students she was on top. That was then.

"I go by Jennifer, now," she told Winnie. Winnie couldn't keep her eyes off the change in Jennifer. Instead of being the slight, modestly dressed girl Winnie remembered, her hair was now very short, spiked, and hot pink. The new "Jennifer" sported a pink leotard and pullover, a green herringbone mini-skirt, and a matching bolero with a <u>very</u> low cut blouse.

"Jennifer" had apparently decided that the quiet life was not for her and had made a number of changes, not the least of which was a <u>very well endowed bosom</u>! She had an attitude to match her new look. She held a strong, edgy opinion on many subjects. Jennifer had traveled extensively experiencing life in some very primitive cultures and providing her some unusual insights into human behavior. She left her audience believing that she really had seen it all.

Jenny moved on to another group. "I would never have recognized her, if she hadn't introduced herself to me," John confessed.

"How did the girl who missed the Hippies and the nuttiness of the Sixties become such a free spirit on her own?" Winnie laughed.

"Now there's an example of nature versus nurture, as we were saying before. I'd almost want to say that nurture has won out in Jennifer's case," Winnie concluded.

"You could make a good argument for that, I'm sure, but there's got to be something of the 'nature' side, too. What caused Jennifer to seek those changes? Was it something deep within her that was begging for expression?" John said.

John told Winnie about his life following graduation. He had gone east to study — to Davidson in North Carolina — where he earned his B.A. in Philosophy and then on to graduate work at Boston University. He was awarded his PhD in 1979, and he moved to Chicago to teach in the early '80s.

John had been tenured at University of Chicago, teaching philosophy since then. He even served as an adjunct professor of philosophy at Garrett Theological Seminary, teaching Introduction to Philosophy.

"So, you've taught theologians!" Winnie interrupted him.

"Yes," John admitted. "Seminarians are usually good students, interested in understanding the rudiments of philosophy. I can always expect to hear good apologetics among my students, defending the influence of Greek thought into Christian orthodoxy. Discussions on how Platonic and Aristotelian thinking has continued to inform Christian doctrine are always vibrant. Those early Greek philosophers gave the church some sound tools for engaging theology. Western Philosophy is foundational to a seminarian's studies."

Winnie didn't offer the fact that she had been to seminary, even if seminary would have been something they would have in common. *I think I'll just leave that subject to rest for now.*

As the evening went on they laughed and laughed, sometimes at things they were discovering at the reunion, like the dramatic change in Jenny, and other times they just seemed to laugh together at nothing at all.

John had never married. His early years were all about school and long hours of study. He spent a year abroad at Queens University in Belfast, Ireland. He was doing doctoral work there. He enjoyed being in the eastern hemisphere, where he could hop over to the continent and spend time poking through history and culture and practicing his French and German.

Winnie wondered about John's mother. *Wonder if she played a role in his not marrying? Or maybe there's another reason. Hadn't thought of that!*

Winnie told John about her world since high school — taking her baccalaureate at Colorado College in the Springs and marrying Mark Taylor, who had been a cadet at the Air Force Academy.

Their life with the Air Force moved them around the States to different bases, as well as to Germany for a couple of three year tours there. Winnie wondered if she and John might have been in Europe at the same time.

The two compared travel dates and times, and it turned out that they were both at the zoo in Dublin on Boxing Day in 1978. "How funny! What a small world we live in!" Winnie giggled. "Did you happen to notice the crocodile there?" she asked John.

"You mean the one who wasn't eating much on his preferred diet?" John asked.

Winnie laughed again. "Right! He was pretty sad, not having any teeth!" They both laughed. "What a small world we live in!" They said together as if they had rehearsed it.

"I discovered that Christmas is not much of a time to go visiting in Ireland. It's all about family time for the Irish then." John observed.

"We drove from Ramstein Air Force Base to Calais and took the ferry over to England; then we drove up the M6 to Dumfries and then over to Stranraer, where we took another ferry to Northern Ireland. We spent Christmas week in Armagh, with friends and drove all over Northern Ireland that week. Unfortunately, as you just said, much was closed because of the Yule holiday. We did get a personal tour of the cathedral in London-derry by the sexton there. We felt like V.I.P's the way we were treated then," Winnie recounted.

"I was at Queens University in Belfast that year, and Christmas break extended into the New Year, so I drove down to Dublin to look around. I ferried to Liverpool from there and drove on to Paris and beyond. I actually got a good three weeks of traveling in then." John smiled at the memory.

On and on they talked. John wasn't always full of big words and ideas. He seemed very down to earth and most interested in Winnie as a person. She enjoyed his humor, too.

Saturday evening was more of the same. Winnie and John sat together at a small dining table in the resort's dining room. John was very attentive to Winnie all evening. He seemed interested to learn whatever she shared about her life. She told him about Mark, about the kids, where they kids were now, and about losing Mark. She explained how becoming a widow at thirty-seven with two half-grown kids had been very painful, of course, but things were better now. She had a full life what with her church work and her children.

Both John and Winnie had flown to Denver for the reunion in order to get away for the weekend. John admitted that he really preferred to drive, when he could spare the time. Driving relaxed him and allowed him to think outside of his busy world.

He said, "I don't do much driving in Chicago. I suppose that's why my car has lasted me as long as it has. I have a '92 Honda Civic, which works quite well. I've hardly had to do anything to it 'cept give it gas."

"I drive a lot, especially since I live in the country. I have to figure on driving into Knoxville at least once a week, and sometimes more," Winnie commented.

"One good thing about not driving much is that I've never had a ticket!" John announced.

"I think I'm a pretty safe driver, too, and I haven't had any citations in years and years, but I have to admit that there was a time, when Mark and I were in Germany and the kids were little, that I managed to gather nine points on my license in about three months!"

John's mouth fell open, pretending to tease Winnie. "No! You had nine points on your license in three months! How did you manage that?"

"It wasn't very funny at the time, but I guess it sounds funny, now," Winnie began to explain.

"It started off with our car. We had a big Ford Econoline van, which was very long and had two little windows in the back; they didn't allow the driver to see below the back windows."

"Our car was parked in our apartment parking lot. There was a large dumpster sitting maybe fifteen feet from the back of our van. I was aware of the dumpster and planned to very carefully back out of the parking lot. Unfortunately, someone was visiting the apartments and had parked his car parallel to the dumpster. I hadn't noticed this small car when I got into the van. I maneuvered our car back, to avoid the dumpster, but the fender of the van managed to hit the little car! I heard the metal meet, and I tried to very carefully pull forward, back toward my parking space. It seems, however, that the fender had hooked onto the fender of the little car, and as I pulled forward, the little car was dragged alongside the dumpster, leaving a nasty gash on the car!"

John had a very difficult time not bursting into laughter at this admission, but he could see that Winnie was not laughing, so he struggled to contain his amusement.

"THAT was considered a MOVING violation, and I had three points on my license," Winnie said.

She waited a minute to see if John would comment, and when he did not, she continued. "A month later I was over at the air base at the chapel, where I was working with junior high kids on a Christmas play. I had parked in the chapel's parking lot. When I got into the van this time, I noted that there was a car parked parallel to my car, and I had to be careful not to hit it when I opened the driver's door. I was completely successful in that effort, but later, as I was backing up, easing out of the parking space, I heard a S-C-R-A-T-C-H-I-N-G sound, and I stopped immediately to see what had happened."

John's eyes were bigger than before, "And?" he asked.

"AND! You remember how my car's bumper that had hooked onto the other car's fender the month before?" Winnie asked, rhetorically. John nodded his head "yes". "Well, we hadn't fixed the bumper on our van, so it was still pulled out several inches, and it had scratched a terrible mark all the way across the side of the car door!"

"I suppose I could have left the parking lot and driven home, but I knew my car had been responsible for the scratch on the car, so I went to the chaplain's office and told him what had just happened."

"This is where the story gets funny," Winnie remembered. "I told the chaplain what had just happened, and the chaplain stood up, his face growing redder and redder. He slammed his fist on his desk and asked me about the color and make of the car. I told him it was a maroon color sedan, and the chaplain told me it was his brand new car; the one he had just bought his family for Christmas. After a moment the chaplain realized it was not his fault that his car was damaged, and he changed his mood. He wouldn't have to tell his wife that he had managed to scratch their new car. NO! It was not his fault, it was my fault!"

Winnie had been watching John's face as she was relating her story to him. She could see the wheels spinning in his eyes, but he never cracked a smile.

Winnie laughed. "As bad as this story is, I suppose it is funny in the retelling!"!

Her admission allowed John to relax and be himself. Then he laughed along with Winnie.

"Anyway, that was three more points on my license — in less than a month!" Winnie added.

"You said you had nine points, right?" John asked, a bit fearful to hear more.

"A month later, one early evening, I was driving out of the base on the access road. You have to creep along at 20 miles an hour on the base, and finally there I was on the road on the outside of the base, and I started to drive a bit faster. I was going, maybe, thirty-five miles an hour, when one of the SP's pulled me over for speeding! Turns out that the speed limit on that road was 30 m.p.h. I felt like a fish that had just been caught!"

"That added three more points — another 'moving violation!' I never did hear anything about the nine points on my license, but you can be sure I was Über careful behind the wheel for a long time!" Winnie concluded.

The reunion was perfect for Winnie and John. They had discovered one another, and they were most pleased with what they found! They talked, and talked, and couldn't stop talking. They felt like they might be able to talk together, non-stop, for a month if it were possible! They each felt something fascinating about the other.

Of course, Winnie wondered how (or if) she might broach the topic of her being a pastor to John. She got the impression that John had had some bad experience with the church and had been turned off of the whole subject. Therefore, she didn't suppose he'd be thrilled to learn that she was a preacher! In fact she hoped to have more time to explore what John meant by his enigmatic inscription in the book he had sent her, before she addressed her work.

* * *

Sunday at breakfast, Winnie's folks were full of questions about the reunion, especially about Dr. Jonathan Daniel, whom, they understood, had spent a good bit of his reunion time at their daughter's side.

"YES! He's very interesting and accomplished, and YES we had a really great time together at the reunion. But, I don't think he's a believer! I can't become interested in someone, if he doesn't follow Christ, I don't care how 'eligible' he seems to be." Winnie sighed.

Chapter 9. The Peace Walkers

"No matter how much I try to get ahead of my work before I leave for a holiday, I still have much more to do when I return. It really makes getting away a hard thing to do;. I have to pay for it afterwards — and before!" Winnie complained out loud. "It's almost not worth the going away, except I really did have a good time."

The trip was good for many reasons, but now, looking at the new week ahead with all its requirements, Winnie wondered how she could get everything done that begged her attention.

The walkers would be arriving at the church on Friday evening, and Winnie wanted to make a few calls to be sure everyone was on line for the breakfast. She also thought there might be some interest among her people to meet these strangers, who were giving up so much of their life to walk for peace.

✳ ✳ ✳

Winnie decided to stop by Sallie's sister's home and see how they were all getting along.

Everything seemed much as Winnie had seen it before she left on her trip. The cottage looked just the same, although there were a few baby items strewn around the living room. There was a large box of New-born Huggies by the kitchen and two infant carriers sitting side by each.

This time Winnie saw the little girls, and they were adorable — plump, blue eyed, with a few wisps of blond hair atop their pates. (Someone had pasted little pink bows on their heads, to announce, "I'm a girl!") They seemed to be good babies, and they were being passed around the room by various family members, holding them and cooing at them.

This seems to be working. Winnie thought to herself.

George was not present, and Winnie inquired as to his whereabouts. It seemed that George was already seeking employment in the community. He was a welder and had several leads on jobs that he wanted to check out. He hoped he would be able to support his new family soon.

That's a good sign. He's not a sluggard.

She wondered about Harry Hardy, Sallie's brother-in-law, and how he was accepting the invasion of this new family into his already-space-challenged, little cottage. He was silent, maybe hoarding his thoughts. Winnie wasn't surprised at his reticence to speak.

The baby girls were definitely the stars of the day. Their needs and their comfort seemed to be uppermost on everyone's mind. Winnie wondered how quickly everyone had accommodated themselves to this whole new situation.

Winnie left the family with various questions, wondering how long this amiable relationship would be able to continue. *After all, the Hardys had just been dumped upon without any warning! And people are people. I won't be surprised if arrangements don't eventually change.*

※ ※ ※

Winnie discovered that she was getting email everyday from John!

His messages invited more 'conversation' as they had enjoyed such banter, and even some deeper thoughts, during the reunion.

He signed his email each day with "Appreciating our friendship more and more! John."

"Hmmmm! That's more food for thought," Winnie said to Bitty, who was sitting at her foot. "We're growing in friendship, according to John. I like that; it has a nice ring."

Winnie responded to John's emails, of course. She thought the banter fun — like playing tennis — you lob the ball back as soon as it hits your court.

Winnie signed her notes with "Your Friend, Winnie"

※ ※ ※

Winnie had a date with Nina late Thursday afternoon. Nina had called earlier in the week to say that she was putting together a new dessert that needed a fresh palate to consider its merit. Winnie told Nina that her palate was a willing volunteer. Thank you! She would come right away!

They sat at Nina's breakfast table in her kitchen. The object of the test sat in the center of the table, a tall, yummy-looking bunt cake with orange icing dripping down its sides. Nina had set the table with a table cloth, napkins, silverware, coffee cups, and bread plates. All was ready for a tasting verdict.

Winnie recognized that this special treat was about to throw her diet completely out of whack, but she decided that she would not disappoint her taste buds. *After all, didn't the Lord enjoy the occasional, lavish party with friends? Such a precedent must not be overlooked!*

The conversation at the table touched lightly on many subjects, the way it does among women. They spoke of the weather, of their children, last week's picnic on the mountain, and, speaking of church, Winnie mentioned the peace walkers who would arrive late Friday afternoon.

Nina was intrigued about the peace walkers coming. She wanted to know all about these people: Who were they? Were they all Buddhists? Did they speak English? How did they decide on Muddy Creek Church to spend the night?

Winnie wondered, along with her friend, about the walkers. She thought it would be especially good for her church people to meet these outsiders and to help them along their journey.

This brought the conversation around to church in general. Apparently, Nina had been married in church, a big United Methodist Church in New Orleans. She and her husband had been students at Tulane, and they were involved in the Wesley Foundation, a campus ministry for young people. The school was just down St. Charles Ave. from the church. They were married in the church's chapel after graduation.

The Mattinglys didn't attend church during the early years of their marriage, but when the children came they took them to church. It seemed like the right thing to do.

They were living in Jackson by then, and they attended a community church. It was friendly, and most of their neighbors were members of the church.

Nina told Winnie, "One day news came out that our pastor had stolen money — a lot of money — from the community! He had 'borrowed' money from various people around town and from the church itself. Then he defaulted on his 'loans'. Altogether, when the loss was added up, it was more than $35,000 that our preacher had absconded with!

"It was dreadful! Everyone at church felt as if we personally had been taken advantage of. We wondered, 'How could we have trusted the man! How can we believe anything he told us? How can we believe his preaching?' Many members left the church then — including us. We were deeply hurt. We didn't know what to tell our kids, Rachel and Perry. We were so disappointed in the pastor and in the way that many tongues wagged for months afterwards. We just left church altogether.

"Maybe there was a better way to respond to it, but that chapter in our lives had closed. We filled our lives with other things. We slept in on Sundays. The kids didn't seem to miss church; they never asked about it," Nina explained.

The Mattinglys moved from Jackson to Misty Falls a year later. By that time they were out of the church habit.

Winnie listened carefully and sympathetically to Nina's story.

"Oh!" Winnie sighed. "I'm so sorry you had to experience such a bad pastor!" Winnie wanted her friend to know she felt for her and her pain. "Too often people of the cloth do great damage to church, to members, and to one another. We should be a whole lot better people than our lay counterparts, but, the truth is, we're not. We stand in the need of God's grace just as much as anyone does!"

Nina was surprised to hear her friend speak so bluntly about the place and the people she was so involved with. "That surprises me," she admitted.

"Don't be surprised," Winnie told Nina. "Although we pastors should be on our best behavior as we live out our lives before the world, we also must lead the way as followers of Christ, and that means we must be first when it comes to being truthful and honest when we fail. Wouldn't our honesty in times of trouble show others how to act when failure comes along for them? There's plenty to ask forgiveness for, and, from what I understand, there's plenty of forgiveness available to those who ask."

Nina let Winnie's words sink in before she answered. "I can see what you mean. You're saying if a pastor is a genuine follower of Jesus, he or she has to be a leader in what he or she does. That means being honest about what you do and say. I like that, Winnie. That helps a little. Thanks."

Winnie was especially pleased to hear Nina's story and her apparent interest in Winnie's response. She seemed to understand how it was that the Mattinglys got separated from church and how painful it had been for them.

✳ ✳ ✳

Linda Anderson, who had visited Muddy Creek's food pantry several weeks earlier, was sitting in her car in the church parking lot Wednesday morning, awaiting the pastor's arrival.

Winnie was happy to show her the church pantry and help her do a little shopping from the shelves. She filled two bags of canned goods, pasta, and paper goods. Winnie told Linda she would like to meet her family, so she hopped in her VW and followed Linda to an apartment a couple miles from the church.

The Andersons lived in a modestly furnished two bedroom apartment; the television was blaring loudly in the living room. Linda's two sons were home with their father, who lay stretched out on the couch.

The room was strewn with children's toys — trucks, blocks, crayons and paper, balls, and stuffed animals. The site took Winnie back to a time when her own kids were about that age. *It's virtually impossible to keep up after them,* she thought to herself.

Linda introduced her husband, Josh, who was a construction worker. He had been learning the trade in Tampa, but he hadn't found a job in Misty Falls, yet. He was hoping to find something soon.

As they were talking, the front door opened and in walked an exceptionally pretty young woman carrying a baby on her hip. Her attitude indicated that she had more than a passing acquaintance with this apartment.

Linda brightened up immediately and introduced her sister to Winnie.

"Miss Winnie, This is my sister Laura Lee." She grinned.

Winnie told Laura Lee she was pleased to meet her. She peeked at the baby in her arms and inquired his name.

"This is Jasper," Laura Lee answered. A young boy opened the door and came inside. "And this is my son, Jason."

Laura Lee motioned to her sister, and the two young women stepped into the kitchen and pushed the door to.

Jason was a good-looking child with a mop of curry blond hair atop his head. Winnie judged him to be about three years old. He immediately walked over to the television, picked up the remote control, and began switching channels. He seemed completely at home in the apartment.

Do both of these families live together in this apartment?

The door to the kitchen swung open, and Linda came out and announced to Josh. "Jerry's missing. Laura Lee hasn't seen him since yesterday."

Who is Jerry? Winnie wondered.

Linda looked at Winnie and explained, "Jerry is Laura Lee's boyfriend. They live in a trailer across the highway."

"I see." Winnie said. "Have you any idea where he went?"

Laura Lee spoke up then. "He's been looking for work, and he left yesterday to talk to somebody about a job. That's the last I saw him." She looked miffed.

"Will you be all right?" Winnie wanted to know.

Laura Lee seemed to think they were okay for now. "Jerry'll show up when he gets hungry."

"I'm glad you have family here," Winnie observed.

When she left the Anderson's, Winnie had the strong impression that she ought to drop by her friend Sheriff Barrymore. She couldn't give a good reason for it, but she felt it might be a good idea.

The sheriff's office wasn't far from Muddy Creek Church. Winnie walked into the office and saw Janice, sitting at her desk. "Hi, Janice! Seeing you reminds me that we're supposed to get together with Joe Ed tonight for the special choir rehearsal. Do you know what time practice will be?"

Janice smiled and said, "He's meeting at six o'clock at the church for 'The Massed Thanksgiving Choir rehearsal.' I'm glad to hear you'll be joining us. Is your choir coming, too?" Janice asked.

"When the folks at Muddy Creek heard that I was to be the preacher for the evening, they couldn't help but commit to showing up" she winked at Janice.

"You know, Miss Winnie, I've never heard a woman pastor preach before, but I've been married to Ken long enough to know that writing and giving sermons is serious business. How long have you been preaching?"

"Well, I didn't jump in with both feet right at the start; in fact I dragged my feet for quite some time. I wasn't aware that women were allowed to preach when I first looked into seminary" Winnie explained. "I had been working part time at a big United Methodist Church in my town. Most of the time, I was working with the youth and Sunday school, but I became a lay speaker. That was when my own kids were early teens".

"Then after Mark died, once I started to get my bearings back, I decided to go to seminary to see about getting a degree that would allow me to work in the church. I had filled in and preached for our pastor a couple of times earlier when the pastor was sick, and that made me think about going to seminary to get a degree for church work, and in the process, I discovered that Methodist women have been ordained to preach since 1956!"

"My first sermons were very painful, probably for everybody, but eventually I came to realize that when I have worked on a message that has some value — something that others would do well to hear — then I got excited about sharing it. Suddenly it was a delight to preach! So, you could say I have come full circle, from not even thinking a woman ought to preach, to being convinced that I have a message I want to share with others at worship!"

Janice listened carefully to Winnie, nodding along with her as her story unfolded. "Yes! We were just studying the Epistle of First John last week, and he said the Apostles were sharing the gospel so that their joy could be complete. That's what you're saying, isn't it? When you have a message that is wonderful and exciting, you can't be fully joyful about it until you have shared it with others!"

Winnie grinned. "That's exactly what I mean! You're not a bad theologian yourself, Janice!"

"Is the sheriff in?" Winnie asked.

"He's down there," Janice pointed down the hall toward the jail. "He'll be back pretty soon. He came in with a man in handcuffs late last night and took him back there."

Winnie didn't think that Misty Falls's jail hosted too many prisoners. She hadn't ever heard Mickey Allen mention having prisoners before. She asked, "Do you know who it is?"

Janice hadn't seen the man before. "No, he's not much more than a boy, though, maybe twenty years old."

Winnie was about to leave when the sheriff came into the room. His face lit up when he saw Winnie.

"Mornin,' Pastor Winnie!" he said.

"Looks like you've had some serious sheriffin' business today." Winnie said.

"I came upon a fight late last night in the parking lot by the highway, and I broke it up. Two of the men took off runnin' before I could find out about them. I think they were Hispanics and didn't want any trouble with authority. The guy I picked up made the mistake of usin' some foul language at me, and I didn't appreciate it. I put him back there (he indicated the direction of the jail) to cool off."

"Is there something I can do for you this mornin'?" he asked Winnie.

"I'm not quite sure why I dropped by here, but I met a young woman about an hour ago, and she was upset because her boyfriend hadn't come home last night. Do you suppose that's just a coincidence?" Winnie asked.

The sheriff cocked his head, thoughtfully. "You may be on to something. M'be I'll mosey on over and see what's up. Where does she live?"

Winnie explained about Linda, Josh, and their kids, and how she had just met Linda's sister, Laura Lee, and her kids. It was her boyfriend who was missing.

The sheriff agreed to stop by the apartments and see what was up.

✳ ✳ ✳

Thursday evening the elementary school cafeteria was full to capacity, or so it seemed to Winnie, as she squeezed onto a bench beside Joyce Ellen Randall (the farmer's wife) and the Washingtons — Bradley, Letitia and Little Brad.

They had all come to hear about a playground building program for Misty Falls.

The mayor had contacted a design firm in Illinois that plans and designs playgrounds unique to a particular community's needs. The plan, from what Winnie had read, was for the playground to be built, "barn-raising" style, with everyone in the community coming together over a weekend to actually erect the playground.

Before that weekend, much work would be needed to raise the money and prepare for all the workers — skilled and unskilled — and all the needed supplies for the project.

Winnie had looked at several large posters hanging around the cafeteria which showed colorful examples of playgrounds that had already been built around the country, using this "barn-raising" method. Winnie

90

could see how this would be a good project for Misty Falls to take on — a positive place for our young families to play in and grow.

The evening was informative and interesting, and, by the end, everyone in the room was excited about having such a playground in Misty Falls. A steering committee was picked to oversee the project. Winnie wasn't surprised when both Joyce Ellen Randall and Bradley Washington were chosen to sit on the committee.

As folks stood up to leave the gathering, Winnie spotted Mickey Allen Barrymore coming toward her.

"Evenin' Ma'am," he said to her. The sheriff leaned closer toward Winnie and spoke very low, "That was more 'n a coincidence yesterday."

Winnie straightened up as she realized he was referring to the young man who had "visited" the jail the day before.

She and the sheriff walked out of the cafeteria together toward the parking lot. The sheriff added, "Yep, he's the boyfriend all right. I drove over to the apartments after you and I spoke and met the family. I learned they're new in town, having just returned from Florida."

"Miss McKinsey asked me if I had heard anything about her boy-friend, Jerry Lane. I told her that was the name of the young man I'd put in jail last night.

"She was all smiles when I told her about him, and she asked if he would soon be free. She was obviously pleased to hear he was fine."

"I released him from jail when I returned from talking to her. He's probably back there by now," the sheriff said.

Winnie thanked her friend for sharing the information about that young family.

※ ※ ※

Tim and Mary Lou Owens and their four charges left Friday morning, before the peace walkers arrived, to drive back down to the gulf. The news had come that the children's father had passed and that the service would be held Sunday afternoon. Before they left, Winnie stopped at the Owens' home to see them.

Mary Lou had called her pastor to advise her about their trip. This final word about the children's father re-opened their wounds, again, and the children were in various stages of unrest and grief.

Winnie quickly gathered up several items from the Sunday school supply closet that might serve to occupy the kids on their trip to the gulf. When she arrived at the Owens' home, she was greeted by the children who wanted her to know that their Daddy was gone. Their tears were real, and Winnie wanted to cry with them, but she decided it might be more comforting to approach them differently.

She was their pastor and the one who should bring the good news, the resurrection joy, to these small children, to let them know how God's love spreads even beyond life itself.

Winnie sat down on the floor with Andy and Carlie, the two youngest, on her lap and the older two seated Indian fashion before her.

She told them about Jesus. She began with the story of the disciples and the others, who were so very sad and in much pain because of losing their dear, good friend, Jesus. He had been with them for a while, traveling with them across many miles, talking with them, telling them wonderful parables and stories — about God's heavenly Kingdom. He was their teacher. He was even more than a teacher; he was a healer. He healed many, many people of sickness and disease. He did wonderful signs like calming the sea in a terrible storm and making a whole lot of wine out of ordinary water! He was so wonderful, and everyone who followed him and heard him speak loved him very much.

"But one day a terrible thing happened. He died. He didn't die because he was old or sick, he died a terrible and gruesome death because of some bad people! His disciples saw him dying, and they were in terrible grief, not knowing what to do. They couldn't help him, and they didn't want him to suffer or die. But he died."

"They felt so badly. Can you imagine how they felt?" Winnie asked the children. They nodded their heads and agreed. Yes, they could understand.

"Three days later, Jesus' friends were sitting together still feeling sad when suddenly Jesus was standing there among them! He was alive, completely alive, and he was standing there with them in the room! He smiled and spoke to them. He talked to them for a while. He was hungry, and they gave him some fish to eat."

"You can imagine the joy everyone felt when they saw Jesus was alive! They had no more reason to cry or be sad. They were filled with joy. They must have sung and danced together; they were so happy!"

"That is the greatest story in the world, isn't it?" Winnie asked the children. "Best of all, it's not a make believe story but an absolutely true story. And it is the reason why we can be glad, even when there is sadness in our lives."

"Your father is in heaven today with Jesus, and that's a good reason to be glad. And more than that, you can have Jesus here with you, too. He wants to be your friend and to go with you wherever you go."

The children had settled down and listened to Winnie's tale. They seemed to appreciate the distraction of her story, pulling them away from their sadness for a moment.

Winnie smiled at Mary Lou and Tim who had listened to her story, too. "You can give the kids the pictures to color on your trip. I also have some CD's of children's Christian music I found at church that you can use on your trip," she told them.

Winnie turned to the kids, again. "This isn't the easiest time for you kids, I know, but can you see how God is taking care of you, even in this very sad time? God has provided a wonderful home for you and a dear aunt and uncle to help you during this difficult time."

✻ ✻ ✻

The peace walkers came and went and everyone who met them was charmed by them! Winnie was pleased that it turned out so well.

She personally enjoyed meeting many of the walkers. Some of them were former Christians before they became Buddhists, and their apostasy caused Winnie to think about what might have happened to their faith in Christ.

One of the women Winnie met told her that she had grown up Christian, but there was Buddhist temple just five blocks from her house, where she would join them sometimes. The woman told Winnie that she was looking for more structure in her life, and she enjoyed the discipline that the Buddhists required.

Winnie noticed a significant amount of discipline among the walkers. They each seemed to have assigned tasks to accomplish — making and cleaning up their evening meal and organizing their equipment. They joined together in an evening gathering where they voiced their thoughts to one another. It was rather like a town hall meeting Winnie thought.

Their leader was a petite, Japanese, woman monk. She had decided to begin a five day fast; the only thing she would allow herself to take in was hot, lemon tea. Winnie noted the reverence that the entire group of walkers held for this minute woman. They were very impressed by her fasting, which she had apparently done on a previous occasion. The diminutive monk didn't speak English, so there was no communication between Winnie and the woman, but Winnie did note her irritation at those in the kitchen having to do with not preparing her hot lemon tea in a timely enough manner.

Discipline! That's what Winnie heard from several of the walkers. They craved the discipline of the community, and they felt they were getting something from the Buddhists.

Discipline doesn't belong solely to the Buddhists, Winnie mused. Discipline's root word comes from the word 'disciple', and aren't we Christians disciples of Christ? *Aren't we to be disciplined about our walk with Jesus? How have we managed not to convey that message to our people? Being a member of a church has become far too easy! Salvation comes from Christ Jesus, but once we realize that it was Christ who has saved us by his sacrifice on the cross, THEN we come into a relationship with him and begin our disciplined life with Him!* Winnie laughed at herself, adding, *Okay, I'm not even preaching to the choir, I'm preaching to myself!*

Just before the walkers left, they gathered together, hand in hand, in a great circle. They included Muddy Creek's breakfast-makers, too — about fifteen of them. They stood in the circle, swaying slightly to the right and to the left and making a low, monotone sound that continued for some time, maybe five minutes. It was not a "note" *per se*, Winnie noticed, but rather a low, sustained vocal sound that anyone could make, musically inclined or not. *Not exactly Amazing Grace.*

The walkers departed by eight o'clock Saturday morning for the next leg of their journey. They left not a trace of their presence at Muddy Creek Church, save the happy memories they had left the Muddy Creekers. They had been very efficient picking up for themselves. The church members were most pleased with themselves for having had the experience and for having stretched themselves beyond their natural comfort zone. They would remember the walkers for some time to come.

Chapter 10. An Invitation

Winnie opened up her email account Monday morning to a surprise.

John's email told her that he had an upcoming meeting to attend at Ole Miss with S.O.P.H.I.A., a group of philosophers in America. They would meet the first week after the New Year in Oxford, Mississippi, and John wondered if Winnie might be able to meet him while he was in the South.

Winnie smiled at the thought. "That's an interesting invitation," she told Bitty. "He didn't say specifically where we might meet. Maybe meeting on neutral territory would be better than one of our own home turfs. There would be no avoiding the fact that I'm the pastor at Muddy Creek Church if he comes here," she commented aloud.

"Dear John," Winnie typed her answer. "Your trip south sounds like fun, and I would be happy to meet you somewhere for a day."

"Have you ever been to the Gaylord Hotel in Nashville? We could both drive a bit and meet there. It looks to be about halfway between Ole Miss and Misty Falls. I've heard the hotel there is a good place to spend time. Over the years I've heard a number of my friends tell me about going there and what fun they've had at the Gaylord. There's a wonderful garden inside the hotel that's several stories high. They have strolling paths all over the place with cute little shoppes here and there as well as inviting cuisines from which to choose. There's also a Grand Ole' Opry museum nearby.

"What dates are you talking about?

"Hoping we can work something out, Winnie"

Winnie hit the "send" button and prayed a little prayer right then that whatever happened would be in God's will. *Please, LORD, don't let this thing go where it should not go, if it is not in your will!*

* * *

Thom Jackson, the church trustee, told his pastor that the parsonage was due for some updating and that he was sending a man to the parsonage to take some measurements of the floors in the kitchen, laundry room, and the bathrooms. "That would be like an early Christmas gift. Nice!" She told Thom.

Jeff presented himself as the man whom Thom had sent to replace the linoleum floors. Winnie quickly learned that Jeff was new to Misty Falls; he had just moved down from Ontario, Canada. Turns out that he had met a woman on the internet who lived in Misty Falls, and they had become friends. Jeff had been a truck driver, and his route took him regularly between Ontario and Miami. He decided to stop one day and meet this ePen Pal of his. When they met, they realized they had something worth keeping. They had each been alone for a long time, so they decided to marry. Jeff would move south, since Jillian didn't like the idea of the colder, Canadian winters.

As they were speaking, Winnie's eyes got wider and wider.

"Are you talking about Jillian Post?" she asked.

Jeff's face lit up. "Yes! Do you know her?"

"Yes, I know Jillian. In fact, we spoke not long ago. How fun to meet you! Obviously, you two are getting along right nicely!"

"We think so!" Jeff said enthusiastically. "We're getting married over Thanksgiving!"

Winnie smiled and nodded. "You've both made some life-altering decisions pretty quickly, haven't you?"

"I'd say! Yes, but it seems so right for both of us. I am in a totally different environment from my Canadian roots, but I'm doing fine. My entire family lives in and around Toronto. Travis, my son, will probably join us down here after school gets out next summer. He's still got a couple years in high school to finish up. He's living with his mom right now."

Winnie showed Jeff the rooms he needed to measure. He said that he'd be back in a week with the new floor to begin laying it.

After Jeff left, Winnie began thinking about how his long-distance relationship had blossomed so nicely. Jeff and Jillian were apparently very happy with their new arrangement. *Wonder if these electronic connections that seem to be developing will continue to be blessed?* Of course Winnie was thinking of her own, personal, long-distance relationship that seemed to be humming right along.

✳ ✳ ✳

Wednesday Winnie spotted Nina as she was stepping into The Depot Diner, so she followed her inside and sat down across from her. Nina lit up when she saw her friend.

"I didn't know I'd be seeing you today, Winnie," Nina smiled.

"Are you on your lunch break?" Winnie asked.

"Yes, I've got 'till one before I need to get back to the office," Nina answered.

"So, may I join you for lunch?" Winnie smiled.

"Oh, please!" Nina agreed.

"I don't eat out all the time, of course, but I was over at the post office and saw you going into the diner, so I decided to throw caution to the wind and follow you!" Winnie teased.

"Would the caution be for the food or the company?" Nina wanted to know.

"It would be for my waistline!" Winnie retorted.

They spent a few minutes deciding what to order, and then returned to their conversation.

Winnie opened with, "I've met a man."

Nina leaned forward, eyes wide, and said, "Tell me!" Nina exclaimed, "I'm all ears!"

"Actually, I knew John before I met Mark. We were in high school together back about the time of the dinosaurs!" Winnie laughed.

"AND! You saw him at your reunion?"

"Yes, we met at the reunion, and we stuck together like two Fig Newtons in a box!" Winnie grinned at her silly metaphor.

"I don't think I've heard that one! Is this a 'sticky' arrangement, already?" Nina teased back.

"No. I didn't mean that. It just popped out right then!" Winnie grinned.

"Actually, I knew John would be there, because he called me the morning of the fall festival, and we talked for quite a while. He had been asked to call a few former classmates and encourage them to attend our high school's fortieth reunion," Winnie continued.

"What's he like?" Nina begged.

"Well! He seems to be very eligible from what I can tell. He's a professor of philosophy at The University of Chicago. He's been teaching there most of his professional life. He's traveled in Europe. He never married. ""

"Uh Oh!" Nina shook her head. "Wonder what that's about?"

"I really couldn't say, but I am intrigued," Winnie answered. "Maybe he sees himself like professors of long ago, when they never married; in fact they weren't allowed to marry.

"We both took the same Latin classes as well as an English class in high school, but we ran in different circles back then."

"Anyhow, we met at the reunion and spent both evenings together. We had so much fun! We laughed and laughed. We even discovered we had been at the zoo in Dublin on the same day back in 1978! How about that for a coincidence!"

Nina was charmed that her friend was finding such an interesting connection. "Where do you suppose this is going?" she asked.

"That's the thing. John knows I live here in Misty Falls. I told him I work in our church office and that I do a lot of things at the church — like the bulletins, teach Bible study, and such. But I haven't told him I'm the preacher at the church!" Winnie confessed. "Maybe I'm lucky that Muddy Creek United Methodist Church doesn't have a website, yet."

"I don't quite understand," Nina said. "Are you ashamed of being a pastor? Why wouldn't you tell him?"

"Of course I'm not ashamed of being a pastor!" Winnie assured Nina. "At first I thought he already knew about my profession, and so I didn't mention it," Winnie started to explain. "And then, when we talked back in September, John said something that made me think he had a problem with church, and somehow, it didn't seem to be wise to drop my vocation into the conversation at that point, so I didn't."

"I can see that," Nina agreed. "What did he say that made you think he wasn't too fond of the church?"

"He said he didn't believe in church.

"He caught me off guard, and I wasn't quite sure how to respond, so I made this lame joke, instead."

"So you actually don't know what he meant by his slur on the church, do you?" Nina said.

"Not really. Maybe it's nothing. Maybe he was teasing me; but who knows!" Winnie said with exasperation.

"John sounds like he'd be a pretty terrific catch, though, don't you think?" Nina asked her friend.

Winnie smiled and nodded agreement. "On one level I do!" she said.

"This morning I got an email from John, and he said he'd like us to meet after the New Year. He's planning to attend a conference with other philosophers at Ole Miss on the first week of January, and he wrote to ask if we could get together afterwards." Winnie told her friend.

Nina's eyes opened wide, and a grin grew across her face. "Now THAT'S got possibilities! Obviously, he's more than just a passing acquaintance!"

"I don't know, quite, what would be good. I can't disregard my feelings. John's fun to be with, and we seem to connect on a deep level somewhere. Maybe this is someone that is right for me. It could be part of God's plan for my life. I really want to be alert to what God wants for me at every step in my life!

"I don't know. Since we live so far apart, it's not so easy to figure things out. There's a lot I don't know about him — why he never married for one thing. What about his discomfort with the church? What about that? How can I be seriously interested with anyone who doesn't follow Christ?" Winnie asked, mostly to herself.

"You don't seem to limit your friends to just those who attend church," Nina winked at her friend.

Winnie smiled at Nina. "You're right. I have no problem with that. After all, Christians are supposed to be IN the world but not OF the world, if you know what I mean."

"IN it but not OF it? Excuse me?" Nina knit her brows.

"We're not supposed to run away from the world — like hermits — but we should be 'counter-cultural' in our approach to the world. We have something different than what the world expects. We are not OF the world when we are following Christ. Christian thinking often flies in the face of worldly wisdom," Winnie explained.

"I see. But it's okay to live among the rest of us, right?" Nina asked.

"Sure. We're supposed to be good examples to everyone — and a blessing to everyone. Maybe people will see our way of doing things and want to follow Jesus, too. Maybe they will see something in our lives that they would like to have," Winnie said.

"Then how would that be different in a closer relationship, say marriage?" Nina asked.

"Actually, St. Paul wrote that if an unbeliever is married to a believer and has no qualms about it then it's fine for them to stay married. It is apparently up to the unbeliever to make the call. The Christian, who is married to an unbeliever, doesn't seem to have the same option to walk away from the marriage simply because the spouse doesn't follow Christ," Winnie answered.

"There you go! You've answered your own question — sort of. If John has no problem with your being a believer ...."

"You're going pretty fast there!" Winnie moaned. "We've just begun this — whatever it is."

"But now you're talking about a time together in the New Year," Nina reminded her friend.

Winnie nodded her head. "Okay, I'm <u>thinking</u> about it, but I won't be other than who I am. If things work out right, I'll still be following Jesus. I'm not turning my back on my faith or on my promise to follow the Lord, no matter what."

They were well into their lunch when Winnie asked her friend, "How about you? Do you date?"

Nina thought for a moment before answering. "In a way I have, but not regularly."

"Uh <u>huh</u>!" Winnie grinned at her friend. "You're keeping something from me?"

"There's nothing, really, to keep from you. I've gone out with Tucker Joe a couple of times, but not recently" Nina explained.

"Tucker Joe!" Winnie grinned even broader this time. "He's a little younger than you, isn't he?"

Nina nodded ascent. "Yes, he is, but that isn't such a big factor in life, since we're both adults.

"Tucker Joe and I have known one another, actually, since Dan and I came here to Misty Falls, but I've been alone for more 'n fifteen years. He's never married. I suppose you knew that." Nina added.

"I always think it's a bit unusual for a man not to marry." Winnie answered.

"We used to call a woman who didn't marry an old maid, and it was a terrible pejorative, but for men there's no parallel nomenclature, like old gentleman. It doesn't have the same snap to it, does it?" Winnie grinned.

"No, it doesn't!" Nina laughed. "Tucker Joe and I went to the theater a couple of times. He's very wrapped up in Friendlie's Foods, of course. Getting him away from the store, he showed himself to be a whole different man. He really gets into acting — even at little theatre. He told me he was in his high school's production of Oklahoma, years ago. He still craves the stage, and the people, and the music, and that whole world. It was fun to see him in that different setting."

"Are you still seeing him?" Winnie asked.

"Well, Tuck's mother got sick, and he had to be totally focused on the store and working with her, and then she passed away, and he got even busier. So, no, I suppose we're not still seeing one another." Nina sighed.

Later Winnie reflected on this new information about Tuck. *Looks like Tucker Joe may be a late bloomer, but I wonder if he's beginning to unfurl his wings to see if they'll support him. It will be interesting to see how things come out.*

✳ ✳ ✳

I knew that wasn't going to work; I could have told everyone right at the start. But no one asked me, of course.

Winnie had just put down the phone after speaking to Sallie. Things were getting touchy around the Hardy's little cottage, so she and Connie and George and the babies had moved to an apartment in town.

Winnie agreed to stop by and see them later in the day.

The place was easy to find, and, Winnie thought, it was surprising how quickly the new apartment had come together. Sallie and the little family had been in the apartment a couple days, already. It wasn't big, but there was room for Sallie in one bedroom and Connie and George and the babies in the other. Winnie noticed that the place was furnished rather nicely, and she wondered how in the world they would have been able to appropriate so much stuff so soon!

She asked about the furnishings, and Connie explained that she had met several of the neighbors in the other apartments. They were all very sympathetic about the new babies and this young family trying to get by on virtually nothing, and, before she knew it, items began showing up at their door. The neighbors had supplied a table, and chairs, and a rug, and various odds and ends. They even had a small, oak, roll top desk that had been given to them!

Winnie saw the baby girls who now had names: Samantha Rose Oliver and Shelby Ann Oliver. They were adorable babies, and Winnie could see how much the family loved them.

Winnie agreed to call the case worker and tell her about her visit. Since she had written the letter saying she knew Sallie and was an interested party for the Olivers, Winnie knew it would be good to keep current with the DHR.

So far, so good.

George had already found a job, so he was busy working. Connie told Winnie that she was anxious to get a job too. There was a small diner across the street from their apartment, which sat just off the highway. Connie would apply for a job in the next day or two. Winnie agreed to be a reference for Connie. Winnie understood that Sallie, who wasn't likely to get a job, would be the perfect sitter for the twins.

✳ ✳ ✳

"Great! I'm really looking forward to seeing you! Love you bunches! Bye, Dear." Winnie put the phone down and smiled. She had been talking to her daughter, Claire, about visiting the O'Neill's over Thanksgiving. She would drive over Monday after her big day of preaching — two sermons in one day. It would be a five hour drive to her place in Kentucky, but Winnie had made the drive before. It was no problem; she was comfortable driving.

The O'Neill's lived nearly over to Missouri. They were a very typical family — a mom, dad, son, and daughter. The kids were still pretty small. Derry (Alexander) O'Neill was in kindergarten, and little Babsie had just turned three. Winnie didn't get to be Grannie as often as she would like, but she was determined to soak in as much family as she could in the short week they had together.

Fortunately, Winnie had already planned to have a substitute preacher for the Sunday after Thanksgiving, which was yet a couple of Sundays off. An old friend from seminary had agreed to preach at Muddy Creek. He wasn't filling a pulpit nowadays, as he was involved in an administrative job for the church, so he was pleased to be able to pitch in. Winnie would be present as the liturgist, but Bob would bring the message. *How nice to have an actual week off!*

Chapter 11. Trouble for Olivers

The fire was not life-threatening, at least that's what the fire chief's report stated, but nevertheless the kitchen was half-charred, leaving a big mess to clean up and rebuild at the Air Force housing apartment complex in Sembach, Germany. The couple, whose residence had been burned, were provided a room in the *Gast Haus* on the air base where they would be able to stay while they awaited the rebuilding of their kitchen.

The McPhersons, the neighbors, who had just moved the day before into their new flat directly above the burned apartment, didn't actually suffer any damage to their apartment, except for smoke. They opened all the windows in their apartment, allowing the breeze to blow through their third story flat, picked up a few overnight items, and left for the night, because the lingering smoky presence was too much to try to sleep there.

As they were coming down the stairwell they met Mindy Moore who lived in the four bedroom apartment on the first floor. Mindy had been watching the entire scene as the fire department responded to the fire across the hall and up one floor from her flat. She was greatly relieved that there was no more damage to the apartment other than the kitchen and that no one was hurt.

When Mindy saw her new neighbors coming down the stairwell, she introduced herself. The McPhersons were happy to meet this neighbor. They hadn't met too many folks, yet, in the community, so it was pleasant to get to know someone in their stairwell. Mindy realized that this new couple might be in need of a place to spend the night, owing to the excessive smoke in their apartment, and she had an idea. Mindy and Dan's apartment included a maid's quarters in the attic on the fourth floor of the apartment, so she invited the McPhersons to spend the night up there. (That room had not been affected by the smoke.) She also invited them to have dinner with her family, an offer that Chet and Angela quickly accepted.

That was the beginning of a friendship that developed quite naturally. It turned out that Chet was a new tech sergeant in the same squadron where Dan was master sergeant, so they saw each other on and off the job. Over time the families grew to be close friends.

Dan Moore, Jr., who was Pearly Mae Moore's younger son, had enlisted in the U.S. Air Force after high school and made it a career. He had become a mechanic, working on just about every plane the Air Force flew. In his current job he was no longer hands-on working with the planes, but he continued to appreciate good work when he saw it. Dan was quick to observe the keenness that Chet approached his work on the planes, and a certain camaraderie developed between the two men.

Dan and Chet happened to learn about a real estate venture in New Mexico through a developer who was building new homes in Albuquerque and offering stock in his company. It seemed a good opportunity to invest, so they did. The two men pooled their money and bought stock in the development, which took off quickly in the early 90's.

Dan's next assignment took him to Kirkland Air Force Base in Albuquerque, which was, coincidentally, close to the development where they had been investing. The two friends kept in contact with one another, and Dan sent Chet updates about the growing development.

Last spring Dan decided to sell their interests in the development, and it turned out to be a fortunate decision to sell the stock when he did. Later in the year the market looked much less hopeful; in fact, as the days wore on, national news was showing serious trouble in nearly every aspect of the financial and business world.

"Boy, did I figure that right!" thought Dan. "I couldn't have made a better decision to pull out when I did, if I had been able to read the future!"

The stock had realized a tidy profit, and half of it belonged to Chet.

Dan had followed Chet's movements when they returned stateside. Chet's Christmas cards told the story. For a couple of years the cards had been signed by Chet and Angela, and then, after missing a few years, Chet sent a preprinted card explaining how he and Angela were no longer married. Five years later, he married a sweet, southern gal named Lucy Jane. They were newly wedded, looking forward to all that married life had to offer; they were living in northern Kentucky.

That was last Christmas, but then Dan heard, through a third party, that Chet had contracted cancer and died very suddenly last May! He hadn't seen Chet for nearly fifteen years, and now, without any warning, he was gone!

Dan wished he could have been there at the end to see Chet one more time, but that was impossible now.

Dan wanted to do something to honor Chet's memory, maybe help his family somehow, and he remembered that Chet had left a widow — a woman named Lucy Jane. There was something about her name that sounded familiar, and then Dan remembered that he used to know a girl named Lucy Jane Smith back in Misty Falls. *She couldn't be the same Lucy Jane, could she? The world wasn't that small, was it?*

Dan typed her name in the Facebook search bar, and up came Lucy Jane (Smith) McPherson — newly married to Chet McPherson and living in Louisville.

"Man! How wild is that!" He exclaimed. "I know her family. Teddy Smith, would be her older brother. He and I went to high school together."

Dan felt for Chet's bride, and he decided he would figure a way to give Lucy Jane Chet's portion of the profit from the investment they had made.

A few clicks of research later Dan found that Lucy Jane had transferred from the Louisville Red Cross office to an office back home, near Misty Falls.

"She's living in Misty Falls again," Dan told Mindy. "I'm going to fly back to Misty Falls to see Mama, and on the visit I should be able to talk to Lucy Jane, Chet McPherson's new wife. I'll be home before Thanksgiving, and I'll bring Mama back with me. It will be good for her to see our family. Do you suppose we can host her through the holidays? Mama's not getting any younger, and it would be a really great visit for us all."

Mindy, who was Pearly Mae's favorite daughter-in-law, was happy to see the holidays developing a theme. "We'll have four generations with us by Christmas. Won't that be merry?"

✳ ✳ ✳

Winnie wasn't surprised to hear from Sallie, but her voice had a serious edge to it. She wanted to know if Winnie could come by today and see her. *I wonder what's come up?*

Winnie was out the door in no time and on her way to the Oliver's apartment.

When Winnie arrived Connie and her mother were very subdued. The baby girls looked well enough, wearing cute, little, matching, pink outfits. *At least the girls are fine.*

Winnie sat in the living room and Connie explained the problem straight forwardly: their secret was out. The DHR woman had made a visit to their neighbors and told them to watch out for any signs of trouble for the twin babies. She told them that the Olivers had already lost other babies to the DHR in South Carolina. The neighbors were instructed to contact the DHR if there was anything they saw that appeared to be the least bit amiss with the Olivers.

Connie was devastated as was Sallie. They felt like their little family was now under a microscope, even being spied upon. All this DHR activity had re-opened the wounds of losing the other children, and the fear of possibly losing these two, precious, little girls was nearly more than either one of them could imagine.

This was a new idea to Winnie. She couldn't fathom the pain that Connie and George (and Sallie) had experienced having had their first three babies taken away from them.

Winnie spent some time with the women that morning. She didn't think she had any really good answers for them except to do the best they could for the twins. She prayed that this situation would resolve itself.

* * *

Thursday morning Winnie turned on her computer, opened her email, and happily found a message from John.

He wrote most mornings, and Winnie was discovering how much she looked forward to these quick, first-thing-in-the-morning greetings from John. *Our friendship is really taking shape.*

The message was about the up-coming, Thanksgiving week. John would be going skiing. He was an avid skier and used holidays to get away from work and visit the slopes.

John would be flying to Aspen for the Thanksgiving weekend. He wondered if Winnie would join him there. He had reservations at a ski resort, same place he'd been using for years. He'd arrive there late Wednesday, since he couldn't travel until his classes were finished that day.

Winnie stopped reading. This offer seemed to involve a step that was probably very normal and expected for adult relationships, but for her, her convictions, and her vocation, it would need to be a different story. Of course, Winnie couldn't know exactly what John had in mind; his invitation was very open — come, enjoy — yet she couldn't assume there were no expectations either.

He's really interested in me, obviously. I don't mind that.

Winnie paused to dream. She had to be honest with herself. Here was an opportunity that had never presented itself before, and she realized at once that she was tempted to accept. Surely, she and John could enjoy one another's company in such a romantic and secluded setting.

Winnie had a very firm respect for the sanctity of marriage and the gift of marital intimacy. God had truly outdone Himself in that department — a great blessing — one she had surely missed for a long time, and, Winnie remembered, this gift ranked very high on most men's agendas. She wanted to respect that, too. She didn't want to toy with the issue.

The temptation for her was clearly there, but Winnie also realized it was just *that* — a temptation. Actually, John had not, in so many words, suggested that such a weekend might develop into this deeper relationship, but assuming otherwise would be a mistake.

Finally, Winnie faced the invitation squarely and decided. *I can't take that step, not yet, besides, I could lose my credibility with my community and congregation simply by accepting such an invitation. A scandal in the church rarely needs anything more than the appearance of impropriety. But, pragmatics aside, the really important thing is, it simply wouldn't be right.*

Winnie had been married to Mark for nearly seventeen years. They had seen their marriage through various struggles, like most young marrieds, and they had watched their marriage mature and become solid and wonderful. It didn't happen overnight. No indeed. It took many trials, some difficult words and misunderstandings, and the advent of their wonderful children with all their added dynamics.

Winnie and Mark had grown confident in their marriage: It belonged just to the two of them. It was sacred, and they were faithful to one another. That was the way God had intended marriage to be. Despite much social and personal pressure they decided to not start their marriage until they were formally married.

They were aware that some couples chose to jump the gun before they married, and many of them never tied the knot. Perhaps this was because they had avoided the commitment piece to the relationship. They seemed to be committed to one another only as long as it felt good.

Marriage, on the other hand, was a commitment, a vow to God, that the two would bring their complete selves — all the gifts they could muster — to help build the marriage. It was not a pledge lightly given.

Those who didn't come before an altar or a judge and make those vows, didn't get that commitment. They didn't have the promise from the other to love, honor, trust, and respect from their partner. They missed knowing the other was committed to their venture.

Besides, giving things away too quickly didn't encourage commitment, rather the gift became cheap. Winnie remembered the old saw, *"Why buy the cow if the milk is free?" Maybe that's a trite saying, but it's still a good question.*

With this in mind Winnie realized she didn't want to compromise a potentially good relationship (might marriage possibly be in their future?) by acting too quickly. Jumping too quickly into some physical arrangement was *not* the way to develop a strong relationship aimed at increasing commitment. It spoke of indiscretion, lack of self-control, and lack of respect for the other person. No, if this fledgling connection had any potential, she and John would need to feel their way carefully through the complicated vicissitudes of getting to know one another.

Now, how to explain this to John?

Winnie wrote,

Dear John, What a wonderful time you will have in Aspen skying over the slopes! It sounds like a grand way to spend the holiday, and it's very kind of you to invite me to be your guest there in the snow and the fun, but I can't accept.

I've already made plans to spend the week with my daughter and her family in Kentucky, and I can't change my plans so close to the day. But, there is another reason why I wouldn't be able to come this time.

I am very aware that we are becoming special to one another, and I have great respect for what our friendship might become. Because of this respect I would not want to do anything that might damage its potential. (Can you understand what I'm trying to say?)

I don't want to be too forward about this, but IF we find our friendship is growing into something greater, something that we would want to make more permanent — down the road — I want to give it the best foundation possible. That boils down to our being very circumspect in our deportment.

King Solomon wrote, "For everything there is a season, and a time for every matter under heaven." Surely that would include adult relationships, wouldn't it?

I can feel myself blushing even as I mention this (in an email, would you believe!), but I feel very strongly that it is right and proper.

I have known but one man in my life, and it is his name that I bear to this day. We had a loving marriage, which began the night we married. I would not want to settle for something less in the future. I pray you understand this.

Have a great weekend; DON'T break a leg!

Your Good Friend,

Winnie

✳ ✳ ✳

Saturday afternoon Winnie saw Pearly Mae at The Depot Diner. She was with a man, who turned out to be her son, Dan, Jr. Introductions were made all around, and Pearly Mae explained to Winnie how her son had come to take her back with him to Albuquerque to be the family matriarch of four generations over Thanksgiving and Christmas.

They chatted together several minutes. Winnie was pleased for her friend Pearly Mae. What a nice way for her to enjoy the holidays, and what a fine surprise Dan had given his mother.

They would be coming to the community Thanksgiving service Sunday evening. Winnie told them that she was preaching then, and she was happy they could come hear her.

✳ ✳ ✳

Saturday evening had arrived, and Winnie was facing two sermons the next day. She hadn't preached two, different sermons on the same day before, but she had been working on both of them for several weeks. They were pretty much ready now.

It was a happy accident that she didn't have to preach the week after visiting with her family. Winnie remembered other times when she visited Claire's or Paul's family, but still had the responsibility of coming up with a sermon for the next Sunday. She had secluded herself in her room, laptop on her lap, working every morning to pull together her thoughts for the sermon, all the while being very aware of her family — those cute grandchildren — waiting her appearance. The one responsibility almost spoiled the holiday time she had come to enjoy.

This time, maybe I've got it right. Bob will bring the message, and I can enjoy my time with the O'Neill's. After all, even God rested on the seventh day!

Chapter 12. The Best Laid Plans

Winnie watched as the road whizzed by under her car and with it the concerns in Misty Falls. Every mile carried her further and further from the town, and the stresses and expectations she knew as pastor faded slowly. Those responsibilities were sometimes heavy and sometimes oppressive — like watching someone else's troubles and not being able to do more than impotently console those involved and pray with them and for them.

Everyone should get away from it all, occasionally, Winnie believed. *Whatever "it all" is — the office, studies, heavy work, the day-to-day grind — getting away is good for a person's interior, and exterior self. No doubt, getting away from the usual grind can be therapeutic and cathartic. It can present a new perspective on one's everyday self and bring new vigor to the humdrum and ordinary.*

Situations that belonged to others came and went, and Winnie could professionally distance herself from them, but the sermon requirement never abated — it came every week no matter what else was happening, no matter how well she felt or what else she needed to do in the world. Giving sermons was in the final analysis much fun, but it was fun that came only after long hours of wrestling her message into a presentable form. Once Winnie found and understood the message, presenting it Sunday morning became a delight, but for some reason that was a lesson she had to relearn each week.

It was quite a paradox for Winnie, a real approach-avoidance situation. She dreaded it and loved it all at the same time. *Goodness, My Dear, I don't suppose I should ever feel so put upon or heavily saddled with that responsibility! After all, I chose to do it. I could have gone into some other area of Christian vocation or even social work, but I chose this. And serving the Lord is a blessing, of course! Oh, Lord, help me put a better face on my sermon building. Help me to recognize the blessing it is – which I definitely feel when I'm actually preaching! Thank you, Lord.*

Winnie could feel herself relaxing as she passed through the new scenery. She was always reminded of God's marvelous creativity and faithfulness when she found herself close to nature, as these great forests and lakes brought to her mind. "*Isn't God great, and good, and incredi-*

ble?" she thought. *"How can anyone look into the immense beauty and grandeur of nature without being thankful?"*

Of course, Winnie had just preached about being thankful the evening before, and she was still filled with her message — being thankful in all circumstances. It was easy to be thankful for such a time as this, but Winnie's message was to remind her listeners (and herself) that even when troubled times come along, we need to stay focused on being thankful to God. An attitude of thanksgiving can push aside other, not so productive attitudes, like fear, or rage, or some other impropriety.

Winnie was relishing this Monday morning, as she did every Monday, because it was so far from Sunday, but this time, of course, she wouldn't have the countdown that she always had as Sundays drew closer. And that was another reason to be thankful!

The week with the O'Neill's in Kentucky was especially good for Winnie, serving as a fresh wind blowing out the (almost) staleness of her workday environment.

The grandchildren stirred memories for Winnie of when Paul and Claire were young themselves. *Goodness, wasn't life different back then?* Winnie used to think that her life was mostly a big blur of activities when the kids were small, running from one event or chore to the next. This time it was possible to engage the children as much as she wanted and then sit back as an observer, watching the flurry of projects and frivolity.

Five year old Derry was already reading. He went with his family to the library each week to hear stories read by the librarian and to pick out books to take home and read with Mommy or Daddy. He was riding a two wheeler, and he was navigating pretty well on his skates too. He was ALL boy! He was enthusiastic about getting outside at every possible moment, no matter the temperature. He climbed the trees in his backyard and around their neighborhood.

Babsie was petite, tall for her age, and wiry. She wanted to do just as her big brother did, and followed closely whenever possible not allowing her size or age to impede her from experiencing all that life offered a pre-schooler. She wasn't quite reading, but she would hold a book on her lap, absorb herself in the pictures, and then tell the story just as well, and, perhaps, more fluently, than if she was reading it. Babsie, like many girls, was all about PINK. She liked all things pink, and her room and her clothes reflected assorted variations on the color. Her favorite doll was a very-much-loved pink bunny called Mr. Flopsy which accompanied her wherever she went. (Winnie thought he was rather like Pooh, who had been dragged along by the leg behind Christopher Robin.)

Winnie's daughter, Claire, was completely focused on her family's well-being. She was a stay-at-home mom, which was a challenge for today's families, Claire and her husband, Alex, had agreed, before the kids came, that she would stay home with them at least until they were safely into school. Claire believed it was a great gift she could give her kids to be home for them while they were young; after all, her mother had been at home when she and her brother Paul were growing up, and she wanted the same for her kids.

Winnie and Claire talked nearly nonstop during the visit. Of course, Winnie told her about John, and they both speculated about what the future might bring — would he stay in the picture or not? Claire didn't seem unhappy with the concept of someday having a step-father. She certainly wanted the best for her mom.

Thanksgiving dinner could have been a scene from a Norman Rockwell painting. Everything seemed just perfect, the children, the dinner, the snowy weather outside, the crackling fire in the living room, everything was lovely. *Didn't Rockwell always have a piece of humor in his depictions of life?* Winnie smiled to herself as she watched a Rockwellian scenario unfold at the thanksgiving table.

The children had spent some time the day before making little place-cards for each family member. The cards were adorned with handmade, three dimensional turkeys. Derry and Babsie had worked hard to put their turkeys together, using pinecones, construction paper for feathers, and pipe cleaners for the turkeys' necks and heads. Each bird was colorful and unique, and the adults were full of praise at the efforts the two children had made.

Winnie asked Babsie if she had named her turkey. Babsie answered, "I shall call my turkey Fred."

"Why did you choose Fred for a name for a turkey, Honey?" her father asked.

"Fred is the name of the dog next door, and he is my friend," Babsie explained.

Everyone smiled at her logical naming of her turkey.

A minute later, however, Babsie came to a terrible realization. It hadn't quite occurred to the child that her place-card turkey and the turkey that had been cooking all day for dinner were in some way related. It didn't occur to Babsie, until that moment, when she realized in horror that she was being asked to take a bite of turkey, which would be like taking a bite of Fred!

Suddenly the lovely holiday dinner table was the site of a very painful expression of unwillingness by Babsie. She dissolved into a different child in mere seconds — crying and wriggling and stretching herself board straight, causing her to slide off the chair onto the floor. The entire meal was stopped mid-bite, as everyone tried to assuage little Babsie's worries about her Thanksgiving meal.

Finally, Babsie agreed to eat the other, yummy foods on her plate and not to touch the turkey. Peace was restored; the dinner continued, and the evening, overall, was still enjoyable.

✳ ✳ ✳

Back in Misty Falls on Monday before Thanksgiving, Dan Moore, Jr. walked into Lucy Jane's Red Cross office, and asked if she could get away for coffee. It was only nine in the morning, but Lucy Jane wanted to give some time to this visitor, so she picked up her coat and handbag and followed Dan out.

They ordered coffee at the IHOP nearby. Lucy Jane's curiosity had been peeked when Dan called her earlier and explained that he was an old friend of Chet's and that he had some business that he needed to do for him. Lucy Jane, being Chet's widow, would be the logical person to receive this.

While they awaited the coffee's arrival, they began to figure how it was that Dan came to know about Lucy Jane.

Sure enough, Lucy Jane knew Dan's mother. Everyone in town knew Miss Pearly Mae Moore. After all Miss Pearly Mae had been associated with the David Crockett Elementary School in Misty Falls for many years. Lucy Jane remembered her teaching fifth grade next door to her own class when she attended school.

They chatted back and forth identifying various personalities that they knew in Misty Falls.

Dan cleared his throat and said, "You must be wondering what my coming here is all about."

Lucy Jane agreed that her curiosity had been piqued after his call.

Dan began by telling Lucy Jane about his time in the Air Force in Germany. He and Chet were good friends then, and they had kept in contact since then. He explained how he and Chet had made an investment in a housing development in New Mexico back in the early 90's. (Chet had paid into it, but the account had been made in Dan's name.) Dan explained how he had been lucky to be stationed near the development when he was assigned back to CONUS (Continental U.S). He had watched the development for quite a while, and then he had decided that maybe it was a good time to cash out the investment, which he did, back in April last year. "We made a good profit, and half of it belongs to Chet!" Dan explained.

Lucy Jane was taking in every word Dan spoke. Her eyes widened and her smile expanded. "Really!" she exclaimed. "You're here to give me money?"

Dan reached into his inside coat pocket and took out an envelope. He handed the astonished woman the envelope and waited. Lucy Jane took the envelope and carefully, almost ceremoniously, opened it up. There was a cashier's check made out in her name for the sum of $15,846.27.

Lucy Jane's eyebrows knit together as she read and reread the number of dollars on the check. She hadn't expected this surprise; it was a really good surprise!

She put the check down on the table and looked at Dan. "Thank you. Thank you, so much! Obviously I didn't know about this investment or that it had been cashed out, but I'm very thankful that you remembered Chet's part and have acted so generously!"

Dan was amused to watch this young woman — her surprise and her obvious pleasure. "Can you think what you'll do with the money? It's not a great amount, but maybe there's something you'd like to do that the money might make possible."

Lucy Jane was thinking. "I can't say this minute. I didn't expect this, and it needs some thought to be done right. I do think, though, it needs to be something that Chet would have liked — some sort of project. I'll give it some careful consideration. Would you like to hear about it when I decide?" she asked Dan.

"I really would like to know, if you will tell me," Dan smiled.

The two finished their coffee, talking about Chet and his earlier life when Dan knew him. Lucy Jane was pleased to hear more about Chet's world when he was a younger man. It was like seeing old photos of times past. Lucy Jane thanked Dan again for the surprise and his thoughtfulness. They each felt a special goodness about the gift.

✳ ✳ ✳

Winnie's drive back home was uneventful. She had not thought of Misty Falls or her church work during her visit and she felt refreshed from the trip.

She arrived at home just before dinner time Saturday evening, unpacked, and made a light meal for herself. *Tonight will be easy. This may be Saturday night, but all I have to do for tomorrow is get the bulletin duplicated, and that will be a breeze!*

Winnie had just put the last of her dinner dishes away, when the phone rang. It was 6:30 p.m, and Bob was on the other end of the line. "Winnie," he said, "I absolutely hate to do this to you, but I'm sick! I've been as sick as a dog this entire past week! My whole family has been sick with the flu. I'm calling to tell you that I can't come to preach for you tomorrow. I really want to, but I'm sick, and I can't make it!"

Winnie listened to Bob's weak and tired voice. She realized this was NOT how she expected her Saturday night to be — figuring out what in the world to do for tomorrow! But, on the other hand, there was a certain amount of irony about it that was not wasted on her. After all, hadn't she wanted to get some rest, away from the constant requirement of building a new sermon? She had had that rest, and she did feel revived.

Winnie dismissed any idea of being angry over this turn of events. She might have nursed some thought of irritation for having Sunday morning just dumped in her lap at the proverbial last moment, but she couldn't do it. *Probably Bob had been hoping that he'd get better, or at least well enough to make the trip.* Winnie checked her anger.

Winnie said, "Goodness, Bob! I'm so sorry you've been sick! How completely un-fun!" Winnie paused for a moment, not quite sure what to do next. Such a situation had never come up before; she had always been so careful to prepare for her Sunday sermons. Before she had time to think, Winnie heard herself saying, "Bob, Don't worry about tomorrow. You remember Dr. Logan in seminary used to say that a good Methodist

112

pastor should be ready to preach, pray, sing, or die at a moment's notice! Looks like it's my turn to rise to the occasion!

"I'm a United Methodist pastor, and it's Saturday night, so what else should I be doing but figuring out what I should say to my people in the morning. Actually, I've had a good rest this week, so I'll just look through my files and find something that's appropriate and use that. "Take care of yourself, and I'll try to get you to fill in another time!" Winnie assured Bob.

That was that. Suddenly Winnie's evening had a new agenda — one she knew very well: Saturday evening — dinner, a little TV, then pick up the sermon and get it ready for tomorrow.

Winnie was thankful that she'd been preaching for a while, and she had a good-sized library of sermons from which she could choose something appropriate. Somehow this thankful sensation seemed to her to have the ironic and typically cryptic timbre of an answered prayer. *Fortunately, that's the only thing in front of me tonight!*

There was no way she could have started from scratch and built a new sermon right then, so Winnie didn't even stress about creating something new. Tomorrow would be the first week of Advent (the church's season of looking forward to the coming of the Messiah), and Winnie had preached a number of times on that subject — Waiting. She would suggest that, as we wait for Christ to come again, we should do it with expectation, intention, and joy. Winnie would use examples of each to illustrate how we can proactively anticipate the return of the Lord. *Yes, this sermon should not be hard to give in the morning.* Preparing this sermon was even fun.

After worship Sunday morning Pastor Winnie stood at the back of the sanctuary shaking hands with parishioners when several folks inquired about their special speaker whom they had been expecting. Winnie quickly explained the situation — the flu, the last minute call, her efforts to pull everything together. She laughed with several of the members when she told the story of her surprising evening. The whole service had come out just fine!

Chapter 13. Signs of Christmas

The newly formed, icy dew created a satisfying "crunch" beneath Winnie's feet and announced that winter was coming as she and Bitty stepped out for their early Monday morning walk.

Mondays are still the best.

The late fall breeze was chilly and scooped up any unbagged leaves and whisked them in whimsical spirals along the streets. Winnie was watching this play of wind and leaves scuttling across the streets, when suddenly a dust devil appeared, coming right toward Winnie and Bitty. Winnie certainly didn't think the dust devil could be dangerous, but nevertheless she began to maneuver herself and Bitty away from the twister's path to avoid the blustery funnel.

Winnie watched the little dust devil in disbelief as it appeared to be following her. It couldn't have been more than fifteen or twenty feet high and, maybe, five feet in diameter, and it was coming directly for her. Winnie began to trot — her top speed — across the grassy field in front of her, when the miniature twister caught her up, spun her several times 'round, and knocked her completely off her feet. Winnie let go the dog leash and closed her eyes tight. The zephyr vanished, but the evidence of the surprising event remained: her hat was no where to be found, her scarf was wrapped awkwardly around her neck and arms; she couldn't have been more blown about if she had walked through an automatic car dryer. As she sat on the ground, legs akimbo, she collected herself slowly and determined that she was totally unharmed, save for her sense of pride and fairness in the universe.

Before the odd pastor vs. nature moment Winnie had been walking over to Main Street to see some of the newly set up Christmas lights, and, although she was now quite disheveled, owing to the brief encounter with the mini-twister, she decided to continue her walk and check out some of homes she had heard about. She picked up Bitty's lead and ran her fingers through her short, wavy hair to settle it a bit and continued her walk.

Some folks in the community had used the Thanksgiving weekend to string lights on their property. There were three houses in town, side by side, that were already well adorned. Winnie remembered hearing about their owners when she first arrived in Misty Falls. They were noted for their lavish Christmas decorations each year. Winnie wondered if the owners competed to make their Yule décor the best in the neighborhood.

The three houses, situated on Main Street and facing the railroad tracks, were owned by three, octogenarian sisters — two who had never married and a widow. All three were members of Muddy Creek Church. Winnie believed someone could write a book just about the three sisters, and it would be quite a page-turner! The sisters didn't attend worship these days, but Winnie had visited them numerous times, hoping to revive their interest in their faith community. The sisters were very good friends. They enjoyed their individual domains, keeping their homes up as they desired, but hardly a day went by without them visiting one another.

The three homes, stood adjacent one another — great, dignified, well-kept, antebellum edifices. Each sported a gracious veranda surrounding the house, which was, itself, surrounded by rolling lawns and tall conifers looming overhead, shading and protecting their homes.

Winnie was surprised the first time she met the sisters — surprised that they possessed such wealth, considering they were single women. The family had once owned a dry goods store in town, started by their father, and they had run the store for nearly fifty years before selling out to a chain store and retiring.

Winnie had tried to encourage the sisters to re-activate their interests in Muddy Creek Church. They had been faithful members in years past, but no longer. Winnie gathered that none of them had attended anything more than a Christmas Eve service for some time. Winnie figured there was a story behind their absence from church, but she had not picked up any clues about why, yet. "Maybe, one day, they will share with me what has interfered with their activity at Muddy Creek," Winnie told Bitty.

※ ※ ※

Winnie opened an email from John on Monday morning. He had returned from his Thanksgiving trip to Aspen and had enjoyed the slopes and the refreshing change in scenery. His skiing holiday was pretty much like what he was used to — the travel, the resort, all the ski paraphernalia, the lifts, the actual time on the slopes —speeding down graceful passages amid magnificent mountainscapes and spotting the occasional wild deer amongst the trees. He wrote about the pristine beauty of the mountains and how he was sure he would never get over the thrill of coming down those slopes at breakneck velocity. "Exhilarating was the only word for it!"

Apparently John had skied in a number of venues downhill as well as cross country. He took opportunities to experience the slopes or a good cross country trek wherever he could, even enjoying slopes in the Andes over a summer in Chili and Argentina. There the snow was in abundance in July and August!

But today John was thoughtful about his holiday. He came home realizing he was missing something. He admitted that he caught himself relishing the idea of seeing Winnie again. He toyed with various scenarios of how they might spend time together. He was finding his mind wandering to thoughts of her each day, and John wondered if Winnie might not be feeling similarly?

John spoke of watching several families at the lodge. These families brought their children — introducing them to skiing, letting them use the "bunny hills," before they ventured onto the steeper slopes. John saw them in the dining room and observed how the children always had so much energy! He wondered if he would have ever been able to work with small children. The children he saw were cute, although some were hyper, and he thought they were exhausting just to watch from across the room. John was thankful that he was not responsible for instructing and correcting children as they sat in the dining room.

That inspired John to ask Winnie how it had been for her and Mark when they had their own children at home? Had it been very trying to have children under foot all the time, or was it something you got used to? Since he'd missed out on being a father of small children, he really wondered how people could keep their sanity with so much commotion constantly going on about them?

John ended his email saying, "I think I'm beginning to realize that I'm missing something, and I've about concluded that what I'm really missing is you! John."

Winnie had come to look forward to John's frequent messages, and today she was warmed inside to read his comment about "missing something" and that the "something" was her. She felt a special closeness to John, and realized that she, too, as busy as her life was, was "missing something." *And I think John may have named it for both of us.*

Winnie smiled as she thought to herself about the time when she had her own little children at home. It didn't seem that long ago in a way, yet, in another way, it was forever ago.

She wrote, "The deal with raising children is that God gives us a deep, deep love for them right from the start. They come to us as extensions of ourselves, so we learn to deal with their needs: the feeding, the changing, the comforting, the crazy hours and lack of sleep that are suddenly forced upon us. We grow along with the kids, re-experiencing life as they learn it for the first time. Yes! They are enormously requiring, especially in the early years, but all their care — all the long hours, changed agendas, new expenses, the loss of independence — all seems to be the right thing to do, even if it demands every fiber of strength we can muster.

"I discovered one weekend when the kids were tiny and Mark was out of town that being a parent can sometimes be *sweet-agony.* The kids had picked up a bug, maybe the flu, and they took turns throwing up all over their cribs the whole night long. I was awakened from sleep by the sound of little Paul retching in his crib. The next thing I knew I was cleaning up a crib, changing the sleeper for a clean one and comforting him;

then a few minutes later, the baby Claire was sick and needing a cleaned up crib and fresh set of p.j.'s, etc.

"This same process continued again and again many times that night. I wondered, then, if I might ever look back on that night and think it was funny! First one child and then the other — then repeat! I was exhausted, but somehow I found the strength to carry on, to care for my dear little ones who were so sick. At one point in the middle of the night, having redone the cribs and the clothes and comforted the babies several times each, I sat on the floor between their two bedrooms and prayed — mostly for strength and for healing for the kids. Then I thought about singing. I don't remember what song came to mind, maybe it was the *Tallis Canon*. (Do you know it?) Anyway, I sang the song again and again, and I came to realize that everything would be fine; I would survive, as well as the kids. Somehow the song, which praises God, helped me pull myself out of some healthy self-pity to a much better frame of mind. (I can see I'm digressing!)

"Parenthood is a wonderful blessing, even as it is a great challenge. It's certainly not one I would choose to miss. I would not want to trade a moment of my time at home with the kids for any other activity. It was just right for me. I wish I could impart some of my memories to you; would that there was a way so to do!

"You may have missed some of the best moments in life — realizing for the first time that you're going to be a parent, holding your new child in your arms for the first time, watching the amazing growth in your child; seeing him stand free for the first moment without anything to hold him up(!), hearing her say "Mommy" for the first time. You get the picture!

"I could wish you had not missed those precious years; I believe you would have loved them. Surely there are many, many different routes to take in life, different experiences we can have. Surely we can't know them all. Some are mutually exclusive; at least they can't be experienced concurrently. I can't know, for instance, the wonder of being a stay-at-home mother and at the same time the excitement of being a single, professional woman. But! When time is added to the mix, then, surely, having numerous, challenging vocations can be had."

❊ ❊ ❊

Joe Ed Rafferty, the choir director at First Baptist Church, was working with children from several churches on a Christmas musical production. This year the Christmas musical was an actual play set to music. There were speaking parts, choral parts, and parts for children of all ages. The play would require a couple of sets and a variety of costumes — mostly angel garb: halos, wings, and long sleeved tunics.

Winnie stopped by to watch one of the rehearsals and saw what a great project it was, giving the children an opportunity to experience being part of a group that was doing something together and being responsible for remembering their parts. *There are a number of really good reasons for children to get involved in little theatre. It evokes their best efforts, and that's a blessing!*

Winnie had spoken earlier to Joe Ed about the show and asked if there was anything that her church could do to help out. Joe Ed had told her that the angel chorus was coming from the four year olds in the pre-school this year, and that they would need eighteen, small angel costumes for the kids to wear.

Vickie Jackson's name came to Winnie's mind immediately, thinking she would be the perfect person to head up such a project. She told Joe Ed that she would check with Vickie and other ladies at Muddy Creek Church and let him know if they could manage such a project.

✳ ✳ ✳

Jeff Plummer called to say that the flooring materials had arrived and to ask if he could come Tuesday to begin work. When he arrived, Winnie asked Jeff if he and Jillian had married over Thanksgiving.

Jeff grinned widely and said, "Indeed! We did tie the knot last week. We took off to Gatlinburg for the weekend. Jillian has some connection there and made arrangements for us to get a one-room place right in the midst of all the tourist attractions. We got hitched first thing. We went to a little wedding chapel there and had the ceremony. It wasn't a big deal; it took less than an hour for the whole business, but I guess that short time is the open door to the whole world of marriage!"

Winnie shook her head in agreement and said, "I'd say that's an understatement! You've been married before, so I guess you know what you're talking about."

Jeff answered, "Well, hopefully I learned from before, and I'm a better man for it. Jessie and I were way too young to get married when we did. I was barely out of high school, and she still had a couple of years more to go, which she hasn't yet finished.

"Jillian and I have talked a lot about what we think marriage means — what it costs each partner, what can go wrong, and what should go right. We talked forever, it seemed, online about our past marriages before we actually set eyes on one another.

"We recognize how it takes two people, each working on the marriage, to make it work. It takes two people who are very interested in communicating — not just to be heard but to really HEAR what the other person is saying. We've set up a time at breakfast every Saturday morning to take five minutes and talk about what's going on — you know: what's on our minds, what's good for each of us, and what's good for both of us, what's working and what's not. We call it our 'Target Time.' So far, which has been just one Saturday, it has worked very well!"

"Our trip to Gatlinburg was pure ambrosia. We took warm clothes for hiking, so we could take long walks each day. We saw the last good days of autumn; most of the colors were gone, but there were still some breathtaking sights up there."

"We had time to talk and share and learn more about one another. Remember, neither one of us is a spring chicken. We still have a lot to learn about one another. It's a little like unwrapping a package that's been bundled in many layers. It's fun and colorful, and Jillian and I think we each have found our 'soul mate,'" Jeff blushed.

*** ***

Lucy Jane had enjoyed Thanksgiving with her family. The week had begun with a big surprise — Dan Moore bringing her the cashier's check, representing Chet's part of the investment the two men had made.

She hadn't told anyone else about it, yet. She deposited the money in a savings account, she would not accidentally spend it down. She wanted to do something with the money that might somehow speak to the spirit of Chet and what they had hoped and dreamed of doing together.

Lucy Jane and Chet had planned to have a family. It would be a late in life family, for sure, but they had wanted to include children in their life together. They wanted to experience parenting — how parents influence their children and help them to develop their personalities and values. They felt their marriage would be more complete with children growing in it.

They had only been married a short while when Chet got sick, and before they knew it his time had come. Lucy Jane realized that she had healing to do before she could think about family or future. She knew she was emotionally fragile yet and needed more time to mend.

She decided that what she could do at this point was begin to think about what she might do when she felt stronger. There were any number of possible ways to use the money, many good places she was sure, but she wanted to remember Chet in some way in the process. She wanted their hope of family to be seen in whatever she decided to do.

Lucy Jane needed someone to talk to — someone she could trust, someone outside her family — and Tucker Joe's name came to mind. Lucy Jane had enjoyed the several conversations she had had with Tucker Joe, and she thought he might be a good sounding board for her.

Indeed, Tuck was pleased to hear Lucy Jane's voice on the other end of the line. Yes, he'd like to see her and could meet this week for a chat. They set up a meeting for dinner in the city on Thursday evening. That would take them away from inquisitive eyes in town here. "It's a date!" Tuck announced. "See you Thursday at six."

*** ***

Saturday afternoon was the time set for the church to be decorated for Advent and Christmas. Of course, the Advent Wreath had already been set up in the chancel at Muddy Creek, and the first candle had been lit last Sunday on Advent One. The chrismon tree, wreaths, poinsettias, and the Advent/Christmas banners would be put out this afternoon by members of the church, followed by a Hanging of the Greens ceremony.

Thom Jackson, the church trustee, had already pulled the tree out of the storage unit and brought it into the sanctuary. The tree would be decorated entirely with chrismons — a crown, a lamb, a fish, an orb, various crosses, etc. Each chrismon was a different symbol of Christ, and had been made painstakingly by hand. The chrismons, along with hundreds of tiny, white lights on the tree, provided an ethereal charm in the sanctuary.

Martha Reeves had brought homemade Christmas cookies to be enjoyed while everyone worked.

In the midst of decorating, Little Brad asked his daddy a question, and his dad referred him to Pastor Winnie. Little Brad walked over to the pastor and asked, "Daddy says I'm s'posed to ask you where the others are who are part of Christmas?"

Winnie crinkled her eyebrows and knelt down to the four year old's height and asked, "What do you mean by the others, Little Brad?"

Little Brad thought he had asked the question as clearly as he could; he said, "You know, the others! There are a bunch of others that are in the stores. Haven't you seen them?"

Winnie nodded her head and said, "Yes, I do know what you mean. I'm so glad you noticed that our church doesn't have those different characters. Can you tell me what you see here at church?" Winnie looked around at the other children to see if they might have an answer.

Brenda Sue, the Barrymore's twelve year old, picked up a lamb chrismon and held it up. "Look, Little Brad, here is a lamb. Do you see lambs in the stores?"

Brad cocked his head and shook it. "I don't think so," he replied.

Matthew Thompson, Marva Lyn's twin brother, spoke up, "Little Brad, you're right; there is a difference between the decorations we see in the stores and the decorations we see here at church. The stores have more cartoon people, I think."

Marva Lyn added, "Maybe they didn't have cartoons back in Jesus' time."

Winnie was enjoying this fun conversation among the children. She said, "Marva Lyn, You hit the answer on the head! Do you know you did?"

Marva Lyn thought for a moment and said, "Well, Christmas is about the baby Jesus, isn't it? At home we have a cretzshe ... Mom! What's that word?"

Sheryl Lynn said, "You mean the crèche. It's a French word for the place where Jesus was born. It looks like a wooden barn with one side open, so we can see into it."

Marva Lyn continued, "And the crèche also has shepherds and wise men and angels and animals in it."

Bobby Jackson asked, "Hey, don't we have a big set like that here? Don't we have one outside by the front of the church at Christmastime?"

Bobby's father, Thom Jackson, answered, "Yes, you and Matthew can help me get it out and set it up later this afternoon."

Winnie thought this might be a good opportunity for the children and their parents to understand more about the difference between Christmas, as the world celebrates it and the celebration of the Incarnation.

She asked, "Who can tell me which came first, Christmas or Easter?"

Letitia Washington was enjoying this line of thinking along with her pastor. She asked, "Do you mean first according to the calendar, or which holiday was first celebrated, or which actually happened first, chronologically?"

Jodi Lee said, "Sounds like there could be three different answers."

Thom Jackson spoke up and said, "If I remember right, Easter was celebrated first. It was the first thing that happened in the church; I'm right, aren't I, Pastor Winnie?"

Winnie agreed, but she didn't want to interject her thoughts as long as there was such good interaction among the folks, so she answered briefly. "Indeed, Christ rose on the first day of the new week, which we call Easter Sunday, and people have been celebrating the resurrection every Sunday since then. Every Sunday is really a mini-Easter."

Letitia continued, "So Easter is the first holy day of the church. Of course, according to the calendar, Easter also comes first in the year, since Christmas falls at the end of the year. BUT! When we think of Christmas as being the birth of Jesus, then his birth certainly came before his death and resurrection!"

Winnie smiled at Letitia and said, "That's a good clarification. So, if Easter was first, when did Christmas come along?"

Jodi Lee spoke up, "I think that Christmas must have come a long time after the church began."

Winnie nodded to Letitia to answer. "Right. It was several centuries after the beginning of the church when Christians decided to celebrate Jesus' birth. They were having trouble with the pagans who held a great Feast of Bacchus, the Greek god of wine and drunkenness, during the darkest time of the year. The Christians couldn't join that drunken orgy, so they decided to celebrate the Light of the World coming into world during that darkest time of the year. Christmas was a counter-cultural way of stating who they were. Christmas for Christians is supposed to look different from the world's way of doing things."

"Can you see why we have different characters in our decorations, Little Brad?" Winnie asked.

Little Brad thought for a moment and said, "I can see why we have Jesus in our church, but why don't we see Him in the stores? And why don't we have the other pictures? They are fun to look at. I like them, too."

Winnie appreciated Little Brad's candor and pointed out to him, "Christmas is all about Jesus and his birth, 'He took on flesh and lived among us,' as St. John says. The other characters that we see in bright, colorful pictures in the stores have nothing to do with Jesus coming into the world. They have nothing to do with God loving the world so much that He gave His only Son, so that whosoever believes in Him will not perish but have eternal life.

"Mickey, Goofy, Donald, the Grinch, Scrooge, and Santa and have nothing to do with Christmas the way Christians believe," Pastor Winnie explained.

The group ended their decorating with a simple "Hanging of the Greens" ceremony, bringing in the wreathes, flowers and banners and turning the lights on the chrismon tree. The sanctuary was now prepared for Advent and Christmas.

Chapter 14. A Busy Week

Winnie had barely opened her eyes Monday morning when the phone rang, and the sobbing voice on the other end of the line was one of her favorite parishioners, Evelyn Hobbs. She was calling from University of Tennessee Medical Center in Knoxville. Her son, Randy, who was just now home from his hitch in the Army, had been in a terrible collision the night before on a country road near their home. He was in the TICU — Trauma Intensive Care Unit. He had suffered a terrible blow to his head as well as a number of broken bones. The bones would heal, but his head injury was very, very severe. He was in a coma and was not expected to come out of it. Evelyn and her husband, Gerald, had driven to the hospital as soon as they heard the news. They would be there with their only son as long as he needed them.

Winnie dressed quickly, grabbed a banana and cup of coffee, and was on her way out the door to the hospital. It was a good forty-five minute drive into Knoxville, and the traffic on Monday morning was just what you'd expect — cars and trucks packing the lanes, everyone intent on getting to work on time. Winnie used her time in the car for a sort of *ad hoc* devotional time, since she was missing her usual time for that at home.

She prayed out loud, especially mentioning this most pressing concern — the young man, Randy, who had grown up at Muddy Creek and Misty Falls.

Randy had come home from his tour in Afghanistan unscathed. He had just completed his enlistment in the Army and was about to begin work back home. Now this!

Winnie met Evelyn and Gerald at the visitors' lounge by the Trauma ICU. She heard the story of the accident from the frightened parents. Driving on country roads is too often hazardous, because one tends to drive down the middle of the narrow road. They didn't know if Randy had been driving in the middle of the road, but another car came from around a bend, and the two met, head on just before midnight. Both drivers were badly injured.

It would be a long haul before this business was done, whatever the outcome. Winnie was pleased to note the confidence that Evelyn exuded in the face of this devastating situation. She was doing exactly what she should be doing in this very difficult time — she was leaving Randy's healing up to the Lord.

* * *

Later that morning after she had returned to the parsonage, Winnie answered a call from Pastor Allen Remington. He was calling the various pastors who were part of the joint community services to update them about the Thanksgiving service.

"Winnie, I thought I'd call and tell you about the offering that came in at the Thanksgiving service," Allen Remington said. "Tinsley Booker over at Faith AME just called to tell me that his treasurer had found an envelope and a note attached to it in the collection plate after that service. The envelope contained cash for the amount of $496.35, and a note inside the envelope said, "I'm returning this money to the community. I found it at the church after the Easter service, and I want to return it to its rightful place. I hope that by returning this money now the missing funds can be 'found' and our community chest will be 'right.' Thank you."

"Do we know who wrote the note?" Winnie asked.

"No name was included on the note; it was written in pencil on a torn piece of notebook paper," Allen answered.

"Tinsley and I talked about it, and we think the matter is closed now. Do you agree?

"Sounds like the thief has a conscience and decided to make amends.

"It's not really our job to determine if someone should be charged for the theft. That falls on the sheriff and the courts to decide, but, from what you tell me, I would consider the matter closed, especially since we don't know who it was that did the deed," Winnie answered.

Allen agreed with Winnie. "That's what I'm hearing from the other pastors, too. We seem to feel that whoever the culprit was, he or she seems to have worked it out, and the community gets the money back for our Traveler's Aide Account. No one was actually harmed or suffered from the theft. We hope that the person in question has grown in the process, which is what we all need to do as we follow Christ."

"I think that Tinsley will take the note to the sheriff along with our thoughts about what should happen. Sheriff Barrymore can use our input to inform his report and/or further investigation, if he needs it."

Winnie couldn't help smiling to herself as she remembered Pastor Allen's unexpected report about the missing funds. "There's a story in that, for sure!" Winnie told Bitty. "I don't suppose we'll ever know who it was that found the money and then returned it, but there's a story there. That's for sure,.." Winnie wondered if it might be someone that she knew in town.

Winnie barely hung up from her conversation with Pastor Allen when the phone rang again. This time the voice was Connie Oliver's, and she sounded frantic!

124

"Goodness, Dear, calm down! Take a deep breath, and then tell me what's happening," Winnie assured her.

Connie tried to follow Winnie's suggestion, but it was hard for her to keep from crying. "The DHR woman just called me ... just a minute ago. She says that she has received a phone call about noise coming from our apartment, and the caller thinks there might be some danger for my girls!" Connie stopped.

Winnie was alarmed, too, and she asked, "Did the DHR woman say anything more?"

"I don't know," Connie answered. "She didn't say we'd lose the girls, but she spoke very strongly about us being very careful with them!"

"So, she gave you a warning? Is that what she did?" Winnie asked.

"I suppose that's what she meant," Connie sniffed. "Now I'm all upset, and that doesn't make things any better."

"Well, it sounds like you've been called to give you a fair warning about the responsibility you have in taking care of the babies," Winnie said. "Was there anything factual about the report that the DHR woman heard?" Winnie asked a little anxiously.

"N-No, there wasn't really anything. Oh, I guess we were all talking real loud last night before dinner. George and Mother don't always see eye-to-eye, and I think he yelled something and walked out and slammed the door. I suppose that's what caused my neighbor to wonder if there was something dangerous for the babies, but, really, they were not in any danger!" Connie assured Winnie.

"Hm. It sounds like you're right about the noise in your apartment," Winnie agreed. "I think you've had a scare with the DHR woman's call, but she's not taking the babies, not yet, so you just have to be especially careful with them. AND watch out about any other loud voices that might attract the attention of your neighbors."

They spoke a few more minutes. Winnie wished like everything that this was not happening to Connie and her family, but she couldn't change the facts. All she could do was to be a friend to Connie and Sallie and hope they could follow through with their best intentions in caring for the babies.

✳ ✳ ✳

John had inquired about Winnie's plans for Christmas earlier. As a university professor the Christmas holidays didn't begin when the students left for vacation. Professors still had papers to read, tests to mark, and grades to be submitted before they could possibly get away.

John explained that his course load this quarter included two Introduction to Philosophy sections, which had several hundreds of students in each section. He had three other, upper division classes and a graduate seminar that were smaller, but which required research papers

20 — 25 pages per student. The finals for the Intro classes were objective in nature and would be graded by T.A.'s, but the research papers were solely his responsibility, and they took significant time to read, digest, evaluate, and grade.

John wondered what Winnie usually did over the holidays, and would she be free at any time. He offered to fly her up to Chicago, if she would like to come.

Of course, Christmastime was a major season for Winnie; she had Christmas Eve service to lead in the middle of the week and a sermon to preach three days later that she would have to prepare and give. Furthermore, Winnie's son, Paul, and his family were coming for Christmas. They would arrive late Christmas Day and stay for a week. This family time had been planned for some time, and Winnie, of course, was looking forward to seeing them.

Winnie wrote,

Dear John,

Sounds like being a college professor has some serious sides to it that we lay folks don't appreciate! And I thought the students were the ones with all the homework! It hadn't occurred to me about the reading and grading responsibilities that professors have following finals. How much time does it usually take you for that work? It sounds pretty detailed and thick. I haven't spent any time thinking about upper level philosophy subjects, but I can imagine in-depth writings would take a careful eye and a thoughtful response by you, the professor. I'm sure you can't just rip through them!"

Winnie figured that Christmas wasn't the best time for the two of them to meet, simply because of the requirements of her job, and now she was aware of the demands of a college professor. Their getting together, especially around this big holiday, posed some challenges. Winnie tried to think more positively to herself. *But then there's our date in January for Nashville; I'm really looking forward to that time!*

Winnie also explained to John about her son's family's visit, which was that week. Paul and his family were coming from Dallas. Everyone had been planning their visit for months, and their tickets had been purchased. Everything was set for them to come, and Winnie, as "Grannie," certainly wanted to see her sweet Taylor grandchildren!

✳ ✳ ✳

Winnie checked in on Evelyn Hobbs every day by phone. She had not left the hospital since the accident, but continued to sit in the visitors' waiting room, making visits every four hours, according to the schedule allowed for family visiting. Gerald had brought her a bag of toiletries, a few clothes, and a pillow and blanket. She was eating from the vending machines and sometimes at the cafeteria. No, there was no good news about Randy; he was in exactly the same state as the night of the accident: hooked up to many machines, not breathing on his own, and no signs of improvement.

Winnie asked Evelyn what she did when she visited her son. Evelyn told her, "I sit up close to Randy's head, hold his hand, and talk to him. I tell him that I'm there with him, and that he's going to be fine. He's going to get through this season of healing, and that he's going to come home and get a job and have a wonderful life. I tell him about how much Jesus loves him, and how Jesus healed so many people that we read about in the Bible, and He heals anyone who is ever healed. I tell Randy that he's got angels surrounding him and watching over him. I sing him songs and hymns he knows."

Winnie was impressed with Evelyn's faith and her determined way of sharing her faith with her son, even as he lay in a deep coma. The doctors and nurses held out no encouraging words about Randy, but that wasn't going to sway Evelyn's faith. She planned to stay next to him, as long as they would allow.

Winnie was thoughtful about how this most difficult time might come out for Evelyn and Gerald. Randy was their only child, and his life hung in terrible jeopardy. There didn't seem to be much hope for him, but Winnie wanted to stay as positive as Evelyn and Gerald were about the future. *It's one thing to preach about having faith and another thing to actually live it!'* Winnie reminded herself.

❋ ❋ ❋

Lucy Jane hadn't thought about getting involved with another man, not yet. Her pain was too close, having lost Chet just months ago. The move from Kentucky had been a good one for her, as it took her mind off her pain, just a bit, and brought her closer to her family.

Misty Falls hadn't changed much at all, not even in the nearly twenty years Lucy Jane had been gone. There were some changes, but the essence of Misty Falls — the people who made up the community — was the same.

Changes that had come to Misty Falls were mostly what Lucy Jane considered "cosmetic." The stop sign in town on Main Street, which had been one of the town's landmarks, had been usurped by the arrival of a traffic light on the highway. The advent of the traffic light had been a big deal for the town — a sure indication of progress!

Lucy Jane was not seeking romance now, but the thought of companionship, someone with a friendly face and an open ear who could help fill up some of the empty hours, would be nice.

The few times that Lucy Jane and Tucker Joe had seen each other, she realized that she felt just a bit better.

Their dinner date was set at a nice restaurant in the city. They met at six at Friendlie's Foods, and Tucker Joe surprised Lucy Jane with a beautiful corsage — red and white rose buds surrounded by a netting of silver stars — it was very Christmasy. They hopped in Tuck's blue, '68 Mustang and drove off to the city for dinner.

It was an Italian place that they finally agreed upon. Soon they were seated at a table near the window, looking onto the bustling, Christmas shoppers outside.

The waiter left them with menus and filled their water glasses. He rattled off the specials being offered and suggested a wine to accompany their dinner.

"That's the big city for you," Lucy Jane observed after the waiter had departed. "They don't appreciate us hometown folks who don't drink, do they?"

Tucker Joe wanted to be amiable and perhaps follow Lucy Jane's lead, but he wasn't a teetotaler, and he needed to state that for himself.

"I know plenty of good folks who don't drink," he began, "and surely there are those who can't hold their alcohol, but I'm not one of them. I have a healthy regard for alcohol, but I have found that a nice, dry wine at a meal is an excellent addition. I wouldn't judge anyone for not drinking, but I think there can be a place for enjoying the fruit of the vine." Tuck completed his thought with a little smile, hoping he had a dinner companion who understood his position.

Lucy Jane nodded her head and admitted, "My husband, Chet, would have completely agreed with you."

"We had the same conversation on our first date. Chet enjoyed a nice wine with his dinner, and he was good about not bugging me to join him. We had a friendly agreement on the subject," Lucy shared.

The dinner was easy and casual. Tucker was a good listener it turned out; he didn't press Lucy Jane for too much information, but he let her talk as much as she wanted.

She told Tuck about her first, dismal marriage, how it was a failure before it got started. She and Frank had met when she was on a trip one summer during college. He was working at a state park, and they had spent many hours wandering around the park. Frank was a mountain climber, and he spent all his money and time running off to far away mountains to conquer yet one more peak. It didn't take long for them to part ways. Their divorce was mutually agreed upon.

Chet, on the other hand, had been perfect. He had literally swept Lucy Jane off her feet, and she knew life had finally begun for her when they married. They had wonderful plans, especially ones that included children.

Chet's cancer diagnosis caught them completely off guard, and there was no time to respond. He came home from the doctor's office that first day, and they were aware that he needed to have some serious-sounding tests to get a handle on his condition. The next week Chet went to the hospital for a whole battery of tests, and he never came home. There was surgery, and waiting, and then he was gone!

Lucy Jane hadn't eaten much of her dinner — she was too absorbed in her tale, sharing her pain with this kind man. She talked on and on, mostly about Chet, when suddenly she made a discovery.

Tucker Joe had been listening and saying little things like, "Yeah," and "Okay," and "I understand." Finally he said, "I know what you mean about the funeral director; the same thing happened to me when Mama died."

Lucy Jane swallowed her Coke and looked straight at Tuck. She knitted her eyebrows, cocked her head, and said, "Did your mother pass, too?"

Tucker hadn't realized that Lucy Jane was unfamiliar with that piece of recent, community history, but he put two and two together and nodded his head.

"Mother died almost a year ago. I thought you knew."

Lucy Jane hadn't heard, but some things did make more sense to her now that she thought about it. She hadn't seen Miss Matilda Tennyson at Friendlie's Foods the times she had been there since she had returned to town.

"I'm so sorry to hear about her passing," she said. "You must miss her."

"Not anything like what you're describing. Sure, Mother passed, and we all miss her, but maybe it was her time to go. I miss her as a friend, and I sure do miss her as an associate at the store. But I don't feel the sort of grief you are experiencing."

Lucy Jane was relieved to hear that. She didn't want to think that she had been terribly insensitive to Tucker Joe's feelings, going on and on, as she had been doing about her own loss and not even acknowledging his. "Oh," she said, "I'm so sorry you lost her. I'm sure the whole town misses her."

Most of the dinner time was spent with such conversation, but that wasn't really what Lucy Jane had hoped to talk about.

Finally she changed the subject and told Tucker Joe about her unexpected gift and how she hoped to use it in some sort of memorial to Chet's fondness for children. That was a new idea, and the two of them agreed to meet again, maybe just after Christmas to consider it more.

The evening went great! Tucker Joe assured himself as he drove home. *Lucy Jane is quite a woman — a woman who has a deep passion for life — and she certainly is devoted to her husband's memory. I expect she'll come to love, again, one day.*

✳ ✳ ✳

Saturday Winnie joined a half dozen other women from Muddy Creek over at the Barrymore's house. Vickie Jackson had assembled the ladies to put together the eighteen angel outfits for the community Christmas show. She had already found a pattern — a simple, wide-yoked gown with long sleeves. The outfit would reach down nearly to a four-year-old's knees. Vickie borrowed her next door neighbor's four year old who, coincidentally, was singing in the angel choir and used him for a model. She also picked up the necessary material and notions that she figured would be needed for the project.

By four o'clock their job was nearly complete. The ladies had become a team of efficient workers, and their results were obvious. Each of the ladies looked forward to coming to the Baptist church the following week to see their work on display in the show. They also realized that they had actually produced a good product in a reasonable time. Maybe they should consider using such a workforce for other needs that might arise. Maybe they could use this ability to help bring in funds for a mission program.

* * *

By Saturday afternoon Winnie's parsonage makeover had been completed: new floors in the kitchen, laundry room, and in both bathrooms. Most of the jobs were not complicated, but the main bathroom floor had to be rebuilt totally. Winnie had watched off and on as Jeff worked to tear out the old, rotted flooring and to install the new. The final result was a fine, linoleum-covered improvement.

The parsonage looked really fresh and clean with the new floors. It would be nice to have fresh floors in the parsonage when Paul and his family arrived.

* * *

Winnie wasn't quite sure how to start her sermon on Sunday. She usually preached from the lectionary, choosing a Bible passage from that list to use as a springboard for finding her Sunday message, but this week's sermon was being stubborn, and she was suffering a bit from writer's block. Winnie had chosen a passage from St. John's gospel about John the Baptist, and she wanted to highlight John's unusual character — he was not part of the pack in any way. John was his own man, God's man. He was the man who had a very special purpose, but she needed a clever segue into her main topic. After twenty minutes of unproductively staring at the blinking computer cursor and surfing the web, she decided that some fresh air would do her some good.

Winnie got all bundled up, as the weather called for layers, unwrapped her earphones for her MP3 player, and put the lead on Bitty.

They had been walking about fifteen minutes when Winnie saw Trudy. Winnie hadn't seen her since she had returned from her Thanksgiving trip, and three weeks makes a difference for an expectant, young lady.

The two women fell into step with one another and started toward the depot. Winnie thought she'd buy Trudy a cup of tea there.

Winnie didn't know Trudy too well. She lived with her mother, Keisha Livingston, in town. Trudy was eighteen years old and finishing her last year of high school. She was due to have her baby around the end of March. That's all Winnie knew about her, except that she had been helpful in caring for Bitty a couple of times.

Winnie didn't want to be too inquisitive about Trudy's situation, but she was willing to be a friendly ear if Trudy wanted to talk.

Trudy was polite but not very talkative during the first part of their walk, but once they got inside the diner and tea had been ordered, she began to speak.

"It's just been me and Ma together always. Ma says that my father was from the city and that he moved somewhere up north. I never knew him. His name is Al Jackson."

"Ma and I get along pretty good, but she's not happy about my present condition. Oh, she's okay with my having this child, as opposed to not having it, but she thinks I'm too young to be a single mom."

"It's a big thing that's happening to you right now." Winnie observed. She wanted to be in Trudy's corner, if she would allow that.

"You're very right about that. I've seen how hard Ma has worked, so that we can have what we need; it's not been easy for her," Trudy added.

"Have you given thought to what you're going to do next?" Winnie asked.

"I'm almost finished with high school. We graduate at the end of May, and I've talked to my teachers and my counselor and they have agreed to help me do some work ahead of my delivery time, so that I can be finished with school by the time Little Mister Child arrives," Trudy explained.

"Is it a boy? Do you know already?" Winnie asked.

"Well, I should know by now, because the ultra sound could have told me, but I didn't want to know when I had the test. These days everyone knows ahead of time about the baby's sex, but I told the nurse not to tell me. Now I wish I had. Isn't that funny?" Trudy asked Winnie.

"Goodness! When I had my children, there was no such thing as knowing the child's gender ahead of time. You had to be prepared with two names before the baby was born; then we'd know which name would fit as soon as it came."

"I suppose there are good reasons to learn about the child ahead of time. Do you want a boy or a girl?" Winnie asked her.

Trudy cocked her head to one side and thought. "I don't suppose I have a preference. Some would say, 'It's a man's world.' and I can see how that could be, and that might have some advantage to a child — knowing he would have an automatic advantage."

"There's good to be said on both sides of that argument," Trudy theorized. "You could make a long list of reasons why girls have the advantage, and another long list of reasons why boys have the advantage. I suppose it's not so much about whether you are male or female, but how well you use what you've been given."

Winnie was pleased to hear Trudy thinking so deeply, and she added, "Goodness my Dear, I think you've come upon a very good thought! You are right. It's not whether a person is male or female that's important but rather how you work with the stuff you have to make this world a little better. God has given us so many incredible gifts, and God expects us to grow up and use them. Men and women certainly do view their worlds wearing different lenses, so to speak, even when we tread the same streets and live in the same houses, we see things differently.

"I'm glad to hear that your teachers and school administration are willing to work with you, to help you through your final semester! I believe that getting the best education we can is important in today's world."

"What classes are you taking next semester?" Winnie wanted to know.

"We're on the block system at school now, so I'll be taking only two classes to finish my work. I'm taking senior English and world history. I could also take an elective, but it's not required."

Winnie lighted up, "That sounds like you'll have a lot of reading and writing in those classes, but working ahead certainly would be a good idea. Do you know that college courses usually work about double speed, compared to high school classes?"

Trudy looked surprised and said, "No! Really? That's hard, isn't it?"

Winnie explained, "It does require your attention and concerted effort."

"It's funny, though. You get your syllabus with the readings and tests and/or papers that will be due, and you plunge into the material, and eventually you see the work getting accomplished.

"The reason I mention it is because if you were to start classes in college next fall, which may be really difficult at this point in your life, you would be seeing that double-time-double-work there. If you are going to work ahead on your English and world history classes next semester, it will be very similar to doing the same requirement in college!" Winnie explained.

Trudy considered this idea and said, "That's really good, Miss Winnie. I hadn't thought about it before, but that does make sense."

Trudy and Winnie talked even after their tea had cooled. Trudy was planning to stay at home with her mother, same as now. Trudy's mother definitely had thoughts on this subject. She believed that her grandchild needed to have a father around. She had struggled hard to raise Trudy without one, and she felt it would have been better for Trudy to have had a father. She could only imagine how fine it might have been to have a father in the picture. She also wanted Trudy to complete her education, even go on to college, and get a place of her own.

"I really appreciate talking with you, Miss Winnie," Trudy told her. "I don't have too many people that I can talk to these days. Most of my girlfriends sort of treat me like I've got some terrible disease. They don't know what to say to me. All they want to know is about the father of the baby. And that's not their business!"

Winnie understood Trudy. She needed to have friends she could trust — various friends — her own age as well as, maybe, an older woman in whom she could confide. Winnie said, "I can imagine your world has changed a lot since you found out about the baby coming.

"You're right. It isn't anybody's business who the father is, although, it may be the father's business. Have you given that some thought?" Winnie asked.

Trudy was silent. She sat across the table and stared into space. Finally, after some moments she spoke. "Maybe the father has the right to know. Maybe that's the law. I don't know ... I'm very confused about it. I don't know what to do. I don't know if I want him in my baby's life."

Winnie could see this topic needed some time to develop, and so she changed the subject. "Trudy, maybe this is something you would like to think about. It's a subject that not only affects you, but also your child and the young man, your baby's father, too. It would have long-term implications. If you'd like, we could talk about it later. What do you think?"

Trudy was nodding her head slowly, agreeing with her new friend. She said, "Thanks. I will think about it. I'd like to know what my responsibilities are, legally."

Winnie agreed to email Trudy some information about paternity rights and whatever she might be able to find that would be helpful in figuring Trudy's decision. They parted when they left the diner going their separate ways. Winnie, who had tied Bitty to the post outside, untied her pup, and the two of them continued their walk back home.

※ ※ ※

By the time she arrived home from her walk, Winnie had thought of a fun opening for her sermon on John the Baptist. *I know exactly what I can say to open my sermon tomorrow. I'll explain about how I use my MP3 player when I go on a walk to listen to music with a strong beat; it gets my feet to moving more quickly and thereby getting my heart to work harder. Then I'll say that John the Baptist was hearing a different drumbeat, a Heavenly Drumbeat different from the rest of the world. He wasn't listening to the drumbeat of the world; he was listening to God.*

Chapter 15. Paul Taylor's Visit

The pre-school, angel chorus for the children's Christmas musical nearly stole the show. They were adorable! Somehow the dozen and a half freckle-faced boys and rosy-cheeked girls, each sporting their newly fashioned, white, angel frocks and golden halos were especially endearing to the audience — they were so cute. These baby angels, being the youngest of the cast members, were seated along the entire expanse of the stage at First Baptist Church's fellowship hall.

They sat on the stage, legs dangling over, watching the audience of several hundred community members watching them. The proud parents, of course, had immediately identified their own youngsters among the chorus. Exchanges of recognition and waves passed back and forth between the stage and the onlookers. Some of the angels having identified Mommy and Daddy waved and smiled repeatedly until Joe Ed, the director, gave several stern looks at the children and the music started, The show had begun.

Of course, one cannot expect four-year-olds to have an attention span that could control them for the entire show, so Joe Ed took a brief, unexpected intermission after the fourth song allowing time for the angelic-looking four year olds to find their parents and join them.

The show was a high moment of Misty Falls' Christmas season, and after the show, everyone — cast, audience, and all — assembled in the fellowship hall for homemade Christmas cookies and punch. It was a good moment for folks from the different churches in town to mingle and congratulate the children. Even Santa made an appearance. It was beginning to really feel like Christmas, Winnie thought. The whole town was merry with the mood of the season.

❋ ❋ ❋

Winnie kept in touch with the Olivers regularly, talking to Connie several times a week. Connie told Winnie that the woman from DHR had come out the day after Winnie had been there, and she talked to them for quite a while. She interviewed each of them — Connie, George, and Sallie — and she seemed to be satisfied for the moment that the babies were not in jeopardy. She did warn the family strongly that another such incident, any other call from one of their neighbors, would result in official action.

"Oh, no!" Winnie exclaimed. "You mean she would take the girls?"

"That's exactly what she meant," Connie admitted.

Finally after waiting a moment, in case Connie had more to say, Winnie added, "I can't imagine how you must be feeling right now, Connie."

Connie remained silent for a moment, and then she answered, "My neighbors are horrible! They're all watching us like hawks! We can't trust them. I don't even want to speak to them. I don't know what to do!"

Winnie felt for Connie. She thought it was almost easier to deal with a personal trauma than to watch on, helplessly, while someone else suffers. She really didn't know what to say or do for Connie. *It's very hard to watch someone else's heart nearly break.* All Winnie could do was to let Connie know that she would be there for her, in any case.

"How are the babies?" she asked.

"They are fine," Connie assured Winnie. "They are sweeter every day. You must come by and see them for yourself."

※ ※ ※

Rev. Paul Allen Taylor was Winnie's son, and he was also a United Methodist pastor. Paul had gone to Perkins School of Theology in Dallas right out of college, so he had been preaching for nearly ten years. Paul and his family would be arriving a bit late for their Christmas celebration with Winnie due to his responsibilities to the church in Dallas. They would be attending Christmas Eve service at Paul's church and then leave on Christmas Day to fly up to Knoxville and drive to Misty Falls for their own holiday with Grannie Winnie.

Winnie loved the times she spent with her children. Sometimes she visited them; sometimes they came to her. Occasionally they'd all go camping or to the beach for a holiday together.

Paul had married Tricia after his second year of preaching. When he arrived at his first church, it took no time at all before the ladies of the community recognized an obvious lack in their new pastor — he didn't have a wife. Rev. Taylor was handsome, well educated, and he definitely *needed* a wife!

Before Paul realized what the church folks were thinking, various young ladies were being introduced to him. Some were daughters or granddaughters of church members. Some lived in the community and heard the word as it spread about Pastor Taylor's "need."

Paul wasn't as convinced as the church was about his need for a wife. He was polite to the young ladies and a bit amused at all this extra attention he was getting. He certainly didn't mind being liked as a pastor, but he would prefer it to be for the right reasons! Paul wanted people to hear his message of Christ's love for all and His invitation to follow Him. Paul's personal life was his own, wasn't it?

Paul was aware of the blatant way he was being introduced to certain young ladies or invited to have dinner with particular families, and he began to realize that these invitations were inspired by his "need" for a wife.

Tricia came into the picture from a different source. She was the sister of a good friend of Paul's from college, so they had met during their college years. Tricia was dating someone else at the time, and then she took a couple of semesters to study abroad. Paul hadn't seen her after that.

Tricia was an accomplished singer, a mezzo soprano, and she had earned a position in a German opera company. She couldn't turn such an opportunity down, so she spent another year with the opera in Heidelberg.

Paul met Tricia again when he visited his friend's home. She had just returned from Europe and was living with her folks while she looked into teaching positions. It didn't take Paul and Tricia long to figure they were meant for one another, and their engagement was soon announced.

Paul's church was all abuzz with the news of his plans to marry, and not a few young ladies were disappointed that they were not the object of the honor of becoming Paul's wife.

Today the Taylors have two beautiful children: Susanna Marie, their lively eight-year old, whom they call Susie, and Paul Wesley, who would be five in the spring.

Winnie planned to celebrate Christmas when the Taylors arrived. They'd have their Christmas dinner and open presents on Boxing Day, the 26th.

Winnie was looking forward to having some "down time". Just being Mom and Grannie to her family sounded delightful!

She did take time early in the week to work on Sunday's sermon, as she wanted to be as free as possible for her family when they arrived. She realized that she was a bit resentful that her professional life interfered so much in her personal life, but then she would remind herself how very selfish that way of thinking was. She'd ask for forgiveness and move on. Winnie hoped that as she traveled this path of discipleship she was learning a thing or two!

❋ ❋ ❋

The Christmas Eve service was beautiful, and everyone said so. At the final carol the sanctuary lights were lowered, save for the candles and the tree lights. The worshipers raised their individual candles high as they lifted their voices together singing Silent Night. All were dressed in festive Christmas attire. The ambiance of love and anticipation stirred in each worshiper as they shared this sublime moment together singing in the Yule.

Winnie walked down the center aisle of the sanctuary during the last verse of the final carol, and as she walked holding her lit candle high she looked over her flock. She saw people, old and young, from many walks of life standing, singing, smiling, and welcoming in the moment — the day of Christ's incarnation had finally arrived! Venite Adoramus — *O! Come Let Us Adore Him!*

✳ ✳ ✳

Christmas morning dawned as an ordinary day for Winnie. Although it was Christmas morning, and at other times in her life she would have been totally engaged in the many responsibilities of the big day; this morning was unremarkable.

Winnie opened her email to find a note from John. He had been up early this morning, already working on his papers. He thought his reading and grading was coming along better than he had hoped, and he believed that he would be completely through with all the papers soon.

John was looking forward to his usual ski trip to Aspen just after the New Year. This trip would come right prior to the philosophers' convention in Mississippi,

John had noticed an advertisement about a ski resort in North Carolina inviting skiers to try the slopes on the Appalachians. He hadn't skied there before, which would mean the challenge of new slopes to ski. This ski resort was offering a special wintertime package for the first week of the New Year, since that was a time when many skiers were already returning to work after the holidays.

It occurred to John that he might drive to North Carolina for his ski trip, and on the way he could stop and see Winnie. He suggested that he drive to Misty Falls and take Winnie out on a New Year's Eve date. He realized that her son Paul and his family would be visiting then, and he hoped he would be able to meet that part of Winnie's family.

Winnie stopped reading and closed her eyes; she needed to think this through.

It was a fabulous idea! Winnie could feel little goose bumps growing on her arms as she read John's email. *Goodness! Look at that*! She touched her forearm. *Wonder what it means? Am I sending myself a message?* She recognized this potential visit had suddenly and completely captured her imagination. She was already relishing an evening with John — just the two of them, not surrounded by hundreds of classmates or anyone else that could project his or her agenda into their company. At the same time she realized that her little secret would finally be revealed — John would certainly discover her pastoral identity!

John was obviously interested in her, and she was thoroughly enjoying the chase. They would be going out together for New Year's Eve — somewhere in Knoxville, some place fancy. *How undeniably delicious!*

John would be coming to Misty Falls in less than a week if she said, "Yes."

Winnie hit the return button on her email and wrote:

John,

It's good to hear your work is progressing so well and you'll be able to take time off afterwards to get away for your own holiday before the new school term begins.

Yes, I'd love for you to come here. Imagine! We'll actually be in the same place at the same time. It's a grand idea! Yes, I'm sure Paul, Tricia, and my grandkids will be happy to meet you.

If I understand you correctly, you'd like to arrive on the afternoon of the 31st, so you'll have time to meet Paul and his family. Then we would drive into Knoxville to some special place for dinner and await the New Year's arrival.

I could offer you accommodations here at my home; I have four bedrooms. Paul's family will be using only two of them, so I would have room for another guest. If you would prefer, though, there is a small motel on the highway here in Misty Falls. They would have room for you; I'm pretty sure.

Yours,

Winnie

Winnie hit the "send" button, and the date was set.

"Goodness!" Winnie said aloud. "That really gives 'shape' to this holiday!"

"John is coming here!" She danced around the room with Bitty, who was surprised to see her owner so animated.

Winnie had a real struggle within herself trying to settle down and concentrate on her sermon for Sunday. Other ideas kept invading her thoughts, and she had a terrible time trying to quell them in favor of focusing on the text she had chosen to use for Sunday. She had certainly preached on that famous passage of Mary's Song of Thanksgiving before, but she wanted to come at it from a slightly different angle this time. Turning her mind to her sermon after the news of the morning was a serious battle for Winnie.

Winnie hadn't mentioned John to her son, not yet. She figured the subject of this very interesting man, who was rapidly becoming an important person to her, would certainly be a topic of conversation with Paul and Tricia. Winnie was especially pleased to think that they would all have an opportunity to meet.

❊ ❊ ❊

Winnie spent the rest of the day doing this and that, readying herself and the house for her guests.

Finally the door bell rang at 8:30 that evening, and Winnie opened her door to the happy faces of Paul and his family! The kids crowded around Grannie Winnie, gave her a hug, and then spotted Bitty. Quickly, the children moved to the pup and showered their attentions on her.

Winnie welcomed the Taylors into her parsonage and showed them their bedrooms.

After all the luggage had been put away and the Christmas presents had been placed under the tree, everyone found themselves sitting in the living room enjoying the ambiance of the moment. Winnie brought in hot chocolate and iced, Christmas cookies for everyone to enjoy. P.W. asked his dad if they could open presents now, and Paul, spying a red, furry Santa hat atop a lamp, placed it on his five year old's head. "Guess you should be 'Santa' this year, Son," he told him.

Paul and Tricia had taken care not to encourage the myth of Santa Claus. They taught Susie and P.W., instead, about the real Saint Nicholas, who was a bishop in the church in what is now Turkey. He spent his life helping people and became known for his generosity to orphans, which was the basis for the story about Santa Claus. Rather than teaching their children a story they would later have to unlearn about Santa Claus, the Taylors taught their children to enjoy the spirit of giving, but they still enjoyed the fun of the Santa myth.

Paul now explained to P.W. how he should pull out gifts from under the tree and hand them to the person whose name was on the package. The family spent the better part of the next hour opening presents and "Ooooing" and "Awwwwing" over them. Soft Christmas music played in the room as a friendly backdrop for their cozy, gift opening time.

* * *

The week spun by. The Taylor family completely filled all the available space in Winnie's parsonage with the sounds of children laughing and playing and enjoying their time at Grannie's home.

Winnie spent time with each of her grandchildren. Susie was very musical, just like her mother. She sang sweetly for Winnie – not being the least bit shy. Susie had a good set of lungs, and she loved to sing all the verses to whatever she was singing. She was already comfortable playing the piano, even at her tender age of eight. Tricia had been working with Susie for years at the keyboard; Susie probably couldn't remember a time when she didn't play the piano.

Susie was gifted in many ways. She danced all around the house; she read "chapter books" and colored in the lines, too.

Paul Wesley, or P.W. as he was called, was already reading well at four and a half years, and he was an avid builder. He was especially thrilled to get several sets of Lego's to construct. Very quickly the front room had become a maze of blocks, tracks, buildings, cars, and miniature characters.

Winnie looked on the newly decorated living room with pleasure and thought, *How well I remember when Claire and Paul were small like these kids. That was a tender age.* She was convinced that her grandchildren, all of them, had wonderful parents! She felt herself very blessed.

❋ ❋ ❋

Winnie brought up the subject of her unexpected guest when the Taylors and she were sitting in the living room after Christmas dinner. She told them some background — how John had phoned her completely out of the blue in September to tell her about Mile High's reunion.

She recounted her trip to Denver and the reunion — how she and John had been inseparable there, how they had talked and talked non-stop, and they had been corresponding via email ever since.

Winnie admitted her interest in John — and her concern. She was hopeful that things would work out well between them, but there was an issue of John's lack of faith in God that was a major concern to Winnie.

"We haven't had a moment when we spoke seriously about faith. I dodged the question about my profession by telling John that I work in the office at my church. I haven't told him I live in the church parsonage and am appointed to preach at Muddy Creek Church! He doesn't know that I'm a preacher."

This confession struck all three of them as pretty funny. Could John really not know about Winnie's work? Paul said, "Mom, if John comes here, he's going to figure it out. Don't you think?"

Winnie had been turning this over in her mind ever since John's email Christmas morning. She said, "Yes, I know he'll find out. I'll be glad to have that silly confusion out in the open. It's beginning to feel like an 'elephant' in the room," she admitted.

"If my being a Christian (and a preacher) is a problem for John then we have a problem and there's nothing more to say. We'll not have wasted time or energy on a relationship that won't work," Winnie stated.

Winnie could tell that the Taylors were pleased to hear about this interesting man in their mother's life and that they would have an opportunity to meet him when he came — not that they would have any serious input to Winnie about John. It was her life and her decision however she chose to go, but they were intrigued to be able to meet this man who was showing such interest in Mom. Their presence would help John to see something more about Winnie's world.

The Taylors had tickets to fly home on New Year's Day, which would be the day after Winnie and John had their date. Paul and his family would drive to the Knoxville airport and fly back to Dallas; Paul needed to be back in his pulpit on Sunday. They would only have a short time to spend with John before leaving for their return trip. Winnie intended to invite John over to the house for breakfast New Year's Day.

Chapter 16. First Date

John rang the doorbell at 2:30 New Year's Eve afternoon. The sound of the bell triggered a not-unexpected response from Bitty who was at the door the next instant barking loudly in her high soprano, doggy voice announcing the presence of a newcomer.

Bitty's demanding announcement paired with the tone of the bell caused those sitting in the living room to cease whatever conversation they were engaged in and to shift their eyes, as if being directed by an unseen conductor, to the front door. Winnie picked up the TV remote, snapped off the program, gathered up Bitty in her arms, and answered the door.

There stood John, holding a large bunch of red roses and a Christmassy-wrapped gift; his eyes were twinkling. Winnie had transferred Bitty to her left arm in order to negotiate the door and the screen, allowing John admission to the room.

The next few moments involved general introductions. Winnie, who was not a little bit anxious, began the presentations, saying, "John, I want you to meet my son, The Reverend Tall Paylor. Winnie's face turned scarlet; she closed her eyes and wrinkled her nose and tried again. I <u>mean</u>, this is my son Paul Taylor and his wife Tisha Traylor. No! I mean Trisha Taylor." At this point everyone was smiling and chuckling and shaking hands all around. Finally the children were introduced to Dr. Daniel. Susie came first. She said, "Hello, Dr. Daniel" in a very soft voice and sat down on the corner of her mother's chair. When it was little P.W.'s turn, he surprised everyone by walking straight over to John and holding out his right hand to shake hands. John raised his eye brows and grinned at the child and held out his hand to shake. The small, child's hand was barely a quarter the size of the grown man's hand, but they solemnly shook nonetheless. After that the two children recognizing that adult conversation was about to ensue left the room. Bitty followed the two, perhaps figuring there would be more activity among the younger set.

Winnie and Tricia excused themselves to go into the kitchen for coffee and holiday cookies.

John and Paul fell into conversation. They both were athletes in their own right. John, of course, was a skier, and Paul competed in triathlons several times each year. After exploring the sports interests they shared John remarked, "So, Reverend Taylor, I gather you are a preacher."

Paul nodded agreement and said he had been pastoring churches for ten years. He told John about his church in Dallas, St. Peter's United Methodist, where he'd been for four and a half years. P.W. was just a babe in arms when they had arrived at St. Peter's.

The church was an older church (meaning the congregation was older), but it was experiencing a revival of young families, like his own, coming now. They had two worship services, one of which was a modified 'contemporary' service.

"We've come a long way with our contemporary service," Paul explained. "The music was too loud at first, so we tempered it, and we've tried to listen to many voices in that community — what they find helpful in the way of connecting to the tastes of an unchurched generation.

"I think our new service is finally developing into a service most of us can appreciate. It seems to be well received. I can use the same style preaching in both of my services, although I wear my black, academic gown with the stole appropriate for the season at the traditional service and less formal attire at the other."

As John and Paul spoke about this contemporary service and how it differed from the traditional service, John reminisced about his own church experience. He remembered going with his mother to a Presbyterian church when he was in elementary school, but his father had teased him about going.

Winnie's ears perked up immediately when John mentioned his experience with church. "Why John," she declared, "I thought you didn't believe in church!"

John shook his head and said, "I guess we did mention church when we first spoke on the phone, but I'm sure I didn't explain myself very well then."

All eyes focused on John, and he took this to be an invitation to share his views on church.

John sat up a little straighter in his chair, cleared his throat, and said, "It's not a very interesting story, really; I just never saw a point in going to church when I was growing up. Like I said, Mom and I attended church during my early years, but it didn't mean much to me. I thought the church services were boring and a terrible waste of a morning. Maybe that was because of my dad's negative comments. I suppose I liked the person of Jesus; he's obviously had an unparalleled influence on the world and could be easily ranked among the most influential moral teachers in the world, but I don't see the connection between respecting him and the thing that church has become."

"I suppose that sounds a lot stronger than I actually feel. I really don't mean to disparage your profession, Paul. I'm sure you're a fine man and a good pastor to your people. I'm just telling you how I see things."

Winnie was drinking in John's every word. Finally John was speaking about his involvement (or un-involvement) with church. She was all ears.

John continued, "I guess what I meant is that I don't believe that you have to belong to a church to live a good life."

"That's quite a statement, John," Paul said. "As a Christian I would define 'the good life' as a life of faith and how one's faith is acted out in the world."

"What do you mean by faith?" John asked.

"Of course there are many definitions of faith, but one that might be helpful is 'living out what you believe each day.' Christians have faith in Christ, but just saying, 'I believe in Jesus Christ' is not faith. It may be an idea, but it's not real faith. Faith is about putting your belief into practice."

John knew well how such conversations had a way of developing into daylong events and realized that this topic needed to be tabled for the present. He had come to take Winnie out for New Year's Eve, and since they needed to be in Knoxville by six they would have to begin getting ready soon.

John said, "I'd really love to continue to explore this subject with you, but I think Win and I must be leaving soon. We are going out on the town tonight, and we have reservations just after six in Knoxville."

Turning to Winnie he said, "Win, (did you notice that's my name for you?) I wanted to surprise you a little, so I made plans for us to take a cruise on the Volunteer Princess tonight for dinner on the Tennessee. We board the boat at 6:15, and if my GPS is right, we'll need forty-five minutes to get into town and a few minutes to park and get to the boat. We should leave here by 5. Can you be ready by then?"

Since the cruise returned at nine, John and Winnie would have time to walk around downtown and end up at Market Square to see the ball drop for the New Year. John suggested that Winnie bring along some comfortable shoes to wear for their walk.

This afternoon is turning out to be even better than I imagined. Winnie considered John's admission about his thoughts on faith, but she wondered if perhaps he had not really heard the gospel message, not really ... not completely. John had not turned it down, he had just not yet heard it clearly. *There is still hope!*

John had reserved a room at the motel on the edge of town, so he zipped over to the motel, picked up his room key, showered, shaved, and put on his suit. He was back at Winnie's home at exactly 5.

The trip into Knoxville was filled with newness for John and Winnie. They found they were able to relax and enjoy one another's company; it was delightful to finally be together, at least as close a bucket seats allowed. They laughed and chatted on and on about current events — Paul and his family's visit, John's work at the University, his new appointment to the Mortimer J. Adler Chair in the philosophy department, and his plans for this coming week. John would have several days for skiing then he would drive to Ole Miss for the philosophers' convention, and finally he would make his way to Nashville to meet Winnie.

John mentioned Winnie's visitors, "I can't imagine having such a family with grown children and even grandchildren! Your family is so warm and welcoming even to me — a stranger. I don't have anything like that. I'm alone these days since my folks passed, and my older brother, Scott, is gone, too. My life is much simpler than yours. I seem to have a lot fewer significant others in my life than you have in yours.

"Your home is so cosy! It's just what I might have envisioned for you," John told Winnie. "How long have you been there? I have to say I'm surprised you have such a big place for a single woman."

Winnie sensed where the conversation was going. She took a big breath and said, "I live in Muddy Creek's church parsonage. A parsonage's size and amenities are determined by a code that is found in the church's rule book, The Discipline, which dictates the number of rooms and other requirements for the pastor's home."

There is was.

John slowly nodded his head. "I was quickly coming to that conclusion. You haven't exactly *said* that you are the pastor at the church, but I should have guessed.

"Did you mean to mislead me?" John turned and winked at Winnie.

"No ... not really." Winnie shook her head. "I didn't want to mislead you about my profession, but when you said you didn't believe in church I quickly squelched my panic and moved to a diversionary tactic. Remember?" Winnie admitted this referring to her silly comeback on the phone — 'You don't believe in church? Why there are several right here in my town!' Please forgive me for my deception!"

"You're forgiven. I think I can see how that happened. I haven't spent any time with pastors before, so I'm on virgin territory here; if you'll pardon the expression!" John laughed.

"How did you happen to get into pastoring? Or do you call it preaching?" John asked.

"Goodness! That's a long story, I suppose." Winnie began. "I grew up in a Christian home, and we were active in our church in Denver. Back then we lived in the city and were members of Park Hill Methodist Church.

"I believe I was called to "full-time Christian service" when I was a youth. Of course being in full-time Christian service could be realized in many ways. When my kids were little, I worked at our church doing Christian education, mostly Sunday school and Vacation Bible School. I became a lay speaker and spoke to women's groups. One time our pastor got sick and I was asked to fill in for him a couple of weeks. That was an experience! I was terrified, but everyone was so encouraging."

"After Mark died I decided to go to graduate school and get my degree, so I could preach. The kids were in high school when I matriculated into seminary, but by the time they were both in college I was at my first church as pastor."

"I can see how that developed. Wasn't it expensive for you to be in school when you didn't have an income?" John asked.

Winnie explained that Mark, who had been an Air Force pilot, had taken out extra insurance for the family "in case." She decided after he was gone to use some of that money to pay for seminary, so she could be earning an income and not just living on what Mark left her.

✳ ✳ ✳

The Volunteer Princess was beautifully decorated for the New Year's Eve party. There were festive hats and streamers and silvery stars all around the hall. John and Winnie were seated at a table right in front of the stage.

After dinner the orchestra began playing Glenn Miller music, and John surprised Winnie by asking her to dance. The smooth, muted tones of the Moonlight Serenade filled the room, inviting dancers to step into the music. The next thing Winnie knew, she was swirling gracefully around the dance floor in John's arms.

Winnie had not danced, not one step, since Mark had died. Suddenly, memories came flooding into her mind. The motion of their two bodies moving together to the lazy beat of the music, the lilting sound of the dance band, the smell of John's aftershave, the squeak of his shoes on the floor; everything seemed to come together, and Winnie thought perhaps she had arrived in heaven!

John held her tightly around the waist and guided her easily across the floor; he was a smooth dancer. Winnie had no idea that he danced, but his moves seemed completely natural. John led Winnie around the room like he was master of the dance. It was spellbinding.

When the music ended, they sat down at their table to catch their breath. Winnie admitted, "This is more fun than I even expected. Getting to know you is turning out to be quite an adventure, Dr. Jonathan Daniel!"

John couldn't have been more pleased. "Indeed it is fun! Win, I think it's too bad we've let so much time pass already."

They danced, and danced, and danced some more. By the time the boat had docked, and they were back on dry land, they both felt they had stepped into a new dimension together.

They returned to John's car, and Winnie changed her shoes for walking shoes. They strolled all around the area holding hands, stopping in a small cafe and ordering hot chocolate. They talked non-stop, completely fascinated with the other.

By the end of the evening they had arrived at Market Square where a big, time ball was about to be dropped. People were swarming from every direction to watch the moment when 2009 would be welcomed in.

Finally the moment came. An announcement from the loud-speaker counted down the last seconds, before the clock would proclaim the New Year's arrival. The crowd began counting in time with the

speaker: "Ten, nine, eight, seven, six, five, four, three, two, one!"

The great, flashing ball began its descent onto the square; the band struck the opening notes of the obligatory Auld Lang Syne, and John put his arms around Winnie, pulled her to him and kissed her tenderly.

On the way back to Misty Falls Winnie and John were thoughtful. Whereas, earlier in the evening they had been talking non-stop now things were different — they didn't need to fill the air with constant conversation. There was a feeling of deep delight, fun, and adventure, and now something new — an added dynamic between them had made its debut.

John walked Winnie to the door of her parsonage and waited while she unlocked the door. He gave her another hug and kiss before he left for his motel room. They agreed to meet later that morning — about nine-thirty for breakfast.

※ ※ ※

New Year's morning Winnie appeared in her kitchen humming a tune — something she'd danced to the night before; she was moving lightly around the room, as she began putting out breakfast goodies for the final meal before everyone left for their respective destinations. John arrived for breakfast just as the grandkids were sitting down to eat.

The morning was filled with the excitement of the day ahead, not to mention that of the previous evening! The Taylors would be leaving for the airport, and John would be driving to his ski weekend in North Carolina.

Tricia inquired about their date, and Winnie quickly produced a colorful brochure she had picked up at the Volunteer Princess the evening before. She passed it around for all to see. She pointed out the great ballroom on the boat where she and John had tarried over their dinner. "Dinner was wonderful. We had shrimp cocktail, a grilled seafood platter with scallops, mahi mahi, stuffed shrimp, and crab cakes; and then, to top it all off, we shared a New York style cheese cake. I don't have to tell you how good it was!"

The best part of the evening, Winnie admitted, came when the band began to play and John asked her to dance. She didn't offer more about the evening, but it was obvious that she and John were happy to have become reacquainted, and that something special was at work between them.

The Taylors had already packed their rental car, so after breakfast they excused themselves to begin their journey. Winnie waved good-bye to them. *What a wonderful visit.*

John needed to leave, too, but he and Winnie found it difficult to say good-bye. Finally they parted, knowing that they would be back together in Nashville in eight more days. They could pick up right where they left off.

After John pulled his car away from the house, Winnie plunked down in her front room and sighed. *I'll never forget this Christmas, and I have a feeling this may be the beginning of something very special! Thank you, LORD!*

Chapter 17. The Week Between

Winnie was still glowing inside from her eventful holiday week. After preaching Sunday, she came home to revel in all her memories!

There wasn't anything about last week that was not good. Of course she was thrilled with the visit of Paul and his family. They were so dear, and she didn't get enough time to be with them. Their visit helped a little. Winnie realized that it's not possible to be bonded with grandchildren when time and distance keep you apart.

Of course, the greatest part of last week was John's visit! Winnie didn't expect to hear from John for a while, as he was off skiing. He wouldn't even be close to a Wi-Fi hook up; he was literally out of touch. This period apart would give them some time to reflect, and that was probably a good thing.

Winnie had plenty to digest. She needed to put her emotions on hold for a bit and try to think clearly about what was developing between them.

They had touched on a few items that needed addressing. She was more than relieved that John now knew that she was a pastor. She had been most uncomfortable keeping that from him, as if it were some dark, mysterious secret that she shouldn't divulge. That wasn't the case, of course, but the longer she had kept it from John, the odder it felt. She was relieved that the "elephant" was finally out of the bag. *Now there's a mixed metaphor!*

John had taken the news quite well, and it didn't seem to change his attitude toward her; if anything, he seemed be pleased about the disclosure. Winnie hadn't expected that. She had feared that John's discovery of her vocation might totally ruin whatever might be developing between them. She was relieved that, in the end, they both laughed about her reticence to divulge her work to him. Maybe John thought he had found a new opponent for arguing philosophy — here was an interesting woman who had a certain perspective, and it might be fun to engage in debate with her on the finer aspects of law, and ethics, and God. Maybe, or maybe not. Whatever the case was, Winnie was most pleased about how the evening had turned out.

❋ ❋ ❋

Winnie gave Evelyn a call to catch up on her son Randy's progress. Evelyn explained that Randy was being kept in a medically-induced coma to let his body heal without his thrashing around.

"Anytime the nurses or attendants see Randy's blood pressure going up or his heart beating rapidly they call me to come sit with him," Evelyn told her. "You know he's hooked up to all sorts of medical equipment, and he can't speak, so when he wakes he gets very agitated and begins to move around. Of course the nursing staff in the TICU can't have Randy pulling on things or moving around in bed, so they come get me. They realize that I can comfort him.

"I go into his room and hold his hand and tell him I am right there. I tell him about all the people who are praying for him. I remind him about his dog, Rascal, how he is missing his master. I tell him whatever comes to mind. I want him to hear my voice and know I'm right there for him. I've told him again and again how God is the master healer, and how Jesus is healing him from the inside out. I'm very positive that he's going to be healed," Evelyn told Winnie.

"I sing softly to him. I sing every song I can think of, especially songs he's heard in church, which I hope are comforting to him. I hold his hand and caress his arm and sing.

"Gerald comes here most evenings to bring me changes of clothes and other useful items. He's very worried about Randy, wondering, if he survives, what sort of life he'll have. I tell Gerald that if the Lord brings Randy through this, it will be a miracle; and if God will do one miracle, God can do another and give Randy a life too.

"I have really been blessed by folks from the church who have come here to see me. They don't get to see Randy, because of the TICU rules, but they have helped me so much in getting through this trial each day. They have prayed with me and for Randy, and they have given me so much to hope for. Their faith and encouragement help me more than I can tell. They keep me going. I don't know what or how to pray, but all the members who came by have given me hope."

Winnie could see how the whole church had been working together to hold Randy up in their prayers. They were a wonderful example of the Body of Christ.

❋ ❋ ❋

Tuesday evening Winnie and Nina had dinner together. They chose a restaurant over in Kirby, the town nearby, for their meal and settled into a large booth. It was a cozy place with various sorts of American memorabilia hanging along the walls.

They chatted about their respective holidays. Nina had flown to Chicago to have Christmas with her daughter, Elise, and her family. "They have a house in Wheaton west of the city. It's a good community. I love what the kids have done to their house. They added an extra room in the back, which becomes a place to put me when I visit."

Winnie told Nina about her date with John. Nina remembered John from their earlier conversation. She could tell something more had been stirring and wanted to know all the details. Winnie's memory of the evening was great fun, Nina thought. She listened with trained ears as long as she could, but finally Nina had to know, "What's going to happen? When will you two see each other again?"

Winnie explained about John's ski trip, his meeting in Mississippi, and their date in Nashville this coming Friday and Saturday!

"Really! You'll be back together Friday night in Nashville?" Nina asked.

"Right. We plan to meet for dinner at The Gaylord Hotel. You've been there, I suppose." Winnie asked.

Nina lit up, "Dan and I went there with the kids right after it opened, in 1977. It really is a grand place. We returned a couple of years later, just the two of us. It's a marvelous place for roaming around, taking in the gardens. The place will be perfect for you two.

"Will you be there for the whole weekend?" Nina asked.

Winnie shook her head, "No" and explained. "No, that's the life of a preacher, I'm afraid. I'll drive back here Saturday night. I can't get a re-placement preacher every time I think it might be nice to get away."

Nina tried to understand her friend's decision about coming back so soon and having just one night with John. It wasn't Nina's decision, of course, but wouldn't Winnie rather take the whole weekend?

Winnie recognized Nina's apprehension and explained, "We both have to get back to our appointed duties. John's classes are beginning, and you know about Sundays for me. Neither one of us can get away longer."

Nina thought it was a fun change of pace to be having "girl talk" with Winnie. She couldn't see exactly where things were going with this relationship, but she was keen on finding out!

✳ ✳ ✳

The first week of January seemed to be just another regular week in the life of a busy pastor.

Winnie had agreed to take Connie and her twins for their doctor's appointment in the next town over. It would be a full morning's outing, so she picked up some study materials to fill up any waiting time that might come along.

Connie was ready with her two, darling babies and all their para-phernalia — two carriers for the girls to be strapped into the back seat, as well as Connie's big diaper bag with all the various items for "just in case."

150

It took the whole morning, and Winnie was a bit set on edge because of the long wait. After an hour waiting in the reception room there was another couple hours waiting in a checkup room before the doctor finally arrived to look at the girls.

While they waited the nurse arrived. She placed both babies on their backs on the gurney and undressed them to check their vitals. Winnie was amused to see the way the two little girls reacted. They couldn't see one another, as they were lying on their backs, starring at the ceiling, but they somehow knew they were near one another. As Winnie watched the babies, they reached out with their arms and touched hands. They each knew the other twin was near. *Their nearness to each other must give them some sort of comfort! What a beautiful sight! I'm watching the Sistene Chapel in real life!* Winnie also thought these two babies had just shown her a tiny glimmer of truth — *would that we could know the 'nearness' of God who is just within reach, right there next to us, waiting to be grasped!* Winnie made a mental note to remember this tender moment, since it could be a good sermon illustration one day: God is in our lives — there within a moment's reach, if only we'd call out.

The nurse left, and they sat a while longer in the room, waiting.

Winnie had spoken to Connie before about her other children, and Connie had not been in the least secretive about them. She had shown scrapbooks she was making for each child and showed them to Winnie. There were pictures of Connie's children in their new homes with their new parents. One of the mothers wrote often to keep Connie informed about how her son was doing. Connie realized that her children had good homes and were receiving loving care. She didn't ever expect to get the children back, but she wasn't totally removed from them. Connie knew they were having a good life.

Connie's acceptance of her first three children's new circumstances was not easy for Winnie to accept. Winnie knew within herself that, had she been in Connie's situation, she would have fought tooth and nail to keep her children with her. Surely Connie had had more time to think about the whole business of losing her children and knowing that other parents were raising them instead of her — that things were now the best for her children. Although Winnie realized how Connie felt inside, about a mother losing her children, she did understand that it was emotionally healthier for Connie to come to the resolve that she had.

While they awaited the doctor's arrival, Connie told Winnie one of the strangest stories she'd ever heard.

It seems that when Connie was growing up, she and her mother lived next door to George *and his family.* George was then married to another woman, and they had five children. Missy, George's youngest child, was Connie's best friend. The two girls were in second grade when they met!

Connie didn't tell Winnie what transpired over the next several years, but by the time Connie was sixteen George had divorced his first wife and married Connie!

Winnie couldn't believe her ears, and it took a minute to process the whole picture. *There is something horrifyingly creepy about that whole scene. Connie has been under the influence of George since she was a child; how does such a 'relationship' begin? What a grotesque, illegal, and immoral situation!* Winnie could see how the DHR, if they had any idea of George's other family, would not be pleased with his presence in the lives of his children.

✳ ✳ ✳

Over in North Carolina, John was thoroughly enjoying his holiday. The whirlwind evening he had just spent with Winnie had turned out to be well worth the effort of getting to Misty Falls.

Winnie brought back fine, old memories of John's high school years, when life was less complicated and going quite well for him. Those old, school times — the memories they shared from times gone by — served simply as a preface for this new saga beginning for them.

John was characteristically introspective and recognized that something was astir within him since last night — something new and fresh. This newness reminded him of another time long ago when he and Helen began to fall in love.

His life would have been so different if Helen hadn't died. Her death had brought John's own life screeching to a halt. When he learned of her death, something inside him died too. He felt completely alone and deserted. He felt dead inside — devastated, hardly able to put two thoughts together in a sensible string. He had retreated into a painful world of wanting to strike out and fight back.

The pain had stayed with John for years, and he knew he had clutched that pain close to him. As painful as his grief was somehow his grief helped him stay connected to Helen, and he grew fearful that if he lost the pain he would lose her, too.

John was only too aware of the long years of loneliness and darkness he had suffered. He felt as if his very reason for life had been completely centered on Helen and what life with her would be when they could be married. All his hopes for their future were sent careening into an abyss that terrible day he lost her.

His response to Helen's death had been to retreat into the world of academia — the place he had always found success before. There in the halls of higher learning John delved into his discipline and found some small peace there.

Now, John found himself tantalized by a new feeling, a feeling that he was young again and that things could be different. The old, nagging feeling of grief had vanished. Hope was returning to him, and he was pleased and reflective of what it might bring.

The weekend raced by as John sped downhill on challenging mountain slopes. He welcomed the strenuous workout of the ski runs. He

152

could feel his mind clearing as the crisp temperatures stung his face while flying down the snow covered mountains.

* * *

Monday morning John packed his car and drove to Oxford, Mississippi and the campus of Ole Miss. John was a philosopher who enjoyed the peace of a long car ride. He arrived at the hotel near the university Monday shortly after dinner.

John noted several S.O.P.H.I.A members sitting around the lobby engaged in conversation, but he didn't yet see anyone he knew. The philosophers' crowd was a good mix of thinkers gathered from every corner of the country — young and old, conservative and liberal. John expected to see several old friends when the conference began in the morning.

* * *

The breakfast items available to the hotel guests included a taste-tempting array of goodies to energize hotel guests for their day ahead. John had been pleased to hear that the hotel included free breakfasts for their guests. He always liked to see his dollar stretch as far as possible.

John was *not* a cook, and most of his meals were either fast food or frozen meals he could zap in the microwave at home. His usual breakfast was oatmeal and brown sugar, which was reasonably inexpensive, especially as John was careful to use store brands and not advertised labels. The many, tasty-looking choices at the hotel invited him to indulge himself today, after all, breakfast came with the price of the room!

He had just chosen a couple of old fashioned donuts to dip in his coffee when he felt a tap on his shoulder. John glanced around and found an old acquaintance of his, Dr. Victor Borkowski, standing next to him.

"Well, I thought I might run into you here!" John smiled at his colleague. "I'm glad to see you were able to make it to the seminar."

John had known Victor when they both attended Davidson College years before. They weren't close friends back then, as they had been separated by a couple of years in school. They did take one class together, share the same advisor, and had many of the same professors since they studied the same discipline. They became better acquainted later at seminars like S.O.P.H.I.A.

The two men found a small table in the corner of the dining room, overlooking the courtyard and exchanged pleasantries — mostly concerning courses they were currently teaching. John told Victor about the new honor he had just received, being named to the Mortimer J. Adler Chair at his school.

Victor was struck by a coincidence when he heard Adler's name, and he interrupted his friend. "I was just reading about Adler. Did you know him?"

"No, I didn't. He left UC in 1952, so I missed him by a generation, but a chair was named for him at the school when he died in '01. The chair was given to the Philosophy Department by a family who had greatly admired Adler's work, especially his work at Chicago, helping to set up *The Great Books of the Western World* and making them available to the masses," John explained.

"What brought Adler to mind?" John inquired.

"I think you and I are good examples of most western philosophers today — not avowing any particular faith. Really, since the Enlightenment we philosophers have not believed in God. We knew better, right?" Victor smiled at John.

John cocked his head slightly and nodded affirmation with Victor's statement.

"There was a time when I thought anyone who believed in God had to be some sort of nut case. Belief in God doesn't seem to bear up to empirical facts," John admitted.

Victor continued. "See, you and I come from a long line of non-believing thinkers. We have been above all that foolishness."

"You've got that right. That's the way it's been for us philosophers, and I admit to having long been among of them!" John agreed.

"Your mentioning Adler reminded me of some research I've been doing recently, which is how I came upon his biography. Do you know that Adler, who was born into a non-observant family of Jews, considered himself a pagan, yet he came to faith in Christ and was baptized when he was in his 80s!" Victor smiled and raised his eye brows.

"No, I didn't know that," John shook his head. "I've heard more about Adler's work. He was passionate about common people being able to learn from the best thinkers of the ages — aren't all human beings endowed with the same basic tools for thinking? Why should anyone be deprived of the great ideas that have been handed down through the ages. Much of Adler's work was finding ways to make great thoughts available to young people.

"What sort of research have you been doing?" John asked.

"I'm not doing this as a philosopher so much as I am searching for my own interests," Victor admitted. "I've been reading about a number of scholars, who represent a host of disciplines, who started off as pagans, or agnostics, or atheists, and later in life came to faith in God."

John cocked his head and nodded. "Sounds like you're pleased with what you've found. One of stumbling blocks to faith for me is the whole debate between science and religion. It would seem there's a great divide between those two worlds, and it doesn't make sense. As philosophers, many of us are sitting in the midst of the two, angry positions, and, as you say, most philosophers would side with the logical, empirical world as science represents it. Yet, some of us have certainly taken a position among theologians. Philosophers had heavy influence on the church over the years."

"And you know, before the Enlightenment philosophers did believe in God; they believed they could get to proof of God through nature. Philosophers used to say that God gives the world a purpose for existence, so humans have purpose because God gave it to us," Victor added.

"John, I have been in the atheist camp for a long time, figuring anyone who admitted to having faith in God was seriously demented — even down right foolish — but very gradually I've come to respect men and women of faith. They seem to be deep thinkers and are genuinely happy in this world," Victor announced.

John listened with interest to Victor's thoughts. His world, too, seemed to be changing — mostly because of Winnie. It was not because he was falling in love with her, which he had to admit was the case, but because she, herself, was obviously, deeply involved in following Jesus.

They hadn't talked about her faith, not much at all, but John was aware of Winnie's commitment to Christ. Her faith informed every part of her life. Wasn't that what her son had said — "Faith is living out your belief every day."

* * *

In his room that night John got on the internet and called up an article about Dr. Adler. Ken Meyers, who interviewed Adler in 1980 just after the philosopher had published his book *How to Think about God*, asked Adler why he had never accepted faith in Christ himself. At that time Adler acknowledged his respect for many Christians, but he hadn't himself made such a commitment.

Adler did eventually commit to faith in Christ and was baptized in the Episcopal Church several years following that interview. He later admitted in *Christianity* magazine: "My chief reason for choosing Christianity was because the mysteries were incomprehensible. What's the point of revelation if we could figure it out ourselves? If it were wholly comprehensible, then it would just be another philosophy."

John added these thoughts to his new and growing catalog of memoranda about faith in Christ.

Chapter 18. Some Answers

Friday had come and Winnie could feel herself getting giddy inside. *You'd think I was a teenage girl!* She chided herself.

She had spent time, on and off, preparing for Sunday through the week — especially her sermon. She hoped she was ready with her message, as there would be no time on Saturday night to work on it. She and John had agreed to meet at the Gaylord Hotel in Nashville Friday night and Saturday, but she would have to get back on the road to Misty Falls sometime that evening, so that she could be up and ready for Sunday morning worship. Winnie couldn't quite let go the image of Cinderella, who had to be sure to be home by midnight or her entire entourage would melt back into barnyard creatures.

Before leaving town Winnie took Bitty over to the Livingston's; Trudy had agreed to watch the pup over the weekend until Winnie could retrieve her on Sunday.

Winnie had plenty to think about on her drive. The roads were packed with cars and trucks on the highway. *What should I expect? It's Friday afternoon!*

"✳ ✳ ✳

John arrived at the hotel before Winnie. He had never been to Nashville before, much less to the Gaylord Hotel, so he was not prepared for the sumptuous mansion that spread before him. The hotel was designed in the manner of an old, southern plantation, complete with the tall, white porticos and spreading verandas out front.

John saw Winnie as she entered the hotel, pulling an overnight bag. She was wearing a green and black plaid, wool scarf on top of her charcoal grey overcoat and matching plaid tam; she looked terrific, John thought. Their final moments together last week had been quite friendly — even amorous — but he didn't want to appear too anxious. in the middle of the day. Instead, he took Winnie's bag and the two proceeded to the registration desk.

A bright-eyed, hotel desk clerk was most accommodating to his new guest. "Yes, Ma'am, how may I help you?" he asked. Then noticing

John, who was standing next to Winnie, he added, "Oh, are you two together?"

Winnie smiled at the desk clerk and explained, "No, we're not together. We are friends meeting here at your hotel today and tomorrow, but we have separate rooms."

"Of course, Ma'am," the clerk nodded his head. "And what name would your reservation be under?"

In another moment the hotel keys had been picked up, and Winnie and John took their bags up to their respective rooms.

The Gaylord Hotel was particularly well known for its botanical wonderland. When Winnie saw it, she remembered the several occasions when she, Mark, and the kids had traveled to castles in Europe — ShÖnnnbrunn in Vienna, Versailles in Paris, and Linderhof in Germany — were each adorned with enchanting gardens in front as well as in back of the mansion. The garden at the Gaylord was several stories high and was under a covered, glass dome, making the weather always perfect for visitors to enjoy.

The hotel itself served as the entryway to an upscale mall — complete with fountains, waterfalls, a river that winds for acres throughout the park, and wonderful shops and restaurants to explore.

John and Winnie stepped from the hotel lobby into the garden and found themselves immediately surrounded by lush greenery and beautifully presented flowers, each looking as if it was vying for a state fair honor; it seemed to the couple as though they had come upon a new world that beckoned them invitingly.

There were restaurants offering enticing cuisines, and as evening was fast approaching, they chose an outdoorsy setting for dinner. The host at The Water's Edge Marketplace Buffet led them to a table right on the river where they could watch the occasional small boat carrying merry passengers slip past them. They were in no hurry tonight; this evening could stretch out as long as possible.

Although Winnie and John certainly were never at a loss to find a subject worthy of reflection, they found it unnecessary to fill every moment with constant chatter, rather they sat and were filled with the charm of the moment — the sounds and sights and even the smells were in their own ways delicious, inviting them to drink in this captivating moment.

John reached across the table, picked up Winnie's hand, and gave it a squeeze. He didn't say a word. Being together, looking at one another face to face, stirred something indescribable in each of them, something that neither Winnie nor John had felt in too long. Loneliness, which had been the dull, aching constant for each of them, had melted away.

While they waited for their dinners to arrive they spoke of the news, which was more and more shocking each day — the market plunging further and further down with no end in sight, the unemployment panic, the housing bubble burst. They exchanged the highlights of the news and speculated on where America was headed in this most unusual time. Discussing the current headlines might have kept them fully engaged in wondering about the country's future or, perhaps, recalling the Great Depression, which their parents had lived through, but as they spoke about these surface items, Winnie was trying to imagine how to bring up a subject that she felt they needed to address, but she was unsure of how to approach.

Finally, just as they were reviewing the terrible housing situation — so many, many home owners being forced into foreclosure — Winnie interjected, "You don't own a home do you, John?"

"No, I don't," John assured Winnie. "I live downtown Chicago near the school. I've been renting the same apartment for nearly thirty years."

Winnie was thoughtful, "So, you've been alone in your apartment for quite a while?"

"I have," John was noticing how the subject had segued into something much more personal.

"And ... you've never married?" Winnie ventured.

John sat back in his chair and straightened up; he thought about what would come next. He realized that he and Winnie had reached the appropriate time to share this piece of himself.

John began, "I was engaged to be married once ...," He stopped and closed his eyes and let a moment pass, then he turned back to Winnie. "But it didn't happen; or, more correctly, it couldn't happen," John dropped his voice, took a deep breath, and continued. "This subject has been difficult for me for a long time. Please understand.

"During my sophomore year at Davidson, I met Helen. She was in my Psych 101 Class; it was one of those really large, introductory classes, but she and I were also in the same, small discussion group. We met there.

"Her full name was Helen Helga Erikson, and I was totally bewitched by her the moment I saw her. She was tall and blonde, a real knock out! She was from a little town in Wisconsin, and she looked like she must have had Viking blood in her.

"For weeks I didn't dare speak to her. Then, about the end of September, we ran into each other at the library and one thing led to another; we ended up going out for a Coke. Helen was easy to talk to, it turned out. In fact she and I had a lot in common — we were both what we would call geeks today; we had both been very competitive in school. We got on splendidly; she agreed to meet me for dinner that Friday night.

"We began seeing one another regularly, taking every opportunity to be together. Since we both had a full load of classes and needed time to study, we worked together, then afterwards we would get a bite to eat or take a walk around campus.

"Helen was a sorority girl, and it was nearly time for the school homecoming when the Greeks were building floats for Davidson's pep rally and bonfire. I got roped into helping with the float along with her sorority sisters and their friends. After that Helen and I attended her sorority's Christmas formal at some fancy resort. Dancing was a great discovery for us that night. We had both attended cotillions when we were young teens, so we knew basics about dancing. We realized how much fun it was to dance. That evening was enchanting — great exercise, growing friendship, festive environment — so we decided to take some dance lessons together. We spent every Friday night on the dance floor, mostly dancing swing and ballroom. It was the perfect way to work out the kinks after sitting so long all week.

"Our romance moved right along, and we dreamed of having a full life together. The night we graduated I gave Helen an engagement ring. Unfortunately, our story didn't have a good ending." John stopped. His voice was noticeably shaky, but he continued.

"Helen and I had a problem; we would be continuing our studies in different parts of the country. I planned to do graduate work in Boston, hoping to get into the PhD program there. Helen, on the other hand, was a scientist. She had taken top honors in her work at Davidson. She even won a government grant for her chemistry studies while she was an undergraduate. She had been accepted to a special program in Berkley, so we would be separated for the next four years by thousands of miles.

"We looked at the programs we were about to undertake and realized that it might be better for us to be separated while we delved into our work. When it was all done, we'd each have more to bring to our world together, and it would be a great reunion.

Winnie was nodding her head, imagining this cute couple with so much in front of them.

John continued. "We each went off to our respective schools. We would talk on the phone and write, of course. That was long before internet or cell phones, so we just had to wait and save up our thoughts for a once a week phone call.

"Anyway, we probably would have tried to see each other during the summer break, but that summer after the first year of graduate school Helen got a job teaching tennis. She played and had nearly gone into professional tennis. I think the only reason she didn't pursue pro tennis was because she was dead set on finding a cure for cancer.

"That summer Helen found a job teaching tennis at a camp in Wisconsin, and she occasionally played in tennis tournaments on the weekends. We had just talked before she left for a tournament one weekend.

"I got a phone call a couple of days later from Helen's parents. Of course, I had met them when Helen and I graduated, and they knew about our engagement. They considered me part of the family, so they called me when the news came.

"Helen had fallen asleep in her car on the highway on her way back from the tournament, and her car had driven straight into an eighteen wheeler parked on the side of the road; she was killed instantly."

John stopped. He gazed beyond the little restaurant out onto the canal, studying it. Finally he turned back and continued, "I couldn't believe that she was gone — that I had lost her! I wanted to scream, and fight, and kick, and gouge out someone's eyes! How do you fight what's not there? How do you fight death?" John whispered; his voice choked.

Winnie's eyes were filled with tears. She felt John's pain with him, and she understood his anger. Having been a pastor for so long, Winnie had come across such pain in others, but that didn't lessen the pain she felt for John now.

She reached across the table and grasped his hand in both of hers.

"I'm so sorry! Helen sounds so perfect for you; you were just right for one another. I can only imagine how you felt when you lost her! It must have been devastating," Winnie said.

"When Mark died it was also an accident. His plane was lost. It varied off its course over the gulf coast and was lost to the air traffic controllers. Later debris from the plane was found in the water near some of the small islands off Texas. That was weeks later, but we knew the first day, when we heard the news, that he and the other pilot were lost.

"It was incredibly painful to think I'd never see Mark again. I was so shocked and disbelieving at first — like you felt. I couldn't fathom the idea that I'd never see Mark again. How could that be? Then, too, my kids had just lost their dad, and I couldn't do anything to help them.

"I guess what I'm trying to say is that I can understand what you must have gone through," Winnie ventured to say.

John was thoughtful again. "Yes, but I didn't come through it very well. You put your life back together and moved on. You've done well, going on to seminary, becoming a pastor, watching your kids grow up and move on."

Winnie looked John in the eyes and said, "Yes, but I wasn't alone. I had my faith, and my family, and my church family that included many, good friends. So many people reached out to me then. They didn't know what to say or do, but they listened to me, and they helped me through the rough spots.

"It was a very hard time when I lost Mark. I can't tell you how many times I cried myself to sleep, yet I felt God was there for me. I began remembering many of the promises that God made to us: that God would be our God, and that we are God's people; that He forgives us no matter what we have done; that all things work together for good for those who love God who are called according to God's purpose; that nothing can separate us from God's love; that Jesus has called us to follow Him to be his disciples. Somehow those promises kept coming to mind, and I was encouraged by them. Very gradually, as I began to pick up the pieces of my life, things began to take on a fuller picture. I still missed Mark terribly, but my life was moving on.

"And ... one more thing that maybe made a difference," Winnie suddenly remembered, "I had read St. Paul's words to the Thessalonians many times, and there were three, little commands that Paul left to the Thessalonians: 'rejoice evermore; in all things give thanks; pray without ceasing.' One day about six months after I lost Mark, I woke up remembering those three — 'rejoice, be thankful, pray.'

"I thought I could understand those three things for most situations, and I agreed with them. But right at that moment I realized that I had not been thankful in some time. In fact, I couldn't remember when I had truly felt thankful at all. And, goodness knows, I had many, many things to be thankful for.

"Anyway, I couldn't get the thought out of my head. Finally, I realized that those commands in the Bible were for me, and that I should pay attention to them.

"And I thought, you know, if I am unthankful in this time, I'm sort of putting my pain and unhappiness ahead of God. That's actually breaking the First Commandment, which, as I understand it, means nothing is to be more important than God, and feeling hurt or grieved for an extended period is doing just that.

"I realized at that moment I had been feeling sorry for myself. You know, 'poor me, I've just lost my best friend and my lover.' I realized that I was enjoying a certain amount of attention because of my loss, and I knew, then, that I needed to begin being thankful to God for all He has given me.

"That was an important day in my life. I think I took a great leap in discipleship that day. I sank to my knees and asked God to forgive me for being unthankful and to ask His forgiveness. That may have been the beginning of the rest of my life," Winnie pronounced. Then she added, "Oh, John, I'm sorry if I've carried on so much about me. I think I was also talking to me just then, as I was telling you about what had happened," Winnie said sincerely.

John was touched by Winnie's admission. It was a strange thing to hear about being thankful to God. It had never occurred to him that believing in God required being thankful to Him, but John respected Winnie's thoughts and the fact that she would share with him now, revealing such a personal story about herself. He felt he almost had some responsibility to Winnie now that he had heard her confession.

"My response when I lost Helen was to bury myself in my work, which first meant finishing up my doctoral work and then landing the position at Chicago. I was miserable inside; I could hardly be with others, because I felt so wretched. I didn't want anyone asking me about myself. I didn't want to have to explain what had happened or how I felt. I just turned away from others and dug into my studies," John admitted.

"Your answer to loss had better traction. It sounds like it was more helpful than sheer work" John said.

Winnie could see now how it was that John had never married. He had withdrawn from society. Perhaps he was afraid of being hurt again. Winnie could only speculate his reasoning.

"I can see why you stayed single," Winnie admitted. "Come to think of it, I didn't remarry, did I?"

They both laughed at her revelation.

"Maybe this is a new day for both of us, Win. Do you think?" John smiled.

This question brought the two abruptly before new questions: What about now? What about the two of them? Is this a new day for them in this New Year? Might they be on a new journey now? Where might this odyssey lead? Were they finally ready to move on to something greater now?

The evening waxed into night, and John and Winnie strolled together through the walks again, stopping frequently to breathe in the beauty of the gardens. It was an enchanting place altogether.

They took a ride on a Delta flatboat and sat close to one another. John put his arm around Winnie "to be sure she wouldn't slip off the bench." They were very pleased with their propinquity.

It wasn't easy to say good night, but by midnight Winnie teased John about the bewitching hour and suggested that they could meet for breakfast and the entire next day together.

John escorted Winnie to her room and waited for her to open her door.

Before leaving John whisked Winnie into his arms and they kissed. This time their kiss was longer and the squeeze that accompanied it more scrumptious.

"See you in the morning, Sweetheart," John said to Winnie. "Shall we say eight o'clock?"

"You've got a date!" Winnie smiled as she slid into her room and closed the door.

✳ ✳ ✳

Saturday brought more of the same; it was all like a dream. John found himself thoroughly amused and enamored by this vibrant woman. She seemed to bring life to him that he had forgotten he had. He definitely felt younger, and he found himself imagining ways that they might be together.

Winnie was also amazed. John seemed to be almost too good to be true. He was brilliant, and accomplished, and had a solid position at the University. He was fun to be around. He made her heart sing. They really did seem to be in sync with one another, even anticipating what the other was about to say. They had quickly become devoted friends, which Winnie knew was a key component to a serious relationship.

John seemed to be perfect, but for one thing — well, actually two.

The matter of faith in Christ was of no small significance to Winnie. She told herself over and over again that she must be careful not to fall for someone who wasn't following the Lord.

By noon Winnie and John needed to be packed out of their hotel rooms as they were not staying a second night. They brought down their bags, paid their bills, and packed their cars. They would need to depart for their respective homes after dinner.

The day had been so perfect neither wanted it to stop. They lingered over their dinner menus not deciding on an entrée for some time. Finally the waitress returned to refill their decaf cups and ask, again, if they were ready to order. So they did.

By the end of the meal John finally asked Winnie what she thought they ought to do? What sort of relationship might they work out?

"I suppose there are several possibilities to choose from, and I think we're getting to the place where we'd like to take things to another level. But! I have to be completely honest with you ..." Winnie started to say.

John already knew where Winnie was headed, and he touched his fingers to her lips, to keep her from speaking the words he didn't want to hear.

"You're about to tell me how your faith in Jesus is more important to you than anything else. Right? And that you can't consider developing a relationship that might lead to a commitment with someone who doesn't believe. That's it, isn't it?" John asked.

Winnie nodded her head slowly. "I'm not trying to say that I've got the right way of thinking and you don't. It mustn't be *sine qua non.* I'm not so self-centered as to think I have to have my own way in this.

"My problem is that my life is not my own. I gave my life to Jesus a long time ago. It belongs to Him. I follow Him at least the best way I can.

"It's actually not wrong for a Christian to marry an unbeliever. St. Paul said that it's up to the unbeliever to stay with a marriage or not. If the unbeliever desires to live with the believer, it's fine. The believer doesn't get the same choice though. St. Paul said that the unbeliever might be sanctified by the believer — meaning the unbeliever could be influenced into following Jesus, too," Winnie explained.

Then she added, "This is very confusing — maybe for both of us! We're being very cerebral about this relationship, which has its merits, but at the end of the day where does that put us?

"I'd like us to have a chance. Who knows where we might end up? Who knows what good things lay ahead? BUT I have serious concerns about the long-term outcome of my getting involved with someone who doesn't believe in Jesus!" Winnie closed her eyes and dropped her head.

John reached over and touched Winnie's hand and said, "We can't make big decisions about our future tonight; that's apparent, but I will make you a promise."

Winnie slowly lifted her head and gazed into John's blue eyes.

"I promise that I'll give it a go. I promise that I'll read your book and ....," John thought for a moment, "and I'll do some outside investigation. I'll see what I can see. How's that?" John asked, hopefully.

Winnie was stunned. She hadn't expected any such offer from John. He had been very open about other things about himself, but as for his interest in things spiritual he had been silent. Was he now willing to consider faith? Was he saying this just to please her? What could he mean by this promise?

"John!" Winnie exclaimed. "That gives me hope. That's a great step to take! I couldn't have asked for more!

"I'll tell you what you can do," Winnie suggested. "Reading the Bible is an enormous project, and I know your time is limited. I would suggest that you start with the New Testament. It's about a quarter the size of the entire Bible, and, of course, it's all about Jesus and the early church."

"I'd also suggest that you pick up a copy of *Mere Christianity* by C.S. Lewis. He was a confirmed atheist in the early twentieth century, but he came to faith in Christ after careful examination of the evidence," Winnie said.

John could sense that his compromise had brought Winnie much pleasure, and that pleased him. As for reading the Bible he found himself growing quite intrigued with the project. Reading was what he did, what he loved to do. *Reading that famous tome will be a piece of cake*, he thought. Already he could see benefits from such an effort — specifically Winnie'a apparent delight at his offer. John nodded his head as Winnie was speaking. He had meant to open the door for them, maybe just a crack, and already he could feel the wind whistling in. It amused him; he smiled.

Winnie changed her tone a bit, saying, "I don't want to force you to be something you don't want to be, but, as I understand it, when we come into a relationship with Christ, we are set on a path to become the person we *were meant* to be — a better person, a person who has a fuller existence, one with real purpose."

They lingered for a while in the parking lot, as they prepared for their trips home. Their departures were inevitable, and they knew it. They would keep in touch, daily. Final good-byes were said; hugs and kisses were lingered over; and they began their journeys homeward.

✳ ✳ ✳

Time apart. This is a new phase for John and me. But we'll be doing a good deal of time apart, so I better get used to it.

The two would talk on the phone each day and be thinking about each other — all the time — but they had their jobs to do in their own parts of the world.

John called every morning before class "just to chat" — a great way to start the day. He bought himself a Bible that had been recommended to him by a clerk at a bookstore, and he began reading Matthew's gospel. *It's funny how much is familiar,* John told himself. He had never read the Bible before, and he supposed it would be new material to him, but he found he recognized much of what he read.

Winnie was delighted to hear that John was being faithful to his promise to her. While she was most pleased to hear of this progress, Winnie didn't want to overwhelm him with her own enthusiasm. If he had decided to take a journey — to delve into faith — it was his journey, and she needed to leave him to it and not be meddling too much. Even as much as she would like to see him come to faith in God in Christ, it had to be his decision. *Of course, if he asks my opinion on something or for some suggestions I'd be happy to speak up then!*

✳ ✳ ✳

The next several weeks went by with the usual community activities. Winnie spent time with Trudy, helping her sort out her thinking and feelings about her baby's father.

Winnie told Trudy that from what she could learn it was up to the mother to notify the father. There didn't seem to be anything that the father could do until he knew he was in the picture.

Once a father has been notified about a child's immanence there are legal steps that could be taken for the father to gain some sort of entrance into the child's life. The father would be given the opportunity to help support his child, and he could be given some visiting rights or even a shared custody of the child.

"I think you're right, Miss Winnie," she said. "I suppose I have several considerations to make.

"Do I want to bring the father into the picture? I'm not sure it would be good for a couple of reasons.

"I don't know him very well. I think my news would totally rearrange his life, and I don't know if I want to be responsible for that.

"As far as my baby is concerned, I don't know that I can make that decision for him or her. Is it fair to make such an important decision that could affect his or her entire life?

"I didn't have a dad growing up, and, so I don't really know what I missed.

Winnie could see that Trudy had been thinking about this and that she wanted to do the right thing.

"What is the right thing to do?" Trudy asked.

Winnie thought a moment and said, "Ask yourself, is this father one who might be prone to hurt your child? Would you consider the man a selfish sort, who would be bad for the child?"

Trudy listened with care to everything that Winnie was saying.

Trudy looked shocked as she heard Winnie's question.

"No! He's a very good person. I think he's one of the greatest guys I've ever known," Trudy answered.

"That's good to hear. There are some men who have fathered children by attacking women. Those men started off with a bad deed, so they are suspect right to begin with. You're telling me this man is good." Winnie repeated Trudy's words.

"Yes'M, he is. I think he's wonderful!" Trudy admitted.

"Okay then, that tells me that he doesn't have any strikes against him already," Winnie pointed out.

"How well do you know him?" Winnie asked.

Trudy was quiet for several minutes before she answered. "I don't know him well. I met him last summer at a party with some friends. We liked each other right off, and he asked me out on a date. We went out just that one time. He didn't have any weird ways, not that I could tell; he was just the best," Trudy admitted.

"So, from what you know about him, he hasn't any objectionable traits that might be dangerous. You're telling me that he's got many good qualities." Winnie said.

"That's the thing. He's got a fantastic scholarship to school. He's on his way to becoming someone important. I'm afraid that once he learns that there's a kid on the way and it's his kid his whole life will come apart, and it will be all my fault!" Trudy had dropped her voice to a near whisper, as she made this final admission.

"How about your life? Don't tell me this baby's advent isn't making a difference for you!" Winnie pointed out, "Don't you have any goals or hopes for a future?"

Trudy hadn't thought about it that way before. She was just like her mom. She was following in her footsteps. What more could she expect?

"I don't know if I have changed my mind about notifying the father, but you have given me some stuff to chew on, as they say," Trudy told Winnie.

Trudy agreed to continue to consider the father. It was her decision, but she had more to think about now.

✳ ✳ ✳

One day in late January Winnie got a call from Connie Oliver. She said that the DHR had just called her and told her there had been another complaint from a neighbor. The neighbor had accused the Olivers of fighting in their apartment. The neighbor apparently had heard loud voices and banging in the Oliver's apartment and was fearful for the babies' safety.

That incident forced the DHR to react — to put the babies into foster care while Connie and George would have to take anger management classes. The classes would last for at least eight weeks. If they completed the classes and passed them, then the Olivers could get the babies back. The DHR would be coming by in the afternoon to pick the girls up.

The news was hard to take in. Winnie knew that there had been warnings by the DHR, but she had been hoping that this time things would be different for her. She had only known the Olivers for a few months, but they weren't bad people, and she had been expecting things to work out better for them this time. She had to have an answer for Connie, and the only thing she could think of was, "I'll be right over." She hung up the phone, grabbed her purse and keys, and headed over to their apartment.

When Winnie arrived, Connie was subdued and didn't want to talk. Winnie could understand her reaction under such difficult circumstances. Winnie talked with Connie and Sallie for a short while. George wasn't present, and no one offered any information on his whereabouts. Winnie would have prayed with them to ask God's help for this new turn of events — to help them get through it — but they didn't seem receptive to such a suggestion. They did recognize that they were being given a way through this trouble by the DHR. George and Connie could attend the required anger management classes and prove to the DHR that they could handle their emotions.

The DHR came later that afternoon and took Samantha Rose and Shelby Ann to a foster home. Connie could visit them at the DHR office every Friday for ninety minutes. *What a painful place to be! What a horrible thing to go through!*

* * *

Winnie spoke with Evelyn on the phone most days, and she learned how Randy's case was evolving. The doctors had decided to do surgery to see what they might be able to do to release the hematoma in Randy's brain. Since he had not died yet and seemed more stabilized at this point surgery might give him a chance to heal.

Winnie drove over to the Medical Center in Knoxville to be with Randy's parents, as they waited through the surgery. Finally, good news came from the surgeon who told them that they had been successful in their efforts to reduce the hematoma, and they expected Randy to come through the recovery and begin the long, healing process.

That was very good news, indeed! Winnie prayed with the Evelyn and Gerald right there in the hallway after the doctor had left, thanking God for the surgery, and the care and healing for Randy.

* * *

Dood-ley-doo! Dood-ley-doo! Winnie's cell phone was ringing. She had set the ring tone to this bright sound to tell her it was John calling.

"Morning, Win" John said. "You're up early."

"Yes, I've been up for a while, of course, I'm an hour ahead of you, too," Winnie laughed.

John wasn't calling just to chat this morning, though. "I was looking at my calendar last night, and I realized that the University will be having a mid-semester break the third week of February. It actually begins after class on Friday the 13th and runs to Tuesday the next week. Anyway, I was thinking I might drive down and see you then," John ventured.

Winnie's eyes flew open wide, and she said, "That's wonderful! But it's a long drive from Chicago to Misty Falls in a short span of time."

John laughed and said, "I don't mind the drive; I enjoy taking trips; it gives my mind some peace and quiet — a good time to think. That's what philosophers do!"

"Of course I'd like to see you then! I'm so glad you'd like to come," Winnie assured him.

"I know you work on the weekends; will that be a problem for you? Will I be in the way, if I arrive on Saturday afternoon?" John asked.

"Yes, of course I work on Sundays in the morning. I'm preaching at eleven o'clock, and there's Sunday school before that, but that doesn't have to be an impossible burden for us. I'll make you a homemade dinner Saturday, if you can get here about six we can eat here at the parsonage," Winnie suggested. "Of course, I can't stay up to all hours that night because of Sunday, but I think we can manage."

"I'm planning on staying at the little motel where I stayed before, so I can just leave and go there when you need to focus your thoughts. I'll be out of your hair as you prepare for your sermon, and we can see one another after church," John added.

"You're very understanding, John," Winnie admitted. "I'll try to have things pretty much *ready* to go before you arrive, so I won't need the entire evening to study," Winnie said.

This weekend visit will be different for us. It won't be decked with New Year's trimmings or the charming gardens, shops, and walks of the Gaylord, but this time we'll be have a chance for a nice, ordinary weekend. "I wonder if John might come for worship? He might, and wouldn't that be special for him to hear the gospel that morning?

Chapter 19. Valentine's Day

Wish there was some way to reduce these butterflies! Whoever suggested that falling in love was a feeling reserved just for young people? Whoever it was, didn't know anything about a mature romance and the erratic way it plays with one's heart! I should know better, yet I can't help how I feel!

John was due to arrive in the evening, and Winnie figured that by now he must be on the road. She planned to cook for John tonight. She had never cooked for him before, and she was looking forward to showing him her domestic side.

Cooking for Winnie had become a favorite escape, a time apart from all those claims on a pastor's time. *"Preparing a meal for John feels so right, so natural. He says he eats out all the time, so this will be a good change for him. How sad — how lonely —to always eat alone."*

Winnie stopped right then and corrected herself, *"Look who's throwing stones at someone else's castle! I eat alone, too! Ninety-five percent of the time, I'm eating all alone,"* Winnie shook her head.

This 'date' is almost more fun than our first two dates. I have a feeling it will be even better in this domestic setting.

Think I'll go with my favorite chicken and broccoli dish but jazz it up using a rotisserie chicken and some shrimp. That's always a big hit at church fellowship dinners. Winnie suspected her church folks liked the chicken dish because she tweaked the white sauce with a pinch of ginger and curry and added a little white wine.

After the casserole was in the fridge ready to be warmed before John arrived, Winnie took time to work out the details of her Sunday morning — both her sermon and Sunday school thoughts. *I can hardly push John out of the house after we eat when he's driven so far to get here, I've really got to focus my thoughts now.*

❋ ❋ ❋

"Oh what a beautiful morning," John sang aloud to himself, as his began driving his Honda down the interstate; "... everything's goin' my way." John's eyes had snapped open very early that morning; this was the day he would drive down to Misty Falls to visit Win for the President's Day weekend. He would make the trip straight through, stopping only for gas along the way. He could be at the parsonage by six, even losing an hour with the time change.

John was relishing this very crisp, Saturday morning and the potential the long weekend held for him and Winnie. He didn't have any specific expectations for the trip, but he was keeping an open mind about whatever might come along.

On the trip south John made a discovery — it was Valentine's Day! He had forgotten all about that popular holiday, but he was suddenly reminded of it when he stepped into a shoppette to pay for his gas. There before him stood a large rack of red, heart-shaped, Valentine's boxes, ranging from minute to oversize.

"By Jove! You've nearly made a fool of yourself," John spoke sternly to himself. *"I can see the egg you would have all over your face if you arrived at Win's house tonight without a Valentine's gift! You really are a cad! But see here, Old Fellow, you can make amends before it's too late, and no one will be the wiser,"* John continued, figuring he had just skirted past a dangerous precipice in this new relationship.

As John was about to make his selection from the sizable array of Valentines, the clerk walked up to him, "I don't know if you noticed our sign over there, but all our Valentine's Day items have been marked 70% off."

"You have just made my decision easier. Thanks," John answered the clerk, picking out the largest Valentine's box and purchasing it. *Timing is very good, and I don't mind saving a little coin in the process.*

Half an hour before he was expected, John drove up the parsonage driveway. He had arrived in town an hour earlier but had stopped at the motel, picked up the key to his room, and taken the time to freshen up before heading over to Winnie's parsonage. John took the big Valentine from the car, walked up the front steps, and rang the bell.

The chime of the bell immediately sent Bitty into peals of barking, as she raced to the front door, and all the commotion caused Winnie to jump up from her seat, forcing her to grab her laptop quickly before it plunged to the floor. She had been sitting on the couch in the family room with her laptop on her lap, concentrating so hard that the sound of the bell snapped her from her thoughts and back to the present: John had arrived; her work was finished; the evening was at hand!

Winnie unlatched the door, opened it, and found John holding a very large, red satin Valentine out to her. "I hope I'm not too early," he smiled.

"Come in, come in! No, you're not too early! I've been thinking about your arrival all day. I didn't expect you'd get here quite yet. You had a good drive?" Winnie welcomed her guest.

"This is for you; Happy Valentine's Day" John offered the big box of chocolates to Winnie, leaned over, and gave her a kiss. "I have to admit, I hadn't realized that today was Valentine's Day, but every time I stopped for gas the shops were full of boxes of candy and red and white teddy bears. Today all the sweethearts in the world are celebrating!" John winked at Winnie.

Winnie flushed bright red across her cheeks. "Goodness!" She replied. "Thank you, John. Did you get the biggest Valentine in the store? It looks like it! I don't think I've received a Valentine in years, and I'm pretty sure I've never had such a big one. We'll definitely share this!

"Is your school really giving you a day off for Valentine's Day?" Winnie asked.

"The University takes off the middle Monday in February because of President's Day, so we get a mid-term break every Winter term for that holiday. The weekend just happens to land on Valentine's Day this year," John explained. "it does make for a fun coincidence, though."

Winnie had set the table in the dining room with a linen table cloth, her good china, sterling silver, and candles — each item adding to the gracious ambiance of the evening.

Winnie's home cooking didn't go unnoticed. "Delicious, Win; this recipe is marvelous! Do you cook for yourself like this everyday?" John wondered aloud.

Of course, Winnie was entirely pleased at John's reaction and assured him, "No, I don't have too many reasons to cook for others these days. I really had fun cooking for you today!"

"Are second helpings allowed?" John picked up his plate and passed it to Winnie.

"Glad you like it. I was hoping that you could have a taste of home tonight. Do you ever cook for yourself?" Winnie asked as she scooped a healthy, second portion onto John's plate.

"Well, I usually have breakfast at home, but I only have cereal or toast. I don't like to mess up the kitchen, and cooking does that," John explained.

The evening was off to a great start; everything was fitting nicely into place — the setting, the meal, the mood, the attitude of lightness and enjoyment for both of them.

Winnie excused herself to step into the kitchen. She had pulled her homemade cheesecake out of the fridge earlier and placed it on the table in the kitchen, so it could accommodate to room temperature before she served it, but, as Winnie walked into the room, Bitty jumped off the table, raced through the family room, and down the hallway. Winnie looked again at her dessert and saw immediately what Bitty had been doing to her creation! That naughty animal had taken a large bite out of the center of the pie!

"Oh No!" Winnie screamed at the dog, who was now far away from her mistress, hiding in the back bedroom.

"What's the matter, Win?" John followed the noise into the kitchen and saw what Winnie was starring at.

"Bitty took a bite out of the center of our cheesecake!" Winnie could hardly contain her shock. She wasn't quite sure whether she should cry or laugh. It was funny, or would be funny someday in the retelling of the story, but at the moment dinner was almost ruined by her naughty dog.

John could see the consternation in Winnie's eyes and voice. "Win! It's Okay. Dinner was perfect even without dessert. Every part of dinner was just right for us, and we're having such fun here, enjoying your home! The cheesecake was one more addition to an already perfect meal." John gave Winnie a big hug.

The evening was filled with laughter and fast-paced conversation.They found much to talk about — history, psychology, music, political and economic news, the wars in Iraq and Afghanistan, and more. Both John and Winnie were well prepared to engage in depth on any number of topics, but, it turned out, they didn't always agree.

The subject of famous people came up, and Winnie remembered a TV show, which was aired just before the turn of the millennium, which counted down the one hundred most influential people in the last thousand years.

Winnie and John had fun listing names of men who might have been included in that notable list.

"Einstein was number one, wasn't he?" John asserted. "He was brilliant in several disciplines that propelled so many of the changes we are seeing today. We can't even understand matter in the same way we did before Einstein came along."

"Actually, it wasn't Einstein who took first place," Winnie replied.

"I'm pretty sure I'm right. It would be Einstein." John said with a confident nod of his head.

"It wasn't Einstein, although he certainly has much to commend him. You're right about that. I remember when the countdown took place on that New Year's Eve; I was watching it on TV, and I actually guessed the right person," Winnie reminisced.

"Are you sure? We're talking about the most influential person in the whole millennium, right? I think it was Einstein." John smiled with confidence.

"I don't want to burst your balloon, but I know I'm right, not that it matters," Winnie didn't want to actually disagree with John, but he <u>was</u> wrong.

"Who do you think it was, then?" John wasn't convinced.

"The top honor for most influential person in the last millennium was Gutenberg — the fellow who invented the printing press back in the fifteenth century," Winnie said. "The reason I figured it out was because I remembered what Dr. Campbell, my Christian history professor, said about why Martin Luther's ideas caused the Protestant Reformation in Europe. Luther happened to live shortly after Gutenberg's press began working, so Luther was able to publish his ideas allowing many people to read his work. He couldn't be hushed up by the Catholic Church because of the printing press. When I remembered that I figured that Gutenberg's invention might make him the most influential person, and I was right."

"I guess I'll have to concede, then," John admitted, pretending to pout. They both laughed at his silly expression.

After dinner John followed Winnie into the kitchen and helped her clean up the meal, before they retreated to the family room.

Winnie had set a fire in the fireplace in her den, so the two sat on the couch, nestling close to each other. They were immediately transported back to the first time they had been close — the time on the Volunteer Princess when they danced together. They had discovered then that their world was changing — the loneliness they each had known for so long had vanished, and in its stead hung a tantalizing hunger for the other. It was a fresh, new feeling, one that neither John nor Winnie had experienced in far too long, and they found they were almost unable to resist its mesmerizing charm.

Winnie might have simply enjoyed the moment; it was totally sublime, but her mind was swirling around on several levels. First she was completely happy and content with the way the evening was progressing. John was a dream, and sitting with him in her cozy den made everything seem so right. On the other hand, a great controversy was waging war within her, causing her to wonder if she might be heading for trouble. *I'm dying to ask John what he's thinking about faith now. He says he's been reading the New Testament. He might even be through most of it by now. How can I gauge where he might be on this journey?*" Winnie thought. *"Could we have a chance to be a real couple? I can't see us having a long term relationship when we are both in such opposing camps, spiritually.*

Could this beautiful friendship become even more than it is now? Could this be coming from the Lord? Might He have brought us together for a purpose?

O, Lord, I do hope so. Please, lead us through this amazing time! Winnie prayed silently.

As these thoughts were busily vying for her attention within, Winnie casually announced, "I'm doing a lesson from John's gospel tomorrow."

"Hm," John nodded, "John's gospel; his gospel is the different one, isn't it?"

"Yes, it is," Winnie agreed. "I especially like to work with St. John; the church uses much of the language from John's gospel to speak about who Jesus is. So, how is your reading progressing?" she asked.

"I wondered if you would ask," John answered. "I've completed the New Testament, except for a bit at the end of Revelation. That's really an odd book, isn't it?"

Winnie shook her head in agreement and said, "Yes, most of Revelation is strange, it's a different sort of writing — apocalyptic material. It is unique in the New Testament. If you haven't read the last couple of chapters, they are really beautiful, all about the end of times when a New Heaven and a New Earth appear. It has a very good ending."

"As I've been reading, I can see my mind working on a couple different tracks at the same time, almost like I'm having a conversation within myself. For one thing, I have heard a surprising amount of the material in the New Testament already. Maybe this is simply because we live in America, a primarily Christian society, and there are many occasions where ideas from the Bible are mentioned."

"There were several parables that I had heard — The Good Samaritan, for instance, and the Prodigal Son, and the Lost Sheep. And then there is the business of Jesus walking on water. And, of course, everyone has heard about Jesus' death and resurrection, but I had never considered that story to be actually true. I believed it was a myth, and like other myths, it was just an interesting tale — you know, like Robin Hood or King Arthur," John explained.

"My world is all about thinking — argument, logic, truth. It's the venue I love. I'm very aware that truth doesn't have to be empirically factual to be true. Like the parables that Jesus told; there's much truth in them, but they are stories. So, maybe I've been figuring this idea of Jesus' resurrection is a truth, like you find in the parables.

"On one level, I was reading the Bible as a piece of great literature — really old, well loved literature. But on another level, I realized that I couldn't just read it as a disinterested party. There is something about the person of Jesus that is calling me to take note of him. It's as if he can make a difference in my life," John explained. "There's something compelling to me about this person Jesus. I've read many, many thinkers and philosophers over the years, yet Jesus stands alone — he truly is one of a kind. His message is also compelling. I like the way he thinks. I like the challenge he presents to his disciples, and I can't seem to get rid of the thought that his challenge is also to me. It's something I need to think about."

Winnie smiled as she heard John's words, because she knew exactly what he meant about not being able to disregard that voice within that challenges and calls one. "John, I can completely appreciate your quandary about that challenge. I know it very well. I've been aware of it for many years.

"I'm glad to hear how well your reading has gone; I think you're on a journey, and it sounds like you are willing to follow it where your investigations take you."

"That's a good way to put it," John agreed. "I do plan to continue my research."

The subject changed. John's visit was short; they had only Sunday and part of Monday before he needed to get back on the road again.

The next several months would bring more separation. Winnie and John took out their cell phones, pulled up their calendars, and looked for common ground — a couple of days when they might get together again — but there was no obvious time before summer.

"Goodness, John, we're going to have to be creative about seeing one another" Winnie sighed.

"We don't seem to find any logical answer for getting together other than just an occasional weekend. That doesn't really cut it, does it?" John agreed.

John picked up both of Winnie's hands and held them in his. He pulled her fingers to his lips and gently kissed them each. Then he looked into her eyes and said, "Win, you must know that I'm in love with you! I want you to marry me, so we can live together for the rest of our lives — under one roof!"

Tears welled up in Winnie's eyes and began their way down her face. She looked deeply into John's face. "I think we should be together, too. I want to marry you, but there are some serious problems to work out ..."

Chapter 20. The Question

The next morning John showed up at Muddy Creek. In such a small church visitors were obvious. Several church members welcomed John, gave him a bulletin, and showed him a place to sit about halfway back in the sanctuary next to Gus and Martha Reeves.

John hadn't been in a church in many years, so he watched carefully what other people did and followed suit studying the bulletin with doctoral scrutiny.

Winnie appeared in the chancel dressed in her black, academic gown with a green stole. She took a seat on a large chair and looked upon the congregation; she was delighted to see John sitting out there.

When it was time for the sermon, Winnie stepped down from her pulpit to the main floor of the sanctuary, as was her custom. Winnie was more nervous than usual, knowing that John had come and would be listening to her talk. *"Look for the blessing; Look for the blessing!"* Winnie reminded herself, trying to calm down. She knew that once she began preaching she would relax into the message, focusing on what she had to say, and she would really enjoy giving the sermon. It was always the time just before she began that caused her agitation. Today was definitely not any easier.

Winnie said a silent prayer, *"Lord, guide my words and everyone's thoughts,"* and began to speak.

This morning Winnie had chosen to speak about two disciples of John the Baptist. They were with the Baptist when he saw Jesus passing by them, and he declared to all, "Behold, the Lamb of God!" John's disciples ran off after Jesus. At first they followed at a distance, but when Jesus realized the men were shadowing him he stopped and asked them a timeless question, "What are you looking for?"

Winnie used Jesus' words as a springboard to elicit ideas from her community about what they might be looking for today in their world: a new tractor, a new job, the pitcher's position on the little league team.

From those answers she moved on to what else people these days might be looking for — things they hope will bring them fulfillment and satisfaction: friends, significant others, spouses, college degrees, bigger cars, houses, even (sometimes) alcohol or drugs. "We spend a lot of time looking for things that won't really give us complete satisfaction. Maybe we're looking for the wrong things," Winnie suggested.

Winnie moved back to the Bible story. The disciples had answered Jesus' question with another question back to Jesus, "Where are you staying?"

"Then Jesus answered, 'Come and see'"

Pastor Winnie added: 'I wonder if Jesus might have meant:

"Come and see...

"Come, and get to know me.

"Get to know **me**.

"Get to know me and the One who sent me.

"Come, become my friend.

"I will be the best friend you will ever have.

"In me you can place your trust.

"In me you can lay down your burdens.

"Come hear what I have to say:

"Come hear about the Kingdom of God

"Come hear my command to love one another

"Come hear my call to discipleship.

"Come witness my ministry:

"Come witness the next few years

"Come witness the miracles I will do.

"Come witness the healing I will bring

"Come learn:

"Come learn my ways and my thoughts

"Come learn about my Father in Heaven

"Come learn

"'Come unto me all ye who labor and are heavy laden, and I will give you rest.'

"'Let anyone who is thirsty come to me, and let the one who believes in me drink.'

"Come and see...

"What I am about to do

"See me heal the sick

"Feed the hungry

"Bring good news to the poor

"Proclaim release to the captives

"And freedom to the oppressed.

"Hear me proclaim the year of the LORD's favor to all.

"Come see how I will turn the world upside down.

"Come be filled with the Holy Spirit.

"Come and see

"Come, see, discover for yourselves

"Discover who I am

"Discover that I am the Lamb of God

"Discover what I can do for you

"Discover that in me you will find eternal life

"Discover who you are in me.

"Discover how you are more fully you when you are in me."

Winnie concluded her sermon with a final question: "Isn't Jesus what we're all looking for?"

John had been listening intently to Winnie's sermon, but not simply because he was interested in the preacher and this was a new facet to her, but he found himself listening to the message itself. John had not heard Winnie preach before, and he appreciated her casual, friendly way of addressing her audience, but he was more intrigued with the substance of her sermon than the method of her delivery. Her final question stuck in his mind: "Isn't Jesus what you're looking for?" John wondered, *"Did Win expect me to be here in the audience this morning? It seemed like she was talking directly to me!"*

❊ ❊ ❊

Following the service, Martha Reeves invited John to join them in the Fellowship Hall for coffee.

"John, this is my husband Gus Reeves," Martha introduced her husband to the visitor. "Are you moving here to this area, or are you just passing through?" Martha asked John.

John wasn't exactly sure what sort of information Winnie might have dropped related to his coming so he evaded, "I'm from Chicago, but I had a couple days free and thought it might be good to get away, so I drove down here."

Before the Reeves could press the question, Winnie came out of her office dressed in civilian clothes and appeared in the Fellowship Hall. "I'm so glad y'all have met. John did you tell these people who you are?"

Martha answered Winnie's question, "John was just telling us how he's here from Chicago on a short trip."

Winnie smiled and said, "John is actually here as my guest. (Martha and Gus exchanged knowing glances at one another.) John and I are both from Denver; in fact we went to high school together."

Winnie turned to John and said, "It was good to see you here in worship this morning, John. I hope you enjoyed our service."

"This is a beautiful church," John answered sincerely. "I especially enjoyed studying the picture windows, and I think I could identify most of the Bible stories that they depict."

Martha spoke up, "Our picture windows are pretty new to us. We had them installed six years ago; before that, the windows were stained glass, but they weren't the wonderful scenes of the Lord we have now.

❊ ❊ ❊

Later, over lunch at the parsonage, Winnie and John had a good laugh. "I really didn't quite know what to say when Mrs. Reeves asked me how I happened to be here," John told her. "I should have thought up something ahead of time."

"There's no need for making up something; you're here as my guest." Winnie grinned.

"Win, were you serious when you said you want to marry me?" John asked.

Winnie looked into his eyes and said, "John, I feel like we've put ourselves into a real predicament. I was afraid something like this might happen, but you'll notice I didn't do anything to discourage it," Winnie grimaced a bit.

"So, what have I gotten myself into?" she said, half to herself.

"Tell me what you're thinking Win," John encouraged Winnie, sensing her discomfort.

"You must know my conundrum," Winnie said, pouting slightly.

John put his arm around Winnie and gave her a squeeze and a kiss on the head. "I hope you know that when you're confused or hurting, I am too," he assured her.

Winnie smiled weakly and answered, "Yes, I love that about you. I think you really are trying to understand me."

"My problem is I feel like I'm being torn between two really wonderful things. How can that be a problem?" she asked. "You've asked me to be your wife, and I don't know how I can say, 'No.' I believe I have fallen in love with you, and I can imagine all sorts of marvelous ways we can have a life together," Winnie smiled at John.

"But?" John encouraged her to continue.

"That's the problem; it's the same thing I've been dancing around since we met at the reunion. By now you must know that my job in life is to follow my Lord. I've been doing that the best I could here at Muddy Creek and the other churches I've served. I've spent nearly twenty years being pastor in one community or another, and I know I can't give it up. I hope I'm making a difference to people I work with. I can't just turn my back on my call to ministry. Can you understand that, John?"

John didn't answer. He sat quietly and let Winnie's words hang in the air for a full minute. Then he asked, "I don't know anything about how the church works with pastors, but I wonder if the system in church is similar to what the university does when it comes to finding lecturers to fill positions?"

180

John's question led to a detailed discussion of how the politics work and differ in the church and the university.

Winnie explained about the different sorts of polity that churches use, some of which were probably similar to the way universities function — searching for prospective candidates and calling them to particular positions. "The United Methodist system of pastoral appointments is different. We Methodist pastors are <u>sent</u>, that is, we are appointed to preach at a specific church, but we are moved to new appointments according to the needs of the churches. There's no guarantee that any of us will be in one spot for very long," Winnie explained.

Their discussion segued into conversation about their own tenures teaching and preaching.

"Which reminds me, Win, I hadn't heard you preach before, but I thought your sermon this morning was wonderful. Are you sure you didn't expect me at your church this morning?" John winked at Winnie.

Winnie nearly laughed at John's question. "Last night nothing was said about you attending Muddy Creek this morning. And although I was hopeful that you might show up, I didn't plan on it. I know attending worship is not part of your normal Sunday morning activity.

"I was thrilled to see you sitting out there next to the Gus and Martha, although your presence didn't do anything to alleviate my preaching anxiety," Winnie explained. "I'm always nervous before I start my sermon, but this morning I had an advanced case of the "*pit.*'"

"I think you're are a good preacher, Win. Of course I haven't heard many others. I have to admit I always change the channel quickly when I'm scanning for something to listen to if I hear someone preaching. This morning I felt as if you were speaking directly to me. You were, weren't you?" John asked half-teasingly.

"I was preaching to anyone who would listen; I have never targeted anyone specifically," Winnie assured John.

"I think I've learned a good bit over the years about preaching, and I feel much more confident nowadays that I am able to share a message once I've worked it out. That's the trick right there — finding what the message is and then figuring a way to impart it to my audience.That's two different problems, and there's no guarantee that I'll find those answers in the time allotted. After I've found the message, I still have to learn the message well enough to know where it is leading. I gave up reading from a script years ago, so I have to know pretty well the main points and in what order they should come when I preach."

"Sounds like you've got an approach/avoidance issue with sermons. Am I right?" John asked.

"Indeed! Being a preacher requires quite a balancing act, trying to do all the right things for your community as well as finding adequate time to study and prepare the new sermon, but I suppose that's what I signed on to do when I agreed to preach," Winnie said thoughtfully.

"I don't think I know a pastor who doesn't have some degree of concern about preaching. Surely we learn a lot about the process of preaching, but it doesn't really get easier. Maybe we just get better at working on the sermons. I keep telling myself to 'look for the blessing' when I'm about to talk because after I'm finished I do feel a certain glow inside.

"The deal is that United Methodists have a reasonably good system of helping people do ministry, and I know I could get into ministry in some way up in Chicago. I am a member in good standing in my conference, so it's quite possible to transfer my membership from here to the Chicago area. I don't suppose I would be appointed to preach immediately, but something would work out, down the road."

John's eyes widened and a smile began to grow on his face. "What are you saying, Win?"

"I'm saying that between the two of us I'm in the more mobile position. I can see that. You have your tenured position and your new chair at the university, and when I think about it, I have no guarantee that they'll leave me here in Misty Falls; I don't know when my superintendent will call and tell me I'm moving; I can't be married to my place here at Muddy Creek."

"Then you're saying there's a way for us to be together! A way for us to get married! That's what you're saying!" John was beaming.

"Yes, I think we've got a workable solution figured out for that part, but my first concern hasn't changed — our difference on the subject of faith. I have a nagging thought in the back of my head reminding me that a believer shouldn't be married to an unbeliever. That's actually another point of wisdom from St. Paul," Winnie said.

"Win, I'm not nearly as worried as you seem to be about that. That's because I'm not worried about me. I know me," John grinned. "I can tell you, though, that in the midst of all that's going on between us, I believe I'm not the same person I was a few months ago."

✳ ✳ ✳

When John finally got to his motel room that night, he sat down on the edge of the bed and began to think. There was much to ponder. This weekend visit had loosed a myriad of thoughts that made John anxious for a few moments of peace to sort things out.

This whole trip is like a dream. What more could I ask? Win says she wants to marry me!

It's almost like I'm back thirty-five years ago, and I have my whole life in front of me again — with a wonderful woman who will be at my side. I love Win's inner happiness — her joie de vivre, her humor, her interest in learning, thirsting to learn more and more — her funny way of springing into a song at the least mention of words from the same.

And! She says she loves me; she feels about me as I do for her. John closed his eyes and smiled.

There's something else, though. Something ... something haunting me — begging my attention," John continued his silent soliloquy.

I feel almost satiated with wonderful feelings — feelings that have been building inside me since I came down here the first time. I don't understand it. John cross-examined himself.

I have such a deep sense of joy. I'm sure part of it is because I'm falling in love. The world knows well of the goofiness of falling in love, but somehow I feel there is more to it. This is not some terrific boon I've been given like when I was awarded the Adler Chair last fall. I was pleased as punch that day, but this is different — it's consuming me.

Win said that when she lost Mark she was grief stricken, and angry, and lost, and hurt. I know so well how she felt, but she came out of her depression. She told me that she had forgotten to be thankful to God. Her grief had prevented her from being thankful or feeling thankful. She admitted that her grief took away her song; she couldn't even sing for a while, and for Win that must have been serious! John announced out loud.

I can totally understand how she felt in her grief, but Win is so full of life and happiness these days. It makes me wonder if she hasn't got a point about being thankful? Maybe it does play into how one deals with grief.

Could that be what's happening inside me? Maybe this whatever-it-is I'm feeling is what being thankful feels likes.

You just said a mouthful! Need I remind you, Old Boy, that you usually stand somewhere between fence sitter and atheist. And for that matter you usually champion the atheist. You know you have, and you've been rather proud of yourself for taking that stance.

So who would you be thankful to? Giving thanks does call for an object of thanks. I feel like I've just stepped into a new world, a place that is calling me — even expects me — to be thankful.

What an odd thought ... Could something expect me to be thankful? How does that happen? Is this a new idea? It's almost as if I'm in conversation with someone else — from within. This is not the same as me proposing two sides of some argument and throwing the thought back and forth. This ... could I call it another voice? ... is different.

Everywhere I look I have something to be grateful for ... I've done well in life. I've gotten an education and a position, which I enjoy. I am well taken care of; I've always had all my needs met — food, shelter, all of it.

And this world is incredible — gazillions of creatures with complex, even exotic, life styles; lands and seas, beauty that takes my breath away; marvelous systems that allow this world to work. Mystery and wonder abound. When I look at this world, I can only gasp in awe at its magnificence. I'm sure I haven't seen all there is to see, but what I know is profoundly impressive, and I am thankful that I have eyes to see and ears to hear and senses to perceive it.

I haven't really had reason to object to anything, yet I lived for years on the other side of that equation. I felt robbed and denied of my future when I lost Helen. I was hurt, and I just couldn't seem to pull myself out of the muck and mire of pain. Too long I allowed grief to consume my spirit," John shook his head.

But, John, maybe you're getting smarter. Maybe you're thinking more clearly. All this Bible reading and the outside reading you've done has given you new food for thought.

That Oursler fellow, who thought he could debunk Christianity, traveled all the way to the Holy Lands to follow the steps of Jesus of Nazareth. He had begun writing a book — An Elevator Boy's View of Jesus — but in the middle of his work Oursler discovered that he had been bitten by the faith bug himself! His novel that was supposed to prove Jesus was a fraud ended up becoming The Greatest Story Ever Told! Now there's a real change of heart! John laughed aloud.

And C.S. Lewis bragged about his atheism for years while teaching at Oxford. He loved to debate in the pubs and would argue his point with anyone who cared to take him up on the subject of God. Yet Lewis later admitted that as an atheist he had to argue that no religion in the world had any merit at all. That's a mentally exhausting position to hold; I'm well aware of that myself! After coming to faith, Lewis realized that the men he most admired in those debates were men of faith, but the men who lacked faith were intellectual lightweights. Atheists didn't have well thought-out reasons for not believing; they just liked to argue. John winced a bit remembering Lewis' words.

It doesn't make sense to be thankful to nothing, and I'm surely not responsible for all this grandeur. I may have worked my tail off to accomplish the few things I've done, but I didn't give myself the resources for thinking or writing or teaching. Somehow those gifts were given to me, and it's not my fault that I have them. There must be a greater being than I am or than is in this world — something, or someone, that has the well-being of this world as its objective, who has given this world, and me, so many good gifts. John announced aloud to the room.

Win is so very clear about us. She can see God's hand working with us, bringing us together, giving us to one another as some sort of blessing. John reminded himself.

She tells me our relationship is like an answer to her prayer, ending our loneliness and opening a new future for us. She's leaning on her faith in Christ to guide us through this whole time. She's even willing to leave her position as pastor to be with me. She's that willing to work things out for us.

But what about me? What am I bringing to the table? What about my commitment? What am I willing to do to secure our relationship and be the best partner I can be?

John had heard a different question in worship this morning, and it had been pursuing him, off and on, all afternoon, even while he and Winnie spoke of their future together.

184

In her sermon Winnie had asked the congregation, "Isn't Jesus what we're looking for?"

That's a very good question. Maybe the answer is what I'm coming around to.

I agree with Lewis when he admitted the thing that really held him back from coming to faith was the great pain and suffering in this world. Pain, evil, and suffering are huge problems in the world. How can anyone believe in a God who allows such terrible trouble to exist?

Here we go again, John, My Boy. You're about to have an entire, full-blown argument with yourself!

John stopped, knowing how well he enjoyed an argument — lobbing questions and answers back and forth to an opponent — the mental competition, the jousting for position. Even without a physical opponent John could have good argument within himself. Arguing in his head was always a good way to hone and sharpen an argument for later when he met a real, flesh and blood adversary.

But this time something else was present, something calling him. *I have to be true to myself, and when I know I'm seeing things differently than before, I have to call it for what it is. I feel as if I've just made a great paradigm shift, and it's a very persuasive position. It feels good to consider this new scene — being thankful, even living thankfully!*

There's the many places in the Bible — verses, that jumped out at me as I was reading them, which I underlined because they were worth remembering. There was wisdom and challenge in Jesus' words; he would not be an easy person to follow; he asks a lot!

Isn't Jesus what we're looking for?' The words returned again. John closed his eyes and said. "God, I think you know my name. I think You've known me all my life. I think You've been waiting for me to say, 'Hello,' to say, 'Thank You.' to say, 'I love You.'

"I'm pretty new at this, but I've got to start somewhere, so here goes:

"God, I'm not a good man. I've been completely focused on myself for a long time. I've tended to my every need without much thinking of anyone else. I think You know how angry I was when I lost Helen. Her death turned my life upside down, and I was a bundle of nerves and pain. I guess You could say I was lost. The only place I could turn was to my books and studies. At least with them I could find some success. I didn't know You, and if I had I would probably have blamed You for Helen's death.

"That would have been wrong; I know that now. I think You are the giver of all good things in this world, and I think I'm just now realizing it. And I'm thankful.

"Somehow, things have changed for me, and I feel differently now. Maybe enough time has passed, and the cloud of grief has drifted away. My world seems to have changed, and I feel deliciously happy. I don't ever want this feeling of being thankful to stop. It feels so right — so very right.

"I'm happy to have discovered You — to know that there's a new relationship that has come into my life — and I am honored and grateful. God, forgive me for waiting so long to come to You."

"Thank you for forgiving me and for the love You have given me and Win. I know I don't deserve her. Right now I'm feeling wonderfully new and different. If You are the author of love, You really are something! Your gifts are far greater than any others!"

John opened his eyes. Tears were streaming down his face, but he felt clean inside, not weighed down with the stuff of old memories and pain. He felt peaceful and content. He slept deeply that night.

✳ ✳ ✳

Monday morning John arrived at the parsonage at eight o'clock for breakfast. Winnie had been up for a while and had already prepared a welcoming breakfast table, complete with coffee and a newspaper at John's place.

John was beaming when he walked into the kitchen. He swept Winnie into his arms and they kissed.

Winnie wondered the source of John's jubilance; she didn't have long to find out.

"What a marvelous day it is, don't you think, Win?" John grinned.

"Absolutely! It's a wonderful day. We're still together, at least for a few more hours," Winnie answered, "but I sense you've got something else in mind. Hm?"

"I slept like a babe last night," John began. "I went to the motel last night with a lot on my mind, a lot to think about, and something happened."

Winnie was beginning to catch John's excitement herself. "And?" She encouraged him.

"I was thinking, and I was reviewing ideas we've been tossing around and some other things that I've been reading, and, I guess, it all came together," John raised his eyebrows and pursed his lips, adding a grin.

"H- Hm!" Winnie was trying to follow what John meant. "And what would you say came together?" she asked.

"Did I mention how happy I was last night?" John's eyes twinkled. "Of course I did. How could I keep that from you!"

Winnie nodded her head and smiled. "We're both happy. Of course we're happy!"

"Well it occurred to me that I'm beyond happy, Win, I think I've fallen into thankfulness!"

Winnie's excitement grew; her eyes opened wide.

"And it occurred to me that being thankful is a two-way street. One is thankful for all sorts of good things, so one gives thanks for it. But the *thanks giver* has to have a *thanks receiver*. Right? And with that thought, I began a long series of questions and answers about the object of my thankfulness," John explained.

"I was about to jump into a long discussion with myself about the pros and cons of having faith in God, when another thought came to me," John paused as he watched Winnie watching him.

"And?" Winnie asked.

"And that thought was that I am a different man today, a new man. I have been feeling nearly overcome with thankfulness, and I want to give thanks. I told myself that I seem to be operating within a new paradigm in life, and I'd better recognize it," John admitted.

Winnie smiled and continued to listen.

"Anyway, I know how much I enjoy a good argument, and there's a place for it, but last night I wanted to stretch in a different direction. I felt called to speak not to myself, but to the the One who has given me, given us, this exciting new chance for life," John explained.

Winnie could hardly keep from interjecting her pleasure at hearing what John was saying, but more than that she wanted to hear him out.

"Win, I'm here to tell you that I actually prayed to God last night! It wasn't a very long prayer, but it was ... it was good. It felt right, and I felt clean, and fresh, and at peace afterwards," John said.

Winnie moved back over to where John was standing and gave him a great hug and a kiss. "Praise the Good Lord!" She whispered in his ear.

After breakfast John drove Winnie into Knoxville and found a jeweler. He bought Winnie a brilliant engagement ring for her to show all her friends — a clear invitation for her to tell them that she would soon be marrying and moving to Chicago.

Chapter 21. Nina's Update

Winnie poured Nina a cup of coffee and passed it to her across the table, then she pulled a chair out from the table for herself and sat down. She grinned at her friend and said, "I'm sure you must think this is all happening too fast, but I can promise you we are NOT having a shot-gun wedding!"

Nina was still trying to comprehend the news that Winnie had just told her. She didn't want to appear judgmental, but really, *What in the world was her friend thinking? She couldn't know the man very well. They'd only spent a little bit of time together — two or three dates—* Nina figured. *What could be the big hurry to get married?*

Things had been really busy since Christmas for Nina. She had extra nursing work to do, and had only spoken to Winnie one time after her first date with John on New Year's Eve. There must have been some important details about what happened next that Nina hadn't heard.

Nina worked full time for Dr. Sedgwick as his nurse, and she had been filling in at the clinic while a fellow nurse was on maternity leave. Unfortunately, when the baby arrived, he was extremely colicky, requiring the mother's attention longer than originally expected, so Nina had been holding down two full time jobs since January. Due to the extra work, Nina realized she was out of the loop when it came to the latest Misty Falls' scuttlebutt.

This afternoon Winnie and Nina had run into one another at Friendlie's Foods, and seeing her friend Winnie immediately held out her left hand and wriggled it before Nina, showing off her engagement ring.

Nina had been too surprised to make a coherent response. Her eyes flew open and her mouth the same. Winnie watched her friend, amused at her consternation, but she didn't say a thing.

Finally, Nina stammered, "You're engaged! When did all this happen? It's John, right?"

Winnie gave Nina a hug right there in the middle of the cereal aisle and said, "Yes, of course it's John. He drove down here over his mid-term break last month and asked me to marry him!"

The two women decided this news was too big to talk about it among the Post Toasties, so they agreed to meet at Winnie's house in an hour. Nina would bring "a little something" to go along with coffee.

Back in her own kitchen Nina put her groceries away. She couldn't get her mind off Winnie's news. She had many questions about this new engagement, but chief in her mind was, *Did Winnie know this man well enough to make such a life-changing decision! How could she really trust him?*

Half an hour later Nina was seated in Winnie's kitchen opposite her friend as she proceeded to explain.

"I think I told you before that John and I both went to Mile High High School in Denver. We were in several classes together then, but we didn't know each other well."

Nina nodded her head to indicate she remembered. She sliced a piece of her new French Apple Cake, slid it onto the Wedgwood dessert plate Winnie had provided, and passed it to her friend.

Winnie's eyes widened at the scrumptious-looking treat; "Thanks!"

Winnie spent the better part of the next hour recounting, step by step, the progress that led up to her engagement to John. She thoroughly enjoyed remembering the entire story to Nina — the reunion, the surprise book, the invitation to join John in Aspen over Thanksgiving.

"John invited me to join him in Aspen for the Thanksgiving weekend. He'd sponsor my skiing, if I would like to try it," Winnie told Nina.

"Of course, my trip to visit the O'Neill's was already planned, and I didn't want to suddenly cancel time with my family, but the bigger problem was the 'adult thing,' if you follow me," Winnie blushed

Nina knit her brows together and leaned forward. She sat silent for a moment and then asked, "Are you saying that you told John that you wouldn't sleep with him? Just like that? Wasn't that a bit awkward?"

Winnie explained her belief on marriage — that fidelity in marriage, which should mirror our faithfulness to God — began with the marriage contract, the commitment the two parties would make to one another. "These days things seem to be so cavalier for people. 'Adult activity' seems to be completely expected," Winnie explained.

"So, the two of you haven't ... you haven't ...'" Nina stammered.

"No, we haven't," Winnie assured her friend.

"I emailed back to John and thanked him for the offer to go to Aspen, but I explained about my prior plans to visit Claire and her family. I also told him that such a holiday for us two in Aspen might lead to complications we didn't need to add to our plate just now. I wrote about my understanding of the sanctity of marriage and hoped he would understand.

Nina nodded her head trying to understand.

Winnie continued he story — their first two dates, admitting that she was a pastor, learning why John had not married, John's promise to her to read the Bible.

Nina gasped when Winnie mentioned John's promise. "That's an enormous book, isn't it? I'll bet not very many people have actually read it — cover to cover — except professionals, right?"

"Well, The Bible is the complete basis for the Christian story. I suggested that John begin with the New Testament, which is all about Jesus' ministry, his death and resurrection, and the beginning of the church. The New Testament is not very long. It has the four gospels, of course, and then there's the Book of Acts, and the letters from the Apostles to the churches. The entire New Testament is less than four hundred pages. That's not so big. I suggested that John be sure to read Genesis and Exodus in the Hebrew Bible to get a flavor of the history of the Israelites," Winnie answered.

Nina seemed satisfied with that, and she nodded, ready for more.

"We continued to call on the phone and email daily, and then John drove down here on his mid-term break, which happened to be Valentine's Day. I made dinner for him, and the next day he surprised me by coming to church! I was so pleased that he came.

"That afternoon John and I talked about marriage. I felt like I was facing a great dilemma — falling in love with him, yet thinking I shouldn't get serious with an unbeliever. But finally I told John that I believe God has brought us together, and that if I marry him I would step down from my position here at Muddy Creek and move to Chicago."

Nina was listening carefully to Winnie sharing her romance. She shifted her weight in her chair, but she didn't say anything.

"The next morning when John showed up here for breakfast, he seemed like a different man — he was jubilant, like a kid at Christmas. It didn't take long to learn that he'd had a change of heart, and he felt that he somehow he had stepped into a new dimension — what he called a personal paradigm shift. He told me that he had been almost overcome with thankfulness for our love, and our plans, and his life, and much, much more. He felt called to give thanks the One who had given him such a wonderful life. He told me he prayed that night, probably for the first time in his life," Winnie let that thought sink in.

"We didn't have much time left, because John had to get back to Chicago, but we drove over to Knoxville to a jeweler, and he bought me this ring," Winnie wriggled her hand again. "We went to a coffee shop next to the jeweler to have lunch, and while we were waiting for our food, John said, "Win, I can hardly believe how much has transpired this weekend. I know I'm on a new trajectory in my life now, and you must be part of it. Do say you'll marry me!"

"Of course, I agreed," Winnie told Nina. "We think we'll marry early this summer," Winnie caught her breath.

Nina waited to see if Winnie would add any more to her reflections — something that would make a more compelling case for such an abrupt marriage. When she was sure Winnie had said her piece, Nina spoke.

"That's so beautiful, Winnie! I can tell you are in love, and John sounds like dream – quite a catch in fact, but I have a problem. I say this, but I hope I'm completely wrong.

"As your friend, maybe it's my duty to be the Devil's Advocate. I think I need to ask you, 'How do you **really** know that John is who he says he is?" Nina had other questions, but this one was good for starters.

Winnie was thoughtful, but she didn't speak. She would have liked to have the perfect response that would immediately and completely exonerate John — something that would prove John's identity beyond a shadow of a doubt — but when she thought about it, she couldn't. She had just spent the last hour enumerating all the delicious times she and John had shared. She felt very sound about John's promise to her, his apparent change of heart about God, and, especially, the deep love she felt in her own heart for him.

"When you ask, 'How do I know if John is who he says he is, all I can say is I **believe** he is who he says he is. I believe him with all my being," Winnie heaved a sigh, bit her lip, and looked at her friend with imploring eyes.

Nina had an idea, "How about we Google him? Let's use some of the new technology that's supposed to be at our fingertips to help us. We could check out the university's web page and see if John's name is on their list of faculty members. How about that?"

Winnie jumped up from her chair and signaled to Nina to follow her to her office. Their query in the University of Chicago's website was initially frustrating, but finally they searched for faculty in the Department of Philosophy, and they found John. There was his name, Johnathan C. Daniel, PhD, and next to it a description of what he taught: Logic, Philosophy of Language, Early Analytic Philosophy, and Introduction to Philosophy.

The two women were elated to find John's name on the school website. It gave him credence — he <u>was</u> a professor of philosophy at UC. They felt the university's assurance was a good step in unpacking John's identity.

"That one piece of information doesn't completely remove all doubt," Nina cautioned. "Just because someone is a college professor doesn't mean he is without fault. I know you want to believe John, and so do I, but I'm just a bit leery of unknowns. It's a dangerous world out there, and you just never know. After all, you're planning to turn your entire life over to this man. He'd better be who he says he is."

Winnie realized that Nina was trying to be fair-handed about this, but Nina cared for her friend and didn't want anything untoward to happen.

"I think I'm fortunate to have such a caring friend as you, Nina," Winnie said. "You've given me something to think about, and, of course, I want to be on guard."

Nina smiled at Winnie and said, "I have no reason to doubt anything John has said or done, but there are so many stories out there that you just need to be cautious."

Winnie asked, "What in the world can I do to get a better picture of John?"

"Well, if it was I, I wouldn't jump into marriage until I was a bit more familiar with the facts. Surely there are people who know John, people who could vouch for his character," Nina suggested.

"I think, maybe, I should get a closer look at John's world. Maybe I should make a trip to the Windy City just to see for myself," Winnie said half to herself.

Nina lit up when she heard Winnie's idea. "Ooooo! I love it! That could be a great way to allay any fears. Besides, if you're about to move up there, it wouldn't hurt to have a look-see at the place," she said. "Now that I'm in on all that's happened, you just have to keep me posted on future events!"

After Nina left, Winnie plopped herself down in her overstuffed armchair and sighed a deep, satisfied sigh. She loved telling the story about John and all the S'wonderful/S'marvelous things they had discovered as they were falling in love. It had quickly become her favorite story. She was glad she told Nina about her adventure. She also realized that, in a way, she was on stage, and Nina was watching. She could see that Nina herself was toying with the idea of trusting Jesus and that she was watching Winnie to see how a practicing Christian makes serious decisions. So Winnie's decisions, be they wise or foolish, could influence Nina's own decisions about following Christ. "*That's another reason for doing the right thing,*" Winnie thought.

✲ ✲ ✲

As evening approached, however, Winnie recognized a certain tense, restlessness inside herself, knowing that John would be calling her soon. Her reticence came from her need to be forthright with John about what had transpired that afternoon. Her conviction that John was exactly who she believed him to be was still intact, yet she knew Nina had voiced concerns that she, too, had entertained. How well, indeed, did she really know John? She found herself in that approach/avoidance place that psychologists mention – wanting to be truthful with John, but at the same time dreading the possible conflict. *"Oh dear!"* Winnie sighed.

✲ ✲ ✲

The phone rang, and Winnie answered her cell the minute she heard it. She jumped right into a confession. "I ran into my friend Nina Mattingly at Friendlie's Foods this afternoon and showed her my new ring."

John was surprised how quickly Winnie jumped into the middle of her thought without even a "Hello" or a "How are you?" He briefly interjected, "You showed Nina your new ring?"

"Yes! Nina was surprised to hear about us, so we met back here in my kitchen, and I told her how our engagement came about! She was excited for me, but she tried to bring me down out of the stratosphere to consider more logically what I'm about to do. She made me realize that I don't know you very well, and she cautioned me to make an effort to learn more," Winnie related.

John's warning antennae had been immediately raised as Winnie launched into her report of the afternoon. He continued listening.

"Then we spent the better part of an hour trying to find something on the Internet that might identify you," Winnie continued, "and we finally succeeded. It's all about doing the right query, you know. Anyway, we were very pleased to discover your name on the UC website! It was very informative! I didn't realize there were so many different areas of philosophy," Winnie caught her breath.

"Glad you found me there. I think my picture is about ten years old," John admitted.

"Even so, your being on staff at UC is only one indicator of who you are, and maybe I need to know more. Nina isn't trying to hurt us, but she's right about my need to be cautious. There are men in this world who prey on unsuspecting women," Winnie stopped.

"I wouldn't laugh at your concern, because there are too many examples of evil in this world — times when women have been seriously hurt. So you have a point. But Win I have to say I'm totally not dangerous. For sure, I want you to have no questions about marrying me, but I know myself, and I know there's nothing to fear about me. I don't suppose that I'm particularly exciting, but I am who I say I am: a professor of philosophy at UC and a man who's deeply in love with you!" John assured her.

Winnie was not sure, and she wanted to be sure. John had not given her the least reason to question who he was or his motives. Still, marrying him was a major change for Winnie: giving up her pulpit and job, moving to a different state, starting her world all over again. She would be trying to fit into John's world — whatever that included — and trying to discover a new way to answer Jesus' call on her life.

Finally, Winnie blurted, "John, I think I should come to Chicago and see your world for myself."

John, who had been straining to understand Winnie's fears, was thinking hard how to bring calm to this moment, when suddenly, as if the clouds parted and the sun came out, there was the answer right before them. The idea that Winnie fly to Chicago to spend a few days with John in his world was just the plan for them.

The conversation made a ninety degree shift right then as they began to consider Winnie flying to Chicago. She could get away for several days the weekend after Easter. As they talked about her coming for a visit, they were nearly transported into a fantasy of what three or four days together could bring them — what they would like to do, and see, and experience.They would stroll along Lake Michigan, walk the campus where John taught, and meet some of his colleagues from school.

The call, which Winnie had so dreaded, quickly filled with fun, and laughter, and excitement as they were already dreaming of the next time they would be together.

Afterwards, Winnie took Bitty out for a stroll, even as late as it was. She couldn't just go to bed with so many plans bouncing around in her head.

Chapter 22. The Windy City

"The Bible tells us not to be anxious," Winnie told Bitty. *There are only so many hours in a day, and there's a lot on my plate just now. I just need to concentrate on what's important, and the rest will have to fall into place.*

Of course, Winnie was thinking about her personal life and the immanent changes that were about to occur, not to mention the Holy Week events, which would culminate with a much-planned Easter morning celebration of the resurrection at Muddy Creek Church.

Winnie would fly to Chicago the Friday following Easter for a long weekend. She and John would have the weekend together, but since John would be lecturing and having class during the week Winnie figured to poke around the city Monday and Tuesday, seeing John when she could around campus and in the evenings.

When she returned from her trip, Winnie would have only a few weeks left to preach at Muddy Creek before stepping down from her pulpit. There were many logistical and relational things to set straight before then, but all that would have to wait until after Easter.

Seek ye first the Kingdom of God and its righteousness, and all these things will be added unto you, Allelu Alleluia. Winnie started singing. She loved to sing; it always helped soften the bite of anxiety, and, so she sang lustily and often around the house to herself.

✳ ✳ ✳

Winnie's plane landed at Chicago's Midway Airport, and twenty minutes later she appeared through the double glass doors by the baggage claim area, pulling her suitcase and carrying a smaller bag and an umbrella.

John spotted Winnie immediately. He couldn't miss her; she was wearing the same, charcoal grey overcoat, black and green plaid wool scarf, and tam she had worn in Nashville. Her short, brown curls, peeking out from below her hat, looked as though they were trying to trade their detention for a romp in the open air. Altogether, she presented a slightly disheveled look, while exuding subtle confidence.

Winnie's and John's first moments together were just a smidgeon nervous. When they had said their last good-byes at Winnie's parsonage in February, they had shared several scrumptious moments of passion. Hugs and kisses were lingered over; sweet murmurs of love were exchanged. They were clearly in love and completely immersed in one another!

Now in the chill of the early evening and the rush and scrunch of so many strangers all about them, neither John nor Winnie were quite sure how to greet the other.

They compromised there on the curb, by sharing a quick hug, putting Winnie's suitcase in the trunk of John's car, and getting seat-belted into the bucket seats of John's Honda.

"How was your flight?" John asked.

"I'm happy to say the flight was uneventful! That's the best sort of flight, you know," Winnie assured John.

"I suppose that's because anything that is worth mentioning about a plane flight might have an element of terror in it!" John laughed and raised an eyebrow.

"You've got it. You don't want anything worth mentioning happening at thirty-five thousand feet up," Winnie grinned.

They were immediately in heavy traffic, of course; it was Friday evening in downtown Chicago. Winnie hadn't been in a really big city in some time, and she had never before seen Chicago. *This city is completely awesome!* She had to arch her back and stretch her neck in order to look up at the ubiquitous sky scrappers. Winnie had been in other big cities, Atlanta, for instance, but Chicago seemed to outdo the others in sheer size and density. *Can little old me really fit into such a strange and busy world?*

John's plan for the evening was to begin to introduce Winnie to his world — the University of Chicago. They would start with dinner at the exclusive Quadrangle Club. It was a members only club for university faculty and staff, which John had recently joined.

Before long they were seated across an elegantly-dressed table in the dining room of the club. Winnie felt welcomed as an honored guest by the well-mannered staff and the beautifully-designed décor of the room. The ambiance of the club suggested the management knew exactly how to cater to its membership of university professors and their guests with gracious attention.

The next few minutes were spent reviewing their menus and making choices for dinner. After the waiter retreated they each felt, finally, that they were free to launch into this most-looked-forward-to time together.

"Win, I made arrangements for you to stay at a hotel in town, but this morning I woke up with a better idea!" John gleamed.

Winnie's eyes opened very wide as she heard John's announcement; her brows knitted together in a curious way. "You've got my complete attention!" she exclaimed.

"What I remembered is that there are accommodations right here at the Quadrangle Club for visiting dignitaries! I don't know why I hadn't thought of it before. A room here will be perfect for you. I called today to see if there was a room available, and when I heard there was a spot I made reservations for a single room for The Rev. Evangeline Taylor. It will be yours as long as you're here. Does that meet with your approval?" John smiled widely.

"I think you've hit on the exact, right solution for us! It couldn't be better. For a moment there I thought you had something else in mind," Winnie teased.

John knotted his eyebrows and began to laugh, "You know I wouldn't do that without your approval, My Dear!"

Winnie nodded her head, partially from relief and asked, "Goodness, how much will staying here, downtown, cost? I have to be careful with my resources."

John shook his head, his eyes twinkled, "No, My Dear Win, you will have no worry about expenses while you're here! That's my treat. I'm so pleased that you have come here to see my world. The least I can do is pay your way while you're here."

"As I was making your reservation this morning, it occurred to me that everyone calls you 'Winnie.' You were Winnie back in high school, so you've been Winnie for a long time. Tell me how you came by that name?" John asked.

"It's simple," Winnie began to explain. "Surely you're familiar with Christopher Robin and his teddy bear friend 'Winnie Ther Pooh!' When I was a child, I loved those sweet stories. Pooh was my favorite character. He was a humble bear — 'a bear of very little brain' — yet he was loving, and faithful, and a great friend of all the dwellers in the Hundred Acre Wood. Somehow I just adopted the name Winnie from him," she admitted.

"*And*! I should tell you that my very worst curse word — my only curse word — although I don't employ it too often, is POOH FACE!" Winnie shared.

"Pooh face?" John asked.

"**POOH** FACE!" Winnie corrected John, with heavier emphasis on the POOH.

"I see," John said. "I'll be sure to take note."

The two sat for a moment in the peaceful silence, awaiting their dinners to arrive.

Then John spoke, "Win, I know you have questions about me, and I think you absolutely must try to satisfy every concern you have."

"I do find myself in a rather odd situation," Winnie confessed. "I want so much for us to get past this business of questioning you and get on with more interesting matters!" Winnie pouted a bit, wrinkled her nose, and screwed up her face to show her discomfiture.

John reached into his suit jacket pocket and produced several envelopes with pages in them. He handed them over to Winnie.

Winnie slowly opened the papers and realized they were John's most recent bank statement and statements from a several investment accounts that belonged to him. She reviewed the pages one by one with careful scrutiny, noting the balances in the accounts.

John watched Winnie's countenance carefully as she poured over his personal finances.

Finally she looked up quizzically and asked, "John! These statements indicate that you are very, very well off! Can that be right?"

"Wealth is such a relative matter," John assured her. "Certainly I'm not hurting, and I am thankful for that. In fact, I have to admit that one of my flaws is that I've been something of a Hoardisaurus — I'm sure I've hoarded my money too much."

"A Hoardisaurus? Goodness, I haven't heard about that funny character since I read that little book to Claire and Paul when they were kids. You know the Hoardisaurus?" Winnie asked.

"My brother, Stewart, had a great library of children's books when his kids were small. I remember reading some of the Serendipity books he had back then. I loved the cartoon picture of the dinosaur with the great bone he carried around in his arm; it tickled me. I don't think I had connected that selfish cartoon character to me and my personality until recently," John confessed.

"One of the things I believe I need to do better, is to be more generous. I've been a bachelor for a long time, but I have not lived like a bachelor — I haven't indulged myself in stuff. Oh, I've kept up with technology — computer, cell phone, car — and I have allowed myself skiing trips. But other than those expenses, I've lived frugally. I've not been quite the Scrooge of Dickens, but I have held on to much of what I've made from my teaching and writing."

"You can see my apartment tomorrow, and you'll understand how I have not indulged in frivolous stuff. You could say I've been a mixture of medieval ascetic and Buddhist, being ultra conservative with my resources," John explained.

Winnie sat absorbing every word John spoke. She was relieved by his openness and candor and intrigued that he was willing to show her his accounts. Winnie had never had much money; she had been happy to get by with what she had been making, and she was not in debt. John's bank accounts and investments added up to much more than a tidy sum; it was so unexpected.

"Goodness, John, it never occurred to me that you might have money! You don't show it off. Money is an important tool, but it takes great care to use it well. Do you remember reading in First Timothy, 'the love of money is the root of all kinds of evil?' That is, no doubt, very true. Certainly when we begin to make any plans cost is immediately a major consideration in the decision process. I can imagine that will certainly be an item in our own future plans."

"I'm sure you're right about that. We'll have to set down some careful plans for a budget for us and work on how we use whatever income we bring in," John agreed.

"Money is a subject that no one can avoid, even if you wanted to. I can imagine you've probably preached on it before. Right?" he asked.

Winnie was about to answer when the waiter arrived with their dinner, delaying her answer while they prepared to eat. Winnie and John had both ordered a cedar planked salmon dish with veggies and a salad. The next several minutes were dedicated to savoring their delectable meals and offering thanks for them.

Winnie swallowed a bite, looked up at John, and said, "Yes, I have spoken on money — the use of money — a number of times. I like to point to John Wesley's view of money: *Make as much [money] as you can; save as much as you can; give as much as you can."*

John brightened up as he heard those words of wisdom. "Isn't Wesley the founder of your denomination? I should add his writings to others I want to explore in my studies. 'M*ake as much as you can.'* That's good. He's not suggesting that having money is wrong or sinful. *Save as much as you can.* I've done that — in spades! So far I'm doing right well in that department, wouldn't you say? And what was the last injunction? *Give as much as you can?"*

Winnie smiled and nodded her head.

"*Give as much as I can.* Hmmm. Well, I haven't done that. Not at all. I've just been trying to hang on to what I've earned. Your man Wesley has an entirely different take on things. Sounds like I need to look into it," John said thoughtfully.

Winnie softened her voice and said, "When we ask Christ into our lives, the Holy Spirit takes that invitation to begin working in our lives, giving us guidance, strength, and encouragement for our walk with Christ. We begin to hear God's voice speaking to us. Many things that are revealed to us are things that help us clean up our lives. From what you've told me, you have been overly careful with your money. That's fine; wasting God's gifts is a different sort of problem. I suppose there is much to learn about using money well."

"When I say that to you, John, I'm talking to myself, too. None of us has arrived at perfection, not yet. We all have a lot to learn in that department," Winnie said.

John was amused at Winnie's mini lecture. He chuckled, "You flip with ease into teacher mode, yourself, don't you! And, yes, you're right. It hadn't occurred to me that this realization might come from the Holy Spirit, but I can see how that works — the little voice within that nudges one to do good. Maybe that's how God's Spirit communicates. I'm sure I need to figure better how to use the gifts I have," John agreed.

"The way you and I have used money is different. We've approached that subject from diverse positions. Perhaps the good thing, though, is that neither of us has become indebted to some credit card or scheme," Winnie added.

"I have tried to be careful with my money, but I haven't made much. I believe in tithing — giving ten percent to God — giving God of my *first fruits*. Whatever I make as income, the first ten percent belongs to God. I have tried to be faithful to that by writing a check for my tithe as soon as it's in my account. Of course, there are other, very good places besides the church to put our gifts, and I do that, too; I don't keep track of that, though. I find it's a great joy to give. Maybe my challenge is to save as much as I can, so then I have more to give," she said thoughtfully.

"I suppose money is always an important factor in life. I hoped that you could see from my banking and investment statements more about who I am. You can see from those accounts that I am solvent — I pay my bills — and I don't owe anyone anything. I have depth in savings. Even in this crazy, financially painful time in our country, my very cautious investing hasn't lost as much as those who speculated more heavily. I lost quite a bit when the crash came, but I've been able to invest in the stocks now at a lower price. It will pay off," John added with satisfaction.

They talked for some time about money. It was the first time that subject had been mentioned between them. Winnie was about to step down from her position as the pastor, which meant she was about to leave her source of income.

She told John about meeting with her superintendent. "He was most jolly when he heard my good news about us!" Winnie recalled. She had asked for a leave of absence from being appointed to a church in the next year. She and her superintendent both recognized that Winnie would probably not be returning to the Holston Conference to preach. Her life seemed to be taking her into a new realm — and something of an adventure. She would be able to connect with the United Methodists in the Chicago area and would be able to seek an appointment there when she decided she was ready for that. The superintendent would write a letter for the Holston bishop to send to the Chicago episcopal office recommending Winnie for an appointment.

John wanted to help Winnie with her moving expenses. She explained that she didn't need to move all the furniture in the parsonage, because she only owned some of it — her bedroom set, her piano, her kitchen equipment and dishes, her china cabinet and related items, and, of course, her library.

As they talked, a couple from across the room walked over to meet them. John immediately stood up to shake their hands and to introduce them to his fiancé, The Rev. Winnie Taylor.

"Well, you old dog!" the man chuckled when he heard that John had an intended. "I didn't think anyone would ever catch you!"

John was smiling from ear to ear; he quickly completed his introductions, "Win, I would like you to meet Dr. Chester Twingate, a colleague of mine in the Philosophy Department. He teaches ethics, metaphysics, and epistemology to undergraduates and graduates, and this is Dr. Marian Quincy-Twingate who is professor of Christian History in our School of Divinity."

Winnie was very pleased to meet this couple who knew John. She stood up to shake hands with them.

Chester Twingate looked at Winnie and said, "Reverend! How good it is to meet you. Are you sure you know what you're getting yourself into by marrying this old codger?" He winked at Winnie as he spoke. She figured Dr. Twingate was teasing.

Winnie smiled at the couple and answered, "Actually, I believe that John is a well-hidden secret, and I count myself as a very fortunate woman to be in his life."

Marian picked up on Winnie's forthright answer to her husband's teasing and said, "Winnie, may I call you Winnie? I think you are quite right in your assessment of John. Chet and I have known John for nearly a quarter century, since before Chet and I were married, and we think most highly of him. He is a man of many fine talents and abilities. He may not have told you, but John is the most popular lecturer in the Philosophy Department. Some students will wait to take the Intro to Philosophy course until they can be sure of having a seat in his class. And now it looks as if he's found himself a lovely companion." She turned to John. "John! You really are lucky!"

The two couples spoke for several minutes, and then the Twingates said good night and hoped Winnie would enjoy her time in Chicago. If there was anything they could do to make her visit better — just call. They would be pleased to help her in any way they could.

When the two sat down again, Winnie grinned and asked, "I suppose you planted the Twingates here? They certainly are in your court! And! I just learned that you're a popular lecturer! Why hadn't that occurred to me before! Of course you're popular among the students! I love listening to you! You're articulate, and passionate about your discipline, and wonderfully able to communicate your thoughts. John, might I sit in on some of your lectures, while I'm here?"

John was pleased to see Winnie's enthusiasm about his work, and he agreed that she could slip into one of his lectures, or several, if she cared to, while she was on campus.

John had not planted the Twingates at the club tonight. He didn't frequent the club, as it was pricier than his thrifty, budget minded self would allow, but he was most pleased that his friends happened to be present tonight. "They are a topnotch couple. Glad they happened to be here for you to meet them!"

"John," Winnie exclaimed. "I owe you a great apology! I am so sorry to have questioned you, or anything about you. I can see I was completely wrong to ever consider questioning who you are or your interest in me. Please forgive me," Winnie asked earnestly.

John looked at Winnie's countenance — so earnest, so imploring — and said, "Of course I forgive you, Dear. I have heard the same things you have about women who have been led astray, or worse, by men. Some have lost money; some have lost much more than that. You do have to be careful in this world. But you don't have to worry about my intentions; I'm glad you believe me. I really <u>am</u> trying to do the right thing for you and for us.

"For that matter, we didn't finish our talk on money," John continued. "It will likely be an ongoing theme for us. It seems the character of money to be that way — always in the picture ... somewhere.

"I realize I'm asking you to give up a great deal for me: leaving your position as pastor; losing your income; moving all your household up here. It's an enormous step for both of us, but especially for you.

"I want to make it as feasible and facile as possible, so I want to set you up with an account for your needs. Once we're actually Mr. and Mrs. (or should we be Dr. and Rev.?), we can get our names on all our accounts together.

"Illinois turns out not to be a community property state, I just discovered, but I plan to make you the beneficiary of my estate, so you will have access to my accounts now and always," John assured her.

Winnie took a big breath and tried to understand what John had just said. "Goodness! I didn't expect that, either! I don't want to be completely dependent on you, though, even if it takes me a little time to get my feet on the ground I do expect to be productive in my new world."

John nodded understandingly, "I can't imagine you not getting involved in some Christian project, which I suspect you'll throw your whole self into. Although I do hope that you'll spare some of you just for me!"

Winnie winked at John and said, "You will definitely be Number One in my book, always!"

"One thing we can do this week while you're here is visit an attorney and have him draw up a prenuptial agreement putting this arrangement in legal form for you," John continued.

Winnie's eyes grew wider, hardly believing this generous offer from John. "You really are amazing, John. I can see I'll need some help, initially, as we figure how to move in together, and I begin to find my way around, but what you're proposing is a fine way of cementing our marriage in a very tangible way. I want to bring whatever I can to our marriage, and, obviously, you do too."

"I expect to take this summer off from teaching," John said. "We lecturers can choose to teach during the summer quarter or not, and this summer I've opted out of teaching. I'm going to be on my honeymoon!"

"I found something in Ephesians when I was reading," John recalled. "It sort of jumped out at me, having to do with marriage,"

"I'd love to hear it. There's much great material in Ephesians about marriage, especially in the second half of the letter," Winnie agreed.

"Ephesians makes an interesting injunction — that married people should be '*subject to one another*.' Have you ever preached about that?" John asked.

"'*Subject to one another*!' Of course, I remember that bit in Chapter Five, and, no, I haven't preached on that. I do think the idea that man and wife are subject to one another is a beautiful picture of love."

"St. Paul doesn't always encourage marriage, but that was because the early believers in Christ expected the end times would be upon them very soon. Paul was probably widowed early in life. The Jews had a very high regard for marriage, considering a man to be only half a man without a wife. Paul was a Pharisee — he followed the law to the letter. He must have been married, but he may have lost his wife very early."

"I really like the idea of married people being subject to one another, because it doesn't make one person always the leader and the other always the follower. People come with various gifts; no one has all the gifts or all the best gifts needed in marriage. Couples need to share from their abilities and gifts with one another. When it comes to being 'subject to one another,' I think that means we are responsible for the other person's well being."

"Which brings us to the Sixty-Four Thousand Dollar Question, when are we getting married?" John looked rather like a woeful puppy.

John and Winnie took out their cell phones and scrolled through their calendars.

"When does your quarter finish up this spring?" Winnie asked.

"We're out the second weekend in June, although I will still have reading and grading to do. Looks like I should be available by the third weekend in June," John figured.

"I know I'm doing a wedding for a couple at Muddy Creek on the sixth of June, and my last Sunday to preach is the next day. I'll be packing out of the parsonage that week. I have to be out of the house by midweek, so that the new pastor can move in then on 'pastor's moving day," Winnie said.

"You're marrying someone else? Tell me about it!" John teased.

"Well, I can't give you names, because this is really a 'hush-hush' sort of thing, but Bert and Naomi are a family at my church. They have two kids — twin thirteen year olds. They are very active at church. Bert met with me last fall and told me that they have a problem — they are not really married! Naomi married another man when she was very young, but they never got divorced! Bert didn't understand there was a problem initially, but after he became a Christian he realized that he was living with a married woman, and that was wrong."

"The two of them wanted to make things right. So he asked me to find him an inexpensive lawyer, someone who could do the divorce for them. I was able to put them in touch with a lawyer last fall. Bert called me in February to say that the divorce was almost final, and that they had to wait ninety days before they could legally tie the knot. They want me to officiate at the wedding for them, so we've targeted the sixth of June for the service. This all has to remain completely quiet. No one at Muddy Creek or Misty Falls must know about it," Winnie concluded.

John was amused by this narrative. He could appreciate the trouble that would accompany any sort of leakage of information in the community. "Well, well, My Dear, you're going to help make those two very happy, I am sure!"

Just then the pianist, who had been playing soft, dinner music as a background for the guests, increased his volume, inviting the room's diners to become dancers.

The first piece he played was *It Had to be You*. John looked at Winnie and sang softy with the music, "It had to be you ..." While singing he held out his hand and grasped Winnie's in his. Standing up he beckoned her onto the dance floor.

Holding each other close and moving to the music was sheerly delightful to the two sweethearts. They swayed and moved together exactly as one body. They seemed to be completely in tune with one another's movements. Words did not need to be spoken; they simply moved together with the mood and the music.

"... wonderful you. It had to be you —!" John finished the song as the pianist completed his coda. "That's how I feel, Win. My life has changed because of you. How lucky I am. How lucky we are!"

The music changed to a medley of Gershwin songs.

John and Winnie melted again into one another's arms as they continued to move gracefully around the floor. They even tried an occasional deep bend or twirl that caused others in the room to notice the new pair dancing in the room. They danced cheek to cheek, as the music invited them, and sometimes they picked up their feet to the rhythm and bounced to a more active beat.

Finally, Winnie begged John to let her catch her breath. They returned to their seats and rested, watching the others still on the dance floor.

"I know something new and wonderful was beginning to blossom between us that night on the Volunteer Princess. We both felt it; I know. I can almost count that dance floor as the real dawning of our love," John's eyes twinkled as he spoke.

Winnie's face was still flushed from dancing, but she entirely agreed with John — they had certainly found something very special in one another.

The sweethearts decided to call it a night and to pick up in the morning with a full day together. John stopped at the front desk to pick up the key for Winnie's room, which the attendant explained was on the third floor overlooking the tennis courts. John went out to his car to get Winnie's bag and bring it up to her room. The two said good night in the hallway outside Winnie's room, promising to meet for breakfast. John would be by to pick Winnie up around nine.

After John left, Winnie plunked herself on the settee and heaved a great sigh. *"I'm so glad I came! There's no need to worry about John; He's shown me some very compelling reasons to trust him. I don't think we'll have any insurmountable troubles facing us."* Winnie sighed happily.

Chapter 23. The Next Right Thing

John knocked on Winnie's door at nine the next morning, and the two went out for breakfast. They could hardly believe they had the entire weekend with no obligations to anyone but to themselves. How delightful!

John took Winnie over to a small cafe for breakfast, before they went to see his apartment in the neighborhood nearby. His apartment was conveniently close to campus, right in the midst of the city. John and Winnie hadn't determined what their needs might be in the way of housing once they married. The big decision had been made — they WOULD be together. That was the important thing; everything else was much less significant, but these logistical considerations needed attention too. Perhaps to begin with they would start out in John's apartment. It had some good qualities — nearness to the university and reasonable rent, and, of course, they would only have to deal with moving Winnie's furnishings.

Winnie wondered if her mental picture of John, sitting by a crackling fire, in a cozy, overstuffed chair wearing a comfortable robe and slippers with a lamp over his left shoulder as he read his papers, was anything like reality. She hoped her picture of his home was close to the fact; she was about to find out.

John tried to prepare Winnie for what she was about to see. "I have to admit that I'm not much of a housekeeper. I get along reasonably well for what I need, but compared to your place — your home — my apartment is rather basic."

John's admission alerted Winnie that it might be wise to be a little cautious in her response when she first saw his place. She had certainly visited many homes over the years — homes of parishioners, constituents, and others — and she was well aware that there were many styles and ways of putting a home together. After all every family has its own way of living, their own way of building a nest and caring for it. Homes were lived in differently by different people. That was just fine. It didn't matter to Winnie about someone else's housekeeping style.

Housekeeping was not an important detail when visiting someone. Winnie was much more interested in the condition of peoples' spiritual selves — clues indicating a person's inner self — worries, hopes, fears, concerns, faith, etc. than their tidiness or lack thereof. Winnie believed she was quite open-minded about a person's homemaking gifts, and, surely, John's housekeeping would not be an issue for them.

John's apartment was on the third floor of the apartment building, so they took the stairs for a little exercise and because the elevator was often out of commission. John's place was one of four apartments on the third floor. The stairwells and landings were a basic tan color — the walls, the tile, the doors to the apartments were all similarly colored tan. John walked to his apartment, unlocked and opened his front door, and then motioned for Winnie to step in. "Win, this is where I live. Welcome," he announced.

Winnie took a couple of steps into the front room and stopped; she gazed around the room and froze. The room, which was good-sized — maybe 18' x 20' — was not what she had hoped. It was the den of a collector! There were tall, library-style bookshelves stretched completely across two of the walls in the front room and a portion of a third wall. The shelves were filled with heavy books, looking much like the stacks Winnie had frequented in college. The shelves stood nearly to the ceiling, providing no visual space for a picture or piece of art to give some color or relief to the scene.

Looking about the room Winnie saw a huge, oak wood, roll top desk stacked high with books and papers. The desk, being a type of secretary, included many, small cubby holes. Winnie noted how all the cubbies were filled with papers and envelopes scrolled up and tucked into a hole. "*I'll bet there's a good portion of John's history there,*" Winnie surmised.

A computer and a printer took up a goodly portion of the horizontal space on the desk top. Winnie mused a moment, thinking how modern technology didn't quite fit into the scheme of the roll top desk. The electronic additions vied for space on the desk top; many wires and small, blinking boxes of a technical nature were also tucked into space on the desk. Winnie could see a nest of wires tangled among themselves at the back of the desk, connecting the electronics to an outlet in back.

Looking around, Winnie saw a large, worn, La-Z-Boy recliner in one corner of the room; it sat in front of a wall of books. A floor lamp stood behind it, capable of shining light over the left side of a reader. Winnie was amused when she saw this chair, because it was exactly what she had imagined the setting would be like where John read his school papers. No, he didn't have a nice, warm fireplace to toast himself by, but the chair and the lamp were there!

Directly across the room from the recliner sat an old TV. It was hooked up to a DVD/VCR player. John hadn't bought a flat screen yet; his was an old, fifteen inch TV, which sat atop a small folding table. Winnie noticed some of the books on the shelves behind the TV were videos and DVD's. "*So! John does watch recreational TV,*" she noted.

There was a window on one wall, which had a heavy drape covering it. The drape was pulled back, exposing the light from outside. Winnie walked over to the window to see the view. There wasn't a view; there was another building, standing five feet from the window. The view from John's living room was the red brick wall of the building next door. Winnie wondered why a window would be put in such a place. Weren't windows for seeing things — like the world beyond. There wasn't much world to be found in red brick!

Winnie realized it would be appropriate for her to say something about the apartment, but as she began to imagine moving into this place, she experienced a strange, dizzy feeling accompanied by an almost overwhelming sense of nausea. She started to sway unnaturally, and John quickly grabbed her arm and led her to his recliner.

Winnie plunked down on the chair and looked up at John. "Goodness! I don't know what just came over me! I was fine one minute, and the next I was lightheaded and woozy, and ... I almost lost it! I'm sorry," Winnie tried to explain.

John left the room and came back a half minute later with a glass of water for Winnie. After a sip and a few breaths, she put on a brave face. "Thanks, I think I'm fine now."

John wondered what might be the impetus behind this sudden attack. "Win, are you sick? Is there something you need? I don't qualify for much in the way of doctoring, but I can call someone."

Winnie was feeling more herself by now. "No, I'm okay. I have no idea what just happened."

John asked, "What were you thinking before you got dizzy?"

Winnie knew she wasn't sick. She assured John, "I'm good now, really. Maybe it was all the excitement of our being together here, but something happened when I walked into this room. I was looking at your apartment and trying to think how I might be part of this (Winnie gestured around the room with her hand), realizing this is going to be our home for a while. I must have been wondering where in this place would there be room for me and my stuff? That's what I was thinking when suddenly I got this crazy, queasy feeling in my head and in my stomach," Winnie explained.

John leaned over and put his arm around Winnie. It made her feel better just having him close.

"Win, I wonder if this little episode could be your body's way of saying that this really isn't the best place for us, not even for a short while," John suggested.

Winnie perked up at John's words and raised an eyebrow.

"How about we take this a different direction?" John stated trying to salvage the situation.

"What are you thinking about?" Winnie wanted to know.

"I've been in this apartment since I moved to Chicago back in 1980. I couldn't afford much rent then; I was only an assistant professor, and I had my school loans to pay back. I was happy to get this place. I could afford the rent, and the location was close enough to the school. I've been here in this one bedroom apartment all these years.

"Since I was alone, and didn't need much space, I got along just fine here. Surely, I haven't spent much on the place, and, as you've noted, it's in serious need of a housekeeper. I have been thrifty, remember? I didn't want to spend money on a cleaning woman, and it's easy to tell."

"What I'm trying to say is we don't have to move into this apartment when we're married, not even initially," John said.

Winnie cocked her head as she heard John's words. "But it will be expensive to do anything else, and I know you are very careful with your resources."

John's eyes crinkled and a smile began to grow on his face. He was touched that Winnie was concerned about his frugal ways. "There's no good reason we have to start here. We've been talking about WHEN we get together — when we get married — we'll finally be in the same place. Our place needs to be just that — OUR PLACE, our very own, personal place. I don't know why we need to wait for some time later to start looking."

"Oh John! That's a really big step for us to take so soon, but I love the idea! Are you sure you want to do that? Can we afford it?" Winnie asked.

John was sure. He hadn't thought it through before, but as he spoke the words into the air, the idea sounded very right to him. It would be an adventure for both of them. Finding a place to begin life together in — fresh and new — would be exactly the right thing to do.

Suddenly their agenda for the day, which had been open, was now spoken for. They spent the next half hour in front of John's computer, looking for a realtor who might be available that afternoon to show them places in the general area of Hyde Park. Fortunately, they were able to locate a realtor quite easily. She would meet them after lunch to show them several listings.

It was exciting to think about finding a house they could call their own. Over lunch Winnie recounted to John the many times she had moved with her family — to various Air Force Bases in the States as well as three bases in Germany. Then after she had been appointed to preach, she moved several more times. She considered herself a veteran mover.

"One of the good things about moving is that you lighten your load. We tend to hang onto stuff for too long, but when you move every few years you toss out items you haven't used. It makes one more streamlined," Winnie explained.

John had only moved a few times, and the last move was thirty years ago when he moved to Chicago. He agreed that Winnie was probably right about his hanging onto things too long, but he didn't know how to go about reducing his inventory.

Winnie assured him that she was an expert at moving. She didn't have a great amount of furniture to move. "We'll have stuff coming from both our homes, and we'll be able to blend them into our new place." Winnie was getting excited about this new challenge, but before any of that could be decided, they would have to see what was available.

After lunch they met their real estate agent, who was most pleased to find someone in the market to buy! The realty world had hit the skids since last fall, and nobody was buying. To find someone who was actually interested in purchasing a house was the best news the agent had heard in some time. It was a very good time to buy a house; housing prices were better than they had been in a long time!

＊ ＊ ＊

Five o'clock that afternoon found Winnie and John sitting on the floor of a living room in an empty row house in Hyde Park. They had been looking at places in the area most of the afternoon — a duplex, a single family dwelling, and a couple of condominiums. Each had good qualities as well as some serious problems.

John and Winnie found nothing of interest in any of those houses. Each time they arrived at a new place, walked through it with their realtor, and realized it was not what they wanted their hopes sank a bit. They wanted so much to love their new place, but each house they saw was missing that certain rightness they instinctively knew they wanted. None of the properties they saw said, "Take me; buy me!," so they were glad there were still more places yet to consider.

And then, at last, they arrived at this row house. It was the second house of six houses on a small, side street. Winnie and John followed their realtor from room to room and up and down the stairs, growing more and more enthusiastic about it with each room. The house had much promise and great charm; already they could feel their imaginations sparking all sorts of plans for various rooms.

As they returned to the living room, the realtor excused herself for a few minutes to answer a cell phone call from her daughter. She left her new clients alone to look around themselves..

The house was completely empty of furniture, so they sat on the newly refinished, hardwood living room floor. It was fun to view the house from this unusual angle.

They had each arrived at the same conclusion about the house: it was wonderful! It wasn't anything like what either of them had ever lived in before. It was not at all what they thought they were looking for, but it felt right — as if it was calling to them.

The house was narrow (maybe eighteen feet wide) and very deep; it had four floors and four bedrooms, which they realized would be useful, since they were going to blend their two households together. They would need at least one whole room for their library, as well as room for guests.

The first floor included the kitchen, dining room, and living room, complete with stone covered fireplace next to the balcony door. Winnie was particularly pleased to see the fireplace. *"There's a perfect place for John to read his papers by the fire!"*

Upstairs on the second floor were three bedrooms and a bathroom, then on the top floor, incorporating the entire floor, was one great, open room, which had been the master bedroom. *"We could dance right here; there's plenty of space,"* Winnie dreamed.

The basement had a laundry room, a family room, and a windowed-in porch, including a walk out to the patio and garden in back.

It was a novel feeling, this fantasy of sharing a future location together in this house. John and Winnie were still just imagining what it would be like to be married to one another, and here was a physical structure that could help shape their future.

The place was perfect; they both agreed. The big question was could they afford it? They didn't want to fantasize about getting the house if it was beyond their reach.

The realtor had already told them that the owners of the house needed to move because of business, and, considering the situation with the economy — especially the housing market — the house might not sell for quite a while, so the realtor was told to lease the house.

It seemed as if they had been sitting on the living room floor for some time when the realtor reemerged. She smiled at the two on the floor and said, "I don't very often find my clients making themselves at home so quickly! I hope your 'sit in' here translates to something positive!"

John jumped up and helped Winnie get to her feet. They admitted that they were very pleased with the house. They spoke about the availability of the house and were surprised to learn that the owners had provided a "rent-to-own" possibility. John pulled out his checkbook and wrote a check to the realtor to secure their interest in the place. They would meet back at the realtor's office Monday late in the afternoon to draw up the necessary papers.

✳ ✳ ✳

An hour later John and Winnie were sitting in a Greek restaurant, waiting to order dinner. What a day it had been! And what a surprise they had found — even putting money down on a house!

The house had added another dimension to their plans, and they were feeling much excitement over it. They were almost giddy with delight, and found themselves laughing together at almost anything — the large cowboy hat worn by that small boy; the very high heels the waitress was wearing; the two, identically dressed, little girls in the company of their grandparents.

Conversation between Winnie and John was focused on their new house. They were trying to remember every detail they had just seen. Did the house include a garage? How high might the ceilings be? Did you notice if the appliances in the kitchen matched? Was there wallpaper in all bedrooms?

John pulled a pen from his pocket and began sketching the floor plans of the first three floors of the house on a large, paper, dinner napkin. Winnie hadn't seen this artistic side of John before, and she exclaimed, "John! I have so much to learn about you and your many gifts! I didn't know you could draw!"

"That's not exactly talent. It's mechanical drawing, which I suppose does require a certain ingenuity. I took the class as an elective one year in school," John explained.

Just then their meals arrived and were placed before them. The waiter brought moussaka for Winnie and lamb chops for John. They spent several minutes savoring their dinners and sharing a bite of each other's meal.

Winnie asked, "Did you notice the size of the bedrooms on the second floor? Are they three different sizes?"

"The two bedrooms on the backside are almost the same size — rectangles — and they are connected by a balcony that runs across the back of the house above the first balcony. The front bedroom, above the kitchen, is a bit smaller than the other two, and it's square like the kitchen," John answered. "What are you thinking about?"

"Well, I was wondering which room would be the best choice for us to make our master bedroom." Winnie smiled slyly at John. "Should it be on the second floor, or should we choose the top floor, the way the previous owners did?"

John smiled at the mention of the master bedroom, because he was quite pleased to note that eventually — maybe even sooner than later — they would have need for a master bedroom. He said, "Well, it might be a good thing to have our bedroom on the top floor; all those extra steps would, no doubt, add to our health, climbing up and down them several times a day."

"I suppose you're right about that; I should look for ways to encourage good health, and those stairs could do the trick for us," Winnie agreed. "Hm, that does bring up a question, though," Winnie stopped abruptly, not knowing how to phrase her thought.

"I like questions. Fire away," John encouraged her.

"Well ...," Winnie stammered, "It occurs to me that one of us has been married before — for a number of years — and one of us has not ..."

John was following Winnie's words, and then she stopped speaking. "I don't think I heard your question, Win. "Yes, one of us HAS been married before, and one of us — meaning ME — has not," John continued. "That doesn't mean that we have a case of The Graduate and Mrs. Robinson, if that's what's worrying you!" John teased.

Winnie flushed, and nodded her head, indicating that John understood her consternation, so she changed the subject. "I know this is Saturday night, but it definitely doesn't feel like Saturday to me."

John wondered, "What usually happens on Saturday night for you? Is there something we could do to help you feel more like it's Saturday?"

Winnie shook her head and laughed. "No, I'm completely content to be here with you. It's great to have a week off from preaching. It's just that I have been preaching every Sunday morning for so many years that my whole system seems to know I should be focusing on my message for tomorrow. Even though I know in my mind that I'm not preaching tomorrow, something inside me won't let me forget what I usually do. That's weird, isn't it?"

"No, I can appreciate that. Being a teacher, myself, I've certainly had the same sort of getting-ready-to-teach syndrome. It's partly nerves and partly adrenalin surging through the body about the new class — or, in your case a new sermon. We all have habit patterns that we get into, and when those are interrupted for some reason, our mind reminds us about them," John reflected.

"That does bring up a subject we haven't mentioned yet. Tomorrow is Sunday; would you like to go to church with me tomorrow?" Winnie asked.

John opened his eyes wider, "Sure, we can do that. I enjoyed the service at your church. Have you got some place in mind?"

Winnie knit her brows together and answered, "No, I don't know any particular church around here."

"You don't have to go to a United Methodist Church, then?" John asked.

Winnie tried not to laugh. She said, "No. We can go wherever we'd like to, but since we'll be making our home here I suppose it would be good to look around the area to find a church where we can plug in."

After dinner they made their way back to the Quadrangle Club and up to Winnie's room.

Winnie had brought her laptop with her, so they were able to access the internet and find a church in the area for Sunday services. They would meet for breakfast first and then attend the eleven o'clock worship.

Winnie and John sat on the settee by the window. Since it was mid-April, the weather was quite pleasant with a soft breeze in the air. Winnie opened the window of her room and the breeze caused the sheers to waft gently inwards. The half moon illuminated the tennis courts across the street. The two sat by the window in the dimmed light of the lamp charmed by the peacefulness of the evening.

Winnie broke the silence saying, "I've been almost afraid to ask you outright about this, but I must admit I'm very curious. You haven't said anything about what's happening for you regarding faith. Can you share with me?"

John nodded his head. "I don't mind your questions," John said turning to look at his fiancé. "This has been the most remarkable season in my life. Not only have I found you, and you have agreed to become my wife, but I believe I have also found faith in God. When you put those two incredible events together, it adds up to a totally changed life. It's amazing!

"It didn't come about instantly, of course. I think I must have been entertaining some thoughts about faith all along, but the thoughts were scattered and not demanding an immediate conclusion," John recounted.

"What sort of thoughts?" Winnie interrupted.

"Many, diverse thoughts. Beauty for instance. There is beauty in this world in many places, every day. When I considered the beauty I've witnessed and enjoyed, I mused about how it came to be. What caused me to recognize beauty? Why do most people agree that something is beautiful?

"Close to that idea is the way my heart feels when I see little animals or small children. There is something inside me that attracts me to them; they are beautiful in a different way. You'd probably call them cute. I'm thoughtful about them.

"Then, following that vein, when you consider the biology of creatures — the many, vastly complicated and intricate systems that operate in living bodies, which are absolutely vital for life to exist, yet it does — remarkably, wonderfully well."

"When I think of all the infinite details in this world, I am impressed, even overwhelmed. This world, this universe, must have had some great mind behind it. It couldn't have just happened!"

"I thought about my own world. I've been lucky when I look back at my life. Yes, I was hurt when Helen died, but I continued on. I was able to finish my studies. I've always had a good job. I've never missed a meal. I've been downright well taken care of," John took a breath.

Winnie interjected, "John Wesley would say that all those things you mention were various ways God has been calling you, evoking you, to look to God. Wesley said that God's Grace can be seen in four ways, and those thoughts you've just mentioned are a good picture of 'Prevenient Grace' — God's Grace reaching out to people, inviting them, attracting them to God.

"It sounds like your reflections follow the actions of Prevenient Grace in your life rather well," Winnie suggested.

"I think faith has been taking root in me for a long time — from an initial recognition of God as a Great Creator; but, as I consider the person of Jesus I see that God truly acted through Him," John said genuinely.

Winnie spoke up, "I can't remember a time when I didn't have faith in God. have known about Jesus since I was a little girl, so I don't have the experience of how faith in Christ changes a person's life. In a way you're in an envious position, because you can see how faith is making a difference in your life.

"Of course, coming to faith isn't like graduation at school. It is not a one-time event, rather it begins, and it grows, and dwells in you as long as you welcome it. It's like a relationship with another person. When we first meet someone, we learn a couple of things about the person, maybe we learn many facts in our initial association. There's more to know, of course, and if we want to really know the person, it takes time and effort. A relationship with Christ, like any relationship, needs to be nurtured, so it will grow. Our own relationship has blossomed in wonderful ways through these past several months, and each meeting is better and more delightful. And it's giving us so much to look forward to. I think that's not a bad picture of our life in faith with God; it grows with time, too," Winnie said.

"The turning point in my life, I believe, was that night in Nashville, when I agreed to read the Bible." John answered. "I hadn't given it a thought until that very moment, when suddenly I opened my mouth, and out came those words, 'Okay, I'll read your book.' Suddenly those words I had just spoken into the air caused me to realize I had never taken Christian scripture seriously, nor had I actually delved into it beyond a verse or two. I had made you a promise that was important for me to keep. Before I knew it, I was beginning to walk a different path than one I had been on previously.

"When I got home I was excited to start my reading project. I stopped at the bookstore and bought a Bible for my own. I began with the New Testament, like you suggested, and as I read the gospels I began to sense that the words on the page were speaking directly to me. It was as if they were written explicitly for me. Jesus' words to the disciples were words for me, too. Jesus called them to follow him, and he was calling me, too.

"It seemed a bit funny when I read about Jesus calling the disciples to follow him, I thought His invitation was also meant for me and that I must follow. I also remember thinking, 'There is no choice in this! I must follow Him; it is the right thing to do! I don't have a choice!' Then I remember thinking, '*Maybe I can just stay where I am and ponder it — slowly*' — but somehow I couldn't let the idea go. It was there, staring me in the face, calling me to act. Finally, I gave in and accepted Jesus' invitation to follow him and recognize him as the Son of God! Since that moment when I made that decision, I have had this tremendous feeling of joy, and peace, and wonder, and excitement. It's really like I'm living on a different plane than I had been before. It's remarkable!"

Winnie smiled broadly. John's words were so good to hear. His admission of coming to faith in Christ and being willing to share it with her was one more reason to believe in him. "John, I'm so glad you are telling me this. I feel very privileged to be part of your faith journey somehow. I think you've had a real conversion experience, and I'm excited for you and with you. Your coming to faith means a great deal to me; you must know that."

John winked at Winnie and said, "I'm sure I have 'miles to go before I sleep,' as Frost so eloquently wrote. I am just beginning this way of life, and there's so much to learn. You know better than I do about the steps I need to take. All my life I've been in the world of academia, and that suits me well. I'm thinking that this new facet of my life will include growing in understanding of Jesus and His call on my life."

"That does make sense — to use your gifts as you begin your journey, following the Lord," Winnie agreed. "There are plenty of academics for you to enjoy. I've learned from a number of them myself, and I'd be pleased to hear who or what interests you as you study. I think Augustine, Martin Luther, and John Wesley were all great admirers of St. Paul. They might be a place to start your investigations.

"I like your metaphor of taking steps when we follow Christ, because a step isn't a very large measure; it's a comfortable, doable, sort of distance. We can take one small step at a time when we follow Jesus, and we can make simple corrections, when, or if, we see that the angle we took wasn't the best one. We might not be able to see too far ahead of where we want to go, but we can pretty well see one step ahead," Winnie offered.

"And the step I'd like to take right now ..." John didn't finish his sentence, rather he pulled Winnie to him and gave her a lingering kiss.

Finally, John took a deep breath and said, "Win, I'm more than convinced we're on the right track," John observed. "You are exactly what I need!"

Winnie responded, "Let's get married!"

John was tempted to do something rash in the fever of the moment, but instead he sat back on the settee and said, "Now I'll use your word, Win, 'Goodness!' Do you think I can't wait?"

This tickled Winnie, and she began to giggle and then to laugh. Then they were both laughing, real, solid guffaws with tears rolling down their faces. It took them some time get control of their laughter. It was a good catharsis and a clearing of the air.

Finally John caught his breath and asked, "Win, have you thought what you might like to do once we're married and all moved in to our new house?"

Winnie thought for a moment and said, "I think I'd like to write a book — maybe something about a woman pastor, who is serving a small church in the South. She meets interesting people and gets involved in their lives, but, mostly, her life is shaped by the task of writing a new sermon week after week to help her community grow in their walk with the Lord. I think that might be a good way for me to share some of the stories and the people I've come across and interject some thoughts on Christian living."

"Might you include this woman's personal journey of finding love in an unexpected place?" John winked at Winnie.

"Now there's an idea!" Winnie laughed. "Of course! That is certainly part of her journey! Romance was not where I expected it, and what fun love can be when faith in God is part of the picture. My heroine's story would be much more compelling when the miracle of love is introduced! The two sweethearts sat by the window, cozily delighting in the closeness of the moment ... and very slowly ... fell asleep!

THE END of *Winnie's Walk: A Journey of Faith and Romance*

Prologue to Misty Falls: The Journeys Continue

Starlight and a great half moon peered in the window of the guest bedroom at University of Chicago's Quadrangle Club, when a chill breeze blew upon a man and woman nestled together, fast asleep on the settee facing the night sky.

The two wakened, almost simultaneously, as the chilly air, wafting indoors, stung their faces and arms, jarring them to consciousness.

"O! Goodness, John!" Winnie exclaimed as she sat up and looked around her trying to get her bearings. "What in the world has happened?"

John, who was coming 'round to the world of the awake, stretched his arms and peered into the darkness of the room. "I think we must have fallen asleep right here, snuggled up together! Looks like we might have slept here the entire night, if that breeze hadn't arrived to waken us."

"Honestly," Winnie exclaimed, "after all our very careful efforts NOT to sleep together, here we are in this cozy place, sound asleep even so! I think, though, we were just exhausted after our very full day yesterday."

"I hope this doesn't worry you about our intentions, Win." John added hastily, squelching his alarm.

"No, not at all, Hun. I know we're on the right track. For now how about you return to your apartment, and we'll pick up as planned later today," Winnie suggested, reminding John that they would be having breakfast and attending church later that morning.

John departed for his apartment leaving Winnie to get a proper night's rest. They would still have several days together left of her visit, finalizing arrangements to take possession of the house visiting an attorney to set up a revokable, living trust for Winnie, and making plans for their wedding, which was set for June 20th in Misty Falls.

Chapter 24. After the Wedding

(June 20, 2009)

Seated on a chair in the corner of Muddy Creek United Methodist Church's Fellowship Hall with her precious bundle in a baby carrier on the table before her Trudy watched the crowd of wedding attendees and well wishers patiently inching their way through the receiving line to give their good wishes to the newlyweds. The exceptionally attractive, young, African American girl was dressed for the special occasion, wearing a swishy, yellow chiffon skirt, a green and yellow printed, sleeveless cotton blouse, which scooped daintily across her back, revealing her graceful neckline and shapely arms. *"Everything seems to take at least three times longer to accomplish than it ever did before!"* Trudy sighed. *"It's all this baby stuff — making sure I've got enough of the right things for a couple hours out of the house along with getting little Kareem ready to go, too. Nothing's simple any more!"*

Trudy had been the bride's puppy sitter on a couple of occasions this past year, as Miss Winnie was getting to know the mysterious professor from Chicago. She had flown to Denver back in the fall to attend her high school reunion when she met Dr. Daniel. Trudy watched the puppy again when Miss Winnie took an overnight trip to Nashville. That trip was for a "date" with the professor. Then several weeks after her baby was born, Trudy and her mother took the pup into their home to watch it, so that Winnie could fly to Chicago to see the professor, who was now her fiancé.

Trudy was happy for Winnie and her new husband, Professor Daniel. She and Miss Winnie, who was the pastor of the United Methodist Church in Misty Falls, had spoken several times about Trudy's quandary having to do with the father of her child.

Miss Winnie had wanted to help Trudy make a careful decision about whether to inform her baby's father of the child's existence. It was a question that had come to haunt Trudy. She certainly didn't want to harm anyone connected to this decision, but she feared that the news of Kareem's existence might cause great trouble in the father's world. She did think, however, that the decision, this momentous decision — to tell or not to tell — should be made soon.

As Trudy watched the sizable crowd of wedding revelers in the room she noticed a young, white woman, not much older than herself, making her way between the tables toward the place where Trudy sat. The young woman was slight in build, like Trudy, but she had a long, blond pony tail and was wearing a sleeveless print dress and sandals.

A moment later Connie walked up to Trudy and asked, "Did I notice you bringing in a baby carrier? Can I see?"

Trudy's eyes twinkled when she heard the question. She answered, "Oh, please do!" She reached over to the basket, picked up little Kareem, and held him for the young woman to see. Kareem wriggled and opened his eyes to his visitor. The little child had a healthy growth of hair already on his head — a mop of finely spun, twisting, black curls — as well as big, chubby cheeks and deep, black pools in his eyes that drew the viewer into them. The baby's eyes had a certain way of tilting up at the corners.

"Your baby's beautiful!" Connie assured the new mother. "Is it a boy?"

"Yes, I call him Kareem — Kareem Lucas Livingston," Trudy announced.

"He looks like a real good baby," the stranger said.

Trudy enjoyed bragging about Kareem. "I think he's the best baby in the world. Of course I suppose every mother thinks the same about her child," she admitted.

"How old is he?" Connie asked.

"He was exactly fourteen weeks old yesterday," Trudy said proudly. "I know it hasn't been long since he arrived, but my entire world seems to have started all over the day he came."

"Children can do that to you," Connie agreed. "You two seem to be getting along real good," she smiled.

"Thanks. I think we are. We're taking this one step at a time," Trudy answered.

"That's an interesting way of putting it," Connie observed. "Is there some problem with your having Kareem?"

"No! Of course not. I just meant that I'm still living at home with my mom, and she's helping me a lot. I think someday we need to get our own place and move on, but I haven't figured out quite how to do that," Trudy explained.

Connie nodded her head in understanding. "My mother has been very helpful to me too. We live together in an apartment over by the highway."

"Do you have kids?" Trudy asked.

"That's a hard question to answer," Connie stammered. "I have had several children, but some of them aren't here. They're being raised by other people."

Trudy clutched! She wasn't prepared to hear this; it was totally unexpected. "Oh ... I'm so sorry," she finally said.

"I have two babies, twin girls, who are just eight months old now. There names are Samantha Rose Oliver and Shelby Ann Oliver," Connie began fussing in her pocketbook to find pictures.

"Twins! They sound wonderful and a handful all at the same time! I'm sure you're glad your mother is around to help," Trudy said. "Am I right? You and your mom are taking care of them?"

"Well sort of." Connie began to explain. "We had some trouble with the DHR before, and so when the twins arrived, the DHR was immediately on our case, and they watched us like hawks. They talked to all my neighbors and had them spying on us too. Finally somebody called DHR, ah, the Department of Human Resources, and told them they were worried about my girls ...," Connie stopped.

Trudy's eyes were getting larger and larger as she listened to this girl's story. "You mean to say they took your babies? Just like that? Is it possible for that to happen? Someone could really come and take your children!"

Connie realized she was causing this young mother to worry and she didn't want to scare her. She said, "I don't suppose it could happen to everyone, but it has happened to me ... more than once!"

Trudy didn't even know how to respond to Connie's tale. Maybe she was a crazy girl who told whoppers. Maybe she had designs on her own sweet baby! (Trudy pulled Kareem to herself.) She was suddenly very aware of not knowing anything about this strange person, and that made her more than a little nervous.

Trudy changed the subject. "Uh, do you know the bride or the groom?"

Connie smiled at the obvious change of subject and said, "I know Miss Winnie. My guess is that you know her, too. I don't think anyone here knows the groom. He's from Chicago."

"You know Miss Winnie. You're right. Nobody here would know her professor friend, ah, I mean, her new husband," Trudy stammered.

"Miss Winnie has been a big help to me ever since I got to Misty Falls ... ever since my girls were born," Connie began to explain.

"I've known Miss Winnie this past year too. She used to drive me over to my OBGYN appointments in the city when I was carrying Kareem, and I've been her house sitter and dog walker on several occasions, too."

The two young women continued talking, sharing about babies and motherhood and living nearby. Finally the crowd around the bridal couple began to dissipate, and the two young mothers moved over to the line to offer their congratulations to the newlyweds.

✳ ✳ ✳

At the parsonage Muddy Creek's new minister, Clive Weston, and his wife Deborah were enjoying a break from their busy day of unpacking. The Westons had not been part of the wedding at the church next door. The former pastor, Rev. Winnie Taylor, was marrying someone from Chicago, a professor from the university, this afternoon. Even though Pastor Clive would normally have been responsible for any of the functions at Muddy Creek Church, now that he was appointed as the pastor there, an exception had been made in this special case. Pastor Winnie's son, The Rev. Paul Taylor, was also a United Methodist pastor, so he was welcomed to come officiate at his mother's wedding.

The Westons noted the many cars in the parking lot and surrounding the community belonging to wedding guests. The cars had been parked for a couple of hours, and finally the guests were beginning to drift away to their own private vehicles and drive off.

Clive was happy to let the community celebrate the wedding of the former preacher without participating. This wedding was the last event before Pastor Winnie left Muddy Creek Church and the Misty Falls community.

Deb and Clive had been surprised when news of their appointment came back in March; they had not expected to move churches this year. When the superintendent called Clive and explained the situation — that Pastor Taylor was getting married and moving away — he could see a new adventure in ministry for him and his wife.

* * *

"Well, Mrs. Daniel, how do you feel now?" John winked at his new bride and gave her a sideways squeeze, as he maneuvered Winnie's lime-green Volkswagen out of the church parking lot and began driving toward Gatlinburg.

"Goodness, John. It's hard to believe, but I think we have really tied the knot. Paul pronounced us man and wife at the end of the ceremony, and we both signed the certificate so it must be so. We just walked through a metaphorical door, and now we're in a new, metaphorical room," Winnie theorized.

"Yes, 'metaphorical' room. We are in a new place; and we're in that place together. That feels really good to me!" John agreed.

"Next stop, Gatlinburg! I think we can be there by dinner. The innkeeper there told me that they serve family style meals between 6 and

7:30 every evening. That sounds like a good way for us to begin our honeymoon."

Winnie laughed and leaned over to John and gave his right arm a hug. "Right now I can appreciate why the Germans call a wedding a Hochzeit — the high time [in life] — because I feel like I'm flying. A wedding really is the high time; it celebrates one of God's finest gifts — the union of a man and a woman. All the wedding guests are aware that the ceremony is the prelude to the finest, most exquisite symphony imaginable, and they get to cheer the newlyweds on toward their new estate of wedded bliss. Talk about an elephant in the room! Maybe weddings were the original setting for that expression?" Winnie wondered aloud.

"I don't think I could get much happier than I am right now," She continued. "I'm all wound up because of so many good things happening at once! Not only are we finally together and finally married(!), but my whole family was able to come for the wedding and many of my church members came, too. How better could it be?

"I didn't realize that there would be so many community people coming today. I expected to see a number of my Muddy Creekers, but I didn't realize so many other folks would want to come. Of course, the wedding was announced in the *Misty Falls Chronicle*, so everyone knew about it," Winnie figured.

"I must have shaken hands with a hundred people or more. Do you think?" John asked. "The only folks I know in Misty Falls are Gus and Martha Reeves, 'cause I met them at the church when I came down here in February, but so many people were gracious to me. I can imagine they have been giving me a careful looking over to figure who this man is that you're marrying and who is whisking you away from them."

"You must be right. I suppose everyone has been curious to get a glimpse of you. I can just imagine what's been going on in their minds — how you seem to have swept me off my feet so suddenly. I'm sure there's been plenty of speculation surrounding us." Winnie smiled as she considered what others may have been wondering.

"John, you were perfect! You seemed every bit the person you are — the highly esteemed professor from Chicago — coming to claim his bride!

"You met each person in that long line, as if he or she came by specifically to meet you. You even tried to place people into the community. There's no reason why you'll ever be back in Misty Falls, but you showed interest in them, nonetheless. That was a classy touch," Winnie complimented John.

"There were two young women, right at the end of the line, that came by together, a black girl and a white one," John remembered. "Did I hear surprise in your voice when you spoke to them? You introduced me to them and told me they were friends of yours, but you seemed, maybe, surprised that they were together. What was that about?"

"You're very intuitive, John. Yes, I guess I was surprised that Trudy and Connie showed up together. I think that they just met at the reception this afternoon, and they discovered they had some things in common, specifically, knowing me," Winnie explained.

"I know you have worked with many people in the community. Maybe they feel related through you. Do you think?" John asked.

"I probably couldn't hide my pleasure, seeing the two of them together. They are both young mothers, and it might be good for them to know one another," Winnie figured. "It could be an interesting liaison."

Winnie's little, lime-green Volkswagen arrived at the foothills of the Smokies and began its upward trek. The newlyweds ceased chatting and just breathed in the verdant scenery, each lost in thought.

John suddenly whacked the side of the steering wheel with his hand, as if he just remembered something, and said, "We did have one memorable moment in the wedding when the whole roomful of people burst out laughing."

Winnie chuckled at the memory. "That was funny, although it's hard to say if Paul really meant it to be. He wanted to introduce himself and the rest of the family to the wedding guests, so they might know who all the strangers in the wedding party were. He simply explained that the whole family was happy about my marrying you and moving to Chicago. Our wedding provided a good opportunity for a family gathering. Each family member had a part in the ceremony — from my grandchildren being flower girls and ring bearers, to Claire and Tricia providing the music, Alex taking pictures, and Paul officiating the service. It was when Paul finished his introductions and said, "... then, after the wedding, we're all leaving for Gatlinburg for a week together."

"Right, and that's when everyone in the audience began laughing, as if the whole family was joining us on our honeymoon! At least, some took it to mean that, and that is pretty funny," John added.

"Okay, it was funny, but, of course, the families just want to spend the time together for a vacation. My folks are with them, and they're all driving to Gatlinburg together. It's a good opportunity for them, too. You and I will get to see them a couple of times while we're there. It will be a good time for you to get to know more of my family, but, for the most part, we have different agendas ...

* * *

A week and a half later Trudy got a phone call from Connie.

"Hi, do you remember me?" Connie asked. "We met at the wedding the other day."

Trudy nodded her head, not that the caller could see her response, and answered, "Sure. You came over and met me and Kareem, and we discovered that Miss Winnie has been helpful to both of us.

"It's good to hear from you," Trudy said. "Is there something I can do for you?"

"Sort of," Connie began. "When we went up to greet Miss Winnie and her new husband she seemed pleased that we had met one another."

"Um Hm!" Trudy nodded her head. "I think she was really happy and a little surprised that we showed up together in the receiving line. You might have thought that she had planned the whole us-getting-to-know-one-another business the way she laughed when we told her how we met!"

"I didn't think I was imagining her response," Connie interjected. "She really did seem pleased that we were getting to know one another, which makes me wonder if she had some ideas about you and me. LIke, do you s'ppose she was hoping we'd meet?"

The two young women spoke for several minutes about the bride and groom. "I think Dr. and Rev. Daniel had a beautiful start in their marriage, don't you?" Connie asked.

"The bride and groom certainly looked pleased to be together — almost like a couple of young kids getting married," Trudy suggested. "I hope they do enjoy their new life."

"I have a feeling they are going to do just great!" Connie said. "They seemed so, so ... well, happy together. I noticed that Miss Winnie couldn't stop grinning."

"Would you like to come over here to my house and visit me and Kareem?" Trudy asked her new friend.

There was a pause on the other end of the line for a moment before Connie answered. "I would like to come by for a bit, if it wouldn't be too much trouble for you."

Trudy laughed. "No, it wouldn't be. You're a mom. You know what sort of things happen when babies are small — they take up all of your time! So, if you're willing to come to me, I can fit you in. I'd like that. Yes, come!"

"Okay I'll be over later this afternoon, then," Connie agreed.

Trudy gave Connie directions to her house, which was only a block off Main Street, across from the depot in downtown Misty Falls.

❄ ❄ ❄

"Boy! Our lives are totally different, aren't they?" Trudy exclaimed. "We are both young mothers, and we each have had our own mothers very much in our lives, but after that our stories go off in different directions."

"You're better off by far, though," Connie admitted. "You have your sweet, little Kareem here with you, and you won't lose him. I only see my girls once a week — on Friday mornings — and then it's only for 90 minutes under the careful eye of the DHR!"

"You're right. I do feel lucky to have my son, and my mom, and a place to live, and so much more," Trudy agreed.

"Maybe life's not fair ... maybe things just happen .... Maybe I made all the wrong choices," Connie thought out loud.

"Life probably isn't fair," Trudy agreed. "It doesn't make sense that some people get so much, and others are starving. I'm sure I don't know all the answers yet, even though I don't have a lot, I've got Kareem, and I think I'm one of the happiest people I know."

"My whole life swings from really, really good — like when I hold my babies close to me — to really, really bad, like most other times," Connie sighed.

Just then Kareem began to wriggle and stretch in his crib, so Trudy jumped up to look after him. She spoke in hushed tones, "He may be waking up. He's sort of on a schedule, but I think the schedule isn't very certain. We'll just have to wait and see."

Connie perked up as she watched Trudy and her baby. "Are you nursing him?" she asked.

"Yes. It's really good, too. I'm glad I decided to try. I hear there are so many good reasons to nurse your baby," Trudy said.

"I couldn't do it, but I sort of wish I could," Connie admitted. "There were too many things happening at the time the girls were born to give nursing a solid try."

Trudy wondered what Connie was talking about. When Kareem arrived in her life, it seemed that everything else in the world took a step — or two or three — backward. "Hm," she said, "Would I be getting too personal, if I asked why?"

Connie figured that her story would eventually come out. She was enjoying getting to know Trudy and her baby, and she hoped that they might begin a real friendship. "It's a long story," Connie began, "and it's not a very pretty one, although there were definitely some high times. Do you want to hear?"

"I think so," Trudy spoke cautiously. "I like you; you seem to be a kind person, even though I think you've had some serious problems. Maybe you need to have a friendly ear to listen to you."

"When Miss Winnie was here, she and I would occasionally talk about stuff that I need to figure out, and I really enjoyed her listening to me and, sometimes, suggesting alternatives," Trudy remembered.

"That's interesting. Mostly I've kept stuff to myself. Of course Mother knows what's been happening, and my husband George knows, but I haven't spoken to too many others about my stuff," Connie explained.

"Of course, when the twins were born we weren't living at home; in fact, we were on a Greyhound bus heading south. We had taken a bus up to Connecticut to stay with a friend of ours. Missy and I were best friends when we were in school, and we've remained friends ever since. She married and moved north two years ago, but we still kept in contact. When George and I realized that we were expecting twins, we were really excited, and at the same time we were scared!" Connie continued.

Trudy's eyes flew open and she said, "Scared! You two were scared?"

Connie nodded her head in agreement, "Yes, we were scared. We had good reason to be scared."

Trudy decided not to interrupt her friend, instead she just made little soft sounds like "hm" and "hm?"

"You see we have had three other babies since we were married, and the DHR has taken all three. That's The Department of Human Resources in South Carolina," Connie stopped to let her meaning sink in.

"You lost ... three ... babies ... to the DHR?" Trudy stumbled over her words.

Connie nodded. She took a big breath and began to explain her painful history. "You see, when I had Jeffrey I was barely sixteen years old, so maybe that's why the DHR was aware of me and my child. The DHR woman visited me when I was in the hospital after Jeffrey was born. She was just doing her duty, making sure that I was aware of the seriousness of being a new mom. I told them that George and I had every intention of making a good home for our new son, but when Jeffrey was still very little, just four weeks old, there was an incident that caused the DHR to get involved," Connie recalled.

Trudy was all ears at this point in the story, so when Kareem began to cry, she quickly picked the baby up and began checking his diaper, all the while listening to Connie.

Connie waited to see what Trudy was doing, and then she continued, "The incident was really more of an accident. I was holding Jeffrey because he was crying. He had been crying for some time. I checked his Pampers and changed him, and I gave him a bottle. He didn't want the bottle, but he wanted something. I couldn't tell what he wanted or needed, so I handed him to George."

George had been with me from the beginning, as I was trying everything I could think of to sooth Jeffery's crying, so George began walking around with the baby, swinging him way high to the left and then to the right. The motion must have soothed Jeffrey, and he calmed down. George thought he had found a good solution to the baby's cries — swing him around, get him moving like when he was inside me," Connie smiled.

"The next day George tried the same solution with Jeffrey when he began to cry. This time we were out in the front yard. Jeffrey was crying and George was swinging him — higher and higher. Jeffrey calmed down a bit, and George stopped swinging, but then the baby started wailing again. This time George sort of shook him a little to remind the baby that he was supposed to stop crying, but Jeffrey stopped everything; he looked like he was asleep, suddenly. Then after a couple of minutes he woke up and was fine.

"By that time there was a woman from next door who had been watching what was happening, and she decided to call the DHR and report this 'incident.' We were shocked, of course. We had heard of baby shaking, and we didn't think anything had happened that was like real baby shaking, but the DHR saw things different. They decided that Jeffrey would be safer with someone else, so they took him. They placed him with a good family, and I hear about Jeffrey regularly from them, but he's gone. He's not mine anymore."

Trudy finished dressing Kareem and began to nurse him; all the while she listened to Connie's terrible story. "I can't imagine how you felt!" she said, shaking her head back and forth.

"That was the first baby I lost. Things were painful for me and George. We didn't exactly blame one another for losing Jeffrey, but we knew that somehow we were responsible for happened. It wasn't long before I was expecting again! The new pregnancy sort of took the sting out of losing our first baby. This time we would be very, very careful. It wouldn't happen again ... but it did!" Connie spoke her words slowly.

Trudy was completely wrapped up in this tale. It sounded like it really happened, yet she was naive enough she knew to wish it had been otherwise. "I'm so sorry, Connie! What in the world happened with your new baby?"

"Have you ever heard of CP?" Connie asked.

"Do you mean the birth defect?" Trudy asked.

"CP, or cerebral palsy, is a birth defect. They don't always know why a baby comes into the world with CP, but some babies arrive with it. I think there are different reasons why a baby might show up with CP, but it's hard to say for sure why."

"Okay," Trudy was trying to follow Connie's story. "What about CP?"

"Yeah. When our new baby arrived, just 11 months after Jeffrey came, he had CP. It wasn't a real bad case of CP, but it could cause little Scott some trouble, especially in his getting the right sort of educational help. His right leg would be a problem and his speech would need specialists for years. Somehow the DHR felt that our baby needed a better chance in life than what George and I could give him, so they took him, too. Scott did come home with us for two weeks, but then the DHR came and got him. I hear from his adoptive parents regularly, and I have books of pictures and notes about how he is doing. I feel like he's doing what he needs to be doing. I'm okay with Scott being with them."

Trudy nodded her head to show she understood what happened.

"That was two babies. Maybe we weren't supposed to have babies. We seemed to be pretty good at losing them!" Connie said with irony. "Anyway, before we knew it, we were expecting again! This time the tests showed that we were having a little girl! Maybe girls would be different. I was older; heck, I was eighteen and a half! We hoped everything would be perfect this time, and we were very excited about the new baby girl. I even changed the color of the walls of the baby's room — from baby blue to soft, little girl pink!"

"But something happened?" Trudy was almost afraid to ask.

"No, that's the funny, or not so funny, part. Nothing happened. Michella was born just fine. We were so excited, but then the DHR came and took her. She didn't even come home with us. They said that their records showed that we had lost two babies already, and they wanted to be sure this baby had the best chance for a good life, and they took her!" Connie stopped and turned away from Trudy, not showing her tears streaming down her face.

Trudy understood how painful this recitation of loss had to be for Connie. She was glad that Connie had shared her story with her, but she recognized the distress it caused her. Trudy could certainly appreciate her new friend better now.

"I wish there was something I could do or say to make your pain more bearable," Trudy said.

Connie wiped the tears from her eyes and turned back to Trudy. "No, I don't suppose there is anything that anyone can do. And most days I'm pretty okay with the way things are — at least with Jeffrey and Scott and Michella, but I'm not so good with losing the twins. I've had them longer, and I love them so much! I don't want them to be taken forever."

Trudy carefully put Kareem down in his crib and walked over to Connie, putting her arm around her shoulder. "I know it hurts; it has to hurt. You wouldn't be human if it didn't hurt. What's happening with your twins, now? How serious is this business with the twins? Maybe the DHR here in Tennessee works different from the one in South Carolina."

Connie looked up and smiled weakly. "Maybe it is. You're right; the DHR woman told us to get some anger counseling, and, if we pass the class, we can get the babies back."

"How long has this been going on with the twins, anyway?" Trudy wanted to know.

"They took the twins away back in March, so it's been three months now. Mom and I go over to the DHR in the city every Friday to spend 90 minutes with the girls. It's the best time in the week. The twins always look bigger, and they've learned new things each week. They're on their knees now and beginning to rock back and forth. Samantha Rose is a little faster than Shelby Ann, but they are pretty close to one another in their development. It's so much fun to play with them, watching them sitting up and even stand up when we let them hold onto our fingers and hang on. I wish I could spend every minute with them, loving them, watching them grow!

"The lady who is taking care of them is a good person. She's trying to be helpful; I understand that."

Trudy asked, "So all you have to do is pass an anger management class, right? Is there a particular time limit on them?"

"The court wants us to have the classes for twelve weeks or more if the counselor thinks we need them. The problem is that George isn't always home in time to get to the class," Connie explained. "And, to tell the truth, he's not always here. Sometimes he goes back to South Carolina for a few days, maybe. I don't know."

Trudy wondered about this George person. "You haven't said much about George. Tell me about him."

"We've been married five years," Connie said with a smile. We got married before Jeffrey arrived. I was just then sixteen years old, and in South Carolina it's okay to be married at that age providing I had parental consent. Mama signed the form giving me permission to marry George."

"How old was George then?" Trudy asked, trying to put this picture in perspective.

"He was forty-three," Connie said quietly.

"Forty-three!" Is that what you said? Trudy was astounded.

"Yes, you heard right. George had been my next door neighbor ever since Mother and I moved into the neighborhood. I was six years old then. So I have known George, or "Mr. Oliver," since back then," Connie told Trudy.

Trudy was trying to get a handle on this information. "I'm not sure what to think about that, Connie. You were very young, and this older man and you got together....

"It's a long story — another long story — and I'm not so sure I'm proud of it." Connie confessed. "You see, George was my best friend's father. Missy and I were like sisters all through school. George and I were going to stay with her up in Connecticut before we came here, just before the twins were born."

Trudy wanted to understand the story that Connie had just told her, yet she felt there was something very wrong with the arrangements — a fifteen year old getting pregnant by her next door neighbor, who was almost three times her age! She shook her head and said, "I didn't know those things happened. I guess I'm naive. I wonder if that's a big piece of the trouble right there!"

"That's the thing, isn't it?" Connie answered softly. When we got married, I thought that marriages were special, and I was very much in love with George. He was so ... so grown up. He knew stuff. He was so much more mature than the boys at school. He was friendly. I'd known him for a long time — you know — as the father of the kids next door. I'm not sure how it all began, our being together, but it happened one evening ... Connie stopped.

"You said he was the father of your best friend, so he was married to the woman next door, right?" Trudy asked.

"Yes, he was, but I thought, I guess I thought, that he was not still in that marriage. He had been separated from Tanya, ah, Mrs. Oliver, for a couple of years. He wasn't always there, but he came by the house, often, to see his kids," Connie explained.

"Hm. So he was visiting his kids when you appeared one day," Trudy asked rhetorically. "I guess I get it. One thing turned into another and voila! A baby is coming. Is that it?"

"That's about it. When I found out I was 'el prego,' I told George. (You know I had a hard time learning to call him 'George' rather than 'Mr. Oliver') ... but, anyway ... I told him about my pregnancy," Connie said.

"That must have been some scene!" Trudy said. "You have a lot more courage than I have; I haven't told Kareem's daddy yet, that he's a father."

This time it was Connie's eyes that flew open when she realized what Trudy had just admitted to her. "You haven't told him yet? Are you planning to tell him?"

"That's the big question, as they say. In fact, that's what Miss Winnie and I talked about. We had tea over at the Depot Diner a couple of times before Kareem was born and spoke about whether I should tell the father or not," Trudy said.

"Isn't he around here? Wouldn't he have seen you ... you know, blossoming out — and now with your new son!" Connie asked.

"Actually, no. He's not from Misty Falls. He goes to college out of state, and I don't think I'm very likely to bump into him," Trudy figured.

"You said that you used to talk to Miss Winnie about him. What did she say?" Connie was curious.

"Well, she was about facts, mostly. She wanted to know if the baby's father was a good person — someone who wouldn't harm the baby. I think she wanted to be sure that the father was not someone who had taken advantage of me to begin with," Trudy said.

"And?" Connie wanted more information. She had been telling her own story, as hard as it was, and she realized that Trudy also had a story that she'd like to hear.

"And ... I told her that Kareem's father is a wonderful guy. I think he's a fabulous person, but my problem is that I don't want to spoil his life by bringing in an already-made-family just as he's getting his education and all," Trudy began to explain.

"See how different our stories are!" Connie observed. "Your baby's father is a good person, someone who will be important someday, and you don't want to hurt him by dropping you and your baby into his life, and my husband divorced his first wife to marry me. He left Tanya and their five children to marry me!" Connie announced, as if she was just seeing her situation from a different perspective.

"Sheesh! How do you unscramble that set of arrangements?" Trudy asked, mostly to herself.

"You said that you used to talk to Miss Winnie about stuff," Connie said. "I know she was very helpful to me — like a good friend. I wonder what makes her the way she is?"

"I think Miss Winnie would say that her faith in God guides her steps everyday. I believe she was hoping that I'd do that too — you know — that I would follow Jesus, too," Trudy answered.

"Miss Winnie never said I had to inform Kareem's father about his new status, but she did remind me that he would have some legal rights to knowing his son, if he knew of his existence. She listened to my fears about ruining his life, if I told him about the baby."

"Sure. Miss Winnie was mostly hands on, driving me and Mom to appointments at the DHR office or taking me places I needed to go. But she listened to me good, too, and, I bet, some of the stuff I told her probably shocked her. I didn't mean to shock her, but I think that's what happened," Connie shook her head remorsefully.

"I wonder what she might say about us now?" Trudy wondered aloud. "I suppose I could call her or email her. Of course, she's probably real busy with her life in Chicago, getting all moved into their new house and being on her honeymoon."

"Well, I think Miss Winnie is a very unusual lady, and I know I'll miss her; I miss her already. She helped me many times, but the thing I remember about her is her positive way of looking at things — kind of like always being hopeful. No matter how bad things got, and, believe me, we were going through some real tough stuff, no matter how bad things were, Miss Winnie had hope. She would hope that things would be better for us ... soon," Connie said.

Miss Winnie seemed genuinely pleased that we met at the wedding reception," Trudy suggested.

"I wonder what she might have said, if you had asked her for her opinion about your baby's father?" Connie asked Trudy.

"I think she wanted me to tell Kareem's father about his son. She was making a gentle suggestion that I might / should tell the baby's father. She wanted to be sure about his character — that he was a good person, which I assured her he was — and then I think she would have encouraged me to tell him. Maybe because that would be more truthful." Trudy answered.

"What do you think about that?" Connie asked. "Do you have a good reason to keep that information away from father and son? Maybe there is a beautiful relationship that would be good for everyone around, if you told the truth and let the guy in on the fact that he has become a father," Connie said and then added, "I don't mean to sound like I'm judging your decision so far, but maybe you haven't thought things through completely. You're thinking of today and now, but there's years more to come, and maybe those years deserve some consideration, too."

Trudy thought. "Hm. My mother brought me up on her own. She's done a reasonable job, I think. She was just about my age when I came along, and that knocked her out of school and put her in a major struggle to raise me, but she did. My father was never around. All I know is his name — Al Jackson. He doesn't live here any more. I never met him, and

230

I have no relationship with him. So, I guess you could say I have no idea what a father could do for a child."

"That's understandable; you didn't have a father in your life, and my father has been in the state insane asylum in South Carolina since I was little. Mom would tell me about him when I was young and I asked about him. He has something called schizophrenia, and he hears weird voices all the time. He can't live with us," Connie explained.

"I can understand that you don't want to force your life on the guy, who you say is so special. You don't want to ruin his chances for a good life, but how do you know that his knowing about Kareem's existence would ruin his life?"

Trudy shook her head. "I don't; not really. I respect him, and I want the best for him, but I don't want to be responsible for screwing up his future!"

"But, Trudy, you have already told me that Kareem is the best thing that ever happened to you and that you love him beyond what you ever thought you could love another. How would that be different for a father and son? Couldn't they also have a beautiful relationship as parent and child? Have you thought about what they might be missing?" Connie asked.

"We're getting really deep, aren't we? I'm not sure how I could tell Kareem's father. Right now he's away at school, and he doesn't live in Misty Falls, so we couldn't just happen to run into one another," Trudy was thinking out loud.

"Talking to you has opened up a lot to think about, at least from my perspective," Trudy said. "What we've been talking about is pretty serious, and we should agree to keep each other's confidence. Do you agree?"

Connie was pleased to hear Trudy make that suggestion.

"You're right. I feel I can trust you, and you can trust me, too. I feel good about sharing my crazy life with you. I don't think you're judging me, like some people do. I appreciate that. Sometimes I feel like the whole world is judging me. I know that I'm not doing everything right, and maybe I've done a bunch of stuff wrong, but I do feel okay about talking to you." Connie smiled.

Chapter 25. A Little History

(July 5, 2009)

Connie had left Trudy with a lot to think about. Connie's visit and her story were different from other stories she had heard before. Oh, there were others girls, like herself, who had become unwed mothers. That story was one she had heard a number of times, and she herself was the star of one of those stories, but Connie's story was not like that. Trudy didn't quite know what to think about it; there were a number of things that didn't add up right, she thought.

"AND, I'm beginning to think I need to include Ned in Kareem's life. I guess I've heard enough reasons for telling him to convince me that he should know about his fatherhood. Ned and Kareem have the right to know that they are family!" Trudy thought. *"I wonder what I might do to break the news to him?"*

This line of thinking caused Trudy to be distracted as she sat with her mother at dinner that evening.

"Earth to Trudy!" Keisha Livingston called to her daughter. "Are you there, inside, somewhere?"

Trudy groaned and said, "Oh, I'm sorry, Mom, I guess I was day-dreaming."

"I can see that," Keisha agreed. "What's on your mind, now?"

"I had a visitor today," Trudy began to explain.

"You had a visitor!" Keisha interrupted. "Who was it?"

"Oh Mom! The girl I met at the wedding last week came by to see me and Kareem after lunch. We had a good talk. I told you about her."

"She's the one that had twin babies that were taken away from her. You told me about her. I'm not sure you want to be associating with her," Trudy's mother wanted to warn her daughter.

"She does have a strange story, Mom. You're right, but I think I should be old enough to decide who I associate with now — at my age!" Trudy stood her ground.

Keisha quickly backed away from her motherly pushing. "You're right. I don't have the right to tell you now that you're a mother yourself. You're eighteen years old, but I guess the girl you're talking about has

232

certainly seen some of the raw side of life, and that's not particularly good for you."

"We sort of see that, too. Even Connie mentioned that to me. She realizes that her life has some real oddities in it. Yet it's sort of like we have been brought together maybe to help each other," Trudy tried to explain.

"Remember, we met at Miss Winnie's wedding last week, and it was almost like she wanted us to meet — that we could be good for one another, somehow," Trudy added.

"I do think Miss Winnie is a good person, and she has done some kind things for us and for others in the community. She's gone now, however, and I don't know what she could do for you now," Keisha said.

"Both Connie and I know that Miss Winnie has very strong opinions, what I'd call a moral code that she lives by," Trudy countered.

Keisha didn't know Rev.Taylor very well, as they had only met briefly on a couple of occasions. She said, "I couldn't say what makes Miss Winnie tick, because I didn't really know her, but she was the pastor over at Muddy Creek Church, so she's a disciple of Jesus, and she wants to follow him. I think that's what pastors try to do — to lead others by example. Sounds like she'd be a good person to listen to. I like those kind of influences in your life.

❊ ❊ ❊

Later that evening, after Trudy had put Kareem down for the night, she found herself reviewing that very special week last summer when she met Ned.

"*I was so surprised that he noticed me,*" she thought. "*The first time I saw Ned he was coming out of the water right after he had made a jack knife into the pool. When he pulled himself out of the water, all dripping wet — the water cascading off his gleaming muscles — I thought he was a living, black marble statue. He was so magnificent! He had shaved his head the way so many black guys do these days, and I noticed how well-shaped his head was — strong with a very high, broad forehead and wide, full lips. I noticed how his eyes tilted up at the corners, just a mite. After he pulled himself out of the water, he began talking to Jeanelle and several boys at the party that I didn't know.*"

Trudy had been invited to come to the party by Jeanelle's cousin, Patrice. Trudy and Jeanelle had been best girlfriends since they were in kindergarten, so they often went places together. Patrice lived over in Kirby, the town ten miles away, close to the big county high school. Patrice's parents owned a large, ranch style house with a pool, and she frequently had parties there. It would be a fun afternoon.

Trudy remembered that both she and Ned were initially shy, but they were on the same water polo team, so there was much thrashing and bouncing around in the pool. They discovered in the process of the game that both of them were capable at the sport, and they were able to work together, setting up the ball for the other to quash into the water on the far side of the net. They crashed into one another on more than one occasion, as they were vying all out for the ball.

After the game Trudy and Ned sat next to one another, soaking up the sun on their backs. Hot dogs had come off the grill, so Ned brought a couple frankfurters over for them. Talking came easier then, as they shared the picnic food. It turned out that they both loved extra relish mixed with mustard on their wieners, but they could do without the ketchup.

Trudy and Ned were on a first name basis in a few moments.

"So, Trudy, you like sports! Do you play anything in school?" Ned wanted to know.

"I've been playing girls' soccer and running track. I lettered in both those sports. How about you? You obviously play a great game of water polo. What else do you do?"

"I'm the kind of person who thinks the sport he's currently doing is his favorite. I like team sports — football, baseball, basketball — but I have done track and diving, too."

"I gather you're out of high school, so you're in college somewhere?" Trudy speculated.

"I thought you knew." Ned replied. "I got an appointment to the Air Force Academy last year, so I've just completed my first year as a plebe."

"That's so cool!" Trudy exclaimed. "Do you love it, or is it just gobs of work?"

"It is work; that's for sure. It requires every bit of me that I can put out everyday, and ... I love it!" Ned admitted. "Fortunately, I was in reasonably good physical shape when I started at the Academy, so the physical side of the program wasn't impossible, and I've always done well in school. I suppose I don't really appreciate the time I have to spend to do those ordinary things like shoe polishing and room tidying. It's not a big deal; it's just a bit bothersome."

"That does sound like quite a program. It's certainly not just the usual college program when you figure in all the rest of the requirements," Trudy said. "Did you realize all that it would require when you got your scholarship?"

"No, I didn't get the total picture, although, I shouldn't have been surprised. The program is designed to make us students more grown up and responsible and able to count on one another when the pressure is on." Ned explained.

"Now I understand your hair cut!" Trudy laughed.

"All us cadets have very short hair, although the females don't completely chop off their hair," Ned returned. "So, where are you at school?

"I'll be a senior at the county high school this fall," Trudy answered. "I need to get a good hold on scholarship opportunities, as my going to college depends on much help. I haven't really scoured the field yet in the way of finding scholarships, but they say there are good ones out there. I should give it a hard look in the next few weeks. I'm definitely looking forward to college."

"Yeah, my scholarship came up out of the blue. I was figuring on going to UT Knoxville, probably, or maybe getting a football scholarship somewhere. But when the senator's office contacted me to inquire about my plans and to ask 'would I be interested in the senator's endorsement to one of the academies,' I could hardly say 'Yes' quick enough!" Ned's smile indicated the delight he felt when he learned about his scholarship.

"How exciting that must have been for you! What did your folks think?" Trudy asked.

"They were overwhelmed, same as I was, but we were excited, too. Of course, the Air Force Academy program covers nearly the entire year. We have programs that begin before the academic year, and we have camps during the summer, too. So I'm not home too much of the time," Ned explained.

"I hope you enjoy the time you get now!" Trudy smiled.

"You bet! This short time is valuable, and I'm definitely enjoying being here today," he assured her.

They talked off and on all afternoon, and before Trudy and Jeanelle left to return to Misty Falls, Ned had secured a date with Trudy for the next day. They would see *Indiana Jones and the Kingdom of the Crystal Skull*, which was just now coming out.

"I loved those first three movies with Indiana Jones!" Trudy said. "I expect Harrison Ford is going to have to be a little less active this time. Hasn't it been at least a generation since he first made those movies? He's got to be a lot older, now.

Ned laughed and agreed with Trudy. "He is something of an icon as an adventure figure. It should be a good flick. What time can I pick you up?"

The date was set — Friday evening. Ned would pick Trudy up at her house in Misty Falls, and they would have a great evening together. Ned would be leaving after that, taking a short trip with his family before he was off to Keesler Air Force Base to work for several weeks to learn about base operations.

Trudy reminisced about that very special evening. The time they spent together was wonderful, but it turned out much differently than she had expected. A couple months later she was acutely aware that things would be very different for her ... from now on!

My life today is not like what I had dreamed about, but I wouldn't change having Kareem. I believe he's the best part of my life! He's changed me in such good ways. I know I've grown in many ways since he came into my life. Being responsible for my young man has forced me to think beyond myself, really, for the first time, and I like the difference it's made in me. I think I'm seeing things in a new way because of him. Life is so important, and even small incidents — like hugging Kareem close and singing him a lullaby — are important pieces of the puzzle of life. He has given me so much, and I hope I'm giving him what he needs, too," Trudy told herself.

Maybe Ned really does need to know Kareem. At least, he should have a choice in the matter. If I leave him out completely, Ned will never have the opportunity to discover this love — how it feels to be in a relationship with this chil', helping to guide a young life, growing in love with this dear little one. How can I deprive Ned of this opportunity? How can I possibly tell him about Kareem? Should I write him a letter or call him on the phone? No. That is too impersonal, rather like getting news from the IRS. Hm. I'm going to have to think about this some more, Trudy decided.

✳ ✳ ✳

Connie was also thoughtful about her conversation with Trudy. She was glad she had made the effort to get to know this girl. They had some things in common — being young mothers, for instance — but Trudy's life was more normal than her own. It wasn't really fair, though.

After all, Connie and George had been married for five and a half years. They had done the right thing about getting married when they realized that there was a baby on the way. Her marriage to George made her baby legal, but something was still not right.

Connie knew that George and his first wife, Tanya, had been having trouble for some time when she and George began seeing one another. He had moved out of the house, but he came over frequently to see his kids.

Connie was a junior in high school when she bumped into George one day at a Target in town. He offered to buy her a Coke, so they sat in the corner of a fast food store snacking on fries and Coke for an hour.

Connie liked George. Of course, she knew him to be her best friend's father, but she hadn't really talked much to him before this chance encounter. As they sat drinking their Cokes, George seemed so much more mature than the boys at school. He knew more about the world than most of her friends did. He had his own checkbook and his own car. He didn't talk down to Connie; he acted as if she was a real person, even a grown up. Connie liked how she felt when she was with George.

George and Connie continued to run into one another over the next several weeks. When they met, they would go to a different fast food place and share a Coke. Then one day George suggested that they might like to go out together; they would have a real date in a restaurant.

Connie agreed with George that their friendship needed to be a secret, so she agreed to meet him one evening for their date.

Connie had some mixed feelings about this arrangement, but she was highly intrigued that this grown man was interested in her. She didn't realize that this liaison might turn into something far deeper, far more complicated.

236

A couple months after that first dinner, Connie realized she was expecting a child. George was the father, and she found herself in a very confused position. She was amazed that she was expecting, but she recognized that she had just turned a corner that she couldn't turn back. She couldn't turn back, unless ... unless she did something about her condition. She knew of other girls who had ended their pregnancies by having an abortion. Connie didn't feel right about that. She knew there was much talk, both pro and con, regarding abortions — whether they were right or wrong. Connie didn't know where she sat on that question, but she decided to tell George and see what he thought.

* * *

George picked Connie up at the high school behind the track to take her to dinner. They had been using different locations for their rendezvous, so they wouldn't catch the attention of community onlookers.

After they had ordered their meal, Connie got up her nerve and said, "I have something I have to tell you, George."

George leaned forward in his chair and said, "You've got news? Is it school related?"

"No, not really. Although I guess my news does affect school — next year," Connie figured.

"Next year? Your news will effect your schooling next year? How's that?" George was curious.

"Because I just found out I'm pregnant, George. We are going to be parents!" Connie admitted.

George sat speechless for some time. Connie was dying to know what he would say. Finally, she added, "Did you hear what I told you?"

"I heard you all right. I've heard the same announcement from Tanya five times before. Oh, I heard you just fine," George said sarcastically.

Connie didn't know what to answer. She didn't want to ruin this relationship with George because she really enjoyed his attention and the grown up things they were doing together. She knew that she had fallen in love with George. She cared very much for him.

"You're not saying anything, and that makes me worry," Connie said. She watched George's face for clues of what he was thinking. "Maybe I should just get an abortion and have this episode in my life taken away — sort of simply erased," Connie ventured to say.

"No! That's not right,' George asserted. You've got a new baby on the way. That's something that God has done. God gives life. I won't let you have an abortion!"

"Then what? What can I do?" Connie asked weakly. Her voice was almost a whisper.

Finally, George spoke up. He began slowly, thinking things through as he talked. "I think I have a bigger problem than you have. You'll be sixteen on your next birthday, right?"

Connie nodded and said, "Yes, I'll be sixteen in January."

"So, the State of South Carolina doesn't smile too happily on men who get young girls pregnant before they're sixteen. I could go to jail ...," George's voice trailed off.

"No! George! That can't be! I didn't know I could get you into trouble with the law just because of my pregnancy!" Connie was suddenly seeing things from a new view. "What can we do?"

"Looks like there's only one thing to do," George said with a flat voice. "I'll divorce Tanya and marry you."

"You would do that for me?" Connie was shocked by the realization that she was causing trouble for her friends, the Olivers.

"Yes, I would do that for you ... and for me," George nodded his head. "As far as my marriage to Tanya goes, you know we've been separated since before you and I began seeing each another. I guess that part of my life is over, and it looks like you and I are the future," George said thoughtfully.

That's how it all came about. George divorced his wife, so he could marry Connie. Connie took care not to be in the Oliver's house; she didn't want Mrs. Oliver to see her as her new shape was beginning to show. She didn't want Mrs. O to figure out her relationship with George until they were married.

Connie's marriage to George was not perfect; it had serious problems, nearly from the first day. Connie had been careful to wear very loose-fitting clothes, so that her condition was not obvious to the world. George had set up the machinations of the divorce after he discovered that Connie was expecting. He needed to move quickly — divorce first, followed by marriage to Connie.

Connie told her mother, Sallie, who had very mixed emotions about the situation. Sallie could see how much George meant to her daughter. He had a good job as a welder. He had been an involved father to his five children next door. He was caring for Connie, as far as she could see, and she wanted the best for her only child.

Sallie gave her permission for Connie to marry George and hoped for the best.

Everything seemed to be happening at an accelerated tempo. Connie's sixteenth birthday was New Year's Day 2004. She and George married the next day, January second, and the baby arrived two weeks later.

The new Oliver family had a small apartment in town, and they began their married life and life as new parents virtually at the same time. Their little son, Jeffery, was a joy, of course, and they were totally focused on meeting their baby's needs.

The DHR arrived at the hospital when Connie gave birth. Since she was just sixteen, the DHR had been alerted to the birth of the child. The case worker was all about business. She recognized that this was not the first young mother to have a child in South Carolina. The fact was, there had been many young women over the years who had begun marriage and family life as teenagers.

The DHR woman met both parents and noted that this new father was not so very young. He had a steady job and had provided for his bride by setting up an apartment in town. Perhaps all would be well. The woman was serious about the DHR's interest in Connie's and George's situation, and she stressed the importance of taking proper care of their newborn.

All went well for several weeks until there was an allegation of child shaking. A neighbor observed George swinging the child up and down and then shaking him. The thing that concerned the neighbor was that the infant, who had been screaming so loudly that everyone in the neighborhood could hear him, had suddenly ceased his cries; he was abruptly silent. The parents, who were watching the baby's apparent sleeping, couldn't seem to awaken the child, even though a minute before that he had been wailing heavily. A couple minutes seemed to elapse before the child awakened. The neighbor thought that this was a case of baby shaking, and notified the DHR office.

That was the beginning of the series of losses for the Olivers. Connie was only too familiar with that story. She and George lost their first three children to the state of South Carolina. It wasn't fair. Connie felt sure it wasn't fair, but her feelings didn't seem to play into the fact that she had born three babies, beautiful babies, and each of them had been taken from her when they were just infants. Her children were now in foster homes, and as far as Connie knew they had good lives; their new parents were taking good care of them.

Life in Misty Falls was different for the Olivers, but the problems over their children had persisted. It was all the fault of the babies' birth place being so unplanned. Connie and George had wanted to make a new start with their twins, but somehow they couldn't get themselves organized enough to manage the change.

Their efforts to move to Connecticut didn't work out. Even though they had stayed with Missy, who was George's youngest daughter and Connie's best friend, something just felt odd about being so far from the South and so far from everything they knew. Truth be known, Connie was a little homesick for her mother. Even though she had been married to George for nearly six years, Connie still hoped that her mom would be around when her babies arrived.

So, in the end, the Olivers jumped on the Greyhound bus and rode all night to get to Misty Falls to be with Sallie. It was still several weeks before their babies were due when George and Connie decided to make the the trip to Tennessee, but the babies began their journey into the world ahead of schedule. By the time the bus had crossed into the Knoxville city limits, the bus driver was advised of the imminent arrival of twin girls. The driver, taking no chances, deviated from his normal route to the bus depot, and made an emergency stop at the ER of the East Tennessee's Children's Hospital. Not too many babies were delivered at Children's, but when Connie arrived at the hospital, the babies were arriving, too. There wasn't much anyone could do about sending the Olivers to a different hospital. This one would have to do.

The Tennessee DHR was immediately notified about the arrival of twin babies to this out of town couple, owing to the suddenness and unexpectedness of the twins' arrival. The twins, as wonderful as they were, added to the Oliver's troubles because the babies eventually were taken by the DHR. Perhaps the twin's removal was not permanent; Connie certainly hoped it was not, but considering the way things had worked out for her in the past, she didn't know what else to expect.

※ ※ ※

Chapter 26. A New Home in Chicago

(June 29, 2009)

Nine days following the wedding a U-Haul packed with Winnie's household goods followed by the lime-green VW, came to a stop on the street where the row house stood. John and Winnie were about to build their nest in this new venue. They had travelled all day in tandem, hoping to arrive at their new home before dark.

The trip had been uneventful, save for the flat tire on Winnie's car. The journey from Gatlinburg had been slowed down by a construction zone in Indiana, which was probably the source of the nail in the tire. Winnie didn't immediately recognize her tire being flat, but when their two vehicles stopped for gas outside of Indianapolis, John noticed the car listing to the port side and a significant loss of roundness to the tire's shape.

"Win, look at your tire! Didn't you notice that your car wasn't acting right?" John asked as he moved over to Winnie's car and began an inspection of the left front tire.

Winnie was surprised. "No, I guess I didn't notice, but it certainly is flat!"

"How could you not know you had a flat tire?" John asked with an edge to his voice.

Winnie wondered, too, how she managed to miss such an obvious problem with her car. "I'm asking myself the same question. How, indeed, could I have missed a flat tire? I really don't know. Do you suppose I had my mind on something else?" She asked whimsically.

After John changed the tire he felt quite pleased with himself. "I hope you'll agree that I passed my first challenge as a new husband."

"You passed marvelously! I'm very proud of you!" Winnie assured John. I didn't know you were a mechanic."

"I'm not. I've never changed a flat tire before, but I'm glad I could fix this one. I wouldn't want to have to pay someone else to do the work. I have a feeling being a married man is going to provide me with many new opportunities to work outside of academic endeavors. That can help round me out," John figured.

"I agree. We will no doubt be stretched in new ways just in the process of beginning to live together and building our new home. Marriage for many couples includes having children, which adds stress and demands to their family life. Of course, we won't have those dynamics," Winnie laughed.

"No, we surely will have challenges; that's what life is about. You never know what will come up," John observed.

"I always liked the old adage, 'It's not so much what happens to you that's important, but what you do in response to what happens that's important," Winnie added.

"It really is amazing how some people respond to problems. It's always heartwarming and encouraging to hear how people can pull themselves up from some seemingly impossible situation and find a new way, a better way, out. It really is amazing," John agreed.

✳ ✳ ✳

"Doodeli-do; doodeli-do," Winnie's cell phone rang about half an hour later. She opened it up and heard, "Hi, it's me. I think you can give Ms. K. a ring now, since it looks like we'll be arriving at the house about seven o'clock," John suggested.

Getting to the new house before the sun was down was possible due to the longer daylight hours of Chicago in late June. At this time of year they would have two more hours of evening glow saturating the city.

John pulled the U-Haul truck to a slow stop, being careful to park just in front of their new row house. Winnie drove her VW up behind the truck and stopped.

John gazed around realizing that this street (this community, this location) was about to become his new home — THEIR new home. It was a quiet street, which, for Chicago, was a blessing. Six row houses stood side by side. Each house had a half dozen stairs leading to a front door, and each had a good-sized window, presumably by the kitchen, to the right of the stairs looking onto the road. The front door of the second house in the row opened, and out stepped their realtor, Ms. Kamaruchi. She had brought the key to the new house for the Daniels, since they would be renting the place initially.

As Winnie turned off the key to her car, she leaned forward on the steering wheel and uttered a short prayer of thanksgiving for her new life and her new husband.

John walked over to the VW, opened Winnie's door, and announced, "Welcome to our new home, Win." Winnie unbuckled her seat belt and stepped out of her car.

John took his bride by the hand, and the two walked up to the front door of their new row house.

"I'm impressed that you two were able to make such good time today!" The realtor announced.

John grinned at the realtor. "It's all a matter of timing. We were up early this morning, because we needed to pick up the truck in Misty Falls. I think I averaged 52 miles an hour in the truck, which is what you might expect."

"Well, I'm very glad you have arrived in one piece ... or two pieces, as it is," Ms. Kamaruchi observed. My son, Eric, and his friend will be arriving in a few minutes. I just called him to let him know you were nearly here. They'll be able to help you get the heavy items in your truck unpacked

The next several hours were focused on getting as much stuff out of the truck as possible and placed somewhere in the general vicinity of where it should go in the house. The two college-aged young men worked hard and were able to place the bed on the second floor and the piano in the living room. Dozens of boxes were carted into the house and left on the floor of the big living room. The boxes would wait patiently for some-one to unpack them.

Fortunately Winnie and John had their overnight bags separate from what had come off the truck, so they were able to find their tooth-brushes and necessaries for the next few days.

After the students carried the piano and the bed into the house and had carted most of the boxes into the living room, John paid them and sent them off.

When he returned he found Winnie sitting on the floor of the living room and joined her there. "I think this was where we were when we fell in love with this house. It looks quite different now, not nearly so fresh."

"It looks like we're moving in, which is how it should look. We're going to have some long workdays ahead of us, but we'll make this house a home before you know it. You might be surprised how much like home it will feel in a couple weeks." Winnie grinned.

"I'm glad you're so sure, Win. I trust you know how this all works. I can't think of anything more we need to do today, though, do you?" John replied.

"There's nothing more we need to do tonight, except figure out where the bedding is and make our bed. We can find kitchen things in the morning. That's a good place to start our unpacking, but that all can wait. It's been a full enough day already; let's go out for a bite," she suggested.

※ ※ ※

For all the excitement of the last two weeks, the long trip from Gatlinburg to Chicago, and after finally settling into their new bed, Winnie couldn't fall asleep. She lay awake and sighed a long, slow, satisfied sigh as she recalled the cavalcade of events she had just raced through.

The memories of the wedding and the ensuing week had become a continuous feedback in Winnie's mind — rather like a brilliantly colored mosaic. Each piece was perfect on its own, yet they harmonized well into delicious thoughts in her re-imagining.

Winnie reminisced over all the moments of her wedding day — each member of her family who had come, the bouquets of garden flowers that had been brought by church members to add to the gaiety and color of the day, the dozens and dozens of well wishers who supported Winnie in her new adventure, the fact that the entire wedding really didn't cost too much (which would please John, no doubt), and, of course, the honeymoon!

The wedding day, which seemed to fly by at mach two speed, unfolded multi-dimensionally in the remembering. *There is enough good stuff in that day to fill volumes!*

Winnie's son, Paul, and his family arrived in their mini van on Friday afternoon about an hour ahead of Claire and her family. The O'Neills had driven over from Kentucky, stopping at the airport in Knoxville to pick up Grandma and Grandpa Bullock, Winnie's parents, who had flown in from Denver.

Everyone gathered at a popular barbecue place in Kirby for dinner that evening. Winnie's parents were thrilled to see their daughter re-married finally after so many years and to be able to spend time with their grand — and great-grandchildren. How much better does it get?

Winnie's final days at Muddy Creek Church had been fully engaged in packing. Fortunately, there had been no pastoral emergencies, which might have complicated her moving efforts. Her last day at church, giving her farewell sermon, was nostalgia- making and full of well wishers. Everyone promised to return the following Saturday for the wedding. The ladies of the church were gracious about planning the wedding reception, including a buffet of finger foods to accompany the wedding cake.

Winnie's friend, Nina Mattingly, had agreed to bake the cake. It would be her first wedding cake, but Winnie was especially pleased that her prize-winning friend would make the cake for her. Nina was one of many people in the community that Winnie knew she would miss once she and John had taken off. *Fortunately you're never completely apart these days, when there is phone and email so available.*

Nina had been a good friend to Winnie as she maneuvered through the complications of her engagement with John. After a heart to heart conversation with Nina, Winnie had decided to fly to Chicago to check out the situation there and to assure herself of John's intentions. That decision had been very helpful to the two affianced, as they made important decisions toward their next step — marriage.

The week that followed Winnie's stepping down from her pulpit and position as pastor remained a great blur — a composite of packing boxes, books, household items, wrapping paper, getting the entire collection into the U-Haul truck, which was then parked at the Reeves' home. All of Winnie's stuff would be out of the parsonage and church, so Muddy Creek's new pastor could begin moving in mid-week — pastors' moving day.

Finally, after reviewing, re-reviewing, and re-re-reviewing those wonderful times, sleep came to a grateful Winnie.

✳ ✳ ✳

After a week of solid work, the newlyweds had accomplished much. They also found that they worked well together, most of the time, making the house begin to feel like home. John especially liked the idea of nest building, as it was his first attempt at preparing a friendly, comfortable place to return after work to get recharged for the next day. It was a worthy project. Although he had not spent time doing household activities before like installing a shower curtain, hanging pictures, or setting up a pantry, John was a hard worker and the new house was taking shape nicely.

Winnie, on the other hand, had moved many times previously, and, so far, the Daniels had only dealt with the items they had carried up from Misty Falls. They hadn't yet been over to John's apartment to begin packing it up. That would happen once Winnie's stuff had found a place to rest. *One set of stuff at a time is plenty enough to work on!*

The honeymooners didn't work nonstop. They took time to enjoy meals together and play around. Often they would stop their work to share an item with the other. When Winnie found her old high school year books she called John to sit with her and look through them.

"I know we both went to Mile High at the same time, and we took several classes together, yet our experiences were very different, weren't they?" Winnie noted.

"I suppose teen boys and girls are worlds apart to begin with," John figured. "I was not particularly into dating or girls, like some guys were, and, from what you tell me, you were not that socially minded back then either. So, we stayed mostly with our peers and studies.

"I do remember you from Latin Club and the parties we had then. Remember the chariot races we had, and the homemade togas we wore? Those parties were about as wild as we got back then," John said.

They spent several hours sitting side by side thumbing through the pages of Winnie's annuals and reading the comments that were left by friends back so long ago. "Did you save your annuals?" Winnie asked John.

"I think so. If I did, we'll find them when we get over to my apartment and begin packing. I don't remember having anything like the number of notes from friends that you have in your annual, though," John tried to remember.

"I'd love to see your annuals; I hope you saved them. Wonder what it would have been like if we had actually known each other back then?" Winnie wondered aloud.

"That can only be speculation, which has no answer. Haven't you told me the same about asking why questions to Scripture? You've said that you can't ask why God sent the Son when He did, rather than at another time. That's not a question that could have a real answer, because that's not the way history happened.

"I do think that you and I met at the right time for us. There was much happening in both of our lives that led up to our finding one another when we did. I think we are building on what we started with, and the more we build the stronger we'll be together," John reasoned.

"I like that, John. I think you're right. We didn't have many solid reasons for our being attracted to one another initially, except how we felt — the chemistry thing — but as we work and play and live together and remain faithful to each other our bond together will grow deeper and even more wonderful," Winnie agreed.

Saturday afternoon Winnie realized that Sunday was the next day. "John, we haven't mentioned it, but tomorrow is Sunday, and it occurs to me that we ought to go to church," Winnie said.

"Sunday already? Seems like our days have been melting one into the next, and it's almost hard to distinguish them," John observed. "I suppose we should take the morning off from our work tomorrow and attend worship somewhere."

Winnie smiled. She was pleased with John's answer. "I suppose we should visit a different congregation than the one we attended in April."

"Wouldn't that church be as good as any other?" John wondered.

"You don't sound very enthusiastic about attending worship. Am I right?" Winnie asked, hoping she had misunderstood John's last comment.

"I'm not quite sure where I come down on church. I do believe in God, and I am working on living thankfully everyday. You know, you're responsible for that. I think I began to understand something about living thankfully once we started falling in love." John pulled Winnie to him and kissed her.

"See, we have one another now, and we're together here in our new home, and I'm certainly enjoying this new life ... and being a nest builder. I don't know that we need anything more," John thought out loud.

Winnie wanted to understand John's thoughts and give him a fair hearing, but she also wanted to be sure that God's actions today, calling the church together and teaching followers of Christ to grow in his commands, would not be overlooked. "Of course, faith in God is foundational to everything else, but there is more to the life of faith ... a lot more."

John wrinkled his forehead in a questioning manner and said, "Of course, you say that because you've been part of the establishment your whole life, but I have to say I still have questions about the validity of the church itself. It's totally manmade (and I do mean MAN-made; women didn't have much to say in the matter, I'd hazard to guess.) It also has been the source of many a war, or terrible pogrom, or other atrocity — enslaving the natives here in the Americas, the Inquisition, and a lot more I'm probably not aware of."

Winnie could see that John was warming up for a full-throated argument, and she realized she didn't have the sort of tools that he had —like rhetoric or debate. Nevertheless, she did have a solid belief that the work of the Holy Spirit was absolutely essential to anyone who would follow Christ.

"I couldn't agree with you more, John," Winnie shook her head. Yes, the church has failed in many ways over the years, but sharing the message of God's love for us in Christ is still the reason the church exists, and that message must not cease. If the story of what Christ did for us is never shared, then what Jesus did for us on the cross would soon be forgotten; it would be lost to the next generations. It would be nothing more than an interesting relic of history. We followers of Christ have a mandate to share that greatest event in human history."

"A mandate? Really? What is this mandate?" John was curious.

"You read it at the end of Matthew's Gospel. Remember? The last four verses in Chapter 28 when Jesus met his eleven disciples on a mount in Galilee and told them, "*... go and make disciples of all nations, baptizing them in the name of the Father and of the Son and of the Holy Spirit, and teaching them to obey everything I have commanded you ... I am with you always, to the very end of the age,*" Winnie quoted by heart.

John was thoughtful for a moment. "I do remember reading that charge."

"It's called The Great Commission," Winnie explained. "It says a mouthful in just a few words. It gives the church her reason for being — to make disciples all over the world and to teach them to follow all the LORD's commands. That's an enormous challenge."

"I don't recall reading a list of Jesus' commands, although He certainly did give challenging guidance for living," John added.

Winnie's eyes twinkled and she said, "That's why study is so important to Christians. There's a great deal to learn, but much of what Jesus meant by obeying his commands is more than just learning his commands, it's learning to live them out everyday. It's one thing to repeat the Great Commandment — "love God with all your heart, soul, mind, and strength and love our neighbor as ourself" — and another thing to actually do it. Sometimes our neighbors aren't all that lovable. Jesus didn't say we are just to teach his commands to new disciples, but to teach them to obey the commands. That's a much bigger responsibility!"

"That gives me something to work on, and you can bet I'll enjoy the learning part. You know, I've been thinking about taking a class at the Divinity School on campus this fall. As a prof at the University I can audit courses for free. I was talking to Marian Q.T. on our drive down to Misty Falls, and she offered to let me audit her course in Christian History this fall," John returned.

"What a great idea! Christian history is a wonderful study! I have always loved history, but the History of ChristianTheology classes I took in seminary were much better than just another slice of history. It was about

247

how understanding the faith evolved in the church," Winnie explained. "It was especially fun to learn how the various, different groups developed over the years."

"The church evolved!" John announced. "It must have, come to think of it. Wouldn't it have been great to be there back then!"

"Yes, wouldn't it! It would be so helpful if we could suddenly find more that was written during those early years in the church. It took several centuries for the church to become really organized," Winnie added.

"I don't know that I've ever heard much about the beginnings of the church. Mostly what we hear today is about the established churches — the different denominations — about completely formed organizations, and they sometimes don't seem all that friendly with one another," John said.

"I suppose the story of how the church got organized is something we'll never have the entire picture of this side of heaven, but, you know something, the fact that the church ever began growing and moved into the world has to be one of the wonders of the world. It was clearly the work of the Holy Spirit. There is no other explanation; seeing the growth of the church is watching God at work in the world!" Winnie said.

"You've just stepped into a whole new realm, Win," John told his wife. "How do you mean the organized church is an example of God's activity in the world? I can see how the resurrection is living proof of God's action in this world, but there's not a corresponding example of the church coming alive, too, is there?"

"I like the way you put that, John," Winnie answered. "I wouldn't call the establishment of the early church a resurrection, but it certainly could be called an incarnation. In fact, the church recognizes her birthday was on the day of Pentecost when 120 followers of Jesus were ignited with the Holy Spirit and danced out of the Upper Room and onto the streets of Jerusalem. Those followers of Jesus were clearly filled with the power of the Holy Spirit that day. They were so excited about the good news of Jesus' resurrection that they stopped everyone they saw and told them about everything that had just happened. They even spoke in languages they didn't know, so they could communicate to the visitors who had come to the city for the Jewish feast of Pentecost. The Book of Acts says that 3,000 people came to faith in Christ that day and were baptized."

"I do remember that part of Acts, and it must have been a remarkable event, but maybe that was just one moment in time that such an outpouring of God's Spirit manifested itself. You can't tell me there were other such events in the life of the church," John wondered.

"Actually, the entire beginning of the church was bathed in remarkable happenings. It's almost impossible to imagine the changes that took place in the early church." Winnie explained.

John was now intrigued by Winnie's statement. "Okay, now you've got my curiosity up. You're telling me that there were many, extraordinary difficulties that the early church overcame, right?" (Winnie nodded, yes.) "Let me see; Okay, I think I know one of them. Those early Christians were Jews, and somehow other people, non-Jews, began hearing about Jesus' death and resurrection, and they wanted to join the Jewish Christians. Is that right?"

"Yes, all the original followers of Jesus were Jews, just as Jesus was a Jew. And Jews had laws about not fraternizing with the Gentiles, but within a generation of Christ's resurrection, the church was almost entirely populated by non-Jews, and by the end of the First Century, it was probably hard to find Jewish Christians," Winnie said.

"That is amazing, I'll agree," John said, "and along with the change in those demographics there would have been a language change. Jesus spoke Aramaic, but the world back then spoke Greek, the lingua franca back then. So, was that another of the changes you're talking about?" John asked.

Winnie was loving this repartee, especially as John was leading it. She continued, "Yes, the language that was spoken by Jesus and which he used to tell his stories and parables, was changed for Greek.

"It was Greek in which the New Testament was written. That's another of the amazing things about the Christian movement. When it began there was nothing written about it. Oh, they had the Hebrew Bible, and they loved it and found a wonderful foundation there preparing the way for the coming Messiah in it, but they didn't have anything like what we have now as the New Testament. The first writings were the letters written by St. Paul, but Paul had no idea his letters would eventually become Scripture. Rather, he was writing to communities, most of whom he knew well, to address concerns he wanted to discuss. There may have been more letters that Paul wrote that did not survive, but those letters we do have make up a large portion of the New Testament. It took nearly three centuries to finally canonize the books we now call the New Testament." Winnie said.

"So, you're saying that the early church didn't have anything written down to guide it, save the Hebrew Bible. So that's three rather strange obstacles to overcome.

"Yes, and there's more," Winnie continued. "Although the church began in Jerusalem on the day of Pentecost, she didn't stay in Jerusalem. There were Followers of the Way in Jerusalem until the city was destroyed by the Romans in 70 A.D. When that happened, they fled to other places, so there really was no particular location or home site of the church. There were several Christian communities in that part of the world, which grew rapidly and became known among the churches — Antioch, Alexandria, Ephesus, Rome — but there was never a Christian 'homeland.'

"And before the First Century was out, all the original disciples had died, yet the church was growing. Like they say these days, 'It had gone viral!'" Winnie concluded, "Can you see the changes that were made in the space of a generation among the early church, yet she grew stronger and greater, even so," Winnie caught her breath.

"That is amazing; I'll have to agree," John admitted. "Those are changes that you wouldn't expect an unorganized group of simple people to withstand. How could it? I've read about others who tried to proclaim themselves to be the Messiah, and some of those men had quite a following while they were on earth, but after they died their movements died, too.

"Yes, I can see that the activity of the Holy Spirit must have been a great influence in the early church, and I'll give the Holy Spirit credit for the communities moving forward, notwithstanding those great changes."

Winnie hoped this discussion helped John understand, better, how much the church is part of God's activity on earth, leading her by the Holy Spirit. "You can see how the church has overcome so many obstacles and continued to flourish and reach out. Does that not speak of how the church is part of God's plan for God's Kingdom?" she asked.

John didn't reply immediately; rather he thought he'd hold his thoughts for now. Instead he said, "Those events are significant, I'll admit. I can better see how the early church began to grow, adding people from all around the known world. I'm looking forward to the studies I want to take this fall, but ... that's not a real answer for me today."

"We don't have to come to a final conclusion this evening," Winnie agreed. "How about we find some place to worship tomorrow and figure out other stuff later?"

✳ ✳ ✳

The church they finally decided to visit was a bit further away from Hyde Park, but they found it very welcoming and attractive. Winnie was pleased to see a wide range of ages as well as ethnicities represented in the church. The building was old, sporting a dense net of ivy growing up the stone walls. The bulletin included several pages of activities for young and old. She listened carefully to the message the pastor gave and was pleased to hear it was well thought out and scholarly. The illustration added nicely to the theme of the sermon. *"He does well preaching; I would enjoy hearing him again,"* Winnie thought.

After church the Daniels stood in line to greet the pastor. Winnie introduced herself to Rev. Moody as an elder from the Holston Annual Conference and that she had just moved up to Chicago. Rev. Moody encouraged the Daniels to come back, to St. Timothy UMC. Winnie hoped that could be the case.

✳ ✳ ✳

The next day John and Winnie left their house after breakfast and drove over to John's apartment. He hadn't returned since he left for the wedding weeks ago. He simply locked the door and left everything for later. Today was 'later'; he and Winnie would begin packing up the apart-

250

ment and moving the stuff over to their new house. John didn't know how much time it might take to clear the entire place, but he expected it might take the better part of a week.

"I have to admit, Win, I have some trepidations about today," John admitted as they drove.

"Really? What's to be nervous about? I'm sure the apartment won't have changed any since you left!" Winnie teased her new husband.

"No. I'm not nervous about the apartment, but about you helping me pack up my stuff. You remember your reaction the last time you came here. You nearly gagged! I don't want you to have to go through that again," John explained.

"I'm quite sure I'll be all right this time. For one thing we're not moving into your apartment, and I don't have to figure how in the world I could possibly fit myself into the place. We've already done much work on our new house, and you know it's beginning to look like home for us. We'll just look carefully at your things and figure what will work in our house and what things might need to be given away. The bedroom next to our master bedroom will make a fine place for your library."

As it turned out, the apartment move went fine. There were a few tense moments when John found he could not let go a volume or some other, favorite object, so Winnie designated a box for those 'special' items. She was figuring that she could set up a corner in the library to display those gems.

Chapter 27. Plans in the Making

(August 27, 2009)

"This committee shall come to order," Mayor Greeley announced to Misty Falls' Playground Committee. The dozen members of the committee fell silent, awaiting their individual turns to present reports.

"I want to thank each of you, hard working committee members for the long hours and great efforts you have put into organizing our new town playground," the mayor continued. "I believe this effort, which has been significant for each of us, will yield a community playground that will serve the families of Misty Falls for years to come. It will provide a safe, healthy, inviting locale for our children to stretch their abilities and grow in confidence on monkey bars, balance beams, and all the Jungle Jim activities, and it will provide countless hours of fun for families of all ages. I so believe in this project that I have spent countless hours communicating my interest in our new playground to every donor I could find. I believe each of you committee members here have acted similarly, and I think we are about to reap the benefits of our time and effort.

"I will now turn the meeting over to our very capable general contractor, Mr. Theo Smith," the mayor concluded and sat down.

Theo Smith, who was Lucy Jane's father, was semiretired when Mayor Greeley asked him to take on the playground project and act as its general contractor. He accepted the post willingly and found it a worthy challenge.

The design of the playground had already been drawn up, presented to the committee, and agreed upon. The playground would encompass an acre of land southeast of the depot. The committee had worked for months pulling all the details together.

Theo stood up to address the committee members. "As you heard from our mayor, the playground project is gaining momentum and I believe we are closing in on the final weeks before Action Weekend, when we will erect the playground. If at the end of our meeting today it appears that the required benchmarks have been met, we shall name the date on the calendar and begin our final surge, which is gathering all the workers — lay folks, 'gofers', and supporters, as well as those who are more at home using tools and building. They will populate our building teams."

The rest of the meeting consisted of reports from the different captains in charge of specific pieces of the project: fundraising events, site preparation, design day, order day, equipment delivery, build day, personnel organizing, and grand opening / dedication day.

Following the reports, the committee agreed that enough progress had been made, and they agreed on a date for Action Weekend, December 12th and 13th.

* * *

The semiannual Misty Falls' Community Pastors' Meeting convened on Thursday following the Fall Festival to plan the next community worship service — The Community Thanksgiving service.

"Good evening, brothers in Christ," Kenneth Creighton, pastor of First Baptist Church, began. Our first order of business is to welcome the newest member of our group — Pastor Clive Weston, who is taking Pastor Winnie Taylor's place at Muddy Creek United Methodist Church.

"Clive, we are happy to welcome you to our community. Have you and your wife made a good landing? Tell us something about yourself and your ministry"

Pastor Weston smiled and nodded his head to his colleagues around the table. "Thank you so much for your kind words Brother Ken. Yes, I think Deb and I have been the recipients of a very warm welcome here in Misty Falls.

"My wife and I have been in the pastoral ministry for fourteen years, and we've served four churches during that time. Before I became a pastor I worked for 23 years as a city planner in Chattanooga, so I'm a retread, you could say. My previous appointment was in Knoxville where I served on staff at First Centenary United Methodist Church for six years, so Deb and I think it's about time for us to get back out in the country.

"My misses and I come from Seymore, TN. We were sweethearts in school, so we come from country stock. It's very good to be here among y'all."

Pastor Ken spoke again, "We have an added piece of agenda that I would like to present this evening. I have been in contact with an old school chum of mine, the Rev. Phineas Cobb. We were roommates at Dallas Theological, and we've kept in touch all these years. Some of you will recognize his name, as he has been doing some really fine work for the LORD with his revivals in the South. He runs his revivals very much along the lines of the Billy Graham Crusades. He will come into the community and work with the local churches to set up a community-wide revival. Local churches will provide volunteers to meet with responders to the invitation, so they can be immediately connected to a local fellowship and encouraged to grow in their faith.

"I discovered that Phineas has an opening for a three-day revival this fall, and, if we decide we'd like to sponsor such an effort, we could have him here on a crusade for Christ then." Ken sat down and awaited reactions.

Matthew Brand, the Pentecostal pastor, began. "Ken, that sounds like quite an opportunity for Misty Falls. We've never had a town-wide revival before, but I think such an event could be very good for us. Think how it would be if we were all revived at the same time!"

Tinsley Booker, from Faith AME (African Methodist Episcopal Church), spoke up saying, "Matthew and Ken are both right. This could be a wonderful opportunity for us, but it sounds to me like we're looking at a very short fuse. How much time would we have, and do you think we could put such a revival together so quickly?"

"You're right Tinsley, but if we all make this a priority and really lean into it, I think we can make it happen," Pastor Allen Remington of St. Luke's Cumberland Presbyterian said agreeing with the Baptist pastor.

Ken Creighton spoke up again, "We would have help from Phineas' team. They have done dozens and dozens of these crusades all across the States. They would help us work with the community ahead of time, so we would have professional help putting this together.

Ed Lorentzen, the Church of Christ pastor, asked, "Money would be a factor, too. I suppose we could borrow money from our community chest to get started, but I have no idea what such an undertaking might require. I don't suppose our little fund could cover it all."

"That's one of the good parts of this type of revival, Ed, it almost takes care of itself. I believe the Phineas Cobb Revival leaves a portion of their receipts to the community. We could even benefit from hosting it," Pastor Creighton responded.

Tinsley Booker, the pastor at Faith AME, spoke up, "Sounds like we all agree about having a revival in Misty Falls. One of the things I particularly like about it is that we would be working together to reach out to our community. Too often when we do revivals it seems like we're in competition with the other churches in town, and that should never be the case. We aren't in competition, we're each working for the LORD, trying to make a good place for worship and learning for whomever He brings our way."

Pastor Remington spoke up, "We've never had a community revival in Misty Falls, and I think we could all benefit from such an event. Like Tinsley just said, 'We're not in competition with one another.' A three day community revival could breathe some healthy Spirit into our town and nourish all our souls. Our semiannual community gatherings always make me wonder what if we extended this warm, thankful, joyful fellowship to something more? We all know the power of the Spirit is there in those occasions, and a community revival could be a great boost for our whole town."

More conversation resulted in the pastors agreeing to work with their church people in the next week and then reconvene the following Thursday to develop a steering committee. Planning this revival would not

take a long time; it couldn't take long. The evangelist's window of availability was only four weeks away!

The revival would not be difficult to pull together. Southern
churches have had years and years of experience putting them on.
Everyone agreed it would be a spiritual boon for Misty Falls.

❋ ❋ ❋

Lucy Jane McPherson lived with her dad and mom, Theo and
Mary Nell Smith, on a ranch outside of town. She had returned to Misty
Falls the previous year, a few weeks after her husband Chet's death.
Theirs had been a short marriage (a second marriage for both of them),
but they had hoped for many, good years of wedded bliss, including children, but it wasn't to be. Chet's illness surprised them both, and he was
gone within weeks.

Lucy Jane moved back to Misty Falls to be near her family. She
was pleased to be able to transfer her job, working with the Red Cross,
from Louisville to Kirby, TN, not far from Misty Falls. It was good to have
the job to give her some structure to her life as she moved through this
time of grief. She still felt the pain of losing Chet, but very gradually her
pain was abating.

Lucy Jane had received a surprise gift just before Thanksgiving
last year. A man named Dan Moore appeared, seemingly out of the blue,
to Misty Falls, looked her up, and gave her a check for over $15,000!
Turns out the money came from an investment Chet and Dan had made
long before when they were in the Air Force. They invested in a housing
development in New Mexico, and the investment had been cashed in earlier in '08. Dan Moore was native of Misty Falls, and his mother still lived
in town. Dan had flown to Misty Falls to visit his mother, and in the process, he handed Lucy Jane the money. What a great and unexpected surprise!

Lucy Jane hadn't determined exactly what she would do with this
windfall, but she wanted to make it count for something that would honor
Chet. One idea in the back of her mind was to use the money in some
way to help children in the community. She and Chet had wanted to fill
their home with children, and that couldn't happen now, but perhaps there
was something she could do for the children in Misty Falls.

❋ ❋ ❋

Trudy was surprised to see how often her thoughts fled to Ned.
She hadn't spent much time dwelling on him this past year, but now, after
she had just relived in her mind those couple of days when they met, she
couldn't dissuade herself of the thought of him. It was as if someone had
ordered her not to think of elephants, which would have the effect of causing her to think of nothing but the great beasts!

Thoughts of Ned filled her mind much of the time. When she gazed into Kareem's face, she saw Ned. The baby was favoring his father more and more each day, and Trudy wondered how much alike father and son might be. Ned was a man with so many God-given talents — his natural athletics, his sharp mind, his kind demeanor. Trudy hoped her tiny child would grow up to be very much like his dad.

Thinking of Ned couldn't help but cause Trudy to consider how she might introduce her child to his father. She couldn't just drop the subject of Ned's fatherhood on him in a casual conversation. Trudy found herself imagining dozens of scenarios involving Ned and herself, and in each scene she would try to casually interject the idea of babies, or children, or Kareem. None of the vignettes she built in her mind worked at all! She found herself quickly denying these imagined occasions.

No, I can't just drop the subject on Ned. I had good reason for not telling him to begin with, and that reason has not changed. I can't tell Ned about his fatherhood, because it could, or more likely, it would, cause him to lose his scholarship to the Air Force Academy. That was the whole reason I didn't tell anyone. I don't want to ruin Ned's life. If I told Ned about his being a father, unless he totally ignored or rejected the news, it's very possible he could put his entire future into jeopardy. I don't think that the Air Force Academy allows students to be parents or to get married or, or, or ...?

"*Maybe I shouldn't even consider telling Ned. Or, perhaps at the right time, with the right words, I could gently plant the idea of his being a father in his thoughts. I would not in any way want to insinuate my world into his, but perhaps he would be interested in knowing he had a son. Hm ....*

As she considered her quandary, Trudy remembered conversations she had with Miss Winnie about informing the baby's father. Winnie hadn't told Trudy in so many words to tell Ned about his immanent fatherhood, but she certainly hadn't told her NOT to tell him. Winnie had asked Trudy about her own aspirations: did not her baby's advent change her life significantly? How was it that it was totally okay to disrupt her own life for the child, but she must never force a change into Ned's world?

As she was tossing this matter around, Trudy remembered something that Winnie had mentioned to her. Trudy knew her friend had made some giant changes in her own life, having to do with falling in love with Dr. Daniel and deciding to marry him. Miss Winnie told Trudy, "I never want to do anything that the LORD wouldn't want me to do. That's one of my rules of thumb, so to speak. If I'm about to do something, and I'm not sure if it's a good thing, then I ask myself the question, "Would I be proud of doing the thing? Would I be embarrassed to tell Jesus about it?" Then Winnie quickly added, "Of course, I think Jesus would know about it before I ever even began to do it. He just knows those things. He knows our hearts."

Trudy smiled as she remembered those words — that the LORD knows our hearts — and she realized that perhaps she had been thinking so much about Ned recently because in her heart she wanted at least to give him the option to know Kareem. *If Jesus already knows my heart, He knows I want to share this beautiful child with Ned somehow.*

Trudy wasn't a regular church goer, but she and her mom were members of Faith AME Church in Misty Falls. She had been active at Faith as a youngster and in the middle school youth group. Trudy especially loved to sing in the choir. She loved being up in front in church, singing her heart out to the LORD. She discovered how natural it felt to swing, and even step to the music and clap her hands as she sang. She would hold the microphone close to her mouth and belt out her praise to the LORD. Singing always felt right inside. She felt like she had been born to sing God's praise.

Trudy hadn't been to church in some time, but she did have faith in the LORD, and she knew Miss Winnie was right about following Jesus the best way she could.

Perhaps this notion of mine is coming from the LORD. Maybe He's putting this thought in my mind. If I use Miss Winnie's rule of thumb I would say, "No, I'm not embarrassed to have Jesus know my thinking — telling Ned that he's a father.

Trudy decided to take a very small step and see where it might lead. She would drop Ned a line just to say "Hi." Trudy looked around her room and found a piece of paper she could use. She was handy with graphics (she had always spent time doodling and drawing little pictures, so she made a cover for a note card.) She drew a picture of an airplane, one she found online, one that she thought might fit into an Air Force theme. The plane was flying into the heavens, nose up, jet stream off the back, small clouds in the background. Inside the card Trudy simply wrote: *Thinking of you. Are you flying high these days? Your Friend, Trudy.* Then, at the bottom of the card, she printed in small, neat letters her email address, so Ned could respond if he was inclined to do so.

Well, Girl, you never know what will come of this, but I'm going to trust God to use it for His purposes.

Trudy found an envelope and mailed the card the next day. She said a small prayer as she put it in the box to be mailed.

* * *

Plans were moving right along for the revival. Each pastor in the community pastors' group had returned to his own church and talked up the idea of Misty Falls having a revival, a real crusade that would attract unchurched people as well as revive church members. Everyone needs a boost from the Spirit at one time or another. We all need a new breath from the Spirit to help and encourage us along our walk with the LORD. Part of the people's enthusiasm came from discovering that so many churches in town were also participating in the revival. It really was as if all of Misty Falls was thinking together on the project.

Churches challenged their members to invite their neighbors to attend, to promise to attend the three nights themselves, to agree to serve in one capacity or another, insuring that all the needed positions for the revival — prayer support, logistical support, monetary support — were filled.

The date for the revival was end of October — the 23rd, 24th, and the 25th. The location of the revival would be First Baptist Church as it had the largest auditorium in town, and everyone was hopeful that there would be a good sized crowd attending.

Churches advertised the revival through their bulletins, newsletters, email, and social networks, The Misty Falls Chronicle, recognizing this was a community event, helped with ads of its own. Ken Creighton had a couple dozen posters made up and placed around town to promote the revival. The three day revival was well on its way to becoming a reality.

Each church provided several, mature Christians to be part of the prayer team. They would make themselves available to pray with and for anyone who responded to the evangelist's call.

* * *

Brother Phineas Cobb and his team would arrive on the afternoon of the 22nd, the day before Misty Falls' Revival. His organization had been in careful communication with the churches that were supplying the infrastructure for the three day event. Every aspect of the revival would flow smoothly, like well greased cogs in a wheel.

Music would be led by First Baptist's Joe Ed Rafferty, who so ably rose to such occasions. He met with the musical townsfolk Sunday evening before the kick off of the revival to run through an anthem for each night as well as hymns they would lead for the audience.

Special music would also be presented by Lydia and Malcolm James. The Jameses had been part of Phineas' team for ten years, and Phineas was well aware of their valuable contribution to the revivals. Lydia and Malcolm were top rate musicians, and their music added wonderful depth and spirit to an evening. They were well versed in several music genres — gospel, country, and classical. Malcolm was fluent in several instruments and would bring out his guitar, keyboard, or clarinet as needed, and Lydia was equally well versed in violin and fiddle playing. The two also included personal testimonies, which complemented Phineas' theme.

The revival team included just four members: Phineas, Lydia and Malcolm James, and Jeremy McKissen, their business manager. The team had come together to respond to the mission they believed they were called to accomplish, namely bringing people to faith in Christ through hometown revivals. It was an awesome responsibility, one they took most seriously.

* * *

Brother Phineas was not affiliated with a particular denomination, but he was well received among Christian groups. His personal charisma, elegant preaching, and history of bringing great numbers of people to faith in God made him an evangelist in demand. He was highly respected in the world of Christian evangelism; his name was becoming very well known, even among the general public, yet he remained a humble man.

Phineas was the brains and the skill that made the revivals work. Not unlike John Wesley, whom he studied, Phineas asked much of himself. Phineas wanted to be the man he projected himself to be — an authentic follower of Jesus.

The remarkable success of his crusades forced him to be especially vigilant about his Christian walk.

Years previous, just following the second revival in 1999, the team gathered in a hotel room after breakfast when Jeremy McKissen interrupted the conversation to say, "As business manager for PCC [Phineas Cobb Crusades] I believe it falls to me to keep us all aware of any situations related to business."

Phineas, Lydia, and Malcolm, who had been half listening to Jeremy when he first spoke, hushed their voices and turned their heads to give him their complete attention.

"We came into this venture trusting the LORD that we would be able to manage the costs of the revival against the receipts that we hoped would come in ...," Jeremy stopped.

"Are you about to tell us that we've incurred a debt?" Phineas leaned forward, crinkled his brows, asking nervously.

The Jameses followed Phineas' lead and leaned forward, looking expectantly at Jeremy.

"No, we aren't in debt," he shook his head.

"Well, if we aren't having a cash problem and we aren't falling into debt, then what are you talking about?" Malcolm James asked.

Jeremy lips began to crinkle, and a smile grew on his face, "I don't think any of us thought that money might be a problem in the way I'm seeing, but I think we need to make some careful decisions about our finances, nonetheless."

"What are you telling us, Brother Jeremy?" Phineas was trying to imagine what decisions needed their thoughtful consideration.

"What I'm trying to tell y'all is that a lot more money came in last night than we ever figured we'd see," the business manager announced.

Jeremy's words hung in the air, as each person in the room wondered what money might mean to them.

Phineas broke the silence, "A lot more money, Jeremy? We're already recognizing that our revivals are more costly to put on than we expected, so it's good that we're not falling into the red due to those expenses. And as we continue no doubt we'll incur other expenses — research, copyrights, music, even sound equipment — not to mention the costs for our travel, lodgings, and what-not. Is there more income than those expenses, including our escrow account for future gigs?

The Jameses nodded their heads, agreeing with their leader.

Jeremy took a big breath, smiled, and said, "Well, maybe this community is especially giving, or there's someone with really deep pockets who was moved to contribute to us, but what I'm saying is that the receipts from this revival are nearly seven times what we brought in with our first revival last month. We were pleased that our first revival broke even with a little left over to help us in the next revival. This time, not only did we clear our expenses and pay each of us for our work, but we have enough to sponsor our next five revivals!"

"I can see your concern, Jeremy, and I'm completely behind you. If this becomes a pattern, and we continue to see surprising generosity from the people, we should have some sort of plan in mind, to protect ourselves from ourselves," Phineas nodded.

This time Lydia James spoke, asking, "Wait a minute, Brother Phineas, I hope you're not going to put us all in a position of poverty. I know there are religious orders whose members live by that rule, and that's fine for them. Those people were called to that sort of lifestyle, but I don't know that our little band has been called for that. I do think we should look reasonably well put together when we're out in front of the crowd."

Malcolm, who was sitting next to Lydia, put his arm about his wife's shoulder and said, "I'm with Lydia on this. I don't know that we can live on peanut butter and jelly everyday, always. I think we do need a plan — one that will guard us against those abuses of money we've seen hurt others in our profession — but let's do it wisely."

The four friends tossed several ideas around that morning, wanting to be fair and wise. Jesus had told his disciples they should be wise as serpents yet innocent as doves. In fact, Jesus said a great deal about money and the use of money. The team spent some time that morning scouring the gospels, searching for wisdom from the LORD, which would help them determine how to proceed in matters of money.

Lydia said, "I really enjoy working with each of you guys. Y'all are men of God, and I count it a blessing to be associated with you. I know we're going to come up with a reasonable guide for our use of money."

It was finally agreed that PCC, their business, would take care of all the logistics for the revivals — travel, housing, printing, etc. Each member of the team would also be taken care of by the business — food, lodging, and revival attire. Beyond that, each member would receive a modest allowance, which they could use for giving and personal items. The allowance was not meager, but it was not audacious, either. What the group was trying to obtain was a simplified living style. They wanted to avoid, at all costs, the troubles that too many others in their line of work had succumbed to. They hoped their efforts in the use of money would be a serious deterrent to such foolishness. They also figured that, in the case of an emergency, the matter could be placed for a vote among the four and determined then.

This plan to handle the proceeds from the revivals worked well. Other funds derived from a revival would go to specific charities that had already been established. The team was proud that they had been able to bring clean water to a small village in Africa, and immunizations to children in India, and meet several other needs, as well.

As for women, Phineas was watchful. While he was in seminary in Dallas, Phineas found himself identifying with St. Paul, the apostle, missionary, and writer of much of the New Testament. The more Phineas studied Paul, the more he wanted to emulate him. Paul was his spiritual hero, the one he patterned his life after. Paul likened following Christ to competing in a race — one engages in a race to win the medal. Paul called his people to run full out, so they could finish well their course. Phineas knew that Paul had followed his own counsel and had run as hard and as long as he could in following the LORD. Paul's challenge became Phineas' theme in life — to run full out as he followed his LORD. Phineas believed that his success in ministry was related to his vigilant efforts to stay on task, to study and prepare his sermons, to walk with the LORD the best way he could each day.

Since St. Paul was Phineas' spiritual mentor, he paid attention to Paul's urging that Christians not marry. Indeed, Paul noted how those who are married use much of their time and resources maintaining their marriage rather than only serving the LORD. Paul did add that marriage was preferred over burning with passion, but, still, the single life was recommended.

Phineas had taken Paul's words to heart, and he decided, for the sake of his ministry, he would not go down the marriage path. Although Phineas was aware that the single life was not an easy path to walk, he believed it to be his calling as an evangelist.

Phineas had had a couple of close calls in this arena when he was younger — there was his high school sweetheart, Tammy Lynn, and Julia in seminary — but both of those women had later found spouses and were now happily married. Phineas believed that he was past that vulnerable time in life, and he was reasonably assured that, as long as he kept eternal vigilance on himself, he would be fine.

The Phineas Cobb Crusade did two, and sometimes three, crusades per month in a calendar year. The long hours, the constant traveling, eating out day in and day out, all were part of their routine. They considered theirs was a much easier path than the one walked by Paul and his band of missionaries 2000 years earlier.

The weekend in October, which was set aside for a little town called Misty Falls, Tennessee, had originally been reserved for another town closer to Chattanooga, but that revival had been cancelled due to the town suffering from severe storms in the late summer. The town needed to spend its efforts and energy on cleaning up the area, so the crusade was put off until next year.

✳ ✳ ✳

Connie and George were not having an easy time. Since the twins were now gone, the Olivers could only see the girls on Friday mornings at the DHR office, and then only for ninety minutes. Connie and George had been drifting apart. George was away some of the time. George and his mother-in-law, Sallie, didn't get along very well, and Connie wondered if George was just avoiding seeing her, but when George was gone several days at a time, Connie knew something else was up.

One morning before work Connie asked, "Do you think we can make it to the classes tonight?"

George was silent, pretending not to hear Connie's question.

"George, please, answer me. Do you think we can make it to the anger management class tonight?" Connie pled.

George raised his eyebrows and turned away from his wife. He mumbled something, but Connie wasn't sure what he said.

"Come on, George. You know we need to attend the classes, and we have to pass them, or we'll never get our girls back," Connie added. "Will you come home in time, so we can get over there tonight?"

George remained silent.

Connie walked up to him and looked him straight in the eyes. "We need to do this together, to show them that we can handle ourselves in a civil manner. I know we can do it. We just have to follow the requirements they set for us."

George finally agreed that he'd be home after work, probably about 5:30 p.m. They would have time to get to the classes, which began at 6:30 in the DHR office.

Connie drew a breath of relief after George had left for work. She and George had attended one of the prescribed anger management classes, but George hated it, and he didn't want to return. That had been one reason that Connie and George had been battling recently, but Connie wondered if George's absences indicated other problems she wasn't aware of. *Where could George be going when he didn't come home at night?*

Chapter 28. Understandings

(late September 2009)

About a week later Connie and George came to an uncomfortable understanding.

George had been away for a couple of days, but he showed up for dinner on Monday night.

"I'm sorry, Connie," George began.

"What are you talking about, George?" Connie answered.

"You've been very patient with me, but you shouldn't be. I'm not worth it," George explained.

"I guess I don't follow what you're talking about, George," Connie answered.

"I've decided I'm no good. I've hurt too many people, and I've really screwed up," George admitted.

"What do you mean?" Connie wondered aloud.

"It seems like everything we do, we end up having trouble. It was bad enough when we lost our babies in Greenville, but I thought, we thought, it could be different by our starting over somewhere else ...," George began.

Connie could see that George was really hurting, and she wanted to help, but she didn't know what to do. She sat and listened. She could feel tears beginning to well up in her eyes.

"I've not been a good husband to you ... I've not been entirely truthful with you," George was saying.

"George, what are you trying to tell me?" Connie was growing alarmed.

"Don't you ever wonder where I go when I'm not home at night?" George asked.

"Well, yes, I wonder," Connie said, wishing this conversation would come out differently than it seemed to be heading.

"You're mom is right ... I've been going back to Greenville to see my other family," George admitted.

"Oh ... I see." Connie said slowly, as the truth began to dawn on her. "You've been going back to be with Tanya, not just the kids, haven't you?"

George nodded his head slowly in the affirmative. "It's not that I don't love you. You know I do, but ..."

"There can't be any **buts** about that!" Connie stood firm. She raised her voice and asked, "How can you go back to Tanya and still say you love me? Your marriage to her was over a long time ago. Wasn't it? That's what you told me! That's why I ...," Connie couldn't continue her thought.

"My marriage was over when you and I hooked up; I think it had been over for some time by then. I didn't have the same feelings for Tanya that you brought out in me back then," George answered.

"This isn't right. It's just not right at all!" Connie was adamant. She turned away and stared at the floor.

"I agree. It doesn't feel right, but I just don't know what to do," George hung his head and wagged it back and forth.

After some time Connie spoke, "I didn't need this news today. Seems like we've had nothing but trouble since we left Greenville — coming here and having the babies and having them with us only a few months before we lost them to the DHR — and now you're acting so weird! How do you think I should feel? You're back with Tanya, and where does that leave me?" Tears were streaming down Connie's face as the realization of her predicament became clearer and clearer.

George left the house, jumped in his car, and drove off.

Sallie ventured out of her bedroom when she heard George leave and said, "I couldn't help overhearing, Connie. I'm so sorry."

Connie ran from the living room to her bedroom and slammed the door. She'd had about as much as she could stand of everything in her life. She felt that her world, which had been tenuous at best, was coming apart at the seams, and she despaired of finding an answer. She fell on her knees at the side of her bed and prayed.

"Jesus, I'm hurting. I'm hurting so bad, and I don't know what to think or do. It's like I'm all covered with mud. I feel dirty all over, and there doesn't seem to be any way for me to get clean.

"You know how bad I feel. I think you know the many ways I've failed. Maybe you know more about my failings than even I do. George and I thought we could right the wrong of my first pregnancy by his divorcing Tanya and marrying me. Maybe that was where things completely fell off the track. I don't know, but I can see I'm experiencing some of the pain of my bad actions.

"Oh, Jesus, if you're real, you're my last hope! Help me, please. I beg you to help me. I really don't know where else to turn."

Connie's tears and sobbing continued for some time. Eventually she climbed onto her bed and fell asleep.

✳ ✳ ✳

Nina kept busy. As a nurse for Dr. Sedgwick she wanted to keep up with the latest in medicine, so she spent much of her personal time reading medical journals and online nursing articles. She was even considering returning for an advanced degree in nursing. She always enjoyed the challenge of learning more about her science, and she wanted to stretch as far as she could professionally.

There was a junior college in Knoxville that offered courses she could take, but that would involve being on the road a night or two each week. Then Nina thought she might investigate what was available online in the way of degree work.

Nina was much more at home in the kitchen than at the computer." *The computer clearly is the new way of the world, and anyone who doesn't use a computer is basically lost in today's world as far as business is concerned*," she thought. Finally, Nina decided to put her toe in the water and try one course online to see how it went. She was happily surprised that it was more interesting and not terribly requiring of computer skills. She definitely enjoyed the challenge.

Nina didn't realize how much she would miss her friend, Winnie. After all the commotion and fun of the wedding in late June and the honeymoon, the newlyweds had departed for Chicago where they were beginning to build their new nest.

Winnie had been super about keeping up with email. That was a fun part of the computer, and Nina certainly appreciated how quickly she could communicate with her children and now Winnie.

Winnie wrote an email to Nina a couple times a week, updating Nina on her progress in the new house. Winnie and John had worked like beavers unpacking and placing the stuff Winnie had brought from Misty Falls; then they attacked John's apartment and figured what could be moved to their new house. According to Winnie, the honeymoon was continuing — what a blessing!

Nina was happy for them, of course, but she missed having Winnie around and hearing her exciting news directly from her. Once Winnie moved out of the church's parsonage in mid-June, she needed a place to stay. She wouldn't be moving on to another church, and her wedding would be at Muddy Creek Church ten days later.

When Nina realized Winnie needed a place to stay, she immediately offered her friend a bedroom in her house. The two women enjoyed some good girlfriend time then.

Nina was invited to join Winnie's family for dinner when they arrived in town the day before the wedding. Everyone went to the barbecue place over in Kirby. It wasn't exactly a rehearsal party, because there had not been a wedding rehearsal. John wouldn't arrive until about noon the next day, just in time for the wedding. He drove down from Chicago with his friends from school, the two professors, Dr. Chester Twingate and Dr. Marian Quincy-Twingate.

Winnie explained to Nina that the university classes weren't out until mid-June, and then the professors had to grade their students' work following that. John's students wrote research papers, which would take him the better part of a week to pour through and assess. He had arranged with the Twingates to drive with him to Misty Falls on Saturday for the wedding. Chester would stand up for John during the ceremony. Afterwards John and Winnie would leave for their honeymoon, and the Twingates planned to tour the area and return to Chicago in John's Honda.

"I have to be envious of Winnie," Nina thought. *"She is on a real adventure in a whole new world with a completely new agenda. John seems to be the catch we hoped he was. He was certainly charming when I met him at the wedding. I just hope they stay as happy as they've started out to be,"* Nina thought to herself.

"*I wonder if I'll ever find someone for me?"* She mused. *"Work and school are fine, and I'm very glad I've got them. I love my job at Dr. Sedgwick's office, and this nursing admin class is more fun than I thought it would be. I shouldn't feel sorry for myself. Winnie showed me that even we widows have a chance for romance. She would tell me that life hasn't left me by the wayside."*

Nina didn't know how or what to do to make a change in her life, but she knew she would be watching for possibilities that might come her way.

* * *

Tucker Joe had a problem. He was very good at figuring out problems; he always thought that was one of his best gifts — problem solving. His knack for solving problems had stood him well in business all these years. Even as a young man, just coming into his folks' grocery business, he seemed to have a way of making wise decisions that would keep Friendlie's Foods strong. The grocery business was a difficult world because of the very slim profit margin they had to work with. Whereas many retail stores figured double-digit profits, grocery stores typically had profits more like 3-5% and sometimes less.

The problem that Tucker Joe was thinking about was not business related. If it were that simple he was sure he could manage it, but Tuck's problem was personal.

Tuck was aware that he was a workaholic — work was what he did, what made him successful. He knew what needed to be done, and he pressed into it.

Personal issues didn't really require work, not work like he knew it. He didn't see a way to work his way through this personal problem

Before Tuck's mother died, he had begun to think of finding a nice woman friend, someone who might turn out to be more than a friend. He had taken Nina Mattingly out on three occasions back then, and they had had some really enjoyable evenings together. Their dates had been to little theatre presentations, and those evenings were full of laughter and lightness. Nina had a wicked sense of humor, and Tuck appreciated it. He also had a special interest in little theatre; he loved live performances and sitting up close to the stage where he could see the players well. Nina was pleasant and friendly, a fun companion. They certainly enjoyed the shows together.

But just as Tuck was beginning to think he had found someone to spend time with, his mother got ill. At first her illness took her away from the store, causing Tuck to have to work longer hours, opening and closing the store each day. Then, when his mother didn't get better, he had to ask his employees to work longer, so he could take time to be with his mom. Mother didn't last long after she was diagnosed with cancer. Her death gave Tuck more responsibilities, being the sole owner of Friendlie's Foods, and his social life plummeted out of existence.

A year ago Lucy Jane returned to town, and she and Tucker Joe had a couple of intriguing encounters. Tuck and Lucy Jane were closer in age than he and Nina were; he and Lucy Jane had both attended the county high school over in Kirby. She was just a year ahead of him. Tucker Joe knew that he was especially attracted to Lucy Jane, but she had just lost her husband last year. Tuck didn't suppose she was ready for a new relationship yet.

So, there were two women in Tucker Joe's life, sort of. What might he do?

* * *

Trudy mailed her note to Ned, crossed her fingers and hoped for the best. *"What is the best to hope for?" She wondered. "What should I hope will come of this small memory jogger I'm sending him?"*

Half a week later Trudy found an email from Ned in her in box. She could hardly believe it. She read each word slowly, hoping the words would stretch just a bit longer:

"Trudy! What a great surprise I got in the mail today! I love your personally designed notecard. Yes, I am flying high these days. I haven't been up in a plane yet; It's not part of my curriculum, but that may come, too. I am pleased to tell you that I am doing very well at the Academy holding down a 3.8 GPA the last four semesters! I especially enjoy the engineering courses, although I find the sciences equally challenging and compelling. Don't know exactly what sort of profession I shall come away with, but since the U. S. Air Force has me in their plan for five years following commissioning, as I must pay Uncle Sam back for my years spent at the Academy, I won't have to worry about a future profession for some time.

I trust that you are also well and enjoying what you're doing.

Drop me another note and tell me more about what you're up to! I can imagine you're enjoying your classes, too.

Thanks for the great pick-me-up!

Your Friend,
Ned

Ned's email made Trudy's day. She quickly memorized every line in the email and replayed it in her mind again and again.

Trudy wanted to reply to Ned's email. He had responded to her little card, and she was thrilled about that. On the other hand, she didn't quite know what to say in reply. She couldn't tell Ned about Kareem, not yet. She wanted to spend a little time getting to know more about Ned, somehow letting him know her personally before she divulged anything about the child they had parented together.

* * *

Chapter 29. The Revival

(Late October 2009)

The days were beginning to act like fall — cooler weather, shorter days, awesome sunsets, leaves changing their hues to everyone's delight, which meant the time for the revival was fast approaching in Misty Falls. Members of every church in town had been charged up by their pastors to prepare for a new experience in town. Each pastor encouraged his strongest leaders, those who were spiritually committed, to join their crusade prayer team. They would meet together initially to learn the procedure — how to stand by and watch for those who might make their way down to the altar rail for prayer. A team member would walk over to a respondent and kneel next to the person and pray with him or her. Then, after the prayer and the music had ceased, the team member would lead the person over to a side room, where hospitality would be offered and a chance for the respondent to ask questions or pray some more. Addresses, emails, phone numbers would be exchanged, so there could be follow up, and helpful literature (Bible verses, tracts, and a list of local churches would be provided to the responders.)

This plan usually worked well. It was low key, but it provided for all who heard the call of the evangelist to be cared for and encouraged along their new walk in faith.

* * *

Connie was not a church goer; not since she'd been married five years earlier had she been to church. Her new life with George just didn't include church. Connie remembered that the Oliver family used to belong to a church, but George had never suggested that the two of them attend worship somewhere. Connie did enjoy listening to the radio stations that broadcast Christian music and inspirational programming. She particularly enjoyed hearing preachers on the radio. They had an important message, she thought, and she loved to hear them preach — especially when those preachers would get loud and begin to holler about everyone being a sinner: *"There is no one righteous, no not one."* Hearing about the sinfulness of humans, all humans, Connie felt she should pay attention; she could identify with others who had failed. She certainly knew she was among them. The preachers would not just stop after proclaiming how everyone had failed, but they would go on to say, because Jesus died on the cross, all our sins have been taken away. Jesus paid the price for our sins Himself. *Somehow, that message felt very good. Could it possibly be true?* Connie wondered.

Connie had been working for months at a little cafe, Countrified Cuisine, just across the road from her apartment. She had started by bussing tables and working part of the time in the kitchen during the lunch period. She really enjoyed learning about the activities in the kitchen — retrieving items from the big, walk-in refrigerator, loading the dishwasher, scrubbing the big, greasy griddle by rubbing a large, pumice stone back and forth over the smooth surface to clean it. She discovered, very quickly, to be most careful not to let the grease swish over her hand, or she would be nursing a second degree burn for days.

The owner, Ms. Reynolds, noticed Connie's diligence at whatever she was asked to do. She never complained about work and was always happy to comply, even for the most unlovely of jobs. It didn't take long before Connie began working the register out front, too. Ms. Reynolds recognized Connie's quickness, and she encouraged her as a protege to learn various aspects of the cafe business.

Connie's work at the cafe was time spent out of her world, and she grew to appreciate it. She could be a different person at the cafe. She wasn't dragged down by her past or her present at work. No one knew Connie or her problems; she could pretend they didn't exist, at least that was so while she was working.

One day in mid-October Connie noticed a small, colorful poster had been placed next to the checkout counter at the cafe. The poster was advertising a revival that was going to be held at First Baptist Church the following weekend. Everyone in Misty Falls was encouraged to come and hear the famous evangelist, the Reverend Phineas Cobb. There would be special music and a warm atmosphere. *If you feel a need to grow closer to God, come. If you feel you've lost your spiritual compass, come. If you would like to be filled with God's Holy Spirit, come. Let God fill you with His love.* Connie read the ad several times while she was working that day, and she decided that she would go ... just to see. Since she worked the lunch shift at the cafe most weeks, her work would not interfere with the revival, and there was nothing else to keep her away. George had vanished again, and the babies were not around. Why not see what the revival was about?

✳ ✳ ✳

Nina didn't think she would be interested in some old revival. She had seen several of the signs around town — at the Depot Diner and even in the doctor's office where she worked. The posters looked inviting, but Nina was not very interested in attending anything like that by herself. She was a bit bashful, and sitting alone among a crowd didn't appeal to her.

271

She happened to mention the revival in an email to Winnie, telling her about the upcoming event, which was being advertised all over town. Nina figured it would be well attended, as the whole town seemed to be abuzz talking about it. One of Dr. Sedgwick's patients even asked Nina if she was planning to attend. Nina blushed a little and admitted that she had not planned to attend. "Oh, but Rev. Cobb is supposed to be a fabulous preacher, a true man of God. I wouldn't miss the revival for anything." Miss Foxworthy assured Nurse Nina. "You really ought to consider attending at least one of the nights. You might find a real blessing there." Nina listened to her patient and dismissed the invitation quickly in her mind. She didn't like others poking her and telling her what was good for her, but when Nina told Winnie about the event in her email, she shouldn't have been surprised to hear her friend's response.

Winnie wrote, "I can just imagine you're not too keen on the revival, yourself. You've been burned before by church, I know, and you're still suspicious of church-related activities. I really don't blame you, if that's how you're feeling. Your experience with church is rather like a grief experience. You were hurt; you lost something you valued — your church community — and you don't want to be hurt again.

"Of course, you and I have enjoyed one another's friendship since we met, and I certainly consider you one of my very good friends! We are close, and I value us. (I also miss our gettings-together and our recipe sampling!)

"You might think of the revival as focusing on spiritual matters, not so much on church. Rev. Cobb is not affiliated with any church, although he is highly respected by many church people. He certainly has done his part in helping people better understand their own spiritual needs, even leading them to a closer walk with the LORD.

"I wonder why you happened to mention the revival to me? Could it be that it's more intriguing to you than you admit? I can see you laughing at me! That's okay."

Nina read Winnie's message about the revival and filed it in the back of her mind. She really didn't think she'd be attending it, but then something happened.

※ ※ ※

Tucker Joe had seen the ad for the revival for two weeks, as it hung in the window of Friendlie's Foods, both coming in and looking out. There were two ads, each telling about the upcoming revival. The revival was Friday night, Saturday night, and Sunday night at the Baptist church's big sanctuary. The revival was being led by the now famous Rev. Phineas Cobb, who was being proclaimed as the twenty-first century Billy Graham. He was bringing people to faith in Christ through his preaching.

Tuck hadn't been to church in years. His family had been members of Muddy Creek Methodist Church, and they always attended services at Christmas and Easter, but Tuck's work at Friendlie's required his attention. When he wasn't at the store, he was home either cooking for himself or hoping to get some rest. *I'm not really doing myself any favors, trying to do this all myself!* He chided himself. *Why don't I have a help-mate who could pick up some of this work?*

Well, Tucker Joe! You haven't spelled out that need in some time! You certainly used to think about meeting some nice, sweet girl, some pretty young thing, who would look good on my arm and make beautiful babies for me, but something happened to that. WHAT? He asked himself. *What, indeed, came of my dreams? Am I about to turn into a middle-aged man who can't have a mid-life crisis, because I haven't experienced the young life yet!*

Mom is gone. She did the lioness's share of the work around the house, along with her work at the store. Now I'm alone, and I need help. Maybe I should do more about this than just complain. What good does complaining do anyway?

Tucker Joe stopped right at mid-step and said, *Okay I'm going to make a real effort to find a wife for me. That's what I'm gonna do, and I'm going to start today.*

Tuck walked over to the ad for the revival and tore it off the window and looked at it. *Hm! This here revival might be a good place to start. A revival is a sort of a show. There will be live music and lots of people in the audience. I could ask someone to go with me tonight. It could be a sort of date.*

Suddenly, Tucker Joe realized that he had two possible women friends that he might ask to the revival — Nina and Lucy Jane.

"*Now that's an interesting quandary to have, I have to say,*" Tuck told himself. "*Before Mother passed I was sort of seeing Nina, and we got along real fine. I think she liked me, maybe as much as I liked her, but things got messed up for us when Mother got sick. Then, there's Lucy Jane. She's a real cutie, especially those long legs of hers (!), but she's still grieving for her late husband. He only passed away a bit ago, and that's hardly fair to her to lean on her for more than companionship. Hmm.*"

After more internal debate, Tuck went into his office and called Nina to see if she might be interested in attending the last evening of the revival.

"Hello, Nina, can you hear me?" Tuck asked over the phone.

"Yes, is that you, Tucker Joe?" Nina seemed surprised to hear from Tuck, calling so unexpectedly.

"You're hearing right," Tuck admitted. "I'm sorry it's been so long since I called you. Things got really busy when Mother was sick and dying, and somehow that threw me off my social world completely."

Nina was shaking her head in understanding, even though her caller couldn't see her response. She said, "Yes, I've noticed you in the store. I could tell you have been swamped, and I hope you're doing better now."

"I am, and I have been trying to be a little kinder to myself. I'm even taking Thursdays off these days, which helps me, I know. The reason I'm calling you today, is that I want to get out and do something out-side the store and the house. I was looking at a poster about the revival here this weekend, and I was wondering if you'd like to go with me this evening to see it?" Tuck said in one breath.

"Would I like to go with you to see the revival?" Nina repeated. "Tonight? You're thinking it's something like a show, like the ones we saw before," Nina was thinking out loud. Tuck didn't answer her, so Nina con-tinued, "Well, I guess that might be a fun thing to do. I hear there's a quite a crowd attending, so I suppose we would need to get there early enough to get good seats. When would you like to go?" She asked.

In a few minutes a time was set for later in the afternoon. Tuck would pick Nina up and they would make it a date. Nina even offered to have a little something for them to eat afterwards.

✳ ✳ ✳

George had been out of town since Friday, the day the revival began. He heard about the revival from Connie, but he wanted to be far away from her, if she was going to attend the revival. She had invited him to go with her, but he wasn't in the mood. He took off after work on Friday and found himself on the road back to Greenville. He would stay there and be out of the way for the weekend, he figured.

Since he had told Connie about his absences — how sometimes he returned to his first family in Greenville — he and Connie had been on very cool terms. He found himself reviewing over and over his admission to her. He had been unfaithful to her and to them as a couple when he went to Greenville. He originally rationalized the trips, saying to himself that he was going over to see his kids, but his kids were not very often home. Most of them had moved out of the house and were living in other parts of Greenville or even further away. When he showed up at the house, he might happen to see one of his kids, but more than likely he would not. Tanya Oliver, his first wife, was the only one still living at home. She had been cool, even angry, the first time George arrived at her house. She had no interest in taking him back and no interest in him spending time around her, but after some cajoling and pleading, George convinced Tanya that they could be friends again. After all they did have a great deal in common — their five children and twenty years of marriage.

One thing led to another, and before either of the two realized how quickly things can happen, they found they had come back together — like old times! George may have been pleased on one hand about that turn of events, but on the other hand he knew he had stepped wrong, very wrong. He had taken the easy road, leaving his apartment in Misty Falls where there was so much pain and so many problems.

LIfe with Connie was no picnic. She and George fought often, especially about George not wanting to take the anger management classes. He was doggone tired of Connie's tears. He was angry with him-self for acting the way he had been acting. Yet he felt he was boxed in on all sides with no right place to go. He didn't like himself in this place he was in, yet he had no idea where to go or what to do about it. There didn't seem to be any obvious answer for him.

George had an odd feeling that he couldn't shake when he awoke Sunday morning. The feeling was different from anything he'd felt before. It was as if something was about to happen; he felt agitated and nervous. He couldn't imagine what was bothering him, but the feeling had come upon him, rather like a personal cloud enveloping him. George felt antsy, like he needed to get moving somehow, and finally about noon he took off to drive back to Misty Falls.

The feeling continued as George drove, but he realized he didn't feel so down the further west he drove. Perhaps there was something he needed to say to Connie. Maybe she needed him. Maybe she was in some danger. George didn't know, but he felt he was headed in the right direction.

It was late afternoon when George arrived in Misty Falls; he found their apartment empty. Connie and Sallie were not there. George glanced around the kitchen and saw literature on the counter from the revival — bio's of the Phineas Cobb Crusade Team, a tract describing the way to salvation, and a brochure filled with lyrics of Christian songs. George figured that his wife and mother-in-law must be at the revival, as tonight was the last night of the crusade.

George felt a let down, as if he had missed whatever it was that he had been driving all afternoon to reach. He didn't know what he was missing, but he had the very strong sense that it was something important to him.

"Great Scott! #$$%^^%&&*&(^^," George cried out, "Now I'm imagining things! What in the world is wrong with me? What am I expecting? What am I searching for?"

George left the house and jumped back into his car. He watched himself turn and drive over to the Baptist church and circle around until he found a place to park. There were more cars parked in the church lot and the surrounding streets than George had ever seen in one place in Misty Falls. He wondered how it was so many cars or people had come to the revival.

George had no plan to attend the revival, yet his curiosity was aroused. He wondered what the big deal was about this gathering of people. "*I'll just slip in the very back of the auditorium and have a look-see,*" he told himself.

The mood of the audience was light and fun, George noted. He could tell the mood from the smiles on faces and the easy-listening sounds and rhythm of the music, which was playing in the background. The setting was not at all as he had expected, whatever that was. "*I guess I didn't know what to expect at a revival. It's been years since I attended one, and I really didn't figure on comin' tonight,*" George thought. He slipped into an empty pew at the at very back of the auditorium next to several older women who nodded to him as he took his seat.

Music was coming from two singers on the stage, and George was caught between paying attention to the singers and screening around the room. The musicians were a youngish couple, possibly a man and his wife, who were singing an old favorite gospel piece, one he remembered from his childhood — *'Tis So Sweet to Trust in Jesus.* The couple's voices blended well, George thought. The song ended, and the singers each picked up an instrument — a guitar and a violin. They began to introduce a new piece, something George had not heard. This tune was faster than the dreamy melody previous. It had a sort of toe tapping beat to it, which George enjoyed hearing. The woman put down her violin and began to sing, accompanied by the man's guitar. The song the woman sang was about finding a new friend, a very good friend, a friend she could count on. The friend was Jesus. This time the woman used the words from the former song and sang it to the new tune: "Jesus, Jesus, how I love him, how I've proved Him o'er and o'er," she sang. "Jesus, Jesus, precious Jesus, be my friend for evermore." The song ended and the instruments played a coda for several bars. Finally, the music ceased and the guitar player spoke.

He spoke in a gentle voice, as if he was speaking to each individual personally, as if he knew each person in the audience very well. "That's one of the greatest things about knowing Jesus — being a friend of His ... and Jesus being a friend of ours. I didn't always know Jesus as a friend. There was a time I thought He was in the enemy's camp. You see, I didn't know much about Him; I thought He was judging me. He asks so much, and I thought I couldn't measure up, and I didn't like what He seemed to be asking.

"But, you know? I was wrong about that. Jesus does ask a great deal from us, but he never asks more of us than we can do. He never puts more before us than what is possible for us, <u>and</u> the greatest thing He does is He forgives us and calls us to be His friend," The singer continued.

"Jesus, Jesus, how I love him. How I love him o'er and o'er. Jesus, Jesus, precious Jesus, be my friend forever more," the singer sang softly, as if he was singing to a small child. "Be my friend forever more."

The two musicians smiled around the room and walked off the stage.

When George had come into the church sanctuary he had scanned the room, just to see who might be there. He didn't expect to see anyone he knew, except, possibly, Connie and Sallie. He figured they were somewhere in the audience, and he was in no mood to see them right now. If he wanted to sit in this place and see what was going on, he didn't need anyone else to tell him or suggest to him that he needed to hear it. He might be interested in hearing the preacher, but he definitely didn't need anyone reminding him of the fact.

George didn't see anyone in the room who looked familiar from his vantage point, but he didn't spend much time reviewing the audience before his attention was directed back to the stage.

A man was walking onto the stage; he was not very impressive to look at. He was not tall. In fact he was about George's size — slightly built and maybe five and a half feet tall. He was clean shaven, save for a triangle goatee below his bottom lip, but his hair, which was mostly brown, hung about shoulder length, reminiscent of actors who brush their hair back. He was dressed in blue jeans and a black cowboy shirt with the yoke embellished by a double row of gold accent thread following the design of the yoke. His shirt was tucked in, showing off a leather belt and large, brass buckle. He wore cowboy boots, which gave him a slight boost in height, not that his increased stature could be detected from the back of the auditorium. The man walked to the center of the stage where there was a podium, placed some papers on it, and then turned to the audience, slowly nodding his head around the room, noting many persons he seemed to recognize in the audience.

Phineas bowed his head briefly and said a short prayer before he addressed the crowd. "It's so good to be here one last evening with y'all. It has been quite a time for us here in Misty Falls, and each of our team has felt your kind hospitality and welcoming." Phineas went on to thank several families in the community who had provided meals for the team members before each of the evening revivals. There had been so many offers to provide dinners for the team it became necessary to split up the team, so that each of our four team members could attend a dinner each night at a different home in Misty Falls. Those town folks who opened their homes to this evangelist and his team were blessed by having a member of the revival team for dinner.

"It is a blessing to welcome an evangelist into your home, and we certainly have been well taken care of by you Misty Fallers. I suppose that's what you call yerselves. So, you know we have been happy to be here. Y'all have made this trip a fine memory for each of us.

"I hope y'all will be saying the same about our visit when you come to remember this year's Misty Falls' Revival. It is my prayer that many of you tonight will hear God's message and open your hearts to listening to His word. God is calling your name and asking you to listen to Him.

Phineas stopped ... and began again, saying,

"A man lay in the ICU at Methodist Hospital in Dallas .... He had been in a terrible accident, a head-on collision — his pickup and another car. He had head wounds, including a broken nose, lacerations and contusions, several nasty fractures and his spleen might not make it. The man had been in a coma, but he was beginning to come out of it. It looked as though the man would survive, although he was facing months of recovery ahead of him.

Phineas stopped to let the scene sink into his listeners. George's attention was caught by this sad situation. He had never had a serious, life and death, medical problem, thankfully, but he understood this man's predicament — he'd be out of work for a long time; he might not come back completely from all the physical troubles he was facing. George was sympathetic toward the man.

"In the morgue in the basement of the same hospital lay the body of a young woman," Phineas continued. "She had been a wife and mother. Her two little girls attended the day care program at the church where I worked. Fortunately, although the girls had been in the car at the time of the accident, they escaped injury. Their safety belts held them in, and they survived the crash .... Not so their mother.

"The little girls, I think their ages were 4 and 6, were left with only their father to raise them.

"The church secretary called me to make the hospital visit to the man in the ICU. I was called to make the visit because the husband of one of our church members was the driver of the truck. The man had been driving drunk. He lost control of his vehicle and crossed the median of the road, colliding head on with the car with the mother and her little daughters. When the news came to the senior pastor at my church, he was deeply struck. He was sickened to his core at the unfairness of the accident and the terrible loss that the young family had suffered by the thoughtless snuffing out of the young woman's life.

"The senior pastor could not bring himself to make that hospital call. He found that he was too angry at what the man had done to minister to him.

"So I went to the hospital in his stead. As it turned out, I was not allowed into the ICU where the man lay because his visitors were being strictly limited, and the man's sister and wife were already with the man. I spent time with each of the women individually, and then we had time together; we talked; we prayed.

"I could certainly understand the anger and pain that the senior pastor felt, and I could see why he didn't want to make that visit to the man who had been the cause of the terrible accident that killed the young mother.

"The man who lay in the ICU bed was someone who had really failed; his whole life was a complete mess. His wife told me several other things about him — the two of them had been having serious problems in their marriage; he'd had several extra-marital affairs; he drank too much. The day of the accident, he had ditched work and had been with another woman. There wasn't much the man could be proud about," Phineas stopped again.

George's interest in this man had changed. He quickly sized up the pain the man had caused the people around him ... and even the young family, whose mother he had killed. George no longer had any sympathy for the man. *He deserved any trouble he got! He was a no good. His life was clear proof of that."* George shuddered.

Phineas picked up his story: "The man's life certainly was an example of a failed life. Through his own foolishness, the man in ICU had managed to kill another person whose loss would be greatly felt by the family she left behind. He also had made a terrible mess of his own family."

George nodded his head in agreement. "*That dope didn't deserve anything. He didn't deserve to live.*"

"But you know something?" Phineas looked around the room at different individuals as he spoke. "As I was talking to the man's wife, hearing all the terrible abuses she had suffered at his whim, I realized that this man was in the same place everyone is. He is a person for whom Jesus gave his life. As foul and stupid and really disgusting as we might think of the man, he is someone that Jesus loves so much that he died for him."

George almost stopped listening; he seemed to be on a dual track of thought — his own musings as well as the evangelist's words.

"This despicable man, who had just eradicated a young wife and mother from her world, this wretched example of a man was someone that Jesus loves! Could that really be so? How, or better yet, WHY did Jesus love that man so much?" Phineas let that thought sink in to his listeners.

"Later I wondered. 'Could it be that my senior pastor, who couldn't bring himself to visit the man in ICU, could it be that the pastor hadn't come to terms with that? Do you suppose he did not realize or believe that Jesus had died for that man and that the man's sins were forgiven? Maybe the pastor understood Jesus' forgiveness in an academic sense, but at the gut level ... he couldn't bring himself to believe it.

"Could it be that the senior pastor had not come to terms with his own, personal sinfulness?" Phineas asked. "That might be the root of the thing. I always thought my pastor was a decent sort of person; he had certainly not done anything terrible, nothing bad or immoral in his life, far as I knew. He wouldn't have been made a pastor if he was obviously a scoundrel, and it occurred to me that he was someone who had really not done much in the way of blatant sinning in his life...."

Phineas stopped, again, and looked directly at his audience, scanning the room and nodding at various people as he glanced among his listeners. "You know, that pastor is probably not the only one who could be like that, being a really, nice guy ...," Phineas smiled at the people and winked at several. Then he opened up his voice and stated soundly, "When it comes to really appreciating the depth of Jesus' forgiveness there is nothing like big, bad, really disgusting sin to clearly show us how obviously in need of God's grace we are!"

George suddenly felt a sharp, visceral pain stabbing him in his gut. It was as if the speaker's words were meant exactly for him. "Really disgusting sin," that's what George felt he was wallowing in. "I'm no better than that fool in the coma. He had nothing to be proud of, and neither do I!"

George struggled to get up; he found he was slightly unsteady as he rose, but he quickly got his bearings. He left the auditorium immediately, walked out of the church, found his car, and drove off.

Far across the room Connie looked up and saw a man about George's size and shape, who had been seated way in the back row of the auditorium, get up and leave in haste. She wondered, *"Could that have been George?"*

* * *

Following the service that night Connie and Sallie walked back to their apartment. They were filled with a variety of thoughts, being intro-spective, so they didn't speak. Even when they arrived at the apartment, they said nothing; they just went to their bedrooms and closed their doors.

* * *

Tucker Joe and Nina were seated in the middle of the front row of the auditorium at the revival, and since they were seated so close to the stage they had a close up view of several dozens of men, women, and youths who responded to the evangelist's plea to come down to the altar and pray — for forgiveness, for new life in Jesus, for answers to current needs. These people came from all over the auditorium down the aisles to the altar railing to kneel and pray. Before the closing of the revival these responders were guided to an adjacent room by prayer warriors.

When the service concluded, and the last song had been sung, Tuck and Nina remained seated while they watched the crowd begin to find their way outside.

Nina spoke first, leaning over to Tuck and whispering, "This wasn't what I expected, but I'm glad I came."

Tuck picked up on Nina's reticence and whispered back, "It <u>was</u> serious, not really like a show, after all. I hope you weren't put off by it."

Nina shook her head. "No, it's not that. I think I'm very glad I came. Rev. Cobb's words deserve reflection. The revival wasn't a show at all. The music was considerably better than I remember, back when Dan and I used to go to church, and the preacher certainly has a way of mak-ing you think about what's important," Nina's voice trailed off as she spoke.

"Yeah, I think you're right. Rev. Cobb put the question out there, and it's a fair question — one I would do well to spend some time working on," Tucker answered reflectively.

"You know I didn't mean for our date to be so serious, and I apologize, if that's what happened. I was just hoping that we could spend a fun, simple evening together here at this community event and enjoy the show," he explained.

Nina, who was almost lost in thought, snatched herself back from wherever her train of thought was heading and said, "You don't have to apologize to me, Tuck. You remember my friend, Winnie, who used to be pastor at Muddy Creek Church. She's been telling me in her email to see some of the revival and the evangelist for myself. Now I can tell her I did; I can also tell her how you and I came together to attend."

Tucker Joe laughed as he rose to his feet and helped Nina get up; they began exiting the auditorium. "I'm glad you enjoyed tonight. I read somewhere that when you are getting to know someone, it's a good idea to experience a variety of places; that way one gets to see his date in a variety of situations and locales. I suppose that would reveal more about the person you're dating."

"Why Tucker Joe, I wasn't aware of your having an ulterior motive for tonight!" Nina teased.

"Please, I don't have anything ulterior in mind, Nina! I have to admit, though, I've been quite thoughtful lately, figuring I need to get on the ball and find myself a significant other."

"There, I said it! I hope I'm not being too forward," Tucker Joe smiled at his date.

Nina nodded her understanding. "I suppose we all have that need in our lives. Not too many people can live without a significant other, as you put it, somewhere in the picture. I guess I qualify for the same need. I've been alone for quite some time, too."

A few minutes later Tuck and Nina were seated in Tuck's car on their way back to Nina's house.

"I was surprised at how many people responded to Rev. Cobb's invitation tonight," Nina stated.

"I'd say there were probably several dozen folks who came down the aisle to the front tonight to pray," Tuck remembered. "I would have been too embarrassed to go up to the altar and pray. I would hate it that everyone else might be looking at me. I don't think I could make myself do it."

"I know what you mean. I'm completely with you on that. I wouldn't want others looking at me while I was doing something so personal — like praying," Nina said thoughtfully.

The two had reached Nina's home, which stood adjacent to the cemetery in town. "It didn't take much time to get you home," Tucker Joe admitted. "I guess I really don't want this evening to be over so quickly. I've enjoyed being in company with you tonight."

"The evening isn't over, Tuck. I promised you I'd have a little something for us after the revival. Don't you remember?" Nina reminded her date.

Tuck jumped out of the car and quickly ran around to open Nina's door and hold it open for her. "I DO remember, now! And already I'm wonderin' what you came up with in such short notice!"

A few minutes later Tuck found himself sitting on the couch in Nina's living room with a plate of her award winning raspberry-apricot-walnut-crumb pie ale mode on his lap. Nina was seated opposite her date in an overstuffed arm chair, balancing a similar plate on her lap.

"I've heard for years about you taking prizes for baking at the Fall Festival, Nina, but this is the first time I've ever tasted the real thing! Yum! I'd say those judges were certainly right about your skills as a baker!

That's another good thing to know about you. You can **bake**!" Tuck was thoughtful for a moment as he continued to enjoy the treat before him. Then he asked, "Pie is wonderful, but ..., do you also like to cook?" Tuck grinned at his question.

Nina laughed. "You'll have to forgive my laughing, but it sounds like you are interviewing me for the role of 'significant other.'"

Tuck laughed along with Nina. "Good grief! I didn't mean to sound like an interview. I live alone nowadays, and you live alone, so I guess I was wondering if you do much in the way of cooking meals just for yourself."

"How about letting your tastebuds discover for themselves how I am as a cook?" Nina's eyes twinkled. "Would you like to come for dinner one of those Thursday evenings when you're free?"

A date was set a minute later; Tuck would come over to Nina's on Thursday for dinner.

"I have to say my mind keeps playing Rev. Cobb's question back to me in my head," Tucker Joe admitted. "For some reason I can't let it go."

"You mean, 'What are you waiting for?'" Nina asked.

"Yes, the preacher laid the ground for his question right well by setting up all the reasons a person should want to follow Jesus — the many blessings we enjoy everyday; the healing that God has already done for us many times over in our lives; the incredible gifts we each have been given; and ... and ... and so many good things we know we are thankful for," Tuck ticked off a few reasons that Cobb had mentioned.

"He said more 'n that," Nina added when Tucker took a breath. "He spoke about how nobody, on his or her own, is good. We all have failed in one way or another, and we all need help —real help — from the Savior."

"I won't forget the story Cobb told about the man in the hospital bed. I began thinking sympathetically about him — he had been in a terrible accident and was badly hurt — and then I was angry that the man had been responsible for the young mother's death. Then the minister pointed out how even that miserable example of a human being was someone that Jesus loves!

"I had to think about it for a minute when he said that because the idea of someone who is so bereft of anything good in his life can be someone that has been forgiven by Christ is amazing to me," Tuck announced.

"I agree. I listened to the sermon thinking the same as you, and I found myself wanting to disagree with Rev. Cobb about that awful man. How could Jesus forgive him for killing that young wife and mother? The man would go to jail for a long time if he lived. Wouldn't he?" Nina asked.

"That's interesting, Nina," Tuck agreed. "I think a person who is DUI and kills someone is guilty of second degree murder — he would be put away for a long, long time — but, somehow, he can still be forgiven his sin by Jesus."

Both Nina and Tuck were silent for a minute as they considered that revelation, then Nina spoke. "Maybe we live on two planes in this world: a physical plane where a consequence is a consequence that we may have to live through, like a jail term, and a spiritual plane where consequences are longer lasting."

"And ... if a person is forgiven some terrible sin or wrong doing, the spiritual consequences of that can be removed, even if there are earthly consequences to endure, there's no eternal judgement to face later!" Tuck announced with a smile, as if he had just answered the Sixty-four Thousand Dollar Question.

"I think you're right," Nina nodded her head in agreement. "I think we're both right. If we're living on two planes at the same time — physical and spiritual — it would make sense that we should be aware of both planes and live accordingly," she said, thoughtfully.

"Okay, I'd agree with that, but what, really, does that entail?" Tuck asked rhetorically. "The physical living is clear enough. We live in society that has laws and customs, and we go about our business everyday, doing what seems right to do, but I don't think I've given any thought to living as a spiritual person."

"Sure, we human beings are complicated people. Ourselves include our mental selves, our emotional selves, our physical selves, even our social and political selves, but I suppose there really is also a spiritual self, too, and we should be aware of it," Nina replied.

"We don't talk much about a spiritual self, but I suppose that would explain why people are aware of God or something beyond themselves — something much greater than humans — and the fact that people around the world bury their dead, have a basic understanding of right and wrong, and all that," Tucker Joe figured aloud.

"Boy! We can sure get deep into the thinking trenches quickly, can't we?" Nina observed. "And that brings us back to Rev. Cobb's question tonight — 'What are we waiting for?'"

"You're right, we do come back to that question," Tuck agreed. "Cobb was talking to a diverse group of people tonight. He specifically mentioned that. He said he knew he was speaking to people who have been walking with the LORD for a long time as well as some folks who haven't yet decided if God exists, and, of course, there were many people somewhere along that continuum. I guess I'd have to place myself with that last group — being somewhere in between the two extremes."

Nina was curious about Tuck's relationship with faith or the church; she asked, "Would you consider yourself a church person, a Christian?"

"Well, sure. The members of my family have belonged Muddy Creek Methodist Church for generations. I think I had a great grandfather who helped build the church, where it stands today, but that was over a century ago. I get to church on special occasions, but Friendlie's takes up a great deal of my life," Tuck answered. "How about you?"

"Dan and I were married in a Methodist church in New Orleans, just after college. We attended church for several years, but something happened that caused us to leave," Nina admitted.

Tuck leaned forward toward Nina, as if she was about to reveal a state secret. "Really! Sounds serious. What happened?"

"We were living in Jackson, Mississippi then, and our kids were little. We thought we should take them to church. It seemed like the right thing to do, and most of my neighbors went to the church. It was just a little country church, some sort of Bible church, I think. Anyway, the preacher stole some money, actually quite a bit of money, from people in the community and the church. He told everyone that he was 'borrowing' the money, but he never paid it back.

"One day the news got out that the preacher had defaulted on his loans and had skipped town. It was terrible! The phones were alive with angry, unsuspecting people calling one another and talking about what had happened. Dan and I were confused and hurt. We didn't lose any money ourselves, but we thought the preacher's words couldn't be believed. He was a crook, and he had torn that little church apart. We never went back to church."

"Hm," Tuck sighed. "You went to church because it was a good, social event, until you realized that the minister was bad, and you left. I can understand that, but what about your faith in God or your faith in Christ?"

This time it was Nina's turn to sigh. She felt as if she was being accused by Tucker Joe. "How can I put it? Maybe I've changed my thinking recently, but back then I don't know that I had real faith in God or Christ. You're right, it was more the social thing to go to church."

"I like our candor, Nina. We're not just talking weather and cooking, we're sharing something deep within ourselves, and I think that's a good thing. I don't know too many people that I'd share my inmost thoughts with, but you're very easy to talk to." Tuck put his pointer finger in his mouth to wet it and then pretended to use his finger to make a hash mark in the air. "There, that's one for us, or is it more than that?" Tuck asked.

"You're giving me, or us, a score for the evening?" Nina laughed.

"Aw, I'm only teasing, but I do like that we can talk about deeper, more significant ideas," Tuck smiled.

"So then, how do you, or how do we, answer the preacher's question?" Nina ventured.

"Right! He made it so simple, asking, 'What are you waiting for?'" Tuck repeated the question.

"His question was about our following Jesus, right?" Nina asked. Tuck nodded his head in agreement. "So, maybe there are steps involved in that answer."

"I'm sure you're right, but perhaps saying 'Yes, I'll follow you, Jesus.' Maybe that is the first step, and then the other steps will follow on the road as we follow Him."

"How do you mean, Tuck?" NIna wondered where her friend was headed.

"Just this. We could spend the rest of our lives thinking up reasons not to say 'Yes' to Jesus, but maybe that is wasted time. Maybe we're supposed to say 'Yes' initially, and let God's Spirit help us along the way as we go. That does make sense," Tucker Joe figured aloud.

"Okay, so saying 'Yes' to Jesus is saying a really big mouthful right at the start, isn't it?" Nina spoke slowly, as if she was putting ideas together.

"Saying, 'Yes,' to Jesus means I believe in Him and what He has done for me ... and for all of us." Tuck began. "I guess I do believe that. I've heard it all my life, and we sure need it. We people can get ourselves into some really nasty pickles, and we need someone who can pick us up and dust us off, so we can start fresh again. That's a great plan!" Tuck announced.

"Wow! This is really amazing. Maybe we could solve all the problems of the world just sitting here talking like this," Nina said whimsically.

Tuck laughed with Nina and said, "It is good to consider these ideas, and I hope we can have many more such times, but I think you know it's getting late, and I need to be off. I do have a terrible schedule for work. Monday mornings I open the store, so I have to be there by 5:30.

The two said good night; Nina walked Tuck to the door and watched while he got in his car. They agreed to dinner in half a week, right there at Nina's house. They would have a little more time to talk then.

✻ ✻ ✻

Although it had already been a very full day for Nina, and normally she would have headed for bed, she realized that she was wound up from all that had been happening. She slipped on her coat, walked out the back door and across her backyard to the cemetery. She found the bench close to where her husband Dan's marker lay and sat down.

Over the years Nina had come often to this peaceful place to be quiet, to think things over, and to relish the memories of her home when her family had been complete — the kids were young and Dan was still alive. This evening, following her conversation with Tucker Joe, she wanted to spend a little time in this favorite spot.

Nina hadn't been sitting on the bench long when she was startled to see someone walking into the cemetery. Her immediate thought was to stay very still in hopes that the stranger might not discover her presence. The bench where Nina sat was recessed in an alcove of trees off the main track in the garden, but the stranger approached along the pathway toward her, even so.

Suddenly the man stopped, maybe twenty feet away, and looked intently in Nina's direction, trying to determine if there was someone sitting on the bench. He spoke, "Excuse me ma'am. I didn't think anyone would be here in this place so late at night."

Nina couldn't see the man very well, but she was relieved to hear his voice, which didn't have a threatening tone. He wasn't trying anything untoward, as far as she could tell. "Good evening," she stammered. "I didn't expect to see anyone out here so late, either."

The man took a few steps closer, so he didn't have too speak loudly to be heard. "This appears to be a fine place to spend time. I'm guessing it is beautiful in the daylight," the man wondered aloud.

Nina could see the man, as the light from the garden pole lamp was shining on him, now. He looked familiar — like the man she had just been looking at on stage at the revival. "Excuse me, sir," Nina began. "Aren't you the evangelist who spoke at the revival tonight?"

"I am he," the man replied. "Phineas Cobb, Ma'am. Good to make your acquaintance. How do you know who I am?"

"I was sitting with my friend right in the front row at the revival this evening, so I recognized you when you stepped into the light. You really are the evangelist?"

"Yes, I am," Cobb answered. "I hope you were pleased with the revival. Did you come just tonight?"

"Yes, I wasn't planning to come at all. I didn't really like the idea of attending something like that by myself, but a friend of mine called me earlier today and invited me to attend with him. So we did," Nina spoke with candor.

"That's one I haven't heard before — your reason for attending the revival — but I like it. You two were going on a date. I hope you took something away with you this evening," the evangelist inquired.

"I think that's what brought me out here now," Nina admitted. "Your question stuck with both of us, and we were talking about it afterwards."

Phineas smiled. "I'm glad to hear you're still working on what I said. My whole purpose in life is to help people examine their lives and see if Jesus shouldn't have a place in their hearts."

"The whole program was better than we'd expected; we both agreed about that," Nina answered. "Tucker Joe and I enjoyed the evening. Since we had seats right in the very front of the hall, we had the perfect place to see everything up close. But besides having really good seats, we were both struck by the question you asked: "What are you waiting for?" Nina explained.

Phineas laughed, "You know, those were not my words originally. I think I heard the same question years ago by a preacher when I was about sixteen. Those words haunted me too, and I couldn't get away from them. So I used them in my message tonight."

"Yes, we heard them, and we spent some time afterwards talking about it," Nina told the preacher. "What brings you out here so late? I can imagine you're exhausted from all the energy you put into the revival."

"Maybe we both felt the need to get to a quiet place and breathe in God's Spirit," Phineas thought out loud. "You're right about my energy level. I must have an adrenalin rush before the service, but I seem to use it up by the end of the evening, yet, even so, I can't just jump into bed. I'm still wound up from the revival. I think it went well, and, God be praised, I saw a number of people responding to God's call on their lives. That makes it all worth the effort for me."

"You are a very gifted man," Nina observed. I could tell by the hush of that audience how well people were listening to your talk. Did you realize that you were holding everyone in the palm of your hand, so to speak? I really think you were."

"That is an amazing thing," Phineas agreed. "Yes, I could feel that power, if that's what it is. I could see the people were focused on me, really sitting on the edge of their seats, intent on listening to every word I was saying, as if my words held something important for them to grasp. I really, truly believe that God has called me to deliver His message to people, to help them navigate through their lives and come out better for it.

"I personally want to live to God, to be focused on God, to use whatever gifts I have to God's glory, but beyond that I want to help others to follow suit. The way I understand it, we've all been saved by Jesus the Christ, and we need to recognize that great gift and respond to Him. Pardon me for preaching again!" Phineas laughed lightly.

"You are the real thing, I believe," Nina announced. "I don't think you're preaching for any reason but to glorify God. I don't know that I've known many fully committed Christians over the years. I'm glad to meet you, sir."

Phineas held out his hand and shook Nina's hand. "This can be the 'handshake of fellowship,'" he said. "Thanks for your compliment, but everyone who is following Christ is somewhere on the path, and I'm sure we all have a ways to go before we've reached perfection."

"Did you or your boyfriend make any decisions tonight?" Phineas asked.

"Tuck's not really my boyfriend. We know we're both looking for someone special, and we are certainly good friends, but we don't have any special understanding," Nina explained.

"Friendships are wonderful and valuable. Whether they later turn into a deeper relationship or not, the friendship is a wonderful bond. The best friend, of course, is the LORD. Do you know Jesus as your friend?" Phineas asked.

Nina thought a moment. "I'm beginning to see how that relationship works. I didn't used to. I have a friend named Winnie; she used to be the pastor of Muddy Creek Methodist Church here in town. She knows Jesus as her best friend, and we would talk about faith, off and on. I'm sure she wanted me to know Jesus as my LORD and Savior, and she would have included His being my friend, too."

"Yes, I think you're on your way to that understanding," Phineas nodded his head. "Is there something that's in your way of making a decision for faith?"

"If I had to point to one thing, I would have to say my pride. That's likely the whole of it. I think my pride has stood in my way of being humble before the God of the Universe, and as I hear those words coming out of my mouth I realize that's a terrible reason!" Nina admitted.

"We all have our reasons for things, and sometimes our reasons don't look so good when they are held up to the measuring stick of Christ. He is our plumb line. His life was perfect; he showed us how to live right, giving glory to God and reaching out to others with care and encouragement. No one measures up to Christ, but He's there to be with us along our own paths." Phineas assured Nina.

"Is there anything I can do to help you?" He added.

"You mean, 'What am I waiting for?'" Nina laughed and asked rhetorically. "I think you're absolutely right, pastor. I suppose I could go on stalling and putting off the decision for another time, but that's really just a big waste of time. Isn't it?

"I think I am ready now to give my life to Jesus," Nina said after a moment.

"Would you like me to pray with you?" Phineas offered.

"Yes, I would." Nina answered, bowing her head.

Phineas put his hand on Nina's shoulder, bowed his head, and prayed, "LORD Almighty, What a wonderful, wonderful God You are. How mighty, and powerful, and awesome, and good You are. Thank You for Your love and kindness and Your many gifts. Thank You for shedding your Spirit across this town tonight and nudging so many folks to trust You. I thank You LORD for all Your good works.

"And Jesus, I especially thank You for this dear sister. She has come here tonight, listening to your voice calling her. She is ready to take the great step to follow You." Phineas stopped to let Nina continue.

After a minute of quiet Nina whispered, "Jesus, You are so good to me! You have been calling me for some time, and I've brushed You off before, but tonight You seem very close and very dear to me. I want You in my life; I want to be part of Your plan; I want to grow closer to You and learn to love You.

"LORD, may I call you LORD? I want You to be my friend, my close friend. I have friends, but I want You to be my best friend. I don't quite know how that works, but I'm asking You to come into my heart and live with me.

"Thank You, LORD, for my children and my grandchildren. Bless them. Thank You for Dr. Sedgwick and my job. Help me to be an even better nurse. Help me to show your love to many others. Help me be the person You want me to be, and thank You for this very special pastor here, who has given his time to help me make this decision for You. Bless him and his ministry. Amen.

"Thank you, Pastor Cobb, for being here tonight. I'll never forget your being here when I really needed someone to nudge me to trust Jesus. I feel so full of goodness right now. Thank you," Nina said.

Phineas walked Nina over to her house next to the cemetery, and saw her safely inside. He got in his car and drove over to the PCC bus where the rest of the team were already bedded down for the night.

Chapter 30. The Next Day

Oct, 26, 2009

Monday morning, very early, just before 3:30 a.m., a train barreling through Misty Falls struck a man who was on the railroad track. The identity of the man who was killed was not immediately apparent. The remains of the man's body didn't leave much to recognize. By the time the sun was rising, about 7:50 that morning, the news of the tragedy of dead man was making its way around the community.

Who might the man be? Was someone from Misty Falls missing? Sherrif Mickey Allen Barrymore had been one of the first notified about the deadly occurrence. He was awakened by telephone as the train people were beginning to investigate the accident.

Sherrif Barrymore was on the case in ten minutes, hurrying over to the spot of the collision just several hundred yards south of the train depot. Apparently the man was alone, and for some reason, he had been on the tracks when the train approached. The man somehow hadn't heard the train whistle, or, at least, he gave no heed to the warning.

The train engineer was very distraught. He certainly had not expected to find a lone man walking down the train tracks in the black of the night. The engineer never saw the man who was dressed in a black shirt and jeans until he was nearly on top of the man. The engineer admitted there would have been no way for him to slow down and stop the train in time to save the man's life, even if he had seen him sooner. "It takes a half mile to stop this train when it's moving as fast as we were going last night," the engineer told the sheriff. I'm so sorry this had to happen. What would have brought the man out to the tracks so late at night? I wonder."

✳ ✳ ✳

It wasn't until she arrived at her job in the cafe that Connie heard about the tragedy — some (yet unknown) man had been killed by a train coming through Misty Falls in the early hours that day.

The moment Connie heard the news she gasped. Immediately her thoughts went to George. He hadn't come home last night. She remembered how she thought she had seen him exiting the church in the middle of the revival last night, and she wondered, no, she feared, that somehow, the unknown man whose life had been snuffed out so quickly was her husband.

Connie, who had been standing in the kitchen of the cafe, quickly found a stool and sat down. All the blood had drained out of her face, and she looked as white as a ghost.

Ms. Reynolds, who had mentioned the news of the fatal train accident, saw Connie's reaction and walked over to her, putting her arm around Connie's shoulder. "What on earth is the matter, Chil'? Are you okay? Was it something I jist sed?" she asked.

Connie didn't say anything for a moment; her throat felt tight, as if she had been crying. "Did ... did they say the name of the man who died?" she managed to whisper.

"Why, no, they didn't. They are going to wait to see if there's any-one missing in town, but I guess they thought the man had been a drifter. He probably wasn't from 'round here," Ms. Reynolds assured Connie.

Too many things were adding up in Connie's mind to be com-forted by her employer's words. She didn't know what to think. "Do you s'pose I could run over to my apartment for a minute," Connie asked. "I need to ask my mom something.

Connie took off her apron, threw it on the back of a chair, and in another minute she was sprinting across the street to her apartment. She opened the door and startled her mother, who wasn't expecting to see her home so suddenly. "Why, what on earth brings you home at this time of day?" Sallie asked.

"Have you seen George? Is he here?" Connie asked breathlessly looking around the room.

Sallie shook her head, 'No.' "Sorry, Kiddo, I haven't seen him since last week, you know. Maybe he's back in Greenville. He told you sometimes he was goin' there these days."

Connie was beyond herself. She didn't know what to do. She was almost convinced that it was George who was on the tracks in the middle of the night and was the victim of the train accident. She didn't want to be worried without cause, but she had a horrible feeling inside about the man on the tracks, and she needed to know for sure.

"What's gotten into you? What's wrong, Dear?" Sallie was feeling anxious because of Connie's unexpected worry.

"Mom! Oh, Mom! I don't know. I just heard from Ms. Reynolds that some man was hit by a train comin' through here way early this morning, when it was still pitch black. The man was killed, of course, but they don't know who he was. They don't think he was from Misty Falls, but they don't know...," Connie's voice stopped.

Sallie sat down on the couch and stared at her daughter. "And you think it was George?" She asked.

"Maybe I'm wrong; I pray to God I'm wrong, but too many things add up and make me think I'm <u>not</u> wrong," Connie plopped down on the couch next to her mother.

Connie decided to call Trudy, who she hoped would know someone in town who could help her.

"Trudy, it's me, Connie."

"Hi, Connie. How's it goin'? I haven't heard from you for a while."

Connie told Trudy what she had heard at the cafe and her fears that the victim was George.

Trudy gasped and cried, "Oh no! Connie, are you sure?"

"That's the thing. I'm not sure, but I'd like to talk to someone about it. Do you know who I could talk to about the accident?" Connie asked.

Trudy suggested that Connie call Sheriff Barrymore, and she gave her his number. The two friends promised to talk again, soon, and Trudy expressed her concern again about Connie's situation.

"In fact, I'll pray for you right now," Trudy promised.

* * *

Meanwhile, George had been driving for some time. He wasn't even paying attention to where he was going. He just drove, mostly on country roads, up hill and down, across little bridges, through forests, past lakes. He couldn't see much in the deep black of the night in the country, but he could see the stars shining brightly.

He was thinking. He had not stayed through the entire sermon that the preacher was giving; he felt too uncomfortable to stay. No, he had to think. He had to get away from people and other distractions and just think.

George didn't want to forget what the preacher had been saying. It had caught his attention; it even followed along with some of what George had been thinking to himself. "*First there was the story about the man who had really screwed his life up. I felt sorry for the man when I heard the story, and then I really hated him for what he done to that young mother and her family, and THEN I realized I WAS THAT MAN. That man was a scoundrel and a scumbag, and so am I!* George accused himself.

I am absolutely no better than that man, and I don't know what to do about it., George thought.

The car had come to a great lake stretching like a grand, glassy, black mirror in every direction, and George maneuvered his car off the main road to follow down to a boat landing by the lake. The moon had come up that night, and it was illuminating the sky. George stopped his car, looked out on the lake and up at the heavens. The view was spectacular. It brought his thoughts away from his punishing, self-accusing mindset for a moment. It felt good to not think of the pain he had been causing Connie and the others for a moment.

"*Wouldn't it be fine if, somehow, I wasn't causing so much grief to others?*" George thought. *Wouldn't it be fine if I could be someone else? What if I could be free of what I've done and start over? Wouldn't that be a miracle?*

"I need a miracle. I **really** need a miracle," George called aloud to the heavens.

"Oh, God, I need a miracle," George cried out. "I have sinned and done so many stupid, <u>stupid</u> things, I've made a total mess of my life. There's nothing in my life that I'm proud of. I've hurt everyone I know, especially my family members, especially Connie and Tanya. I've been living just for m'self for so long. I've lied and lied to others to get around things — to get my way.

"*I really don't know what to do. Connie doesn't deserve the trouble I've brought her. She's young. Yet she's been so faithful and loving to me. (God, thank You for Connie!)*

"LORD, will you forgive me for all this foolishness? Please forgive me! Please, please, please forgive me!" George pleaded; tears flowed freely over his face and down his shirt.

George stopped his prayer and thought again. "*The preacher was beginning to talk about how Jesus loves us, even when we have failed in life, even when we don't deserve it. I barely heard those words tonight; I was too much wrapped up in realizing my sinfulness. I had to get away and think.*"

"*But that's really neat, if Jesus loves people, even those of us who don't deserve it. That's completely cool.*

"*God, I think I remember that your Son, Jesus, died. He didn't deserve to die, but he did, and his death turned out to be a good thing.*" George was remembering what he had heard years and years ago from the pastor of the church he attended with his first family in Greenville.

"*Like the preacher said tonight, Jesus loves even bad people, people who have done plenty to make them unlovable and unwanted.*

"*Jesus, I'm crying to You. I think You know me very well, and You know how bad I'm hurting. You know that I'm real sorry for all the trouble I've caused, and I want your forgiveness. I need Your forgiveness. I guess that's what the preacher was gettin' ready to say to us — get right with God, come down to the altar here and give your troubles to Him who loves you best.*

"*I didn't stay for the whole revival tonight, but I knew what was about to come, anyway. I've heard those words before. I suppose I should have stayed and gone down to pray down in front.*

"*LORD, will You forgive me for that, too? Will you forgive me for not going down to the altar, like we was s'posed to, to talk to You?*" George asked.

He sat silent for some time, listening to the sounds of nature around him — the occasional howl of a coyote, the screech of an owl, the rush of river water flowing into the lake nearby. George enjoyed listening to nature and watching the silhouettes of the trees across the lake. Best of all was the great expanse of sky he could see as he walked past the trees closer to the lake, where the heavens opened up to him. The stars were dazzling and thick in number. George remembered an old verse from his Sunday school days when God had promised Abraham that he would be blessed with so many children they would number more than the stars in the sky.

"*Wonder what brought that to mind just now?*" George thought. "*That's odd. Why would that verse jump into my mind tonight?*

"*Well, I guess it's the stars that are telling me to remember that promise,*" George said to himself.

"*Boy, that was a long time ago. I wonder if old Abraham ever stood out under the stars and tried to count them? He couldn't; I'm sure. Nobody can. Although Abraham would have seen the same sky that I'm seeing tonight. He would never have been bothered by the city lights covering up the stars.*

"*God made Abraham a promise. A long time ago, he made a promise to him, and I think God still makes promises to people today. It doesn't make sense that God would promise one man something and not make promises to other men, too.*

"*I was asking for a miracle; I was begging for a miracle,*" George stopped and thought. "*Maybe, just maybe, there is a miracle here! Think about it, George. If that preacher was right when he said, 'There's nothing like a really fouled up life, someone who truly knows how bad he or she has been, to really understand the gift of God's Grace.'*

"*Oh God! I need Your Grace, Your forgiveness, Your love,*" George breathed the short prayer.

He sat on the rock, gazing out at the scene before him. It was enchanting. The scene was mostly devoid of color, due to the blackness of the night. All he could see were bare outlines — the trees, the hills across the lake, the vast expanse of the heavens, the canopy of space with a host of uncountable stars. "It's so peaceful here, so still. It's starkly beautiful, and a kind of blessing.

George sat on the rock breathing in the peacefulness of the moment and began another thought. A cool breeze blew in from the lake, chilling George as he sat on the rock, so he returned to his car and got in. He felt a lightness of spirit, something that he had not felt in a very long time. "I think this is a miracle, and I'm experiencing it right now!" George said aloud.

George sat in his car, looking out at the lake for some time. He sat and he thought. As he thought the heavens began to change, slightly. There was the first hint of a rosy color insinuating itself on the sky above the lake. Morning was making its way upon the land, but George was ready to sleep. He climbed into his car's back seat, pulled his coat over his shoulder and fell fast asleep.

* * *

Back in Misty Falls, Connie returned to work, but she could hardly focus on what she was doing. Her mind kept churning around a horrifying picture, and she didn't know how to break the worry cycle. She had talked to her mom about George, but Sallie had no more information than Connie did about George's whereabouts. She called Trudy and told her the problem. Trudy was sympathetic, and she promised to pray for her, but she didn't know where George was. After a half hour of fretting, Connie decided to return to the cafe to finish out her shift.

"What's going on?" Ms. Reynolds asked Connie. "You took off out of here like a scared rabbit a bit ago." Then her employer remembered her announcement about the unfortunate man who was killed earlier that day, and she asked, "Was it something about the man they found this morning?"

Connie nodded her head affirmatively, but she couldn't make her voice work. Finally she said, "I don't know any more than you do, but it could be my husband who was the victim. The reason I ran home was to see if my mom had heard from him today."

"Oh, Hun! That's terrible! I'm so sorry! I hope you're wrong and it wasn't him! I wonder if they know anything more about the person who was killed?" Ms. Reynolds took out her cell phone and called the sheriff's office.

"Good morning, Ma'am," Ms. Reynolds said to the secretary, Janice Creighton. "This is Juanita Reynolds over here at Countrified Cuisine. I heard about the tragic accident that happened this morning on the tracks. Can you tell me if there has been anything more discovered about the identity of the victim?"

"No, I'm sorry, Ms. Reynolds. So far what we know is that the man was alone, walking down the rails. He was wearing blue jeans and a black cowboy shirt and sneakers and a suede jacket. The body has been sent to the medical examiner in Knoxville for an autopsy, so maybe more will be known in a couple of days.

"Since you're calling, do you know anyone who has disappeared?" The sheriff's secretary asked.

"Well, I have an employee who says she's concerned that the victim might be her husband," Ms. Reynolds explained.

"I see! I believe the sheriff would like to make a stop over at your place. Will she be there in a few minutes? I'm sure he would like to follow up on this," the secretary suggested.

Ms. Reynolds raised her eyebrows and cocked her head to one side, as if asking Connie's permission for the sheriff to come. Connie hung her head down and slowly nodded her assent to the sheriff's visit.

After the call, Ms. Reynolds took Connie by the hand and led her into the back of the kitchen. She put her arm around her employee's shoulder and said, "Would you mind if I prayed with you, right now, about this? I think we need to invite God into this situation and trust Him."

Connie was relieved that Ms. Reynolds had the presence of mind to turn to the LORD in such a moment. "Yes, please ... thank you."

The two women bowed their heads and prayed together asking God for help and courage and wisdom and whatever they would need for whatever else was about to happen.

Mickey Allen Barrymore arrived at the cafe a few minutes later and talked with Connie. There was nothing particular about Connie's fears that could connect George Oliver to the victim who was hit, so the sheriff wrote down all the information about the missing man and thanked Mrs. Oliver. He would be in touch if anything more was learned about the man.

Chapter 31. Chicago, Again

Fall had arrived in Chicago, and the city was clearly experiencing the new season. The trees were rich with autumn tones, and the temperatures had cooled down considerably, requiring added layers for warmth. The icy wind off Lake Michigan could bring a chill to anyone not warmly dressed. Winnie and John had taken to walking a couple evenings each week after dinner, and at this time of year they were careful to bundle up.

They discovered walking together around their area after dinner was good exercise. They also found it was good for catching up on the news, both local and beyond, as well as continuing to learn and understand their new neighborhood and each other.

On one such walk Winnie began their conversation by saying, "Personalities are complex; maybe we will never thoroughly understand one another. Time is no doubt a factor, too. We can't reveal all the layers of our personality at once. I'm sure we don't even know them ourselves."

"Our personalities are surely a mix of our past — events, learning, associates, hope, faith, and, no doubt, much more. Probably there are certain natural tendencies, mannerisms, and behaviorisms that we come with — you know our genetic leanings — which play into our initial responses and may have significant influence on our tenacity for something," John theorized.

"I don't suppose there's any real scientific way of getting to know and understand one another. Maybe there's good reason for mystery in one's spouse. Maybe really knowing all about your spouse would take some of the fun out of the relationship," Winnie laughed.

John nodded his head in agreement with his bride's words. "There are psychological tests that can sum up a person's innermost thinking, but those tests aren't available to the general public, and they don't touch on other aspects of one's person — mental, physical, social, and more."

"I've taken the Minnesota Multi-phasic Personality Inventory several times, and the results of that test are quite humbling," Winnie replied.

"You took the MMPI?" John was instantly curious.

"It's part of a battery of tests that the United Methodist Church requires their ministerial candidates to take. You know, the responsibility of bringing God's word to a congregation every week isn't something the church takes lightly. Some people might think they are called to preach the gospel, but they may have other motives that are not healthy for a congregation, and they could devastate a church. Such people must not be given a license to preach," Winnie noted.

"Strike one more for the church," John counted. "I can imagine that there are some people who might like the notoriety or the community standing or some other misbegotten reason for wanting to be a minister, but that would be a terrible motive for choosing such a profession.

"There are probably more wrong reasons for wanting to be a pastor than there are good reasons. You'd think if men or women manage to get into preaching for the wrong reasons, they'd quickly discover their error and leave," Winnie said, "but that's not always the case."

"I'm sure churches need to have good preachers. There's so much to learn and so much to change in one's life, that a good preacher / leader would be critical piece for its well being," John observed.

Winnie was pleased with John's comment. She wondered, now and again, if he was cooling off about his interest in faith. It seemed, sometimes, that he thought the church was all well and good for her, a lifelong Methodist, but she feared that John had not really changed his attitude about the church since she met him, although he had made a strong profession of faith in God.

"Good observation, John," Winnie agreed. "That's an important function of the church — to keep a vigilant eye on the pastors who represent a denomination."

John shook his head. "You're very involved in church, of course, and you think that all believers in Christ should belong to some church. Right?"

"Yes ... I do. Why?" Winnie answered slowly, wondering what was behind John's comment.

"I'm just not convinced that we can't follow Jesus on our own. [Pardon my double negative!] Church is fine for you, but I don't know that it's a requirement for heaven," John conjectured.

Winnie shook her head. "You're not alone in that thinking. I've met many people who have become inactive from their home church and others who consider themselves good Christian believers, even though they have nothing to do with church.

"It seems that coming to faith in God doesn't necessarily lead one to church, but it should," Winnie stated.

"Don't be hard on me, Honey." John pleaded. "I don't want to disturb you. I'm just telling you how I feel. Can I help how I feel?"

Winnie squeezed John's hand and looked at him, "No, Sweetheart, I'm not angry with you, but Christians follow Jesus. Our feelings are not the first things to consider. Feelings, which can give us a glimpse about what's going on inside us, as well as around us, shouldn't be the first or the only thing to consider when making a decision. I'm sure there are plenty of times that we don't particularly feel like getting up in the morning or going to work, but we have to look beyond our feelings and remember we have responsibilities, so we need to get a move on. Even love is not so much a feeling as it is a decision to do something. Nobody feels exactly the same all the time. You could get very swept up in a feeling, like our romance, for a while, but it won't remain like that forever. When the feeling goes away or changes, we still have our commitment and our love to guide us."

"You're right, and I shouldn't have suggested that my feelings should trump my thoughts. That's very unlike me, anyway," John admitted. "Although, I have to admit I certainly let my feelings carry me away when I lost Karen. Hm. Maybe I'm more feeling oriented than I was giving myself credit for being." John laughed at himself.

"As far as activity with church is concerned, I'm thoroughly enjoying auditing Marian's church history class. We've been marching through the early centuries of the Common Era, seeing how various aspects of the church became organized — the leadership, the monastics and religious, the saints. I have particularly enjoyed studying the ancient councils as they negotiated and hammered out some of the basic doctrines of the Christian faith — how Christ is related to Almighty God; how the Holy Spirit is related to the Father and the Son; should Mary be called the *Theotokos*, the Mother of God?" John used his fingers to tick off some of the decisions made by the Ancient Councils.

"I loved the two semesters I took on Christian history," Winnie interjected. "We viewed historical events with the lens of the church, rather than from some military or political vantage. I think the church had to organize to defend herself from the many outside groups that were trying to use the name 'Jesus Christ' for their own purposes. The name 'Jesus Christ' has been a catch phrase for a long, long time, really since Christ rose and the followers began calling Jesus LORD and Christ," Winnie observed.

"I guess I can see why the Church got organized back then. Organization is a human activity, and we people are the most social of all creatures. We don't get things done too well on our own. We form corporations, offices, groups, businesses, colleges, universities, political entities, churches, and more. I can see how the church became increasingly organized, but I don't see how membership in any particular church is critical to my salvation. I thought what Jesus did for us on the cross satisfied that," John rested his case.

"You're completely right, for a start," Winnie agreed, "but there is a difference between justification, that is being reconciled to God, and sanctification."

"Sanctification?" John repeated. "You mean to make holy? Surely that idea is outmoded these days. What's holiness got to do with faith?"

Winnie laughed at John's query. "That's a great question. There is an old argument about what is more important — faith or works. Faith is what it takes for you to become justified (or saved) and works, which is what the rest of life is about, is doing whatever we can to make this world a better place — bringing heaven to earth, feeding and caring for those in need, and working for peace and justice. It isn't a matter of one or the other. Both faith and works are essential.

"When we are justified we are exercising faith — faith in Jesus' work on the cross — but the plan doesn't stop there. Except for the thief on the cross, who asked the LORD to remember him when He came into His kingdom, we have life to live after we trust Jesus. (The thief died that day, along with the LORD, so he couldn't have gone on to do any works.)

John nodded his head, as he remembered that scene in Luke. "Okay, the thief on the cross didn't join the church, did he?"

"No, he didn't, and a deathbed confession, like that of the thief, is recognized as sufficient, if someone is honestly coming to faith in Christ on his or her last moment of existence, but who can ever tell when that would be?" Winnie asked rhetorically.

"So ... sanctification is necessary," John surmised.

It's all about obedience to Jesus," Winnie replied.

"Obedience? Oh, I remember. You were talking about the Matthew 28 passage before — the one where Jesus met his disciples for a final time and sent them into the world to make disciples ... to baptize them ... and teach them to obey his commands. That's what you're getting at. (Winnie nodded her head and smiled.) "So, you think I should be baptized." John deduced.

"It depends. You said that you and your mom used to attend a Presbyterian church in Denver when you were small. Do you know if you were baptized then?" Winnie wondered.

"No, I wasn't. I was christened. How about that?" John raised his eyebrows hopefully.

Winnie grinned widely and said, "Then you have been baptized, John! You have, but you didn't know it."

"I didn't know that christening and baptism were the same thing. I thought christening was when a baby is officially given a name," John said.

"The term christening is often used in lieu of baptism when it is done for a small child, but it's the same sacrament in the church. The difference is that the parents or sponsors of the child take the vows, promising to bring up the child in the knowledge and admonition of Christ, rather than the individual taking those vows," Winnie explained.

John nodded with understanding. "So, I don't need to be baptized then, do I?" He smiled.

"No, one baptism per person is all that's done, or all that should be done. I know there are folks who would like to be re-baptized later in life, realizing that they don't remember their baptism, because they were infants," Winnie added.

"I can appreciate that," John said. "If my future includes being a member at a church, then I suppose I need to do the whole thing, including the baptism. Wouldn't that be a good beginning?"

Winnie was thoughtful for a minute, then she said, "There is a provision for people who have been baptized as infants. The same ceremony is held in the church, and the vows are taken by the person, just like any new believer who will be baptized, but the water is used to 'remember your baptism and be glad.' The pastor wouldn't pour or sprinkle water on your head, but you could dip you hand in the water yourself and place it on your head to remember your previous baptism. That would work, but there is a problem."

"And what would that be?" John couldn't imagine what more might be required.

"We haven't decided on a particular church, yet," Winnie laughed.

"So, now I know what I'm looking for in church — a place to plug in," John announced.

"Indeed. It's been some time since I have had the choice of selecting which church to attend, since I've been an itinerant preacher for so long, but yes, we should look for a place that will help us grow in our faith and help us to do some good in this world.

"It might also be fun to find a church that has a couples group that we could join. So far the only couple we know in town are the Twingates. We should invite them over to our house before long, don't you think?" Winnie suggested.

"I've never entertained anyone before, probably because my apartment wasn't exactly conducive to that sort of thing, but I get the feeling that you like to entertain. It would be fun to get to know the Twingates better," John said.

"I suppose a Saturday evening might be a good time for them to come, do you think?" Winnie suggested. "Weekday evenings wouldn't work."

"Working three nights a week does seem like a lot for me to be away now, when I have my bride at home waiting for me!" John's eyes twinkled, as he smiled at Winnie.

"Evening classes must be par for the course at the university. I knew that your Tuesday / Thursday evening Intro to Philosophy class would keep you on campus extra long. Then you added the church history course you're auditing, which makes Monday evenings out for you, too.

"I love getting up early to fix you breakfast, so we can have some time first thing in the day, and I love knowing the times you'll be home for dinner, too. Our dinner times work well as a prelude to our whole evenings. I think we're even beginning to get comfortable being around each other at home. Neither of us have had anyone living with us in some time," Winnie noted.

"You once told me you thought I was made for the domestic life, and, having had a brief taste of it so far, I quite agree. I think we've slipped easily into nest building. I find I really enjoy doing those things that need doing around the house. It's a different sort of challenge, and I am having fun with it," John thought aloud. "I didn't know how easily I'd be able to come 'round to marriage, especially given the long time I was a bachelor, but I think with your help I've done remarkably well."

"You always have been a fast learner," Winnie teased. Yes, I think you were made to be married, and I'm glad you found me — that we found us — and you gave it a try," Winnie's eyes twinkled.

✳ ✳ ✳

John came bounding up the steps the next day, as he returned from classes. He had a question for his bride.

He found Winnie in the kitchen preparing dinner. He swept her into his arms and kissed her.

"Goodness, John! Would I be right in assuming you've had a good day," Winnie grinned.

"My day was fine, but as I was driving home I suddenly remembered that we had to put off a date last year, and now, this year, I think we should definitely manage it," John explained.

"You're being mysterious, John, what are you talking about?" Winnie wondered.

"You remember. Last fall we started emailing each other, and the Thanksgiving holiday presented itself, and I asked you if you would like to join me in Aspen where I planned to ski that weekend," John had a gleam in his eye.

Winnie laughed as she realized what John was leading up to. "So, you think this year I should say, 'Yes' to your invitation. Indeed I shall. We can make up for missing Thanksgiving together last year."

"When you answered my email last November and told me your concerns about 'adult activity.' I was initially taken aback. I had to think it out a bit. I knew that you worked at your church — in the office — but I didn't have the whole picture," John teased his bride. "So when you laid down your expectations for our getting to know one another, I thought you were a bit old fashioned. I also wondered how many other areas of life you might be old fashioned about. I decided I'd put up with your rules and see where it would take us, and ... I'd say things have turned out quite nicely."

Winnie was remembering along with John about that time, just last year. At the time she felt she was tiptoeing cautiously through a virtual maze of possible scenarios that John's invitation had suggested, if she joined him in the chalet in Aspen. It probably hadn't occurred to him that she would object because of her faith. She had worried about his reaction — would he just drop their correspondence and forget her? That might have been the case, but John had been a gentleman and agreed to be circumspect.

"So you came home to invite me to Aspen for Thanksgiving?" Winnie laughed.

"How about we have a second honeymoon there," John's eyes twinkled.

Winnie stood back from John and looked at him squarely in the eyes. "I didn't know our first honeymoon was over!" She winked at John.

"You're right about that, Win. Our first honeymoon is definitely not over. We'll just have to move the site from here to there!" John scooped his bride back into his arms.

Chapter 32. A New Start

After George's great internal struggle that evening by the lake, he was exhausted. He slept for hours on the backseat of his car.

As noon approached, the sun, being at its zenith, shined warmth into the car. George was unceremoniously yanked awake by a sharp Charlie horse in his left leg. Thinking he was in bed he immediately sprang out of bed to attend to the fiercely, painful knot, when he found himself on the floor of the backseat of his car. "%^&^*&^&$#$#," he yelped. "How in the Samhill did I get here?" George asked no one in particular, as he struggled to open the car door and tumbled onto the dirt.

Of course his leg cramp was still demanding his attention, so George pulled himself off the ground and began to dance around the forest floor, gingerly trying to step his foot flat on the ground — the method he had always used in times past to alleviate such a leg cramp. His effort, he found, was hindered due to his stockinged feet. It seems he had slipped his shoes off just as he was sliding from consciousness, leaving his feet clad only in stockings. George continued his belabored dance on the rocky and stickery ground for a few minutes longer, when nature called with a different, albeit urgent, voice, and he realized that he needed to find a convenient tree without delay!

George was now completely awake. His leg was functioning normally, and the drama he experienced the previous night came flooding back to his memory.

"*I think I saw a miracle last night!*" He told himself. "*I know I saw a miracle. I have been given a bone fide second chance, so today is a whole new beginning for me. At least I'm going to treat myself as if that were so. I'm going to be a better man, a kinder and gentler man — a man who is willing to do the right thing. That's what I'm going to do!*"

George got back into his car, started up the engine, and began the drive back to Misty Falls. Although it would be hours before he would arrive back at the apartment, George spent his time thinking of how he could explain to Connie what had happened to him. She was first; he figured. He needed to make things right with her. Then, if she would take him back and forgive him, he would begin to address the other areas of his life that needed his attention.

* * *

Connie got home from work about four in the afternoon. Sallie was waiting for her daughter, wondering what might happen to them, now.

Connie didn't say anything when she came in. She disappeared into the kitchen almost as if she was sleep walking and began taking things out of the refrigerator and arranging them on the narrow counter.

Sallie stood at the door of the kitchen, watching her daughter. Finally she said, "I don't suppose you've heard anything more, have you?"

Connie shook her head 'no' and began to stir a pot she had put on the range. She sighed and told her mother, "I had to tell Ms. Reynolds, because she could tell I was upset."

"What did she say?" Sallie inquired.

"She took me over to a corner of the kitchen and asked if she could pray for me," Connie told her mother.

"She did?" Sallie showed surprise.

Connie said, "Uh-huh. She did, and she prayed right then a real good prayer asking God to help me through whatever is coming.

"I think that was real kind of her ... to be so concerned for my worries. I didn't expect that from her, but it was nice."

"I remember when I used to pray," Sallie said. "I think I've almost forgotten about praying, but your Ms. Reynolds is right. We have to look to God now. We don't have any other good places to go."

"Oh, Ma! Are we supposed to use prayer as a last resort — you know, when there doesn't seem to be any other way out, then we ask God for help?" Connie whined. "Somehow, that doesn't sound right.

"If God is up there, and He knows what's going on, then He also knows we haven't been praying to Him since ...," Connie stopped.

"Since a long time, and we were wrong," Sallie finished her daughter's sentence. "I like Ms. Reynolds even better now."

Dinner wasn't a big item for Connie and her mom. Neither of them had an appetite. They settled on splitting peanut butter and strawberry jam sandwich; it was good, comfort food for them.

They sat in their small living room, wondering what would happen next. What should their next step be? "I talked to Sherriff Barrymore today. He drove over to the cafe to interview me in case I had information that might lead to identifying the victim of the railroad accident. He couldn't tell me anything more than I had already heard — a man was dead, killed by the train.

"Oh, Mom! What's going to come next? What should we be doing? I don't know if we can stay here in this apartment. If George is gone, we couldn't afford to stay here. My little salary at the cafe won't pay for this place.

"And we can't leave Misty Falls! The twins are here in Tennessee. We can't go back to South Carolina because of the twins. I **have** to be able to see them, even if it's only once a week for an hour. I have to be there for them," Connie spoke as tears raced down her face.

"I don't know what to say, Honey," Sallie answered. "I have very mixed feelings about George."

"We weren't getting along very well," Connie admitted. She was beginning to realize how she was carrying a number of unresolved feelings and concerns about her husband. "We haven't been getting along very well, but you know what? I love him, and I wouldn't know what to do if I never saw him again. I'd be lost."

"Oh please, dear LORD, don't let that be so!" Connie sobbed. Sallie went over to her daughter and gave her a big hug to comfort her.

Just then the front door opened and in walked a bright and smiling George. He had a large bunch of cut flowers in one hand that he had picked up at Friendlie's Foods before he made his appearance at the apartment.

Connie and Sallie were startled the minute they saw George and ran to the front room to see him.

"George! You're home! You came home, and you're ... you're all right! I can't believe it!" Connie flung her arms around her husband. "You're really okay. You're not dead!"

George had dropped the flowers and opened his arms to allow Connie's embrace.

To say that George was surprised at his reception would be to understate his reaction. He had hoped that he might somehow ask Connie's forgiveness for all the painful things he had done to her, AND he wanted to tell her about the miracle that he had experienced the night before.

He had stopped at the grocery store as a last minute thought to pick up some flowers for Connie, hoping to be granted an audience from his wife for what he needed to say.

George took a step back and looked at Connie and Sallie. "I can't believe this is happening! Connie, Miss Sallie, you both seem as if you're glad to see me, and yet I can't imagine why you would act that way."

Connie began to reach out to George. "Just let me touch you. I want to be sure you're really for real and that you're not some sort of hallucination" she laughed.

George wanted to say what he had come home to say before he lost his nerve or changed his mind. He looked at his mother-in-law and said, "Miss Sallie, I'm glad to be home, and it's good to see you, but would you mind if Connie and I talked alone here for a few minutes?"

Sallie took the hint and exited into her bedroom, closing the door behind her.

George took Connie by the hand and led her over to the couch in the living room; they sat down facing one another.

George spoke first, "Connie, I don't know what's been going on here, but I've come home to tell you something miraculous happened last night, and I want you to be the first to know about it."

Connie interrupted her husband, "George, today has been a nightmare! All day long today I've thought or feared you had been killed in a train accident over by the depot, but instead, you're telling me that something really good happened to you. You're acting very unlike yourself. It's not like you to be so, so ... so happy. I can hardly remember you ever being like that. What are you talking about, and where were you last night?"

"It's sort of a long story, but I have to tell you about it. The truth is, I think God did a miracle for me last night!" George gleamed at his wife.

"I don't understand, George. What do you mean, a miracle?" Connie cocked her head, listening to this unexpected tale.

"Okay, Let me start from the beginning," George suggested. He explained about his weekend trip back to Greenville how he felt inside, becoming totally convinced of his faults — hurting everyone around him, being unfaithful to Connie and uninterested in the anger management classes. "I realized how far I had failed in so many parts of my life. I drove back here yesterday afternoon; I felt as though I was mysteriously being drawn back here, but when I got to the apartment you and Miss Sallie had already taken off. I think you had gone over to the revival. I didn't want anything to do with the revival, but somehow I found myself driving over to there anyway. I slipped into the back of the church and sat down. The preacher had just come out and begun telling this story about a bum, a real pathetic character. The preacher was about to explain why Jesus loved him, but I was so angry with myself — I could see myself in that fool — I ran out of the church and drove off. I wanted to be alone and think things out."

Connie listened carefully to her husband. He seemed so earnest and eager to share what had happened to him. She was amazed at what he was telling her.

"I drove and drove. Last night was so peaceful, and the sky was crystal clear. I could see a gazillion stars you don't usually see in the city. It was breathtaking — absolutely gorgeous. Maybe I drove into Kentucky; I was on back roads most of the time, so I didn't keep track of where I was going. I didn't care. I was disgusted with myself, and I was shocked to realize how far I had fallen. I used to think I was a fairly stand-up guy. But, if I ever was one, I know I haven't been one for a long, long time.

"You have to understand, Connie: I think I finally got it. I finally understood how rotten I'd become, and I was really mad at myself. I was horrified to realize how low I had managed to sink as a man. I felt there was no hope for me. I had failed in every part of my life, and I was not worth anything to anybody. That's how I felt," George spoke in a near whisper, struggling to speak such painful words.

Connie disagreed with George. Despite his faults, she wanted to tell him she him loved him and was in his corner, but she decided to let him finish his story.

After a minute George continued. "You know it was a funny thing. I was feeling so bad, yet there was something inside me pulling me to reach beyond my misery and my self-disgust. I remember crying out, "God, I need a miracle, a real miracle. I need to be different from who I am. I need to be a better person.

"I remembered what that preacher was saying, something about the people who really appreciate God's forgiveness are the ones who are convinced they have failed. Those people absolutely know they need God's grace."

Connie took a deep breath and looked into George's eyes, trying to understand how this tale would end.

"I knew I was one of those convinced people. I knew I was a failure. I knew I needed God's love in my life.

"Last night I prayed to the LORD. It's been years since I prayed — before you and I were married — probably a long time before we got together. I think I knew we were wrong when we did what we did, but I think I turned off that little voice inside me that was trying to warn me about the stuff I was fooling around with. I just turned off that little voice of wisdom, and I did what I felt like doing.

"Connie that doesn't mean I don't love you, because I do. We were wrong in the beginning, and we've been living with the consequences of our foolishness since then. But, I want to tell you that after the miracle that happened last night, I think I'm a different man. I think God has forgiven me for the past, and has given me a new start.

"I think I can do better. I know I have failed you. I've been playing hide and seek with the anger classes, and that's one place I intend to do right. I know I can take those classes and pass them, and if we get a good mark in those classes, I think we'll get our babies back," George stopped.

Connie had been listening to her husband's declaration — how he had changed, how he had experienced a miracle — and she was amazed. So much had happened in the last twenty-four hours, and she recognized the emotional roller coaster she had been on: the trouble she and George were having; then fearing she had lost him to that tragic train accident; and finally almost miraculously, George returning and being so ... so changed, so excited, so happy!

"A lot happened last night — something wonderful happened to you — it must have been a miracle," Connie began to speak. "What else could it have been? The minister said the same thing last night — that God loves us all. Even when we hurt others or don't live up to our best, we still have God's love.

"Do you know we thought you had died last night — that you were gone forever?" Connie asked? "There was a train accident last night over near the depot. A man was on the tracks and was hit by the train. He died, of course, but no one has been able to identify him. When you didn't come home last night, I began to think you were the man.

"I thought I saw you at the Baptist Church last night; you stood up and left in the middle of the preacher's sermon. I thought it was you, and then you didn't come home, so I thought you somehow had been on the train tracks ...."

"Oh, George! I'm so glad it wasn't you! I was beside myself thinking I had lost you. I realized how much you mean to me, and how horrible it would be to lose you." Connie touched George's hand and smiled at him with eyes that glistened from the tears that were in them.

"Connie, please forgive me for being such a dunderheaded fool! I have been so wrong so many times, and I want to make it right for you now," George implored.

"I don't know what to say. Yes, I want to forgive you, but you should forgive me for badgering you about stuff. I've been crying and carrying on about the girls — wanting to get them back. I'm sure I haven't been easy to get along with.

"When I thought I'd lost you, I realized what real pain could be, and now suddenly you're here! You're alive! And something wildly wonderful has happened to you!

"Are you sure you're the same George that I know and have been married to for almost six years?" Connie reached over and pinched her husband ... to be sure he was real.

George laughed at Connie's teasing and said, 'No, that's what I'm trying to tell you. I don't think I am the same man at all. I was begging God for a miracle last night, asking the LORD to take my sin away, to make me whole, and I think He did! That has to be a miracle. I feel so clean inside, so ready to do things right this time."

Connie was still trying to take in all that George was telling her and make sense of it. She had a myriad of questions, which she began asking. "Okay, then, you're telling me that you're going to be a different person. What will make you different?"

George shrugged his shoulders and explained. "Honey, the only thing I can tell you now is how good I feel inside, and it isn't from alcohol or junk. I just feel great inside — like somehow I've done a really good thing. I know I haven't done anything yet, unless you count my prayer last night asking God to forgive me and to set me straight. I suppose that was something.

"But I also understand that even though Jesus forgave me, I still have to deal with people that I've hurt, so I'm starting with you. I need your forgiveness. I want us to start over, and this time we'll do it right.

Connie gave George a big hug and kiss. They would work things out together.

✳ ✳ ✳

Nina hurried home from work. Tucker Joe was coming for dinner tonight, and she wanted everything to be just right.

She had prepared the meal ahead of time, so there wasn't much to do except take things out of the fridge and warm them up. Tucker Joe had been so obvious when he asked Nina if she liked cooking along with baking.

Nina had decided to make stuffed bell peppers for the main dish, which might be an unusual item as an entree, but she really liked the peppers, and they were very healthy. With the peppers and the filling of meat, rice, and cheese they made a complete dinner, she thought — although she did add fresh rolls and butter, to make it perfect.

Men always enjoy having a piece of bread with their meal. No matter what else is being served, they always expect to have bread or rolls or buns with butter.

She was moving about the kitchen doing all the final finishes to the meal, when a knock came at her door.

Tucker Joe opened the door and peeked his head inside. "May I come in?" he asked.

Nina moved swiftly to the living room to welcome her guest in. "Of course, come in, and make yourself at home.

"I was just finishing up a few details in the kitchen. Can I pour you something to drink?" Nina asked.

"I'd like some Coke, if you have it, or how about diet Coke?" Tuck corrected himself. "I'd like not to add empty calories."

Nina smiled at her guest and showed him where the ice and Coke were, so he could prepare one for himself.

She had set up dinner at her kitchen table; she offered her guest a seat there.

"I'm sorry you had to do this dinner for me at the end of your workday," Tuck admitted, "but I'm not sure if there's ever a time when one of us isn't working, is there?"

"Come to think of it, you're right. I work weekdays for Dr. Sedgwick and some weekends at the clinic, and you work, when?" Nina asked.

"Most of the time, but I have been taking Thursdays off for several months. Of course Friendlie's doesn't open until noon on Sundays." Tuck explained.

Nina placed a wide-rimmed bowl before each of them containing a large, stuffed, green bell pepper; she also brought a pewter tray with fresh rolls.

"This is great," Tucker started to say. "I know I've had stuffed peppers before, but I don't remember eating a whole one like this. It looks a bit like a work of art; I hate to dig into it. I suppose I should carve it delicately with my fork and knife."

"Please enjoy the pepper however you're comfortable. I usually chop mine up so there's a piece of pepper to go with the stuffing in each bite. You might like to try that," Nina laughed. "I didn't realize that I was presenting a problem with this meal."

Tuck pretended to use large gestures to approach his pepper and cut it into bite sized pieces. "Mmmmmm! This is scrumptious! It's not as good looking now, but who cares? It tastes great! "I think I can absolutely declare that you really are a good cook!" He winked at Nina.

"I have to tell you about what happened last Sunday night after you left," Nina changed the subject.

"You went to bed, right? It was already late for a school night." Tuck guessed.

"Well, I did get to bed eventually, but not before I went over to the cemetery to think. I go there sometimes, since it's so close; it feels good to be near Dan's marker. Anyway, I was sitting there on the bench soaking up the peacefulness, when I saw a man entering the garden and coming my direction.

"At first I was alarmed, being alone and this stranger coming into the cemetery so late at night, but then he spoke and I realized who he was," Nina told Tuck.

"Really! Who was it?" Tuck sat up taller in his chair.

"We had been watching him on stage all evening, so I knew it was the same man. It was the preacher. He had driven over to the cemetery to find a place to think and pray. He explained to me that after a big revival he's too wound up to just go home to bed, so he seeks out a quiet spot.

Someone told him about Peace of Heaven Cemetery, and he drove over here," Nina remembered aloud.

"I'm glad he wasn't someone else, someone with the wrong sort of motives," Tucker observed.

"No, he is a good man, a man of God, I believe," Nina stated.

"We talked about faith, and I told him about the conversation you and I had just been having. He seemed to be pleased that we were still thinking about his revival challenge.

"We talked about following Jesus, and he asked me what I was waiting for.

"It occurred to me that my pride has been the major obstacle that keeps me from saying 'yes.' I like doing my own thing, and I have never wanted to be considered weak — like going down to the altar for prayer. I didn't want to be lumped in with some Christians I've known who are real hypocrites. I figured I could do better than they do; I'm afraid I thought I am better than they are," Nina admitted.

"Sounds like you know yourself pretty well," Tucker Joe commented.

"Yes, but when I said that to the preacher, speaking those words out in the air, I could see how anemic my thinking was. Who was I kidding? Did I really suppose I could handle everything without God's blessings? I can't, and neither can anyone else. We all need God's care, and healing, and goodness, and love. It occurred to me that God is the God of the good things in life, and I want and need to be on God's team. It might / could be that if you're not on God's team, then you've put yourself on some other team, and that's bucking God. How stupid is that?" Nina asked.

"So, you just figured out why waiting is wrong for you." Tucker thought he could see where Nina was going.

"You could say that. I've waited too long to come to that conclusion. But once I realized it was a matter of choosing which team I needed to be associated with, the decision was obvious.

"Before Rev. Cobb left he prayed with me to accept Jesus as my Savior, LORD, and Friend," Nina told Tuck.

"I believe that Rev. Cobb is a real Christian; he's definitely on the right team," Nina seemed to be telling herself. "He's so dedicated to his work and truly trying to lead the Christian life. He's also brought many others to faith in Christ, and I guess I'm one of them."

"What an evening! I'm glad you made that decision and that Rev. Cobb happened to be there to talk to you.

"I remember the pastor used to talk about coincidences that were really 'God-incidences', when things happen to come together, or like you and that preacher just happening to be in the same garden way late at night. That sounds like a 'God-Incidence' to me," Tucker said.

"A 'God-Incidence.' Yes, I like that. It must have been," Nina agreed. (Tucker nodded his head and smiled, knowingly.) "Since then I feel like I've been living with two, almost opposite emotions. I've been feeling very pleased inside, and I feel like I named a problem in me that I wasn't consciously aware of before — my pride — and now that my awareness has been sparked, I'm seeing my pride pop up all over the place.

"It's an interesting phenomenon, feeling pleased AND askance at myself all at once," Nina tried to explain herself.

"Pleased and askance at self? Can you break that down a little?" Tucker asked.

"Okay, the pleased side of me is tickled when I realize that I made a good decision, one that should have been made long ago, but still I made it, and it feels very right inside — deliciously happy.

"Feeling askance at self is because I find myself continually uncovering more examples of my pride. Seems everywhere I look I have been prideful — in so many aspects of my life I find I've been too proud," Nina shook her head.

"I see. You're happy about joining the winning team, as you put it — being part of God's family. Then you're being introspective, and you're seeing your former, prideful self, so you're shocked and dismayed at that. How 'm I doing?" Tucker asked.

Nina agreed, "I think you understand. That does make sense. It occurs to me that not only am I recognizing all the different ways I've been prideful, but maybe, as I see these unattractive / prideful ways I have been living, I realize I need to change that ugly attitude for something better. Pride has to be the opposite of humility. I remember my friend Winnie used to say we should walk humbly with God."

The conversation moved on to mundane matters — the national news, which was still reeling from the economic woes of the country, the wars in Iraq and Afghanistan, and the new community playground that was in the planning.

Nina felt she needed to address one more topic, "Sunday you said you were looking for a 'significant other.'"

Tuck laughed and said. "Yes, I probably shouldn't have said anything so awkward as that, but truth be known, I find myself in a bit of a quandary, and I really don't know what to do about it. I suppose there are other ways of finding the right someone, but I was hoping the old fashioned way — boy meets girl; boy falls for girl; they get 'twitter-pated' and live happily every after — would work for me."

Nina laughed at Tuck's streamlined system. "Only in the fairy books does that happen. What would you consider a 'significant other,' anyway?"

"That's just a catchphrase these days. I don't really mean a modern sort of arrangement like we see on TV, but I do feel life is passing me by. I've been working 'nose to grindstone' for so long, and I haven't taken any time to get to know anyone special, yet I figure I should have someone in my life by now ...," he stopped.

"Tuck, you and I are good friends, even buddies, but I don't know that we would ever be a 'match.' There isn't anything for us in that way. Do you agree?

"I think we enjoy being in one another's company, like last Sunday at the revival, when we can spend time together and talk out hard questions, but I don't see us ever stepping beyond that," Nina admitted to Tuck.

"I'm glad to hear you say that," Tucker agreed. "I've been wondering what it is that doesn't seem right for us, and I think there may be several items. For one thing, even though age shouldn't matter — we are both adults — I am younger than you, and one day I'd like to have a family. I think that's not part of your agenda."

Nina could hardly contain her mirth at this suggestion. "Amen, brother! I have had my family, and I have grandchildren, now, so that answers that question. Doesn't it? I can imagine you do want your own children; most people do, but I'm afraid you'll have to look somewhere else."

Both Nina and Tucker Joe were relieved to have addressed the issue of their relationship, and they parted friends.

✳ ✳ ✳

Trudy wanted to tell Ned about Kareem. She now knew it was the right thing to do. He deserved to know about this charming young man who was his son. Trudy knew she had been vacillating for too long about telling Ned; the time had come for action.

Thanksgiving was approaching soon, and Trudy wondered if Ned might be home for the holiday. If he was coming home over the long weekend, maybe ... perhaps, she might have a chance to see him. Somehow she hoped to find a way to insinuate the idea of Kareem's existence into Ned's thinking.

Trudy hoped an email would do the trick. She wanted to learn Ned's plans for Thanksgiving and possibly secure a 'date' with him when he was in town. She typed:

"Hey there, Ned! Your name came up the other day, and it occurred to me that you might be coming home for the holidays. Do you get time forThanksgiving and Christmas at the Academy, and will you be home then? I hope that answer is 'yes,' and I'm hoping that we might see each other somehow if you' ll be around.

How's that for being forward? That's not me, usually. I'm too shy most of the time to assert myself, but I remember the fun we had before ....

Anyway, I expect to be home over the holidays and would really love to hear from you.

Trudy"

"Well, that's that. Who knows if your daddy will answer, or if he'll think I'm too pushy, almost inviting myself on a date with him, or ... or ... I don't know what. Well, I can hope, can't I?" Trudy told her baby.

That evening following dinner, after Trudy had finished feeding Kareem and putting him down for the night, she opened up her computer, just to see if there was any response, and (!) Ned had seen her email and promptly replied.

"Trudy,

"Good to hear from you, again. It's been a while since I got your card, which is still tacked on my bulletin board.

"Yes, we cadets get both holidays, and yes I would love to see you again. Are you commuting to school, or do you live on campus? For that matter, I didn't hear what school you finally chose. I'm imagining you chose UT Knoxville — it's reasonably close and has a great reputation.

"Aren't you loving the whole college scene? I suppose you have a beau, but maybe you're between beaus, since you said you'd like to see me when I'm home.

"Sure, I get a week for Thanksgiving as well as a two and a half week Winter Break in December, and I'm definitely looking forward to having a reprieve from all this heavy studying I'm doing.

"How about we go out on Friday, the day after Thanksgiving? The Friday after Turkey Day is open on my calendar, and seeing you sounds more than fun.

"Would you like to go somewhere special for dinner? I don't get out much due to my busy schedule. It's the mess hall that fills me. Not that it's not good food; it is good, but having a real date without a tight curfew could make for a great evening.

315

"I need to get back to the books for now. Let me know if Friday will work for you and if you have any particular restaurant you'd like.

"Already looking forward to a fun evening, Ned"

Trudy could hardly contain herself; she was so excited. It was late. Kareem had been down and asleep for an hour, and she found herself wound up like a top, desperate to start spinning. She had to tell someone about the fantastic message she had just received from Ned, but ... she couldn't.

Trudy hadn't told anyone the identity of Kareem's father. She had kept his name out of her baby's history. She had protected Ned's scholarship by not dragging him into her world of unmarried mother and child. Now, having decided she was wrong about not informing Ned, she realized that she couldn't tell anyone.

Trudy was almost beside herself; she just <u>had</u> to tell someone the news that Ned was coming to town and was looking forward to taking her out.

Before she knew it, Trudy had tiptoed down the hall to her mother's bedroom and knocked lightly on the door.

Keisha Livingston, being a light sleeper, was quickly awakened and rose on one elbow to see what could be the matter. "What's up Honey?" She asked her daughter. "Is Kareem Okay?"

Trudy ran over to Keisha's bed and sat down next to her mom, leaned over and gave her mother a big hug. "Oh, Mom, the baby's fine. I just have to talk to you," Trudy explained.

"Well, of course," Keisha assured her daughter as she sat up on her bed. "What's on your mind?" Keisha wondered what possibly could have happened since dinner that evening.

"I just got some fabulous news, and I have to share it with someone or I may explode!" Trudy explained.

Keisha was now fully awake and beginning to share her daughter's excitement about this mysterious event. "Whatever are your talking about? Has something changed since dinner?"

Trudy shook her head and said, "No, nothing's changed, yet maybe everything is about to change."

"Such a mystery!" her mother teased. "Tell me what's goin' on."

"You know I've been worried for some time about what to do about Kareem's father — what is the right thing to do in this situation," Trudy stopped.

Keisha was suddenly very interested in Trudy's news. "And?" she encouraged her daughter.

"And I finally decided that he really does need to know about Kareem. In fact, I think he shouldn't miss out on being a father to his wonderful son," Trudy announced.

Keisha was nodding her head, following Trudy's words, agreeing with her.

"So I decided to tell him," Trudy continued. (Keisha listened, nodding her head in agreement.)

"I sent him a card that I made several weeks ago. I drew one of those cards like I used to make with colored pencils. I wrote, 'Hope you're flying high these days,' and I put my email address in the corner, so he could respond, if he wanted to.

"And he did email me back, saying he was really busy and happy, and he hoped I was doing the same at my school.

"I didn't quite know what to say about what I'm doing, so I didn't reply.

"Then, tonight I thought I needed to push this ball a bit further down the road, so I emailed him and sort of suggested that I'd like to see him if he happens to be around over the holidays," Trudy caught her breath.

"You did?" Keisha asked her eyes widening. "That's a big step. Did he answer your email?"

Trudy bounced up and down on the bed. "Yes, that's what I came here to tell you. He did! He read his email and replied right then. He wrote back, saying he would love to see me. He said, he'd like to take me out the day after Thanksgiving! I can hardly imagine it. I feel a bit like Cinderella and the missing slipper. The prince is coming, and I'll get to see him."

"Do you suppose we could put a name on this young man, now?" Keisha asked. "I know you don't want anyone to know who Kareem's father is, and I gather he is not from Misty Falls. I won't tell anyone, but I'd like to know."

"Oh, Mom, of course. His name is Ned, Ned Wilson. We met at Jeanelle's cousin's swim party a year ago summer, and we liked each other a lot. Ned was a couple years ahead of me in school. He had just finished his freshman year at the Air Force Academy when we met."

"He's at the Air Force Academy?" Keisha exclaimed, trying to put this picture together. "I can see why you'd like him."

Trudy grinned even more. She was so elated from Ned's email, and now telling her mother about him seemed as if she was the star of a chick flick. "It all happened so fast. I liked Ned from the moment we started talking, and I think I fell in love with him before the end of the afternoon. He's so cool — a real hunk! He's smart, and tall, and good looking, and kind, and good. I was totally surprised that he would be interested in me, but after we started talking we seemed so right together. We had a lot in common — sports, doing well in school, growing up around here, looking forward to good things in life.

"We had one date to the movies the next night. You'd have to say that was memorable! Ned was going with his family on some trip after that and then back to some Air Force base for several weeks for training. We only had that one date, but of course, there were lasting consequences.

"When I realized I was expecting Kareem, I was afraid that if Ned found out, somehow, he would lose his scholarship, and I would be blamed for ruining his life," Trudy confessed to her mom.

Keisha was following exactly what Trudy said, and she certainly appreciated her daughter's feelings about not wanting to destroy this young man's future. "But now you're thinking differently about telling Ned? What made you change your mind?"

"A number of things. You remember I told you about Connie, the girl who lost her children. She started me thinking about Ned. I told her most of my story, and she was shocked that I hadn't told Kareem's father about his son. Then, earlier this year, before the baby came, I was talking to Miss Winnie, and she told me that she likes to use a 'rule of thumb,' — 'If I am ashamed to tell Jesus about something I'm doing or have done, that might be a strong indicator of it being wrong.' I have to say, in no way would I be ashamed to tell the LORD that I want to tell Kareem's father about him being a parent.

"And then there's Kareem, himself. He's so adorable! You know that, and he's looking more and more like his daddy every day. I can hardly look at him nowadays without thinking of Ned. And I love my little guy so much; I think I've come to the conclusion that I don't have the right to keep Ned from having an opportunity to know his son," Trudy sighed.

Keisha wanted to support her daughter's decision. "Trudy, I think you've done the right thing. I don't know how you're going to tell Ned, but I'll be happy to be your sounding board if you want to talk. I'm real happy that you shared your special news with me tonight."

Trudy felt better, having told her mom about Ned. She gave Keisha a big hug and headed back to her room. Before jumping into bed she kissed her baby gently on his cheek, dropped into bed, and fell fast asleep.

※ ※ ※

Thanksgiving week had arrived, and all around Misty Falls preparations were being made for family celebrations of giving thanks. The community Thanksgiving gathering had been at Muddy Creek UMC this year, and Brother Tinsley Booker from Faith AME Church was the preacher. Following the service as everyone was enjoying goodies in the fellowship hall, Clive Weston, the new pastor at Muddy Creek Church, greeted Tinsley and thanked him for his message. "It's good to experience the Misty Falls community coming together like this, and it's especially good to see so many folks from various places in town all praising and thanking God.

Your sermon was completely on target for us as everyone is trying to understand what it is to be thankful, especially in light of the current economic bust," Clive began. He lowered his voice, raised his eyebrows and said, "Tinsley, I heard something about the odd business that occurred with the community offering a couple years ago — how initially the money hadn't been picked up from the trays, and then later it was missing, and then six months after that the money showed up in another community offering! What a strange turn of events. Sounds like whoever it was had a real lesson to learn, but it also sounds like things turned out right. Do you suppose we'll ever know more about that?"

Tinsley shook his head 'no.' "I think you've heard right. Somebody, somehow, managed to pick up the offering that evening, and it sounds like the person was highly tempted to use it. But whatever happened, the individual eventually made everything right, so we're happy to leave it at that. It was the source of a good chuckle when the funds were returned and we were able to put them back in the community chest."

✳ ✳ ✳

Lucy Jane came to the community Thanksgiving service with her family. Since her dad, Theo Smith, was the acting general contractor for the playground committee, and Action Weekend was just a couple of weeks away, she was preoccupied with thoughts about the project.

Theo had asked his daughter to help find extra helpers who would come and lend a hand in the many not so technical aspects of the weekend — food and water providers, "gofers", set up and clean up personnel, and team members. Lucy Jane used every spare minute she had outside of work, enlisting people to sign up to help.

At this point Lucy Jane had found most of the people she needed for Action Weekend, and she discovered she was enjoying the extra responsibility, getting people to sign up to help for this good, neighborhood cause. Lucy Jane was a people person, although with the recent loss of her husband and moving back to Misty Falls, she realized she had not been her usual, outgoing self. This job she was doing for her dad helped her to begin to open up more with others, and as she spoke to increasingly more people, she felt she was more relaxed and like her old self. She enjoyed interacting with folks, helping them to see the need for a playground in the community. She had hoped that she might run into Tucker Joe at the community Thanksgiving event, because she wanted to enlist his help on Action Weekend. Besides that she was looking forward to seeing him again. It had been some time since they had dined together and she told him about her unexpected windfall — the money that had come to her from her late husband's investment.

"I really hoped to see Tuck tonight," Lucy Jane said to herself. *Maybe I'll have to make an appearance at Friendlie's Foods sometime soon."* She decided to try to catch Tuck at his store sometime this week, since she would be shopping for last minute items for her family's Thanksgiving.

✳ ✳ ✳

Lucy Jane stopped at Friendlie's Foods grocery store Tuesday afternoon before Thanksgiving to buy apples and a large can of pumpkin for the pies she planned to bake. She also picked up some Parker House

319

rolls and butter and ice. The store was packed with shoppers, each intent on finding just the right items to complete their holiday fare. Lucy Jane squelched a smirk from her lips as she gazed at the unusually large crowd of folks in the store, jamming all the aisles and creating long lines at the checkout.

Lucy Jane hoped she might run into Tucker Joe while she was in the store, and she had been keeping an eye open to find him. She had about decided to ask a store employee about Tuck, when she saw him. He was deeply engrossed in conversation with a couple of men wearing suits and ties and carrying clipboards. They were standing in the meat section of the store.

Lucy Jane maneuvered her basket over to where the three men stood and waited to be noticed. When Tuck saw Lucy Jane standing nearby, he excused himself and turned to speak to her.

"Well! Lucy Jane! It's good to see you. I suppose you're doing your last minute shopping for the big day?" Tuck asked.

"Like everyone else here!" Lucy Jane admitted. "You've got quite a monopoly on groceries here in Misty Falls. This must be one of your busiest times of the year."

Tucker Joe wrinkled his eyes and smiled wearily. "I'll say! "Yes, this certainly is a crazy time for us, and especially since I'd like to give my employees time off for their own celebration, Friendlie's will only be open 'til two on Thanksgiving Day. Hopefully, that will allow folks who need this or that to get in early for what they want, and we can still have some family time for ourselves."

"I can't imagine what it must be like to always be open and available for the community!" Lucy Jane thought out loud. "It would have to be exhausting. No one can work all the time. We're not built for that. We're not machines."

"Friendlie's is only open to midnight, of course, and it's a matter of staffing to keep things running well. As the owner, I'm in and out all day long. I take time when I can for myself, and I do take most of Thursdays off, just for me."

"Tuck, what are you doing this Thursday?" Lucy Jane suddenly wondered if Tuck had plans.

Tuck shook his head. "No, I guess I don't have plans. Things change when you're the only one left in the family. I've been telling myself for a while, now, that I really do have to get movin' on doin' somethin' about my personal life. I just haven't fig'red it out, yet."

Lucy Jane's eyes grew larger as she realized what Tucker Joe was telling her. "You really don't have an invitation to Thanksgiving?" (Tuck wagged his head back and forth, 'no.') "Then I'm asking you right now to come join me and my family for the holiday dinner."

"You mean it?" Tuck said hopefully. "I'd love to come. Thanks for the invite.

"Can I bring something?" He offered.

Lucy Jane was warming up to this unexpected change in her holiday. "There's nothing you would need to bring, except your merry self," she assured her guest. "Everything is already set for the dinner, especially once I get these things home and start work on the pies.

"You DO like pie?" Lucy Jane teased.

"How can you go wrong with pie?" Tucker assured Lucy Jane. "I'm already looking forward to the dinner. You've certainly helped change my feeling about Thanksgiving — from a major work time to something I actually would LIKE to do.

"What time should I be over?" Tuck asked.

The two finished up arrangements for the dinner, happily anticipating what might be developing between them.

Chapter 33. The Secret

Trudy had hardly been able to enjoy Thanksgiving with her family, knowing that she would be seeing Ned the next day and that their meeting might promote serious consequences.

She didn't know what to expect on her date with Ned. She hoped that their time together might just be the beginning of a real friendship. But considering her objective, disclosing Ned's family relationship, she wasn't at all sure of the outcome.

For one thing Trudy was a little concerned that Ned might have completely misunderstood her email. He might have thought she had more in mind than a 'date.' "*I tried to be so careful in composing my message to Ned, so as not to be too forward or suggestive, but somehow the words I wrote — 'the <u>fun</u> we had before' or 'hoping we might <u>see</u> each other' — in light of our previous date, could have been read with a double meaning, and I sure don't want Ned thinking <u>that's</u> what I have in mind. Of course, I **don't** have that in mind. I made a mistake once, but that doesn't mean I would make the same blunder again. I don't want him to misinterpret my intentions.*

I want Ned to have a relationship to his son — have some part in Kareem's life. There must be various scenarios that could work. I have no idea what he will decide to do about this new addition to his life, but I can't expect him to suddenly want me in his world, too. It's one thing for Ned to find some way to be part of Kareem's life, and it's completely, another thing for him to be interested in me! That's not my objective tomorrow," Trudy tried to convince herself.

Ned has probably dated a dozen other girls since we went out; a year and a half can make an enormous difference in the life of a cadet, I'm sure. I'd be totally surprised if he doesn't have several girlfriends. Why not? He's so yummy!

Trudy couldn't stop her musing about Ned as she and her mother and Kareem walked over to Gram's house. Gram had a house further down the road, just beyond the Misty Falls town limits. Keisha, Trudy's mom, had grown up in that house with her three siblings. Her father had passed away a couple years ago, but her brothers were nearby, and her sister came back when she could. Thanksgiving Day was one of those days when the entire clan would be together, and Trudy should have been especially pleased to be there. And she was.

She had been looking forward to the holiday, when so many kin folk would be at Gram's. She would be seeing cousins she hadn't seen in months and she could show off little Kareem.

Everyone brought food to share. Gram cooked the bird. She had stuffed him earlier and popped him in the oven before breakfast. Besides the traditional American Foods — turkey, mashed potatoes, and cranberries — their table would include mac & cheese, pork chitterlings, yams, turnip greens, a green salad, potato salad, rolls, and sweet potato pie. The food would be much enjoyed, of course, but the best part of the day was getting to see family members who had been away for a while.

As much as Trudy wanted to immerse herself in family and cousins, her new status as a mother and her need to watch over Kareem took precedence over hanging out with the siblings.

The baby was getting closer and closer each day to standing free and beginning to walk. Kareem wasn't quite ready to balance himself, but he would pull himself up on whatever convenient chair or table was nearby, grasp it with his strong, baby fingers, and then begin to edge his way around the room, moving from one piece of furniture to the next. He was the newest family member and, therefore, a big star at the Thanksgiving party. Trudy loved being the mother of this newest youngster. She was also pleased to note how her own status had modulated due to her new title — Mother.

For all the fun of the day, Trudy's mind dwelled in the morrow. She was nervous, excited, terrified, and hopeful all at one time. She and her mother shared a secret — knowing that Ned was coming to take her out, and that she was going to, somehow, tell him about his being a parent. She found herself relishing this little secret she was sharing with her mom. Their secret made the day special. Every so often Trudy and Keisha would exchange glances and smile, eyes twinkling, knowing what was coming.

✳ ✳ ✳

Lucy Jane told her folks that she had invited Tucker Joe Tennyson to Thanksgiving dinner. She explained how she happened to see him at the grocery store, and that he had no plans for the holiday. "I couldn't just leave him without an invitation to dinner. His store does so much for our whole community, and then he didn't even have an invitation to dinner. So I asked him. I hope that's all right with y'all."

The invitation was perfectly fine with Mary Nell and Theo, Lucy Jane's parents. They exchanged glances and raised eyebrows in a knowing sort of silent communication as their daughter was explaining how she had invited Tucker Joe to dinner.

"I told Tuck that we'd be eating about four o'clock Thursday, and I think he'll arrive sometime before that." Lucy Jane added.

323

✳ ✳ ✳

Tuck arrived at the Smith's house by 3:15, carrying a large bouquet of flowers for Lucy Jane and a bottle of Riesling for his hosts. (He
had picked up the items just before closing up the store and leaving for
the Smith's home. He congratulated himself for being in the business that
would allow him that advantage — having access to quick gifts like the
wine and flowers — not that he would take anything without reimbursing
the store.)

The Smith's dinner table had been stretched as far as it would
extend with leaves to accommodate nine people — Theo and Mary Nell,
Lucy Jane's older brother, Teddy, her sister Carol and her husband along
with their two children.

Tucker had been looking forward to a pleasant dinner with Lucy
Jane and her family from the moment she asked him to come. His anticipation of the event [might he call it a date?] had heightened over the last
several hours, and he found he was more than just a bit hopeful that Lucy
might be similarly interested in him. *"Previously she's been understanda-
bly preoccupied with the loss of her husband, but I wonder if she's beginning to find her way through that maze of emotion?"* Tucker Joe thought.

The dinner conversation was especially lively with the addition of
a guest. Tucker Joe was seated opposite Lucy Jane and next to her dad,
Theo. Tucker was amused to note how everyone seemed to be focused
on him. He answered questions from all around the table about his work
at the store and his presence in Misty Falls. "Yes, both Mother and Pappy
were from here; I believe their grandparents were even native of Misty
Falls. Back then, their families were in farming, like everyone was,"
Tucker told Theo in response to his question.

Mary Nell, sitting at the other end of the table, asked her guest,
"We know your family because of the grocery store, but are you the last
Tennyson, or are there more like you at home?"

"No, I'm afraid I'm the last of the bunch. Mother and Pappy should
have had more children; I used to think they were too busy to have others, but that probably wasn't the case. I've always wanted to have a big
family, but the best I can claim these days is a cousin who lives in Nashville with his wife and kids. That's hardly big," Tucker shook his head in
dismay.

"I'd say you've added a fine element to our family today, Tucker,"
Theo assured his guest. "We'd be pleased to have you come whenever
you'd like; wouldn't we?" Theo asked his clan at the table

Lucy Jane was amused by the somewhat obvious way Tucker
Joe was being courted at the table. *"My family is acting conspiratorially
about Tuck. He seems to be playing along with them, but still, I hope this
silly show doesn't embarrass him or worse,"* she worried.

"Oh! Dad, You're embarrassing him!" Lucy Jane complained to
her father. "Really, Tuck, you have to understand how worried everyone

has been about me, since ... you know ... since Chet died. They've wanted to kiss me and make it better, but that's not the way grief works." Lucy Jane told Tucker.

"I'm very pleased to be here with y'all today." Tuck smiled and nodded his head around the dining table. "If you hadn't invited me to join you, I'd be home microwaving a Marie Callender frozen meal, so you can see how better life has suddenly become for me!"

"I can't imagine anyone having to eat Thanksgiving dinner by himself. That's just not right," Mary Nell stated. Then, turning to her daughter she said, "I'm so glad you ran into Tucker and invited him to join us today."

The conversation moved to a more pressing topic — Playground Action Weekend. Since Theo was deeply involved as general contractor for the project, he told Tucker Joe about it.

" ... and so, with all the many pieces coming together we should have our new Misty Falls playground erected weekend after next."

"I have heard that Misty Falls is working on the project, but it's really interesting to hear more detail about it. You're certainly the man with the plan. I haven't been involved at all, I'm sure you're aware, and the only thing I can claim is the usual business — Friendlie's monopolizes my life. But since I'm sitting at the table of the very one who would know, tell me, is there anything I can do for the effort at this late date?"

Lucy Jane picked up on this cue and said, "Tuck, there is something you can do to help us. Would Friendlie's be able to provide the soft drinks and water for our volunteer workers? That would be the perfect gift you could provide, and it would be very appreciated."

"That is the perfect fit," Tuck agreed smiling at Lucy Jane. "I can get coolers over to the site with ice and drinks. Do you know approximately how many volunteers we might be wanting to provide for?"

Lucy Jane and Theo talked more about the plans for Action Weekend, and Tuck was pleased to be thinking about something beyond groceries, inventory, and delivery schedules for a change.

At the end of the dinner, before the pies were brought out, Tuck spoke up, "I just want to say thank you to each of you here. You've made my day, and I am very glad you included me in your Thanksgiving celebration."

"Tuck, you make a fine guest, and I hope we will see you again soon, but we're hardly finished with our meal," Mary Nell assured her guest. "We have pies yet to be enjoyed." She and Lucy Jane exited the dining room and quickly returned with the home baked pies along with ice cream and whipped cream.

After the meal Tucker and Lucy Jane went into the small den and sat in a corner where they could to talk somewhat apart from the others.

"I'm really glad you came today," Lucy Jane began. "Thanksgiving is one of my favorite holidays. It's not so jammed with gifts and paraphernalia, like Christmas, but there's a good feeling of being thankful in all circumstances of life. Everyday should be a Thanksgiving!

"I'm really thankful for today." Tucker admitted. "I think your home is so warm, and loving, and gracious, and inviting.

"How are you doing these days? I mean, how are you feeling about yourself? I know you've been through a tough season, but from what I can see, you're doing well. Am I right?"

"When Dad asked me to look around for volunteers for Action Weekend, I saw a need that I could fill, and I've been trying to do more each week. I can see I'm getting stronger and feeling more like my old self these days. I have to say that seeing you here today has lifted my spirit in a good way," Lucy Jane smiled at Tuck.

Tuck changed the subject. "A few weeks ago I asked Nina Mattingly to go with me to the last night of the revival. We used to go out occasionally before Mother got sick, and I was looking around for someone to go with to the revival. I was hoping it would be rather like a local show with good music and stuff. The revival turned out to be very good, although it wasn't like a show. Nina and I had a deep conversation afterwards about a question that the preacher has left everyone thinking about."

"A question? I thought revivalists would be calling people to give their lives to the LORD. Is that a question?" Lucy Jane was now curious.

"I suppose it all works together. The question the preacher asked, after he had said all those things about following Jesus, was, 'What are you waiting for? What's keeping you from answering Jesus' call to follow?'" Tucker explained.

"'What am I waiting for?' That's a great question; it could cover a multitude of reasons, couldn't it?" Lucy Jane asked rhetorically. "I like that. Did you and Nina make a decision?"

"Well, we talked about that question and what it requires — saying, 'Yes,' to Jesus entails beginning to follow Him and includes all the other 'yeses' that will come up later on," Tuck explained.

"That's deep, but it does make sense. No one knows what tomorrow will involve, and I guess, when we follow the LORD we rely on His guidance and power and healing, even when we can't see clearly ahead," Lucy Jane suggested.

"Spoken like a true woman of faith," Tuck grinned.

"Nina and I came to a good conclusion a couple days later when I had dinner at her place."

"And what was your conclusion?" Lucy Jane was getting very interested to hear about Nina.

"We realized that, even though we're very good friends, and we enjoy tossing around ideas like how faith can affect our lives, we are just that — good friends, almost like brother and sister. It was a great discovery, and one that gave us our freedom.

"You'd be surprised what the straw was that broke that camel's back," Tuck mentioned.

"The straw? What are you talking about?" Lucy Jane's curiosity was suddenly aflame.

Tuck laughed and explained, "Yes. You see, I still hope to have a family of my own, in the not too distant future, but Nina definitely doesn't need that. She has children ... and grandchildren! When we realized the disparity in our ages was really significant that sealed the deal. We will be great friends, but nothing more."

"You want children. Of course you'd like children! That's a very normal part of growing up. I read this article by a human growth and development expert from Sweden, a man named Erikson, who wrote about eight stages of a person's life, and one of those stages was called Generativity. It refers to the time when adults begin to pass their values and culture on to the next generation. Erikson believed that each of these stages of development in life can result in success or failure.

"You and I would fit in the stage of life when we want to share ourselves with a new crop of people. I certainly don't want to fail that stage of life development, and I think that's where you are, too," Lucy Jane caught her breath.

"Are you saying that if people don't reproduce then they will fail that stage of development?" Tuck asked knitting his eyebrows together.

"No! That's not it. Having children is one way to start passing on the wisdom we've gleaned, but there are certainly other ways to influence the younger set. You could be a mentor, or an adoptive parent, or a teacher, or scout leader, or some other way of working with the next generation. All of those are ways to be generative," Lucy Jane pointed out.

"That's a relief!" Tucker Joe pretended to wipe perspiration from his forehead. "I have to be honest with you, though, I really look forward to having my own children, and at my age I realize that it couldn't be any too soon."

"Tucker, I didn't expect you to bring so much with you today. It's a holiday! Are we supposed to think on our day off?" Lucy Jane teased her friend. "Well, maybe we should. The question, 'What am I waiting for?' calls for a thoughtful response, and you raised your own question about us both being in the same place — wanting to be generative.

"I like your challenges, and I shall work on them," Lucy Jane promised.

✳ ✳ ✳

Thanksgiving weekend in Aspen was a glorious, snow-covered wonderland, and Winnie and John were certainly enjoying their holiday getaway. "Last year when you emailed me your invitation to join you here, I have to admit that I dreamed just a bit about coming up here with you. I knew that I couldn't join you here, but that didn't stop my mind from taking a short vacation into the land of temptation, imagining us being here together. I knew I couldn't accept your offer, but still I wondered ...," Winnie winked at John.

"We can't go back to a year ago and reenact that decision, and I wouldn't want to, but I have to say, everything turned out so well. I'm not the least bit sorry that the tryst didn't develop. It makes our trip here this year that much sweeter. Don't you agree, Mrs. Daniel?" John reached over and tickled his wife in the ribs.

Winnie jumped back to avoid John's fingers and said, "Of course I am; you know I am, and I'm glad you admit the same. This year we have a different story. We can be here and enjoy the amenities at the inn and the town here, as well as the snow, and all the fun all we want."

"I think I'm still in that first phase of marriage when the romance hasn't even begun to tarnish, Win. I still wonder if my feet will ever touch the ground again," John crinkled his eyes and looked whimsically at his bride.

The Daniels picked up their room key and took their bags up to their second floor room. John unlocked the door and held it open for Winnie to enter. "Welcome to our new honeymoon venue, Win." John looked around the room. It had the usual things one would expect in a hotel room — a big, a kingsized bed, dresser, TV, an arm chair, an alcove opening to the bath area, and a big picture window looking out on the town with an expanse of Aspen Mountain silhouetted at the horizon. As the hour was late, the town below was sparkling with lights describing the town of Aspen.

"Oh, look John," Winnie moved over to the window. "It looks like a fairyland, all twinkly and cute."

"Cute isn't a man's word, but the town certainly does resemble something out of a storybook," John joined his bride at the window, putting his arm around her waist.

"Seems we were looking through a different window at the night sky just a few months ago, the night we set our wedding date, weren't we?" John reminisced.

"John, you are a romantic! Indeed my trip to visit you in Chicago was perfect in so many ways. I'll never forget it; we certainly realized that we needed to be married." Winnie remembered.

"Yes, well, this is even better. You won't send me home at the close of the evening!" John sighed.

"We can't really see the mountains with the pitch black out there, but can you show me where will you be skiing tomorrow?" Winnie asked.

John stood behind Winnie and pointed his arm over her right shoulder to help her find the area where he would be. "Follow my finger there. See? That high slope to the left. It looks more like a negative picture right now in the dark, but in the morning it will be gleaming white and very picturesque."

"I'll be sure to watch that slope tomorrow; I don't suppose I'll be able to see you skiing, but I'll be thinking about you."

"Are you sure you wouldn't like to ski on the bunny slope? Skiing is fun," John wanted Winnie to know she was welcome to try the sport.

"I am quite sure, but thanks for offering. I'm sure I'll find something to do here," Winnie replied.

"You'll be here all day by yourself, and it's Thanksgiving Day. That does seem a bit odd for you, doesn't it? I'll bet this is the first Thanksgiving you won't be totally enmeshed in making the dinner, either for your own guests or at one of your children's homes." John seemed anxious considering how alone Winnie would be.

"I relish the time to have to myself, and I'm not in the least bit concerned about being alone. You don't have to worry on my account," Winnie assured John.

"What do you plan to do all that time?" John was curious.

"I think I'm ready to begin writing my book. Remember? I did want to write something, probably a piece of fiction that could describe the life of a woman pastor," Winnie reminded him.

"I remember you telling me that you'd like to write, but you can't have had time to get anything on paper, have you?" John asked.

"Before I can write I have to think, so that's what I've been doing," Winnie said. "I have some ideas of where I'd like to go with my plot."

"Thinking should always come first, of course. This ought to be a fine place to work; I am almost envious of you for that, but I shall do my downhill thrill instead.

"Tell you what, Win. How about I cancel my final downhill run tomorrow, which should be about 3 o'clock, so I can get back here and clean up for dinner? We could still have a Thanksgiving meal at one of the restaurants around here," John suggested.

✳ ✳ ✳

Trudy and Keisha planned to have the baby out of the house when Ned came to pick up his date. That would give Trudy a little time to work up to the announcement she hoped to make. Keisha got Kareem bundled up with his diaper bag and toys and snacks, and they left. Keisha would push the baby stroller over to Gram's house.

Trudy didn't have anything fashionable to wear for her special date, so she chose a pair of jeans, a long sleeved, gray orange sweatshirt with a big, orange "T" on the front. Her nervousness had not abated; it seemed there was nothing she could do to assuage her angst. *I can sure see why some people use stuff to help quell nerves, but that's not me. I'll just have to deal with it.*

It occurred to Trudy that there was something she might do. Maybe it could help. *"LORD Jesus,"* she prayed, *"You know what's going on, and You know I've never been so nervous. I don't know exactly what will happen or how I'll find the words to speak to Ned, but I really think Ned deserves to know about his son, and I think You would be pleased that I'm taking this step. Please be in this day with me. Help me do the right thing ... say the right thing. Please lead us not into temptation. Bless Ned and this whole business. Amen."*

A knock came at the door, and Trudy froze. *Well, here goes.* She felt as if she had just jumped off the high dive at the county pool. She was trusting the LORD to help her through whatever might happen this afternoon.

She opened the door just as Ned was about to knock a second time and said, "Welcome to my humble home." She stepped back, allowing her date to enter the house.

Trudy left Ned standing in the living room saying, "I'll just get my jacket; I'll be back in a minute."

When she returned Ned asked his date, "Did you say that you live here with your folks?"

"No, I live here with my mom. I don't have a dad; at least I never met him. His name is Al Jackson, but he's not from around here, and I don't know him," Trudy explained. "Mom went over to Gram's house; she won't be back for a while."

"I'd like to meet her someday," Ned commented. "She's raised a beautiful daughter."

Trudy giggled at the unexpected, kind words. "Well, thank you, sir, for the compliment."

The two buckled themselves into Ned's blue Chevy and drove off.

"You haven't told me yet. What or where is our objective today?" Trudy asked.

"I don't get to drive much at school, since we cadets live on campus at the Academy. Some cadets have cars, but it's not really needed. Anyway, I thought it would be fun to drive up into the hills; we might like to take a hike somewhere in the woods. I'm sure we can find something to eat along the way. Would you be up for a little adventure?" Ned suggested.

Trudy was all smiles. "After that big meal I had yesterday, a hike in the woods sounds like the perfect antidote. It would be good to get out and stretch and see some of the Smokies, and I have to say, your company makes it all the better."

"Well, thanks. You, too. I kinda like our company — you and me. Do you get out here much?" Ned wanted to know.

"No, I don't. I'm just from Misty Falls, so already I'm loving gettin' out of town today," Trudy assured her date.

Ned wondered at Trudy's answer, figuring that she probably went to school somewhere outside of town, but he didn't pursue his question.

330

Ned drove for a while and then pulled his car over to a rest stop adjacent a ranger station; there was a large sign with a map of the area indicating a hiking trail nearby. "What do you think of this place to hike? Looks like it's got some marked trails, so we won't get lost."

The weather, even for late November, was cooperating well for the would be hikers. The temperature was in the mid-forties in the late afternoon, although it would probably drop to a significantly cooler degree once the sun set. Ned figured they could have a good hour to hike before the sun retreated.

Ned and Trudy took time to review the map next to the entry of the path into the woods; it detailed three suggested hiking trails. They chose to follow the shortest route — five kilometers — considering the hour they had to spend. Ned and Trudy were initially able to walk the path side by side but as the trail began climbing at a severe angle, Ned stepped forward to lead the way.

The slope caused Trudy to pant for breath, but she was determined to keep up with her date. Ned found a level section of path with a turn out and a sign, indicating a lookout to the east where giant mountains in dark violet hues could be seen in the distance.

Ned motioned to Trudy to check out the view. "Look at those peaks! They totally take your breath away! Come see!"

Trudy panted, "Let me catch my breath." She stopped to look out at the majestic scene. "What a view! I've never seen the Smokies like this. They are awesome! I love how you can see so many rows of purple mountains, one behind the next, all surrounded in clouds. It feels like you're looking over heaven."

As Trudy and Ned were enjoying the view, a young girl, maybe high school age, came running quickly down the path. When she saw Trudy and Ned she stopped and cried, "My brother! I've lost my little brother, Mitch. We were on this path, following along; he was running ahead of me, turning a bend, and when I tried to catch him, he wasn't there. I've been all over this area, but he doesn't answer me. I'm going for help right now."

The minute Ned and Trudy understood the girl's alarm they wanted to help. Ned said, "There was a ranger station at the start of this trail, and someone there might be able to contact more help. Trudy, I think we should split up, so we can cover more area. How about you return to the station, and I'll go up the path with this young woman. What's your name?"

The girl's name was Yolanda. The three agreed that Ned would return with Yolanda, staying on the pathway, so they could be found. Trudy would run back for help and bring it A.S.A.P.

"You do have your cell phone, don't you?" Ned asked Trudy.

Trudy shook her head and answered, "No, I don't have one, but do you?"

Ned answered nodding his head 'yes' and told Trudy his cell number, so when she brought help they could be in communication. Trudy repeated the number several times to be sure she could remember it.

"Okay. Everybody agrees that's what we need to do?" Ned wanted to be sure they were working together. Both girls nodded agreement. "Yolanda and I will search 'til sundown, and then we'll start back down the trail when twilight comes. I hope you can bring others before that." Ned took off with Yolanda calling, "Mitch, Mitch, where are you?"

Trudy raced with all her might down the trail to the little hut. She completely forgot the anxiety about her own situation and replaced it with genuine urgency for the lost child.

When she arrived at the ranger station, she found the ranger and Yolanda's parents, who had already returned to the station. She quickly summarized what was happening for everyone, and after the ranger made a quick call to his headquarters, explaining why he would be away from the post, the four of them began hurrying up the trail to find the missing child.

Meanwhile Ned and Yolanda were calling and hoping Mitch would show up at any moment. Ned was already concerned that the daylight was diminishing, especially inside the forest, where tall trees shaded it from much sunlight. The two searchers made their way a good quarter mile up the trail when they noticed that the path turned decidedly to the east, but a second path continued on straight ahead.

"Look here!" Ned exclaimed. "Did you get this far up the path before?"

Yolanda didn't think she had seen the divergence in the path, and she told Ned, "No, I think I was getting so worried about Mitch, I had turned back for help before I got up this far."

"So, we don't know if Mitch might have taken this other path," Ned figured. "Perhaps we should try both paths. How about we go up one a ways and then return and make our way up the other?" The two agreed.

Yolanda followed Ned, who was a very quick hiker, on the lesser used path. They had been on the path about ten minutes when they came to a creek with water splashing down. The area was filled with fallen leaves from many deciduous trees around as well as large, smooth rocks in the stream.

"Great! The trail stops here at the creek. I wonder if your brother might have crossed here?" Ned observed, as he noted that some of the rocks were reasonably flat, and that they were scattered across the stream in such a way as to invite one to traverse them.

"What should we do?" Yolanda moaned. "Mitch ... Mitch!" She called out, hoping to hear a response from her little brother.

For a moment the two stood silently listening to the brook gurgling along and the trill of a screech owl, and then they heard a different sound, a soft moan that alerted them immediately.

"Did you hear that?" Yolanda asked Ned.

"Shh, I'm listening," Ned cautioned.

They both stood stalk still hoping to hear more of what they hoped had come to their ears.

Nothing.

Ned motioned the young woman to remain quiet and listen.

The sound came again — a soft moan not far off.

They turned toward the direction of the sound and began walking along the stream. They were bothered that their feet crunched on the dry leaves beneath them, making noise as they walked.

The sound came again, and this time they were sure they heard it; it must have come from the child.

Ned was the first to see Mitch. The boy had been following the river, which suddenly dropped off, becoming a waterfall with a fifteen foot drop. Mitch had fallen down into a ravine.

Ned carefully climbed down the steep incline, holding on to roots and rocks, until he found the bottom of the ravine. He called out "Mitch! Can you hear me?"

A moan came again, and then a weak voice crying, "Help me."

Ned called up to Yolanda, "Mitch is here at the bottom of this ravine. I don't know if I can move him by myself to get him back up the hill."

Yolanda called back, "Is he all right? Maybe I should come down to help you."

Ned wanted to try to assess the boy's condition, if that was possible, before he encouraged the girl to come down the slippery cliff.

"Wait a minute. Let me look at him first," Ned called back.

He moved closer to where the child must be, and called his name, again.

"I'm over here," came a voice. "I think I hurt my leg; maybe it's broken."

Ned found Mitch lying on his back with his leg crumpled beneath him.

"I'm Ned. Your sister found me and told me you got lost, so we've been looking for you," he told the boy. "Does anything besides your leg hurt?"

"Sort of. I fell down those rocks, so I hurt all over, but maybe those are mostly scrapes and scratches," Mitch offered.

"How about your neck or your head? Do you feel any pain there?" Ned wondered if he'd have trouble transporting the boy. Maybe he would need to wait for help to bring a stretcher and a neck brace. He had noticed that sort of thing was SOP [Standard Operating Procedure] for emergency crews on TV.

"I think I'm okay," Mitch admitted. "I'm glad you found me. I was beginning to think this could be a real bad time. Do you think help, ah, more help, is on the way?"

Ned was pleased to see the spark of humor from the child. It indicated that he wasn't too badly off. "I think we'll be seeing help come soon," he encouraged the boy.

Within the next half hour much had changed. The ranger, along with Mitch's parents and Trudy, arrived at the spot where the accident occurred. The ranger called Ned on his cell phone to ascertain exactly where he was. With all the help, they were able to move Mitch up the ravine to safety and then help him down the path to the ranger station. Very soon Mitch and his family were on their way to the hospital to have his leg x-rayed and fitted for a cast. The family was very, very indebted to Ned and Trudy and thanked them profusely for their kind and prompt response to their son's need.

Suddenly the fun afternoon date had developed into a whole different occasion for Ned and Trudy. The time had flown by, and already it was well after dark.

When they were back in the car and beginning to resume their date, they realized that they might need to be turning back toward Misty Falls.

❋ ❋ ❋

Chapter 34. The Truth

"We haven't even had a bite to eat," Ned pointed out. "Let's look for somewhere between here and your home to stop for dinner."

"Food does sound good. I'm famished. In all this excitement I couldn't even think of food, but you wouldn't have any trouble talking me into eating now!

"We haven't really had much time to be together. Finding Mitch and getting him to safety was a lot more important than anything else we might have done. I have to say, though, I'm real glad we happened to go on that hike. I think we learned something rather interesting about each other in the process. Don't you?" Trudy mused.

"I agree," Ned picked up on Trudy's train of thought. "I suppose an ordinary date, you know — dinner and a movie — isn't the best way to get to know another person. I think today we saw each other in action in a real, live situation — how we responded to the emergency and how we worked together to find a solution to the problem. Those are really good things to know about someone else. We weren't together much searching for Mitch because we each had a task to accomplish, but working that way helped to solve what could have been a serious, even life-threatening problem."

"I was thinking the same thing." Trudy agreed. "We couldn't have set up that scenario if we had tried, but it came right to us, and we responded. I'm so glad we could help that family. Gads! Can you imagine how awful it would have been, if Mitch had to spend the night alone, having fallen down that cliff and his poor leg hurt. Everyone would have been terrified, too."

Ned drove his car west, down out of the hills and toward Misty Falls. A sign advertising Home Cookin' appeared, just as they turned due west. "Look at that!" Ned pointed at the sign. "You wouldn't mind a little home cookin' would you?" He smiled.

A few minutes later Ned and Trudy were seated in the small diner and had ordered a meat and three — turkey with corn, smashed potatoes, and okra, along with dessert. They sat in silence for a moment, enjoying the friendly atmosphere of the diner.

Trudy suddenly remembered she should ask about the time.

Winnie's Walk / Misty Falls: Journeys of Faith and Romance

"It's a quarter to eight. Is that all right? Are you worried about the time?" Ned inquired.

"I'd just like to call my mom and tell her where I am." Trudy said simply.

Ned raised his eyebrows and asked, "Do you usually check in with her? Is she the nervous sort?"

Trudy wasn't quite sure how to answer Ned's question, but she did need to let her mom know that they were now having dinner and would be home later than she had originally expected to be. She figured her mother would be okay with watching Kareem longer this evening, but it was a good idea to call, just the same.

"Well, I'm not sure if Mom had plans for this evening, and I just thought she'd like to hear from me," Trudy stalled.

Ned reached in his pocket and brought out his cell phone and handed it to his date. "Here you go," he grinned.

"Thanks." Trudy punched in her home phone number and waited while the phone rang. "Hi, Mom?" Trudy began. "How are things?" Trudy listened for a moment as her mother spoke about her day with her grandson. Trudy kept the cell phone close to her ear, so her mother's words would not be overheard across the table.

"Ned and I had something of an adventure up in the foothills this afternoon. We were able to help find and save a young boy who had fallen into a ravine. He's doing fine, now, but that event changed the plans for our date. We're at a diner about an hour from home, but I just thought you might like to know what's going on."

Keisha, realizing that Trudy had not yet be able to say anything about Kareem's existence to Ned, quickly assured her daughter that all was well and not to worry. She told her to take her time. Everything would be fine at home.

Trudy handed the phone back to Ned and thanked him."I suppose that seems a bit weird for me to be calling my mom when I'm out with you, but sometimes it's a good idea to keep parents informed."

"Tell me," Trudy changed the subject. "You're already more than halfway through your course work at school, right?"

Ned lit up with the subject of the Air Force Academy. "Glad you asked. That's one of my favorite topics. I absolutely LOVE the Academy, and I feel so honored to be there. The school is completely free to me — my uniforms, my food, and medical care — and all my living expenses are paid for. Of course, I do have a five year commitment to the Air Force when I graduate, but that's looking really good to me these days. Too many young people are not finding work, even after they worked hard in undergraduate school to learn something they want to do."

Trudy nodded her head and smiled as she listened to the passion in Ned's voice as he spoke about the Academy.

"It does sound wonderful," she agreed. "You'll always be able to remember those years with your fellow cadets as something very special, I'm sure.

"You mentioned doing real good in your classes. That's great. Would you ever be interested in flying?" Trudy wondered out loud.

Ned cocked his head to one side. "That might be fun. Some of the cadets have already been selected for a pilot track, and there are tests done each year for other cadets to apply for the pilot program. There are many requirements — aptitude, for one. Grades are important but not the only requirement. There's a long list of prerequisites for pilots. The school expects their pilots to have their Bachelor's of Science degree when they graduate."

"How about you and your school? I haven't heard anything about what you're doing. Are you enjoying your classes?" Ned asked.

Trudy sat silent for a moment, wondering where to start. She was tempted to say something to dodge the question, thinking maybe she needed more time to figure out how to present her story.

"It's a long story, Ned, and it's something that I need to tell you about."

The conversation was suddenly sounding odd to Ned. He hadn't given a thought to what Trudy had been up to since the summer before last. He wondered what in the world this classy young miss might have to tell him.

"You know that I'm still living at home." Trudy began.

Ned nodded his head.

"I haven't left home for school or to move out and be on my own," she continued.

"I figured that much when you called home just now. I suppose everyone is different that way. Some of us get nifty opportunities for school and can make the big step out from under Mom and Dad more easily," Ned theorized.

"You're right. My best girl friend, Jeanelle, lives at home and commutes to the junior college over in Strawberry Plains. She really likes it there, and the drive isn't bad," Trudy offered.

"And you're attending UT Knoxville? At least that's what your sweatshirt is saying," Ned's eyes twinkled.

"No ... I'm not," Trudy admitted. "I do hope to go, but I haven't made it there, yet."

Ned was confused, but he did understand that finances can be a great problem, and he had just been in Trudy's very modest home. He didn't want to press the issue, because he didn't want to cause Trudy embarrassment or pain, as if he was judging her. Ned nodded his head slowly up and down and smiled at his date. "I'm sure when the time is right, you'll take advantage of school."

Trudy realized the time had come for truth to be said. She reached into her pocketbook, took out her wallet, and pulled out a small, color picture and handed it to Ned.

"This is what I've been doing," she said.

Ned reached for the picture and held it in his hand. It was a snapshot of a baby boy, wearing a blue outfit; he had a headful of springy, black locks, and bare feet. He was a good looking child — plump with high cheek bones and a broad nose; there was something that fascinated Ned about the picture, as if he had seen that face before, but he couldn't put his finger on what it was. "Good looking child. Do you watch him? What's his name?" Ned asked looking up at Trudy.

"His name is Kareem," and, yes, I watch him. I'm his mother," Trudy looked straight at Ned and smiled.

"You're ... his ... mother?" Ned nearly fell over his words. He tried to regain his composure, so he quickly added, "He's a beautiful child! You must be very proud of him."

"I am! I believe he's the best thing that ever happened to me in my life!" Trudy nearly sang her words. Finally, she had told Ned half the story, and it felt very good. Of course, there was a lot more to divulge, but at least now he had heard that much.

"Okay. Now I understand your phone call to your mom," Ned said slowly. "She's watching Kareem, is that what you said his name is?"

"Yes, do you like the name? I named him Kareem, after the basketball player. I hope he will enjoy sports someday. I certainly do."

"That is a good name — easy to remember. I can see why you haven't had time for school. I'm sorry if I was assuming too much," Ned tried to rescue his earlier words, presuming Trudy's involvement with college. "It didn't occur to me that you had a different agenda."

"When we met, you had just finished your plebe year at the Academy, right?" Trudy asked. Ned nodded 'yes'. "And I was about to start my senior year in high school.

"Back then I was definitely looking forward to going off to college, even living away from home, if I could figure a way to pull it off. I've wanted to be a school teacher ever since I went to kindergarten, but, as you can imagine, things have changed for me," Trudy quickly reviewed her history.

"Maybe you'll get there down the road," Ned suggested, hopefully. You know there are new ways to get to college, and maybe there's a way for you to begin without leaving Misty Falls," Ned said, wanting to be helpful.

"I hadn't thought of that, but I'll bet you're right," Trudy thought out loud. "I do have a computer at home; it's one that was given my mom, when computers in the office were changed out for newer ones. So I have a PC, and I'm online. Maybe there are some courses that I could take, even just one at a time. That way I might afford the class and would have time to take it. I like that idea, Ned, I'll look into it," Trudy smiled in agreement.

"Wow! This day has turned out so differently than I ever thought it might," Ned changed the subject. "Our whole afternoon turned into a story that ought to be on the news. I'm awfully glad we were at the right place in the right time. What happened to Mitch could have been a whole lot worse than it was. I felt like maybe God was using us right then to be his hands and feet for Yolanda and her brother. Didn't you?"

"I'm glad you see it that way because I do, too. I think God put us there in that woods at that exact moment to be there for that family, AND I have to be honest with you, I'm glad to hear that you're a person of faith. At least it sounds like you are. Am I right?" Trudy ventured to ask.

"My whole family are members of Ebenezer Missionary Baptist Church in my town. My granddad was the pastor when I was small, and my father is the minister there now. So, yes, you could say I come from a believing family. I have been a follower of Christ since I was baptized at eight years old." Ned explained.

Trudy's eyes lit up, and she couldn't keep from smiling broadly as she heard this confession by Ned. "I used to be real active in the youth group at the AME Church in Misty Falls. I loved to sing with the choir, too. Those were great times."

"You used to go?" Ned asked. "But not now?"

Trudy sighed and answered, "Having a baby seems to slow me down. It always takes three times longer to get ready to go out with Kareem than it ever took before he came. That's a terrible excuse; I should make it to church more often than I have."

The two had finished their dessert and paid their bill, so it was time to start back to Misty Falls.

As they drove Ned thought out loud, "Obviously Kareem's appearance has made a great difference in your life. A baby would do that, of course. Do you get any help from the father?"

Trudy wondered how to respond to Ned's question. He really didn't realize his involvement in her plight. Trudy answered, "No, he doesn't know about Kareem; he doesn't know he has a son."

Ned was listening to Trudy's words, which were getting softer and softer as she spoke, until it was barely audible to him. He slowed his car and pulled off the road, set his emergency blinkers on to alert any cars coming along and turned off the motor.

Ned turned to look straight at Trudy. "You're telling me right now, aren't you? You're telling me that I'm the baby's father."

Trudy hung her head down and nodded 'yes' and she said, "Yes, you are Kareem's daddy."

Ned didn't speak for a minute, analyzing everything that had been going on that day — the crazy events in the mountains when he and Trudy helped to find and save Mitch; the picture Trudy showed him of the baby boy, who reminded him of something ... a picture his own mother had on her dresser, a photo of Ned when he was about a half year old. The two pictures could have been of the same child.

Ned held out his hands to Trudy and took hers in his. He grasped her hands and pulled them to his lips and kissed them gently. "Oh boy! Lady, you have just changed my life. I think your life must be crazy different today from what you'd dreamed it would be. Somehow you've been able to keep things together, you and your mom, even though, I can imagine, it hasn't been easy for you. But what about me? I haven't had to scrimp or do without or anything to help care for my boy.

"**My boy**! Listen to how that sounds!" Ned let the words roll off his tongue. He felt as if he had never heard those words before. "I didn't think I was ready to be a father, but guess what? I think that's not really a choice now, is it?"

Trudy shook her head and laughed lightly at Ned's question. "No, I guess the choice has been made."

"Should I ask why you didn't tell me before?" Ned voice rose as he questioned Trudy's reticence to inform him.

"At first I was in shock, myself. I didn't realize that a child could be conceived so easily — one time. I was totally unbelieving, but then I knew that the night you and I went out had a lasting consequence. I couldn't hide the fact from myself ... or from anyone else after several months. By Thanksgiving last year I was well along in my pregnancy; all my school friends begged me to tell them who the father was, and I decided not to say. I didn't think it was anyone's business but mine.

I was afraid to tell you, Ned. I wanted you to know, but I thought about your wonderful scholarship and how well you were doing at the Academy and how important you will be someday, and I was afraid that if you knew about a baby coming, you'd end up, somehow, losing your place in the Academy. I didn't want to be responsible for your losing that. Can you understand what I'm saying?" Trudy was nearly in tears as she confessed her difficult quandry.

Ned, put his right hand on Trudy's shoulder and massaged it for a moment. "I think I can understand what you were thinking. You mean nobody else knows about my being Kareem's daddy? You didn't tell anyone?"

"I didn't tell anyone until a week ago when you emailed me to say that we could go out today. I was so excited I had to tell someone, so I ran and told my mom about you and how wonderful you are," Trudy told Ned.

"I don't know why you think I'm so wonderful. There's a lot a man should be doing for his family, if he knows about them. So far I've done nothing except cause you much trouble," Ned accused himself.

"No! Ned, you had no idea, and I wanted it that way. At least I wanted it that way until I started seeing you in Kareem's face. He really favors you. I wondered if you saw the similarity in the picture I showed you. You seemed to fixate on the photo for a minute, and I figured you knew then." Trudy remembered.

"You're half right. There was something that tickled my memory when I saw the picture, but it didn't come to me until you told me about my connection to Kareem. My mother has a picture of me, when I was about the same age; it's sitting on her dresser, and I've seen it thousands of times. The two babies' pictures look nearly identical. I suppose that's proof enough; I must be the father," Ned announced.

"I want to meet him. When can I?" Ned asked.

"That's another reason I decided to tell you about your fatherhood. Kareem is so perfect, so dear, so cute, so adorable, and so many other wonderful adjectives. I love him so much. I have such great hopes for him. He's going to be just like his daddy, I think, and I believe you two deserve to know one another," Trudy shared.

"He sounds perfect. Does he talk, yet? How about teeth? How many teeth do babies get when they're ... how old? When is his birthday? I think I've got a gazillion questions for you to answer!" Ned grilled Trudy.

"Maybe we should get back on the highway and head toward home," Trudy suggested. "I think Mom is okay with Kareem tonight, but I don't want to be out too late."

Trudy and Ned talked nonstop all the way to Livingston's door. Ned was taking the news a lot better than Trudy expected. She really didn't know how he would react, but she was impressed with his initial response to the news.

When they arrived at the Livingston's home, Trudy brought Ned inside to meet her mother. Kareem was already down for the night, but when Trudy explained to her mother that Ned now knew his status as father, Keisha led Ned into Trudy's bedroom and over to the small crib where little Kareem lay sleeping.

The light was very low in the room, but Ned leaned over the crib and put his hand on his son's back; he held his hand there feeling the slow, deep breathing of the child raising and lowering his hand. He leaned over the crib and kissed the nape of Kareem's neck.

Everyone tiptoed out of the room; the bedroom door was closed. Keisha offered a chair to Ned in the living room, and everyone took a seat.

"He's amazing!" Ned spoke in hushed tones. "He's warm and soft and ... and amazing! I can see why you love the little guy," he turned to Trudy.

Trudy was delighted with Ned's response. "Oh, yes! He is that and so much more. He's smart. He's already beginning to talk, you know, simple things like, 'Ma ma.' He's pulling himself up on whatever is around; his legs are getting stronger and stronger. When he holds my fingers, he can stand up and move his legs like he's marching. He's on the verge of so much. I'm so glad you like him!"

"This is all so new to me, but I already know I have to <u>know</u> him, and I want him to know me.

"What a gift! Trudy! What are we going to do?" Ned asked.

They both fell silent. Keisha wondered if she should be sitting there in the midst of this rather personal discussion, but nobody suggested that she leave. She sat quietly, praying silently that things would work out well for everyone.

The hour was getting quite late, so finally Ned said he would go home for now.

Trudy said good night to Ned, and closed the front door. They would talk on the phone in the morning, and, hopefully, get together again later that day. Ned's head was spinning with many deep thoughts as he drove home. "LORD in heaven, hear my prayer. I really need your guidance on this one. Thank you for the incredible blessing of being a father. Help me to figure how to respond as you would have me to. Amen."

* * *

Winnie was completely delighted to spend time on her own agenda Thanksgiving morning. She had wakened early to join John for breakfast down in the lobby of the hotel before he took off for his day at the slopes. She returned to their room to begin working on her new book.

"Goodness! I've never tried my hand at fiction before, but it is probably a good choice for general public reading. Everyone loves stories; we've grown up on stories, and we each have one. They are fun to hear; they catch the imagination; they are conveniently versatile. I don't suppose a writer has to stick too closely to the facts, but I think, for my book, I'll try to use the background of what was happening on the calendar and in the news last year. The world was floundering as the housing bubble burst and companies and banks were failing right and left. The election was coming up, and the government needed to borrow enormous sums of money to get the economy moving. The market was diving dramatically down further every day, and no one knew what the bottom would look like.

That makes a colorful backdrop for Miss Vangie — that's what I'll call my alter ego, Vangie, like my nickname used to be. Pastor Vangie's been at her church for a couple years, and she's getting into the community now. I'll try to show what a pastor's life is like — the weekly countdown toward the next sermon, the emergencies, and the unusual situations that come along, and, of course, continually seeking God's guidance.

I'll figure a way to introduce John. Hmm. He needs a fictional name. I shall call him Sam, Dr. Samuel McKay. That story will probably be the best part of the book, and the most fun to write. I will enjoy telling the story of how John and I fell in love.

Winnie was warming up to her task, and the time flew by, she was deep in thought when the door of the guest room opened and John stepped in.

"Hi, Honey, I'm home!" He announced happily. His face was still flushed from his day of working on the slopes, yielding a ruddiness to his complexion.

John's arrival spelled the end of writing and the beginning of Thanksgiving Day for the Daniels.

✳ ✳ ✳

Ned didn't speak to anyone when he got home that evening. The whole house was quiet, and he didn't want to disturb the sleepers. He had BIG news that he would share, but his news would wait 'til morning.

✳ ✳ ✳

Saturday morning Ned was awakened by sounds coming from the kitchen. His father was up and preparing breakfast for his family.

"Morning, Dad, whatcha makin' this morning?" Ned asked.

"Pancakes and sausage. Since everyone's home today, I wanted us to have a family breakfast. Would you put the coffee on, please?

"We missed you last night, you know. We don't get to see you much, now that you're away at school, so we were hoping to see a great deal of you while you're here this weekend.

"You must have gotten home late last night," Ned's father continued in an inviting way, hoping his son might volunteer something about what he had been doing.

"No one was up when I got in last night, so I just turned in myself," Ned explained.

Half an hour later Ned's family had assembled at the table for breakfast.

"Just like old times, isn't it?" Ned smiled at his mother and dad and younger brother, Jason.

"I remember helping Dad make breakfast on Saturdays. He's always been the early riser, and his making breakfast for us called everyone together — a way to start the weekend off," Jason added.

Breakfast conversation revolved around the news the two brothers had from their respective colleges, but five minutes into the discussion Ned made an announcement.

"I need to change the subject, Guys. Something came up, and I want to share it with you," he began. (Three pairs of eyes instantly snapped onto Ned, and Henry Wilson's fork dropped with a clang onto his plate as he focussed his attention on his son.)

"You know I went out with Trudy Livingston yesterday. She and I met a year ago last summer at a swim party, and we went out the next day.

"She's sent me a couple of cards and emails when I was at the Academy, and we planned to go out together while I was home this weekend.

"Trudy's a really cute kid, and we had an amazing time yesterday. I mean it, from beginning to end, it was amazing," Ned stopped for to catch a breath.

"I don't remember this young lady, Son," Ned's mother interrupted. "Is she important to you?"

"I'd say! I think Trudy and I may have a future together," Ned said. "That sounds mysterious, and I don't mean to be. There's just a jumble of puzzle pieces I need to figure out."

"Puzzle pieces? What are you talking about?" Ned's dad was now curious.

"Let me start from the beginning and explain ...." Ned shared the events of the previous day as they had unfolded to him — the trip into the foothills, the emergency, finding the lost boy, stopping for dinner, Trudy's revelation about her motherhood, and ..."

"She hasn't told the father of the child about him?" Ned's dad interrupted.

Ned was working up to the big announcement, "Dad, Mom, I just found out last night that I'm the father of Trudy's son! The boy's name is Kareem."

Silence, or was it shock, dominated the table for a moment, which, to Ned, seemed much longer.

"You're ... a ... father?" Ned's mother asked. "How can you be sure?"

Ned explained about Kareem's picture that Trudy had shown him. "We were having dinner last night, and I asked Trudy where she was going to school. Seems like we had only been talking about the Academy, and what I'm doing, but she hadn't mentioned her college, even though I knew she had been planning on college.

"As I was interrogating her about her life, she pulled out her wallet and showed me a picture of a baby, maybe half a year old. When I looked at the picture of the child, I had this odd sensation of having seen the picture before, and then I remembered that it's nearly identical to the one you have on your dresser, Mom. The picture looks just like me!"

Silence, again. Then Ned's dad spoke up. "That's great news and, at the same time, it's life altering news, Son."

"It is life altering, but there's so much to consider," Ned stated. He hoped he could review some of his options with his folks.

"Have you seen the child?" Ned's mother asked.

"I took Trudy back to her house after she told me about Kareem. Her mother was there, and Trudy told her mom that I had just learned about being Kareem's dad.

"Miss Keisha took me to Trudy's bedroom and let me see him sleeping.

"He's incredible! I couldn't see the baby very well — the room was dark, and the only light was coming in from the hall — but there he was, lying on his tummy, his arms stretched out over his head. His face was turned toward the wall. I put my hand on his back and felt him breathing; his little body moved gently up and down. He was warm and soft and, and, and ... I'm his dad!" Ned announced with a look of amazement.

Jason, who had been listening to this surprising exchange asked, "Boy, your life has just changed ... in an earthmoving way! What do you think you'll do?"

The family talked for some time about what this news meant for them — for everyone affected by the advent of this little child — but before the family adjourned Henry Wilson, Ned's father, led the family in prayer for guidance and blessings for this new member of their household.

Ned phoned Trudy and told her he would be over to her house and that he hoped to spend some time with her and Kareem, if that was okay with her.

"Of course it's okay for you to come over and see us. You are very welcome to come and meet your son. I'll tell him you're on your way," Trudy was happy to answer.

Ned realized that his head had been spinning since the minute the news was revealed to him about his son. Thoughts had been flooding his mind, all sorts of thoughts: What was his child like? What would he need? How could he become known to his son? There were so many possibilities that were demanding Ned's attention. He knew it would take some time to sort out what needed to happen.

"I should to take this one step at a time, and today will be about Kareem, getting to know him and for him to begin to know me." Ned decided.

The car pulled to a stop outside the house, and Ned looked around the neighborhood. The street, which was a block behind Main Street across the road from the depot, had a dozen small, wooden cottages standing in a row. Most of the houses sported a wooden porch, leading to the front door. A window overlooked the porch from the living room.

Ned hadn't noticed much about the neighborhood the day before when he came to pick up his date, but today he took greater interest in the surroundings. Trudy's house was old, and the paint was chipping, but he noticed a small vegetable garden on the side of the house. The garden was fallow, being that it was late November, but Ned appreciated how the two women had been growing some of their food at home. *We don't garden much, but I've always enjoyed the tomatoes and peas we did plant. Looks like Trudy and her mom have been doing what they can to make ends meet.*

Trudy appeared at the door and called to Ned, "Good morning, Ned. I see you're checking out my neighborhood. (Trudy stepped on to her porch and down the steps to the front yard.) This is where I grew up," she waved her arms to indicate the area.

"Come in and meet Master Kareem." Trudy ran back up the stairs and held the door open for Ned to enter her house.

Ned stepped inside the living room and glanced about. Kareem was sitting on a rug on the floor. He was dressed in a powder blue crawler, which snapped up the front. His legs were sticking out before him, and he was holding a yellow, rubber ducky in both hands. When he saw the visitor, he held the duck out to him for inspection.

Trudy came into the room, scooped up Kareem in her arms and brought the baby over to Ned.

"Kareem," she spoke to her son, "I want you to meet a very important person in your life. This is your dad. His name is Ned Wilson, but you can call him Daddy," Trudy made the introduction. "Is it all right that he call you Daddy?" She asked Ned.

"I should say!" Ned was pleased to agree. "Yes, Young Man, you certainly should call me Daddy, although I have to admit, it's going to take some getting used to on my part."

"May I hold him?" Ned asked Trudy, holding out his hands.

Trudy carefully placed Kareem in Ned's arms, showing him how to support their nineteen pound child.

Ned didn't speak; he held his son tightly at first and stared into his face. He was cradling Kareem primarily in the crook of his left arm, so he was able to caress the baby's hair with his right hand and feel the fine spun softness of his jet black curls.

"He's so beautiful! I know that's not a word you use for boys, but it fits. He's really beautiful, and I'm beginning to understand what you were saying about him. Is it possible to fall in love so fast? Can that really be?" Ned asked.

"Here, Ned, would you to sit down with him?" Trudy guided Ned and Kareem to the couch.

Ned obliged and sat down with his precious bundle; Trudy took a seat beside them.

Trudy and Ned spent the rest of the morning together talking about Kareem and many of the minute details about his life. Ned was soaking up all he heard. He found he was fascinated to learn all there was to know about his son.

Ned set Kareem down on the ground and held out two of his fingers for the child to grab onto. Ned had never experienced a baby pulling himself up to make his legs take initial steps on the floor.

"He's so strong! Just look at those legs! They will take him far, and you should feel his grip on my fingers. He's got quite a grasp! Do you think he'll be walking soon?" Ned was delighted with the novelty of his son. Babies — having anything to do with them, learning about them, discovering their world — had been the furthest thing from Ned's interests before, but he was quickly realizing that in this one short hour, little Kareem had walked right into his heart, and Ned realized he was hooked.

Lunchtime arrived, and Trudy showed Ned what feeding time was about. She set her baby up in a highchair and buckled him in. Then she brought out a small container of baby food from the fridge along with finger food items — a piece of a banana, some Cheerios, and crackers.

Ned watched as Trudy sat before Kareem and tried to help him with the meal. Some of the food went successfully inside the child's mouth; most of it didn't. Much food ended up somewhere on the tray or on the floor. Kareem seemed more interested in watching Cheerios fall to the floor when he let them go. The baby repeated this discovery many a time, watching this astounding fact of physics: *stuff falls down when you let it go from your hand.*

"Sorry this is so messy, but it takes time for kids to figure out how to eat right. Of course, there are some mothers who only nurse their children for the first year or so, and they don't have to fight the mess of food everywhere."

Ned was not quite clear about where he and Trudy stood — what their relationship was all about — but he thought it might be appropriate to ask her, "May I ask you a question?"

"It's fine with me. Ask away. What have I got to hide from you?" Trudy laughed.

"Did you nurse Kareem?"

"Yes, I did. I was nursing him completely until about a month ago. He was getting real hungry, so I supplemented my milk with some cereal. That got us started on other foods, and now he's mostly weaned," Trudy explained.

After Kareem's lunch Trudy set Ned up to feed the baby his bottle, then, once the child was asleep, Trudy showed Ned where to lay the sleeping infant down in his crib.

"Now we can have some time to ourselves," Trudy whispered to Ned as they tiptoed back to the kitchen. "How about I make us lunch?"

Ned found that he was seeing a new side to Trudy. She was very responsible and caring for her son, and she was also interested in him — Ned. Those were important pieces to the puzzle he was trying to assemble in his mind.

"I think things are making more sense to me now," Ned was thinking aloud.

"I know you held my identity close to you and didn't reveal it to anyone until now, and I think I understand why you did.

"And I know that today has been, perhaps, the most important day of my life. I met my son today, and now that I have met him, I also know I have to be part of his life," Ned announced.

Trudy realized that Ned was working hard on this business that she had just dropped in his lap, and she didn't know how or if she could help him in whatever decision he would make. "Can you think of anything I can do to help?" She asked.

"That's the thing. We're a fractured family, right from the get go. The perfect picture of a family is a man, a wife, and child, but we're not there. We may never be there, but maybe we should at least keep all our options open," Ned thought out loud.

"Ned, please remember why I was silent for so long. You know I don't want you to do anything that will upset your future. That's important, too." Trudy pleaded.

"My work at the Academy is another piece to the puzzle, and I will deal with it," Ned admitted.

"But how? I'm sure there are rules about cadets and families. What do you suppose those rules say?" Trudy asked.

"It's one thing for you and me to be Kareem's parents. There may be some regulation about a cadet being a parent, but I never had reason to look into it. The bigger question is about you and me.

"We really don't know one another very well. Except for the fact that we are Kareem's parents. Obviously we have that really important detail in common, but I don't think we know each other well enough to determine if there's a future for us," Ned reasoned to Trudy.

Trudy nodded her head up and down slowly to agree with Ned's observation. "You're right. We don't really know one another. We come from different communities; we've certainly had different experiences recently; we may have different goals and hopes and dreams. I don't know. I have to say I don't know what or how much you should know about another person before you get more serious," Trudy answered.

"It's quite a dilemma. In most ways we're just two young people, who are friends, who might have a beautiful future together, and on the other hand we've already jumped past the entire business of courtship and begun a family.

Ned stood up and walked around the living room, not really looking at anything, just stretching his legs and thinking out loud. "Trudy, what I know of you and me I like very much, but reason tells me that we really don't know one another well, and it would be wise to spend some time doing just that ... learning more about one another.

"I have to agree with you. I know too many people who come from broken homes, not to have a great deal of respect for a good marriage. My mom never married. She was just out of high school when I came along, and my dad was never part of my life. So, I'm hardly knowledgeable about marriage, but I do hope that Kareem will have a stable family life as he grows up," Trudy added. "I want the best for him."

Ned smiled at Trudy and said, "There's one difference we have. My mom and dad are truly in love and have been as long as I've known them. They have shown me a fine example of a Christian couple working together to give glory to God and to love one another.

"Before I came over here this morning, I had breakfast with my folks and my brother, Jason. We have a tradition of having breakfast together on Saturday mornings and checking in with one another.

"This morning I told them about you and Kareem!" Ned told Trudy.

"You did? Already they know about me and our son?" Trudy seemed surprised.

"Yes, I did. This can't be a secret. The situation might be a big puzzle right now, but we won't gain anything by being secretive about it. In fact we'll need their help. They can encourage us and pray for us and be emotionally supportive of us. We need whatever help we can get, I'm sure," Ned assured Trudy.

"I've tried to keep this all a secret for so long; I hadn't thought about the way you're explaining it — that people who know what's what can be helpful. I like that," Trudy smiled at Ned.

"Good. I'm glad you understand. I think we should be upfront with your family as well as mine about what we are trying to do," Ned said thoughtfully.

"What will you say to them?" Trudy asked.

"Kareem comes first. He's the reason for everything else. I want to know him, and I want to be part of his life, and if that might somehow develop into a family with the three of us, so much the better," Ned began.

"Yes! Kareem does come first. He's been first in my book since that day back in March when they first put him in my arms. He stole my heart that day the same way I think he has just stolen yours," Trudy agreed.

"Second, I think you and I should begin courting," Ned winked at Trudy.

"Courting? That's a really old expression. What do you have in mind?" Trudy was most curious.

"Courting was when a guy wanted to keep company with a young lady to get to know her with the possible consequence of betrothal. I think that's what we should do." Ned suggested.

"That does sound fun," Trudy agreed. "I like how you phrase it, 'keeping company for purpose of possible engagement.' That has a very positive outlook, yet you and I will have free will to change our minds. Either one of us could decide this isn't right. Do you agree?"

"Yes, either one of us could decide this isn't working out for us. We could do that if we decide that we have serious problems about us being together, but that wouldn't change our relationship to Kareem. No matter what, I want to be part of his life, however we figure things out." Ned agreed.

Trudy and Ned didn't have too much time to themselves that afternoon, as Kareem awakened at three, and their attention shifted to him. Ned was introduced to even more about the world of babies — diapers, dressing, preparing and warming bottles, etc. He got a crash course in baby handling that day.

Keisha arrived home from her Saturday job cleaning the mayor's house, and she sat and talked with Ned. She was very impressed with the maturity of this young man, and she was more than pleased to hear his thoughtful approach to this strange new world he was discovering.

"Your folks already know about Kareem," Keisha repeated. "I'm glad to hear that. We've had enough secrets, and maybe with a few more folks who are aware of things you'll get more emotional support and encouragement."

"What did your folks say when you told them?" Keisha was interested to know.

"They were surprised, of course, the same as I was, and my mother wanted to know for sure if the baby is mine. I told her about the picture that Trudy showed me last night, and how much that picture looked like a photo of me that my mom has on her dresser," Ned recounted. "I think we're all satisfied about that now."

Keisha nodded her head with approval as she listened to Ned's words. "I'm glad you told them. It sounds like you've got good parents!"

"I'd say. Dad and Mom are very special people, and I've always known how lucky I am to have them in my court," Ned agreed.

It was about time for Ned to leave for home. He was torn between wanting to do something for Trudy and Kareem, yet he couldn't figure what that could be.

"Trudy, today was a day out of time and space, totally special, and I loved it! It felt a bit like I had been hurled somehow into the future — what it might be like for me to be a father someday, but obviously I don't have to wait for years ...," Ned stopped. He didn't want the day to end, yet his world was calling him back.

"I leave for school tomorrow afternoon. I'll be taking the four p.m. flight back to the Springs, which means we need to leave right after church for Knoxville. I will be home for two weeks at Christmas, and then we can spend more time together."

✳ ✳ ✳

The Daniels thoroughly enjoyed their time in Aspen. John enjoyed his time on the slopes, and Winnie had built a community and populated it with characters that she drew on from people she had known in one church or another. The two would be leaving for the airport at noon on Sunday, so there would not be time for more skiing. Winnie thought it would be good to attend worship somewhere in town. She Googled "Aspen Church" and found one church that held three services on Sundays.

"John, since you won't be skiing tomorrow morning, how about we go to church here in town?" Winnie asked hopefully.

"Hm. I thought we are on a holiday. I suppose you're going to argue that you go to church, wherever you find yourself — holiday or no. Right? (Winnie smiled 'Yes.') I suppose we could do that. Do you know of a church around here?" John walked over to where Winnie was peering into her laptop.

Winnie laughed. "Are you suggesting we take a holiday from the holy day? You know there's a commandment just for that — the Fourth Commandment tells us to remember the Sabbath and to keep it holy. I wouldn't even try to suggest that Christians follow the Sabbath the way that the Jews do. They dedicate the entire twenty-four hours to attending Sabbath services and to doing no work, but I do attend worship on the LORD's Day, Sunday, if at all possible. Maybe that's how I keep that commandment."

"Is that getting around the edges of the commandment?" John teased his wife. "Why don't Christians worship on the Sabbath, anyway?"

"The earliest Christians did. They were Jews, and they worshiped on the Sabbath with other Jews. When Jesus rose from the dead, he rose on the first day of the week, Sunday — the day after the Sabbath — so Sunday became known as the' LORD s Day. It was such a remarkable event (the disciples had suddenly changed from being in deep grief and

351

depression to feeling alive and thrilled and overcome with delight at Jesus' returning from the dead!) they wanted to remember and celebrate the event. I think Christians have been celebrating and worshiping God on the first day of the week every week since then without missing a Sunday!" Winnie explained.

John nodded his head. "So Christians eventually forgot the Sabbath worship?"

"That's another piece of history. It became a matter of choice for the Jewish Christians — they could remain as Jews or leave their community and be Followers of the Way.

"The Jews had strict laws about associating with non-Jews, but the new Christians saw many non-Jews coming to faith in Christ and wanting to become part of their faith community. The Jews couldn't have Gentiles worshiping among them. One day something new appeared in the Sabbath worship. Their service included eighteen benedictions, which were repeated by the congregation, but one of the benedictions was a curse on Christ. That caused the Jews, who were following Christ, to have to make a decision: would they curse Christ and remain in the Jewish fold, or would they walk away from everything to follow the LORD?

"It must have been a terrible decision for the young Christians, as the choice they made had grave consequences. If they cursed Christ, they were no longer one of Jesus' followers, but if they left the synagogue they were losing culture, community, and family. Everything they had grown up with had to be left behind. That must have been an impossible decision," Winnie said.

"I'm sure it would have been devastating to the believers in Christ." John smiled. "You're a pretty good prof yourself, you know. I'm surprised I didn't hear that bit in my church history course."

"So, would you like to see the place I found for tomorrow?" Winnie pointed to the screen on her laptop.

"Right here; I think it would be within walking distance from our hotel, if we're up for a stroll tomorrow morning. There's a service at 8:00, which ought to fit our schedule nicely."

"Okay. We can plan for church in the morning. I suppose the dress would be casual? I didn't bring a suit and tie," John asked.

"I'm sure whatever you wear will be fine, Dear," Winnie answered.

"What sort of church is it?" John inquired.

"This church is a newer variety; it's called Simply a Christian Church. That would not be a particular denomination. The members have searched the scriptures and found the good news of God in Christ there, and they gather for worship and mission work," Winnie answered.

Before bed John checked Winnie's laptop and signed on to his bank account. It was his custom to check on his accounts regularly, just to see how he was doing.

Once the screen came up with his account on it, John stared at it for some time. Eventually, Winnie noticed that John was not getting ready for bed, but seemed to be stuck in front of her laptop.

"What are you looking at?" Winnie asked curiously.

"My checking account. It seems that my being married is making serious dent in my bank account. I knew it would, and that's okay. But this trip to Aspen is making itself known in a bigger way, and I'm just trying to take it in," John said with a moan.

"Maybe we need to scale back on our holiday expenses," Winnie suggested.

"That could be a good option," John nodded his head.

"What do you suppose this hotel suite costs us here?" John remained intent on the screen.

"I don't know, but I have a feeling it's rather pricey," Winnie answered.

"It's definitely more than it cost me in the past. That's because we're enjoying a nicer location, two sets of meals, two plane tickets, the cost of the equipment and the lifts for each day. It does add up," John spoke with a slight pinch in his voice.

Winnie came up to John, who was still seated, staring at the machine, and encircled him with her arms. She placed her cheek on his head and spoke softly to him. "We have been enjoying some of the finer things in life, but we don't need to have the best or the most expensive. We don't even need to run off at every holiday to the slopes."

"You're right. We have been having fun here; and it was especially good to make up for last year's non-event this Thanksgiving. I'm glad we came to Aspen, but I don't know that we'll do it every holiday, or even every year.

"I appreciate your sensitivity to my natural thriftiness. I know I need to learn to be more giving, but that is different from being a spendthrift. I'm sure there's a big difference between happily giving to those in need, and spending big bucks on self," John moaned.

"You are so good to me and for me, Win, and I do appreciate your humor, your wisdom, and your thoughts. I'm glad we are who we are — happily married people."

✳ ✳ ✳

Chapter 35. Action Weekend

Dec. 12-13 2009

Action Weekend was a grand flurry of work, assembling the various pieces of playground equipment on the already prepared site for Misty Falls' new community playground.

Friday, the day before the building began, the team leaders responsible for their sections of the playground, along with other volunteers, met for training and site prep for the new playground. The actual, barn-raising project would come together the next day because of the efforts of their preliminary work.

Saturday morning Lucy Jane sat with her father at the registration table, which was the single point of access to the work area. All volunteers would check in and out of the playground work area via their table.

"Finally, it looks like things are beginning to settle down. Do you agree?" Lucy Jane asked her dad.

"It's ten o'clock and our workers have been here on the job since eight this morning. Looks like we've managed to get things going and fielded the concerns that came up," Theo Smith answered his daughter. "Everyone appears to be hard at work, so you and I are seeing a break. I don't expect it to last too long. We're here in the heart of this project, and, considering all the possible snafus that might arise, I think we're doing rather well."

Both father and daughter looked at the playground before them, watching the many industrious people working in half a dozen areas of the soon-to-be, new playground. Each working unit was pulling hard to assemble, construct, or fit together their section of the project.

The main structure of the playground, its centerpiece, was a two story high tower with a rope ladder hanging down the center. Four great arms extended from the tower, and each led to a different activity and a new challenge. One arm led to a slide that twisted and bumped steeply down to a sandbox area. A second arm would lead an explorer over to a second tower, where a child could descend on a rope or pole. The third arm, fanning off from the main tower, led the adventurer to a metal ladder which could be crossed by swinging with hands from one bar to the next. The final arm was a large cylinder described by ropes, which hung between the main tower and a second platform.

"Maybe we could take advantage of this moment of calm to take turns walking through the playground to see how things are coming along," Theo suggested.

"Sounds good, Dad. You go first; I'll make my turn once you're back," Lucy Jane agreed.

Lucy Jane sat at the table watching all the commotion and the teams of people, each intent upon accomplishing their set task. The teams had only been at their project for a couple hours, so significant progress couldn't yet be expected.

About the time Theo Smith returned from his inspection of the site, Lucy Jane spied Tucker Joe's truck pull up. He parked and walked over to the table. "I'm here with more drinks," Tuck told Lucy Jane. "This is my second trip today, bringing sodas and water. I left a load yesterday and one earlier this morning.

"How are things going?" He wanted to know.

Lucy Jane smiled at Tuck. "The project seems to be going quite well. We did have a bit of a snag with the slide. Maneuvering it off the truck and over to its place in the yard required a number of able-bodied persons, but when the call went out for help across the yard, we had more than enough respondents, They were able to haul the slide to its proper location. See!" (Lucy Jane pointed to the bright yellow slide coming off the center tower.)

"That is a mighty fine looking slide!" Tuck nodded his head. I can see this place is transforming nicely into the playground Misty Falls will be proud of."

"Thanks for your help, too, Tuck," Lucy Jane said.

"Can you stay a while?" She suggested.

"Might as well stay for a bit. Martha's in charge at Friendlie's for the next while," Tuck replied.

"Do you have a schematic or a drawing or an artist's rendition of the end product?" Tuck wondered.

"Come! I'll show you around," Lucy Jane motioned with her index finger to Tuck to come, follow her.

The two began to walk around the periphery of the playground. "We'll go around the outside of the park, so we won't be in anybody's way," Lucy Jane explained.

As Tuck and Lucy Jane began walking around the acre of new play park, Tuck reached over to Lucy Jane's right arm and slid his hand into hers. It was an unexpected advance, but Lucy Jane responded easily with a squeeze to Tuck's hand, and the two continued along in company.

Nothing was said about this novel arrangement, but they seemed to accept the change gracefully with a natural rhythm and continued as if such had always had been so.

355

"There are several units here, you can see (Lucy Jane pointed around outsides of the playground) that are not working on the central playground structure, but each of these special units are responsible for building picnic tables and benches that will be scattered about the park. We also have two other units who are setting up a swing set and a tire swing." Lucy Jane pointed to the workers for these areas.

"What a great example of a community working together!" Tuck announced. "I didn't know we had it in us to pull something like this off! How did it all happen?"

Lucy Jane tipped her head to an angle, remembering, and said, "My dad was one of the first people enlisted in the project. Mayor Greeley was the one who initiated the idea of Misty Fallers building a playground.

He contacted several playground businesses online and researched what he wanted for our playground. Do you remember the meeting last year at the elementary school? That's when the idea was presented to the community. The mayor appointed a steering committee of a dozen folks to help get things off the ground.

Dad asked me to find volunteers. There are some people from Misty Falls who are good with tools and building, and they are the key team leaders for the castle and the main equipment installation. They each have a team of volunteers, which are erecting their section of the playground. See, the main attraction — the castle — will have four major entrances opening to the castle. The playground is set up for kids from four to twelve years old, but we will also have swings, balance beams, a geodesic dome, and rocking horses for younger kids to enjoy, too.

As Tuck and Lucy Jane continued their trek around the new playground area observing all the activity, others took note of them. Not everyone recognized Lucy Jane, but Tucker Joe was a community icon. Everyone knew Tuck, because of his ever presence at Friendlie's Foods. Not only did they notice the couple walking about the building site hand-in-hand, but their obvious closeness was also observed. Nothing was said by anyone, but the event was noted nonetheless — *Does Tucker Joe have a lady-friend?*

When the two returned to the registration stand, Lucy Jane needed to get back to work. Tuck asked, "Would you be interested in having dinner with me, soon?"

"Gee, yes, I'd love to go out with you again, and soon, but this weekend is seriously demanding my presence. We only have these two days to get the entire park put together, so I know I'll be on the phone tonight checking on all my volunteers for tomorrow. Some people who agreed to work both days may be exhausted and want a reprieve, which means I'll need to find other volunteers for their jobs. Already I feel like I've shaken the volunteer tree pretty hard, and I'm not sure where I'll find any more helpers, if I need them." Lucy Jane shook her head.

"I see," Tucker Joe nodded his head slowly. "I can understand that. Work does come before pleasure. At least that has always been my mantra. Maybe, though, there's a third option available to us. If you agree."

Lucy Jane was intrigued. "A third option? What could that be?"

"Hows about we make it a Coke date tonight, rather than a whole dinner?" Tucker Joe was not to be put off.

"I suppose we could do that. We really mustn't be out late though, because tomorrow will be a full day," Lucy Jane answered, realizing that between church in the morning and the finishing of the playground in the afternoon, her day was completely spoken for.

Tucker Joe figured that Lucy Jane was not wanting to avoid him, but she did have a responsibility. "I think I see a plan coming into focus for us, LJ. Is it okay for me to call you LJ? What time will you be home tonight after things close down?"

"We're working here 'til five, and then we have to secure the area. I suppose we'll be home by six. Can you come then?" Lucy Jane asked.

"I'll give you a call after that, and we can make a plan," Tucker answered.

✳ ✳ ✳

The playground building was moving along quite nicely, George thought. He hadn't planned to participate in this community event initially. He had only recently heard about this barn raising effort to build a community playground, but when he learned there was a need for people experienced in handling tools and building he realized he had the needed skills, so he decided to volunteer.

George called the number on the flier and found he was talking to Theo Smith, the general contractor for the project.

"Yes, how can I help you?" Theo Smith answered the phone.

"My name if George Oliver. I'm a welder by trade, and I know tools and building. I heard you might need someone with my expertise to honcho a team of builders with the new playground. 'S'that right?" George began.

"So glad you called, ah, George," Theo assured the caller. "I am looking for some skilled workers, people who are comfortable at a building site and can oversee volunteers to get a project done."

"That sounds like quite a challenge," George noted. "What are these projects you're talking about?"

"The Action Weekend for building our new playground will involve setting up and installing pre-fabricated lumber and plastic pieces, already made sections, into their appointed spots. The steering committee decided on a castle theme for the park, and they chose the sections they want installed there. When we come together on Action Weekend, we'll simply be putting the pieces together. That will involve screwing or ratcheting certain pieces down and lifting and placing other parts. It all depends on the various sections of the playground," Theo explained.

"I see. So I would have helpers to carry and install the equipment. Right?" George asked.

"You would have between six and ten volunteers, depending on the particular project you'll be given. Some of the lumber pieces are good sized and need a colony of workers to move them. Hopefully, you'll even have some semi-skilled folks working for you," Theo answered.

"And this playground raising will be accomplished in one weekend?" George asked incredulously.

"That's the plan. Hundreds of communities across America have built community playgrounds that way — barn raising style. The whole business is about pre-planning, getting everything worked out ahead of time, preparing the work site the day before, and ordering all the pieces for the specific theme we're using ahead of time. We raised money to cover the playground. That was the hardest part, at least to begin with, but after we repeatedly explained how truly valuable a community playground would be for Misty Falls, people began opening up their pocketbooks and adding to the pot. We were happily pleased with the results," Theo said.

The two men continued talking about the upcoming building and what George could expect for his crew.

"There's a training time on Friday the eleventh, the day before Action Weekend. The team leaders will all be present, and we'll review what has to happen and work to set up the grounds, so we can be ready for the build the next day. Can you be there Friday, too?" Theo needed to know.

"I think I can manage that. I'll explain to my boss about this being a community project, and that everyone is coming together to build on Action Weekend. I think he'll be okay with letting me off then," George explained. "Uh, do you need unskilled volunteers?"

"We need all the hands we can get for the project. We'll need close to two hundred people of varying abilities and skills to help make this park happen. Do you have someone in mind?" Theo asked.

"My wife would probably be happy to lend a hand," George offered.

"That's good to hear. What's her name? I'll get my daughter to call her and let her know about the volunteers," Theo began to write Connie's name down.

After that conversation George told Connie about the playground. "I saw this flier about a new playground for Misty Falls, and that they were looking for volunteers to help erect it in December. So, I decided that our participating in the playground building would look good as community service. Don't you think?"

"A playground? Who's building it?" Connie asked.

"Sounds like it's the brainchild of the mayor in town. He has had some committee researching playgrounds around the country. The whole idea is to get all the necessary pieces figured out, purchased, and delivered so that the entire playground can be installed in a weekend, sort of barn raising style. I'm thinking we need to show the DHR that we are contributing members of this community, and that we can be counted on, so I called the man in charge and volunteered to help. I also gave him your name." George explained to Connie.

Connie was still musing over the changes she had observed in George. He had come home several weeks before, declaring that he was a new man and that he wanted to start fresh with her and their marriage. "You are so amazing, George," Connie cooed. "I know you told me you would be different and that you would show me the difference, but what you're doing is a lot more than talk! You're applying what you said you would do. You've stuck to your word, and I'm so ... what' am I trying to say ...? impressed. Yes, I'm impressed with how you're thinking and what you're doing.

"What do you suppose I could do for this playground?" She asked.

Connie was quickly connected to Lucy Jane's volunteers, and she agreed to work in the food tent, which would be set up for meals for the workers. She would help by keeping the food line moving and well supplied for the volunteers. "*This sounds like a fun way to meet more town residents!*" She thought.

※ ※ ※

The playground building was working at full tilt by Saturday afternoon. The park's castle shape was beginning to appear. The tallest structure in the very center of the park was the main castle, and it had been securely installed after lunch. Four large 6" x 8" x 24' posts needed to be placed, one in each corner of the central castle room. These beams would serve as load-bearing structures to which the other pieces could be affixed — plastic walls, pressure treated wood for the floor and roof. The posts sat deeply into holes that had been pre-dug during the prep day on Friday.

Jeff Plumber (the handyman from Ontario, who had married Jillian Post) was the team leader for the main castle section; he recognized the criticality of the four posts being well set in the ground. All the other sections of the castle would hang from those four, great posts. Moving the posts across the ground to their proper locations would take some careful handling.

Jeff Plumber and Homer Randall (the farmer) had already prepared the holes the day before Action Day. Now they needed to manhandle the posts, one at a time, and place them well into their spots. After the posts were set in the ground they would be secured with quick hardening cement at their bases.

Jeff was pleased to see that his volunteers seemed strong and willing to work with the large poles. Jeff assembled his team: Homer Randall, Mickey Allen Barrymore (the sheriff), Kevin Thompson, Joe Ed Rafferty, Josh Anderson, and Dick McBride.

"Gentlemen, we have a challenge before us, and I believe that if we put our minds and backs to it, we will prevail," Jeff addressed his team. "We need to move these four posts from here (Jeff pointed to the four, giant beams on the ground) to the middle of the playground. We will begin with the first post, and we'll work with it and learn how best to negotiate it into place."

Homer Randall spoke, "Jeff, I have a small wagon in the back of my truck. I'm thinking we would do well to walk the beams over to their spot, using the wheels as far as we can."

Jeff's face lit up with that suggestion. He replied, "Indeed. that's a fine addition to our team." The wagon was quickly brought into service.

The four posts didn't take an hour to be planted and cemented in the ground, which established the location of the rest of the teams' work. Each team was able to build their portion of the castle project from those anchored posts.

✳ ✳ ✳

Connie was enjoying her job in the food tent. She was pleased to have a chance to meet a number of Misty Falls residents who were working on the playground project. *"Working here puts me in a new light,"* Connie thought. *"I feel more like I'm part of this community, because I'm involved in helping feed the volunteers. It's like I belong here. I like that.*

"George was right about our doing this community service," she thought. *"He's been right about a number of things, and I hope we'll begin to see a real turn around for us ... someday."*

Because Connie had been working inside the tent much of the day, she almost missed seeing Trudy, who had taken Kareem out for a stroll. Trudy heard about the new playground and that it would be built this weekend. She wanted to see what was going on. This new playground was being built behind the depot just across the street and down the road a quarter mile from the cottage where she and her mother lived.

Connie took a break from her work and walked out of the food tent to see how the building was coming along. She walked around the outside of the park and watched the workers busily at their tasks. *"This reminds me of what a multi-ring circus must look like,"* she thought. As she was making the final turn, back toward the registration table, she saw Trudy and Kareem.

Connie walked over to where they were standing and said, "Hi! I didn't expect to see you today, but here you are!"

"Hi! Good to see you! The new playground will be a great place for Kareem to play and learn and be challenged, and it's practically next door to us. How convenient! How nice of Misty Falls to build a playground for us so nearby!" Trudy said.

"Maybe coming to the playground will become a daily activity for you two. Kareem can meet other kids over here, too." Connie was thinking aloud.

"That would be fun," Trudy answered. I've heard about play groups that moms and tots have, and this could be the perfect place to meet such children and parents.

"Since you're here, I guess things worked out for you," Trudy remembered the anxious phone conversation she had had with Connie several weeks previous.

"I should have called you to tell you what happened," Connie admitted. "George didn't die, obviously. In fact, he had some sort of miraculous experience, something related to the revival. He drove around all over the country that night, and by the time he got home the next day he was a different man. I mean REALLY a different man!"

Trudy wondered how that could be. "Your husband is different?"

Connie laughed, "Yes! He's like a new man these days, I hardly know him. He used to be sort of mean, and distracted, and he wasn't around our apartment much at all, but since that night he's been like my sweetheart. He keeps finding things to do for me. He brought me flowers that first day, but he's done so many kind things for me since then. I hardly know him, BUT I have to say I like whatever it is that's changed him. He volunteered for us both to work here today, and I'm meeting more Misty Fallers — people who have been in this town for generations, who are real good folks. And, the best part, is that they seem to like me."

"How cool is that? It sounds like George had some great change inside, and it also sounds like it's made an important difference to you both. I'm glad for you two." Trudy smiled.

"How about your situation? Have you made any decisions about Kareem's dad?" Connie asked.

Trudy's face lit up with her news, "I told him!"

"You told him," Connie repeated. "You told him? Tell me about it! What did he say?"

"He took me out Friday after Thanksgiving, and I told him. It was a strange day, because we saved a boy's life first, and I wasn't sure how in the world I could ever find the right words to tell him, and then, suddenly, it all just came out. It felt very good to finally tell him," Trudy admitted.

"So ... what did he say? What's going to happen now?" Connie asked.

"We don't know. There's so many things that need to be decided, but the fabulous part is that Ned (that's his name) loves Kareem! He is so excited about his son; he wants to be part of his life, somehow, and I'm thrilled about his response," Trudy shared.

"Sounds like you've made some important steps toward being a family. You have big decisions to make, obviously. I can imagine that you won't figure it all out overnight. Gads. We should talk more often. Too much has changed since we talked before," Connie laughed. "I'm real glad to hear your exciting news."

They chatted for a few more minutes before Connie realized she needed to get back to work in the tent. The two young mothers promised to stay in touch.

✳ ✳ ✳

Tucker Joe knew that he was imposing himself on the Smiths, especially in the middle of their very busy weekend. He knew that Lucy Jane wouldn't be very available to see him that evening. She needed to make the necessary phone calls for tomorrow's continued work, and she needed to get to bed early, considering the second day of the playground build. Tucker Joe knew all this, yet he couldn't convince himself to leave Lucy Jane alone. He wanted to be with her, and he wanted her to know that's what he wanted.

"This is sounding a bit like a young teen's yearning, but I can't seem to help myself. I think the time has come, and I think the right girl has arrived, and I want to move things along however I can," Tucker Joe mused to himself.

"That really doesn't sound all that good. You're beginning to sound like some sort of weird person who is after some object de amor. I'm not in that category; I have more depth than that, I think," Tuck assured himself. *"I'll just take Lucy Jane out for a Coke, and that will be that."*

Tuck arrived at the Smith's house at 8:45 that evening. He had phoned Lucy Jane and learned that she would be finished with the phoning by then, and that, yes, she would go out with Tuck for a Coke.

Tucker Joe rang the bell at the Smith's home, and Mary Nell, Lucy Jane's mother, answered the door. "Well, it's good to see you, young man. It is a bit late to be going out, though, isn't it?"

Tucker Joe felt the blood rush to his face, but he replied, "I suppose it does seem a bit odd for us to be going for a Coke at this hour, especially on this busy weekend, but somehow it seems right for us."

Mrs. Smith stepped aside and let Tucker Joe enter the house. Lucy Jane walked into the front room just then; she had her coat on. She spoke, "Hi, Tuck. Mom, Dad, we're off to have a Coke. We won't be long."

"I don't think I've ever had a date quite like this one," Lucy Jane exclaimed as they began their drive. "It feels more like some sort of goofy thing we did in high school when we were tagging someone to be in our club."

Tucker laughed. "I'm really out on a limb here. Something is happening to me, and I think it's happening to us, and I just want to understand it. Can you follow what I'm saying?"

"I didn't before this afternoon, but something was happening when we held hands and walked around the playground site," Lucy Jane answered.

"That was it! That's what I felt, too. You have to understand, LJ, I have put off having a relationship with a woman for ... well, really, until right now. I was even fearful that having a relationship with a real girl had passed me by. Maybe if you don't find someone special when you're young you can't make that connection later on. I hope that's not the case, but I was beginning to wonder if it was so."

This tickled Lucy Jane, and she laughed. "I'm pretty sure that isn't the case." I don't think you have to have a girlfriend before you're, say, eighteen or nineteen or you lose the potential of ever developing such a relationship. I'll bet there are numbers of people who were December brides (or grooms, if you would).

"Is that why we're going for a Coke tonight?" Lucy Jane asked.

"Something like that," Tucker Joe nodded his head. "I have to tell you something has happened. Maybe it's been on its way, but I can say for sure it happened today, and I have to admit it to you. I think I'm in love with you!"

Lucy Jane startled a bit in her car seat when Tucker made that admission, so out of the blue. "I don't think I've ever been told that quite in that way before.

"I believe we're on that track. We've been enjoying each other's company for a little while now, and I believe we're very good buds."

"Don't go saying that!" Tucker jumped onto Lucy Jane's words. "This is more than friendship! I believe there's more, maybe a lot more, between us."

Lucy Jane smiled at her friend. "Yes, I agree, but don't put down friendship. It's an important and necessary piece to a good relationship. Before a man and a woman begin becoming intimate, having a solid friendship should come first.

Tucker drew the car up to the Wendy's diner and parked. He opened the door for Lucy Jane and held out his hand for her, helping her out of the car. He quickly slipped his hand into hers as they walked towards the enticing smells coming from the restaurant.

After filling their cups and snapping the tops on their Cokes the two sat down in a corner of the dining room. "LJ, I'm so pleased you have come into my life," Tuck began. "Do you suppose we could consider ourselves officially dating ... with a purpose?"

"Dating with a purpose? Is that sort of like being engaged to be engaged?" Lucy Jane's eyes twinkled at Tucker.

"Sort of. Years ago people 'kept company.' They began courting, which was seeing one another for special occasions, with the objective of learning the other well enough to become engaged and later married. So I guess that's what I'm hoping we could consider ourselves to be," Tucker Joe explained.

Lucy Jane nodded her head. "I think you're right; we do seem good for one another. I've noticed that when you're around I feel good; I feel lighter and happier and looking forward to the next thing. I don't know why that's so, but you seem to be good for me somehow."

"Good for you? That's great to hear, because I know you are good for me. These days I wake up and wonder if I'll see you; I look forward to seeing you; I can't wait to see you and be with you.

"Does that sound a bit goofy?" Tuck asked her.

"Sounds like we're becoming very important to one another. I don't know that it's possible to totally understand what happens to people when they begin getting close. Surely some psychologists have studied the matter, but maybe we can just enjoy it," Lucy Jane suggested.

"I'm learning so much about you. I've been watching you this weekend with the playground program, and I can tell you are really well organized, putting people and needs together. You also work well with many different people. I'd say that is a forte of yours — working with people. You are a very gifted person," Tuck told her.

"I like working with challenges, and I especially like to work with people. I do like to be organized, as opposed to flying by the seat of my pants," Lucy Jane replied, "but I used to hope that I could also be involved in raising a couple of the next generation kids. I haven't spent time with kids, aside from baby sitting when I was young."

"I'm glad you added that, because I have that on my to do list," Tucker Joe nodded his head in agreement. "I think you mentioned that before, when you were talking about you and Chet. Didn't you say something about your dreams for having a family?"

"Yes, we did. We included having children as one of the major goals for our marriage, but obviously, that didn't pan out," Lucy Jane said thoughtfully.

"You and I are both from Misty Falls. We know what a beautiful community it is for growing up, for raising a family. I hope to have some kids to bring up in this place, and our new playground will be a great addition to our town. I can just see dozens of children clambering over the equipment there, learning to stretch and balance, and gaining confidence for trying new things in this world," Tucker Joe added.

"It occurs to me that the playground might be a place where I could put Chet's money that could serve a host of children. I was thinking about it today when you brought the water to the volunteers. Water is so basic to life, and having a couple fountains is really necessary for the playground. I don't think our plans include a drinking fountain, but that could be my gift to the project." Lucy Jane suggested.

"You're thinking about using that windfall from Chet's investment to put a drinking fountain into the park?" Tucker Joe asked. "That's a great idea! A fountain would be a perfect addition to the park and one that would be forever appreciated, I'm sure."

Lucy Jane was happy that Tucker Joe agreed with her idea. "I have no idea what the cost would be to put a a fountain in there, but I did a little checking online, and the actual fountain isn't all that pricey. Getting the water over to that spot would be the bigger cost, I imagine, but if we could get volunteers to help lay a water line, I think I could manage the cost. I'd have to rent something to dig up the ground from Main Street to the playground, and I'd have to buy the pipe that could connect to the fountain. Since this is a town project, I expect they would pay for the water. It wouldn't be an exorbitant amount of money, anyway. It's just for children drinking water when they're thirsty."

Tuck could see that Lucy Jane had been looking into this idea, and he wanted to be supportive. "Sounds like you've put some thought into giving a fountain for the playground already. You ought to put a plaque on the fountain somewhere in memory of Chet's love of children."

After their Cokes were finished, the two returned to Tucker Joe's '68 Mustang and began driving back to the Smiths' house. Tucker held Lucy's hand as they walked toward her house. When they arrived at the porch of the house, Tucker stopped walking, turned to Lucy Jane, looked deeply into her eyes and said, "LJ, I'm beginning to feel like a new man ...." Tuck stopped speaking and drew closer to the tall, brunette beauty, leaned over and kissed her lightly on her lips. Lucy Jane responded to his touch invitingly. A second kiss was more eager and delightful, being accompanied by hugs and caresses.

Not a word was spoken, keeping the spell of this new understanding alive. Lucy Jane slipped into her front door, closed it softly behind her and leaned against it, revisiting those final, tender moments.

Lucy Jane waltzed into the living room and down the hall to her bedroom. Her head was spinning full of thoughts of the evening, especially the last few minutes. This situation was not something she hadn't experienced before, yet it was unique, even so. Surely she had been in love before, and she recognized the symptoms, feeling light as air and so very alive. Thoughts of Tucker — his new passion, his desperate hoping that she felt the same — and the kisses they had shared a moment before spoke so much more eloquently than mere words could ever accomplish.

Somehow, in that fraction of time, she felt she knew more about Tucker Joe Tennyson than she had ever known. There was excitement, interest, desire, and thrill all wrapped up in that moment; Lucy Jane was fully aware of the implications of their kiss. It carried a promise. If she and Tuck had talked non-stop for a month, they would not have been able to achieve the promise their kiss had spelled out.

Lucy Jane was not ready to give herself to Tuck, but she recognized that they were now on that road toward such a full relationship. She believed that there were some important details left yet to be worked out.

"O, Miss Lucy Jane! You are beginning something very new and wonderful — a new possibility — and it feels so good and right!" She told herself. "Tuck wants us to be engaged to be engaged. I suppose it's all about timing, but I have a feeling our fuse is rather short. If we want to include children in our lives together, we'd best not wait too long." Lucy Jane thought. She began singing a song to herself. I'm as corny as Kansas in August ....' She danced around the room.

✳ ✳ ✳

Chapter 36. Almost Christmas

Trudy and Ned emailed back and forth daily after Ned returned to school. Life for Trudy now had an added dimension. Instead of her entire life being centered on Kareem, she also had this new relationship slowly developing online. *"Baby, Baby, Baby! What you have done for me — and for us!"* Trudy told her son. *"You can't understand all that has happened, but I can tell you that your daddy is now part of our lives! It's still hard to say how it will finally turn out, but I hope, no, I pray, that God's will is done for us all. I really don't know what exactly I mean by that, because whatever steps Ned decides to take will involve change, but I'm trusting him to make a wise choice.*

Finally, the days of waiting were over, and Ned would be returning home for the Christmas holiday. Trudy expected that she would be seeing Ned some of the time over the seventeen days he had for school break. She didn't know exactly when he would be able to see her and Kareem, but she recognized that she and their son had become a priority for Ned.

The emails they had exchanged were wonderful, Trudy thought, but they were all about information. Trudy could appreciate that Ned wanted to learn as much as he could about his son, and he also wanted to know about Trudy — her interests and hopes.

Ned would be arriving in Knoxville Saturday afternoon before Christmas on a flight from Colorado Springs. Trudy figured that Ned's family would pick him up from the airport in Knoxville and take him home for dinner that first day in town.

When the phone rang, Trudy ran to answer.

"Hello," she said.

"Trudy, Is that you? It's Ned. I just walked in the door at home, and I'm wondering if we might have a date tonight." Trudy was caught off guard, but she wanted to be ready for whatever Ned might have in mind.

"I think you sound nearer than when you called from the Academy. That doesn't make any sense, of course, because calling me from Colorado or from ten miles away in Kirby shouldn't make any difference. Maybe it's just my imagination. Yes, I'd be happy to go out with you tonight. What have you got in mind?" She asked.

"I want to introduce you and Kareem to my folks. Would that be okay with you? You don't have to get dressed special for this; we're all very casual. "My mom wants to meet her grandson, and I told her I'd call you and ask," Ned explained.

"Yes, of course she wants to meet Kareem. I know you've already told her how this all came about, and I'd like to meet your parents. What time should I expect you?" Trudy asked.

"How about I pick you two up at five? We could have dinner together with the family," Ned suggested.

So plans for the evening were set; the families would meet. Trudy was a little apprehensive about meeting Ned's parents, but she knew their meeting would eventually have to happen, so why not now?

When Ned arrived he helped Trudy get Kareem settled in a child's seat that his folks had borrowed from a member of their church. "We have to be compliant with the law, which demands a child seat for babies. Mom knows a family who has car seats they're not using, so she was able to borrow one for us now."

Trudy was excited and nervous. "*Everything is happening so fast,*" she thought. "I know you've been doing a lot of thinking about our 'situation.' Have you made any decisions, yet?"

Ned was enjoying this time with Trudy and Kareem, and he wished it could stretch out longer than just the twenty minutes it took to get to his house. "I've been reviewing various scenarios for us, Trudy. I talked to my counselor a couple days ago about you and Kareem, and I want to tell you what I learned then, but I think I'll wait until after tonight. Right now we're doing the family thing — introducing everyone to everyone. That will probably be plenty of agenda for one night."

❋ ❋ ❋

The evening had been a smashing success. Everyone thought so. Trudy hadn't realized that she was coming into a pastor's home, although Ned had told her that his grandfather had been the pastor of Ebenezer Missionary Baptist Church in town and now his father was the pastor.

Kareem had been a perfect jewel. He was smiley and happy and adorable, and everyone admitted he was the hit of the evening, being passed around the room from one set of anxious arms to the next.

"Let me hold him, now," Sara Wilson begged her husband.

"Be careful to support him; this boy is a chunk, and he's wiggly," Henry Wilson laughed and passed his grandson over to his wife.

"Oooo! He's so soft and warm!" Sara held the child up close to her face. "You forget how warm babies are when your own are all grown up," Sara nodded to her sons. She held Kareem carefully and watched him hold her little finger in his hand. "He's so alert! I'll bet he's smart, just like his dad is!"

Trudy was enjoying Ned's family and especially enjoying the way they were taking all this newness in, apparently without judging her. She was thankful for that.

"How close is he to walking?" Henry asked Trudy. He held out his arms toward Sara, indicating that she could set Kareem down on the floor and help him make steps toward his grandfather.

"I think he's getting there. He certainly wants to walk. He's forever pulling himself up on furniture at home and trying to use his feet. He cruises around our little living room easily, hanging onto chairs and the couch. One of these days I think we will see him take off completely on his own," Trudy told them.

"I gather you live with your mom," Henry spoke up.

"Yes, we've been in our house just off Main Street in Misty Falls, since I was little. I guess Mom and I lived with Gram and Papaw for several years, but then Mom got her job at the elementary school cafeteria, and we were able to move into our little cottage not far from the depot in town. Our house isn't very big, but it's good enough for the two of us, I mean the three of us," Trudy corrected herself.

"You're from Misty Falls, and you grew up there. Sounds like your mother is helping you with Kareem. Am I right?" Sara Wilson asked.

"Mom is very helpful. She remembers how it was for the two of us, when I came. I know that I need to find a way to venture out of the house someday. She found a way, and it's probably better to be on my own, eventually, but right now we're with her," Trudy answered.

"Tell me about your family. Are your folks people of faith?" Henry wanted to know.

"My whole family has been part of Faith AME Church in Misty Falls. I used to be real active there, especially in the church choir. I loved singing back then. It felt so good inside when I was singing to the LORD," Trudy explained.

"You'll have to come over here and sing for us one of these days," Pastor Wilson suggested. "I'm glad to know you're a person of faith."

"I don't know what I would do without my faith in God," Trudy admitted. "I haven't been so faithful to worship recently, though, and that's a mistake."

"Well, I can imagine you've been busy, but that shouldn't stand in the way of worshiping the LORD. It's helpful to be among fellow disciples. We all need a spiritual boost at one time or another, and the best place to find that is in church," Henry said.

"I'm sure you're right," Trudy smiled at Ned's father.

"I can imagine you two young people have a great deal of thinking and deciding," Henry continued. "Your situation is not the first that has ever occurred, and it won't be the last."

"Henry, do you suppose this would be the time to share our story?" Sara asked.

Ned looked quizzically at his mother and sat up straighter in his chair. "Do you have a story to tell that I don't know, Mom?"

"It was a long time ago, but, yes, I do have a story to tell, if you're all right with it?" (Sara turned to her husband, cocked her head, and raised her brows.)

"It's your story, and if you think it's the right time, I'm fine with it," Henry agreed.

"Like you, Trudy, I was an unwed mother twenty-one years ago," Sara began her story.

"Mom! You never said anything before!" Ned gasped.

"No, I guess I didn't, but I think you're old enough to hear about it now.

"Like I was saying, I was an unwed mother, and I tried to keep everything a secret for a while. Of course, when Ned arrived, I had to tell my folks, and they accepted the baby into their home. We were members of Ebenezer Church. One day we were there, and I started talking to Henry. I introduced him to Ned, who was just a year old. Henry asked me about the baby's father, and I told him that the father had just completed his Army basic training and was about to be sent to Germany for his first assignment when I met him. Unfortunately, I lost track of him when he left town, and I never heard more from him. All I knew was his first name — Matt. His name was Matt M. I remember how he laughed when he told me that some of his friends would call him 'M&M,' like the candy. I never learned what the second "M" stood for. He was from around here, but I didn't even know exactly where."

"Yeah, something like that happened to my mom, too," Trudy piped in. "My father's name is Al Jackson, but I never knew him or spoke to him."

"You know his whole name!" Sara raised her eye brows. "Too bad you haven't met him.

"To return to my story, Henry and I began seeing one another. He was going to Bible school over in Knoxville, but he hoped to return here and work with his dad in the ministry and eventually take over the job as the senior pastor. When we were dating, Ned, you were always part of our date. We'd do picnics, or take a hike, or go to the movies. We always included you, Ned, in our time together. We were like family right from the start. Then, as we fell in love, we knew it was just right for us to include family in our plans. Jason came along a year after we were married."

Ned's eyes grew larger and larger as he listened to the tale of his origin. He looked at Jason, "So we're really half-brothers, but I don't think that makes a bit of difference, do you?"

Jason gave his big brother a mock slug to the arm and said, "No way. We're bro's however we came to be linked."

Ned was thoughtful on the way back to Misty Falls. "I had no idea about the story my mom told. It's really amazing. I'll have to think about that one. It won't make any changes in my life, now, but it is interesting, and I learned that my biological father's name was Matt something. I wonder if I'll ever meet him? Probably not, considering Mom didn't know his full name."

Trudy was thoughtful, too. She was reveling in all the kindness that the Wilsons had shown her and Kareem. They were a loving family. Ned was not the only good thing that came from that home. "Ned, I'm so glad you introduced me to your folks today. I think Kareem has wonderful blood in him!"

✳ ✳ ✳

Sunday, after church, Ned arrived in his car and knocked on the Livingston's door.

Trudy opened the door and said, "Hi, glad you're here. I just put Kareem down for his afternoon nap. You can go in and peek at him, if you'd like, but he'll be sleeping for another two hours."

Ned smiled and said, "I was at church this morning, so I didn't get over, but I think it's about time that we spent some one-on-one time together, don't you?"

Trudy responded with a big smile, "Yes, please. Do you have anything special in mind?"

Keisha picked up on the conversation as she was coming into the living room. "Hi, Ned. Good to see you. Sounds like you two would like to be on your own this afternoon. I'll be happy to watch Kareem, if you'd like."

That being settled, the two young people walked over to the Depot Diner.

They chose a table in the back corner and sat down. Ruby Anders quickly brought them water and asked what they might like to have.

"How about two pieces of your bread pudding, or would you rather have the banana pudding?" Ned asked Trudy. The order was made — two puddings, one bread and one banana.

"I need to tell you about the conversation I had with my counselor," Ned began.

"I met with her just before finals, and I told her everything about us. I find that's a good policy — being truthful. It keeps things cleaner and simpler."

"What did the counselor say? Did she give you any suggestions?" Trudy wanted to know.

"First, she was very kind. I liked that. She wasn't judgmental or angry or shocked. She asked some questions — to ascertain the validity of my fatherhood — and she explained my options."

Trudy watched Ned's body language carefully as he was speaking. He was relaxed and casual about what he was saying. "Options? Oh, of course you would have options. What sort of choices can you make?" She asked.

"To begin with, I'm a cadet at the Air Force Academy, and I'm in very good standing with the Air Force. My record is unblemished, and my GPA puts me close to the top of my class. It looks like I can write my own ticket however I like. Of course, I must follow the rules of the Academy, which do not allow for spouses," Ned explained.

Trudy nodded understanding. "I see," she murmured.

"There's more. Because of my contract with the Air Force, I an obliged to serve with them for five years following my four years at the Academy. I knew that when I signed the contract with the Air Force, and I rather thought it was a good plan. These days it's cool to have a guaranteed job somewhere.

"My counselor did point out that, if I so desired, I could curtail my time at the Academy any time, but that would still leave me with several years of pay back time to the Air Force. If I choose that option, I would be placed immediately in the enlisted ranks and put into a squadron at the Air Force's discretion, following basic training. That sort of step would allow me to marry, have my family, and be employed, without skipping a beat. I would be enlisted, but there would be a possibility of attending Officer Candidate School later. Of course, I would have to complete my baccalaureate degree somewhere first," Ned took a breath.

Trudy shook her head. "I don't like that option, Ned. You don't even know if I'm the woman you want to marry. You'd be giving up your career, and look how well you've done already! I can't let you consider that choice. It's just not fair to you."

Ned reached across the table and picked up Trudy's hand. "This is a really big decision, and it needs to be done right.

"Somehow I feel like we made part of that decision back two summers ago when we created Kareem. You and I are not meeting like normal people do with all the chips on the table, so to speak. We're already in a kind of a family arrangement, and that changes things for us," Ned said earnestly.

"This whole thing is not normal. You never hear about people like us, yet there have to be many men and women in the same boat — having put the cart before the horse," Trudy laughed. "I think I just jammed two metaphors together, just then. Sorry! You never hear about pre-families in a fairy story. It's always, 'boy meets girl; boy falls in love with girl; boy gets girl, and they all live happily ever after," Trudy sighed.

"That's why I thought we need to begin our courtship now, Trudy," Ned explained. "We skipped a number of stages, but that doesn't mean we can't visit them now.

"I propose that we go out every evening for the rest of my time home and see what we've missed."

Trudy's eyes opened wide as she heard Ned's suggestion. "Really? You want to go out with me, every night while you're here? That does sound fun. Where would we go? I have to tell you, I don't have much in the way of party clothes."

"I'm thinking we will be taking a cram course in going together. Remember our trip to the Smokies? We weren't expecting anything like what we found, but I learned so much about you that day ... and then later on that evening you told me about Kareem and my whole life turned upside down!

"I think we should go window shopping downtown Knoxville and get a few Christmas toys for Kareem. It is his first Christmas, isn't it?"

Trudy nodded, "Yes."

"And I'd like to meet your Gram, so that could be an afternoon event.

"I'd like it if you'd come with me to Christmas Eve worship at my church.

"And we should go out for a special dinner on New Year's Eve," Ned suggested. "And we'll go wherever you'd like one night, too."

Trudy was beaming with delight after everything Ned said. "It all sounds real good, and you know I'll go wherever you want. Maybe this will be the foundation for our friendship to grow and blossom."

"I want us to do the right thing. I've been praying about this whole thing and asking the LORD to guide me through the maze we seem to have fallen into," Ned said thoughtfully. "I do expect our way will become clearer as we keep watching for it, and another thing — I think you'll agree — even though we know one another (in a Biblical sense) I believe we should refrain from further such activity for now. We know the consequences, and we know how good we'll be, when and if we decide that's what we want," Ned smiled at Trudy and winked at her.

"I'm glad you mentioned that, because I've been thinking the same thing. We don't, for sure, know what's going to happen, but until that time, we can respect one another and watch out for one another, and we can look to Kareem to remember ...." Trudy stopped mid-thought and decided to leave it at that.

❋ ❋ ❋

Christmas was fast approaching, and Connie and George were getting along well. George had continued to stay on the course that he had set for himself. He came home every evening from work and spent the evening with Connie. Even Sallie saw the change in her son-in-law. Although the weather was chilly outside, now that winter was approaching, the Olivers would put on warm coats and take a walk together. They started walking over to the new playground, since they had taken part in building it. The trip was a couple miles round trip, but they reminisced about the fun they had helping build the playground, and Connie told George about some of the new people she was getting to know after working in the food tent.

Connie also told George how much she was learning in her job at Countrified Cuisine. She realized that Ms. Reynolds was helping her to learn the restaurant business, and Connie believed she was catching on well. She especially liked cooking and running the register out front.

One day, a week before Christmas, Connie took a look at the wall calendar and cried out, "Oh, no!"

"What's the matter, Dear?" Sallie asked her daughter.

"Look at this calendar. The twenty-fifth is on a Friday this year!"

"Why is that a problem?" her mother asked.

"We see the girls on Friday mornings, and when it's a holiday, I'm sure the DHR won't be open," Trudy cried.

"I see what you mean," Sallie said.

George was in the living room as this conversation was taking place. "Honey, what are you talking about?"

Connie ran out to the living room. "Did you hear? I was just looking at the calendar, and I realized that my next visit with the girls, which is always on Friday, won't happen. Friday is the 25th of December, Christmas. I'm absolutely sure the office won't be open on Christmas Day, and I won't see the girls for two weeks then! That's horrible! I don't know what I can do! I want to give the girls the presents I bought for them, and I want to sing them Christmas songs, and I want us to all be together for Christmas. Now, it looks like it's going to be one big, fat disappointment!" Connie dropped onto the couch, sobbing.

George heard Connie's fear, and he felt for her. He had never taken time off work for the weekly visits at the DHR office, so it had been some time since he had seen his twin girls, but he understood and was sympathetic to his wife's pain.

"How about I try to talk to the DHR woman, and see if we might see the girls on a different day?"

"Oh, George! I should have thought of that! Maybe Ms. Richey will take pity on me and allow me to have my visit next Thursday or something." Connie was hopeful.

George found the number and made the call. "Hello, this is George Oliver over here in Misty Falls, and I would like to speak to Ms. Richey. Is she there? ... Thank you. I'll wait."

"Hello, Ms. Richey? This is George Oliver. I'm the father of the twin babies that you're watching over. Yes, that's right, George Oliver. My wife is Connie Oliver. She and my mother-in-law have been coming to your office Fridays to spend time with our twin girls, but we just realized that the next visitation date will be on Christmas Day. We were just looking at the calendar and realized the visitation would not be happening on Friday, because of the holiday," George explained to the woman.

"Yes, ma'am. We've both been attending the weekly anger management classes; I think we're halfway finished with them.

"Oh, you heard from Dr. Rogers, our counselor, and he has told you that? I'm glad to hear that," George listened carefully to the DHR woman's comments.

"Yes, that would be a special arrangement. I think I can speak for my wife and say that it would be a wonderful blessing for us ... especially on this holiday!

"You say we could meet late Thursday in your office?" "Yes! We can be there ... four-thirty? That's fine. Thank you so much!" George hung up the phone and looked at Connie.

"George! What was she saying?" Connie asked excitedly, anxious to hear the verdict. "Did she say we could see the girls on Thursday? Is that what I was hearing?" Connie was dancing around the floor, hoping to hear she would somehow see her girls to wish them a Merry Christmas.

"No, she didn't say we could change our meeting to Thursday," George began slowly. "She told me that since we've been successfully working on our anger classes that we could pick the girls up on Thursday evening and keep them for the long weekend! We will need to return them on Monday after Christmas, but Ms. Richey thinks it would be good for the girls to be with their own family on Christmas!"

"You're not kidding?" Connie asked incredulously. "You're sure she said we could have the girls for the entire weekend? Three whole days?"

"It's no joke! I don't exactly know why Ms. Richey is allowing this, although she seemed to think we are making progress in our classes; apparently Dr. Rogers called and spoke to her and gave us a glowing report. That didn't hurt us, I'm sure," George winked at Connie.

Immediately Connie was making plans. "We have so many things to do before the girls arrive! We only have four days before we pick them up! There's shopping, and wrapping, and decorating, and planning to do! George, I'm so excited! This would never have happened except you changed, and we've been working on getting us in shape, and, and, and," Connie stammered. "It's working!"

George took hold of Connie's hands, bowed his head and thanked God right that moment for the good news they had just received and God's guiding their lives.

✳ ✳ ✳

Lucy Jane met Tucker every day for the next week. Since their late evening date on Action Weekend and Tucker's declaration of affection, they had managed to eke out half an hour at different times each day to be together. Lucy Jane usually went to Friendlie's to meet Tuck, but twice they had dinner together over at the Depot Diner just across the street from the grocery store. They had an hour for each of those two dates.

Their second dinner they sat in a back corner at the diner, which was as far away from other guests as they could manage to be. Tucker spoke, "LJ, I'm beginning to feel like my life is revolving around the moments we're together. Time seems to drag along between times, and then our moments together fly by much too fast."

"I have to say you've certainly got a different sort of timing. I've never been so squished for time before. Is that the way your life goes?" Lucy Jane asked.

Tucker was thoughtful for a moment. He gazed out into the diner and watched Ruby Anders, the owner's wife, talking to other customers; he saw the Charlie Brown Christmas tree that was sitting atop the check-out counter, and he heard the holiday music surrounding them. "This is a colorful time of year, isn't it?" He asked changing the subject.

"I've always loved Christmas. I think it's my favorite time of the year. It's full of peace and good will and chilly weather, so we have to wrap up tight, but it's full of fun, gift giving, and thanking God and one another, and many fun surprises," Lucy Jane reminisced.

"What would you say we get married, this week, like Christmas Eve? Wouldn't that be perfect? We'd never forget that date, and everything is already decorated and looking so festive," Tucker Joe declared.

"You're serious! Aren't you?" Lucy Jane could hardly believe it. "You're right about everything being set for fun, and as far as we are concerned, I suppose we could take our time for a few more months, but what's the big deal? Getting to see one another a half hour, or maybe a whole hour, once a day is hardly satisfactory. If we're married we'd get more than that, for sure!"

"So, you're willing?" Tucker Joe was almost unbelieving. "Will you marry me, ah, this week?"

Lucy Jane thought for a minute. She had already been married twice, and both times she had big weddings. She had already done the big wedding thing with strings of bridesmaids and fancy gowns and glorious flowers and guests and sit down dinners. She knew that the wedding day with all the trappings was not nearly as important as the marriage itself. "I might not be so inclined to do something so suddenly, if I thought I was missing the big-to-do wedding, but, you know what? I've already done that. I suppose we could still invite friends to come and witness us taking our vows. The important question is, 'Are we ready for marriage?', and I'm not sure we're not. That's a terrible double negative, but you know what I mean. I think I am ready to be your wife and bear you wonderful children."

Tucker Joe couldn't help grinning broadly. He was thrilled that Lucy Jane agreed with his whim. "It's not like we'd be eloping or something; we'll have guests and witnesses and whatever you'd like. Would you like to have a dinner or a finger food type of party? How about music? We could mix Christmas music with some of our favorites for the party."

"Uh-oh!" Lucy Jane exclaimed. We do have one serious business to agree on before we get the minister out of bed."

"What's that?" Tucker Joe pulled back and looked with apprehension at his soon to be bride. "What haven't we talked about?"

"Well, the reason we're letting this idea about getting married take over is because we can't seem to find any time to be together, and you have to admit, it's your fault!" Lucy Jane pretended to pout.

"That's true. I am a workaholic, and because I work long hours, we are choosing to marry so we <u>can</u> spend more time together. 'Sides of which, we both want family, and if that's going to happen — starting our family — we need to get with the program!" Tucker exclaimed.

"Yes, you've got it. Maybe in a saner moment we'll laugh at our reasons for this shot gun wedding, but my real question to you is how much do you expect me to work in the store after we're married?" Lucy Jane raised her eyebrows in a questioning way.

"Gottcha! That's a good question, and I can see how you might think I'm marrying more help for the store, but that's not why I'm so excited about us marrying," Tucker said. "In fact, I was going to surprise you with this when the final pen strokes have been scratched on the contract, but since you brought it up I'll tell you. I've been in dialog with a national grocer, and things are looking very good for me to be bought out by them. I'll retain a 35% interest in the store, but it will mean that I'm not working so hard. I can work as much as I want or don't want, and I'll be making a very generous stipend to boot."

Lucy Jane sat back in her chair and tried to take in what Tucker Joe had just told her. "You mean you're selling Friendlie's Foods? You're really selling it?"

"The fifteenth of January will be the beginning of the new store. It will be expanded and modernized over the next year, but it won't be mine anymore, and best of all, I won't be a slave to Friendlie's anymore, either," Tucker shook his hands, as if to free them from some chain.

"So which date would you like — the twenty-third, the twenty-fourth, or the twenty-sixth? I'll let you choose the date and time and the place, and I'll be there to say, 'I do!'" Tucker grinned.

After they parted, Lucy Jane made a bee-line for St. Luke's Cumberland Presbyterian Church to talk to Pastor Allen Remington.

"Pastor Allen, I expect you are surprised to see me here this afternoon," Lucy Jane began.

Allen Remington was always pleased to see a parishioner, "Merry almost Christmas to you, my Dear. What brings you here in such an apparent hurry today?"

"Would you believe I want to get married?" Lucy Jane smiled.

"Married! That would be a great blessing. I don't recall seeing you with someone special, though; who might you be marrying?" Allen inquired.

"Tucker Joe Tennyson asked me to marry him, and we want to have the wedding this week!" Lucy Jane announced.

"This week? This week! My, my, my ... my, my! Isn't that just a bit fast? How long have you two been engaged?" Pastor Remington glanced at Lucy Jane's left hand to see if she was wearing an engagement ring.

"Yes, it is sudden. In fact, we just decided a few minutes ago, but we are very serious. We just want to get on with the program. We want to build a home and family and all the trappings, and we don't want to wait any longer than necessary," Lucy Jane explained.

"If I remember correctly, you've been married before, and so you know, more or less, what you're jumping into, and you're of age, for sure. I can understand your wanting not to waste precious time planning and setting up a big wedding. You've done that before, too. I remember when you married Chet McPherson. That was less than two years ago, wasn't it?" Remington asked.

"Actually, we married the first of October in '07, so it's a bit over two years, now," Lucy Jane grimaced and then picked up her thought. "So, you can see why Tucker and I want to have a simple ceremony this time," Lucy Jane admitted.

"The timing is not such an important matter, but are you really sure about Tucker? Have you given yourself enough time to grieve your loss? Do you know Tucker well enough to want to be his wife?" Pastor Remington asked.

"Yes, yes, and yes!" Lucy Jane proclaimed. "I'm sure no one knows everything about one's intended; I'm sure it will take a lifetime to truly understand Tuck, but I think I've seen the important things, and I like what I've seen. Yes, I think I know Tucker Tennyson well enough to want to be his wife."

Pastor Allen nodded his head. "I suppose younger people need more time to sift through things than you do. You must know your mind by now. I don't remember Tucker ever being married. Is that right?"

"No, he hasn't been married before, and from what I understand, I don't think he's ever had a girlfriend, either. He tells me that he had been rather afraid of having totally missed out on romance. He hoped he hasn't missed that boat. He really wants to have a family, and he wants me to be his wife!" Lucy Jane began talking faster and faster.

"So when is this wedding going to take place?" Allen asked.

"Could you marry us on Christmas Eve?" Lucy Jane asked hopefully.

"I suppose that could happen. Do you want it to be part of the service on Christmas Eve?" Pastor Remington wondered.

"Hm. Maybe just following the service we might add the wedding vows. Would that work?" Lucy Jane was thinking aloud.

"That would make the Christmas Eve service even lovelier. Christian worship services are always a celebration, and Thursday night we'll be celebrating God sending His Son to earth to initiate the kingdom of heaven. A wedding celebration would just make the evening that much more joyous. We could even print an invitation for worshipers to stay and be witnesses to the ceremony, if you'd like that," The pastor offered.

Lucy Jane was pleased that her pastor was so willing to do the marriage ceremony following the Christmas Eve service. She and Pastor Allen spoke a bit longer to figure how much of the wedding service would be used that evening.

"What you want and need is to have the vows spoken and rings exchanged. Ah, you DO have rings, don't you?" Pastor Allen asked.

Lucy Jane rolled her eyes and exclaimed. "No! We don't have rings yet, but I'll be in Knoxville tomorrow, and I'll pick them up then. Thanks for the reminder!"

❄ ❄ ❄

Christmas Eve was fast approaching. The Olivers had prepared their tiny apartment for the advent of their twin little girls for the Christmas weekend.

The moment they realized that the girls would be coming home for Christmas, they went out to the stores and began shopping. They picked up a small tree and bought some simple ornaments for it. Connie thought they could pop some corn and string it to add to the decor on the tree and around the room.

They bought new outfits for the girls and several toys that were for 18 months up to 3 years old. "I love these colorful toys!" Connie picked up the box of stacking donuts and tossed them in her basket. They look so joyful!"

Sallie wanted to cook a turkey for Christmas, even though the twins wouldn't be eating much of it. "We can get a small bird, and we can add a can of cranberries, a can of yams, and some corn. I love to make stuffing, so that will be fun to have — like a real Christmas party."

George helped with the stockings for the girls. He picked out two Christmas stockings — one red and one green — which had stars and angels and trumpets above a small creche. "The girls can grow with these stockings. I'm so glad we'll have them with us for Christmas, and I hope that it will be the beginning of their coming home for good in the New

Year. Connie, I believe we can begin to count down the days 'til they are with us permanently."

"Do you really? You think we'll be getting them back next year?" Connie questioned.

"If things continue as they have been going — with us continuing our anger classes and doing well in them — I think I could say we'll have the girls back by Easter! I don't guess we should set our hopes too high, but still, I'd like to believe it can be done," George predicted.

"I hope so, too. It would make life easier to be able to count down the days till we get them back," Connie smiled.

* * *

Wednesday, two days before Christmas, Ned stopped by the Livingston's house for his visit. He wanted to take Trudy and Kareem to meet Trudy's grandmother, Gram. Ned believed in family, and he wanted to get to know as much of Trudy's family as possible.

Trudy had Kareem dressed in layers, so they could be out in the cold weather. "I think we'll drive over to your Gram's today, so we'll have more time to spend with her," Ned suggested.

"Let's do it!" Trudy smiled. She was thrilled that Ned was apparently so interested getting to know her family.

When Ned and Trudy arrived they discovered that Gram had a visitor, an old friend of hers who Trudy knew, Miss Pearly Mae Moore.

"Ned! We're in luck. Miss Pearly Mae is one of Misty Falls' notable citizens. She has been a teacher and principal at David Crockett Elementary School here for many, many years. I'm so glad you'll get to meet her," Trudy explained.

Gram welcomed her new visitors into her living room, and she introduced them to her good friend Miss Pearly Mae Moore.

After introductions were made, everyone sat down.

Pearly Mae spoke first to Trudy. "Your little son is a real looker, isn't he? You know, he reminds me a little of my first boy, Matt. He has that same way with his eyes, how they almost tilt up at the corners. I used to say to him, 'Matt, my boy, you're just like your daddy with those eyes, my dear. You are truly a child of his!'

Ned was suddenly very interested in this friend of Gram's. He asked Pearly Mae, "So you're from Misty Falls. Have you always been here? I mean, are you a native?"

"I love to tell folks about my family. Yes, I'm a native of Misty Falls. The fact be known, I am a direct descendent of a slave — my grandmother was born in 1860 right here in Misty Falls. She spent her early years as the property of the Randall family. Of course, the emancipation proclamation freed all the slaves in '63, so she didn't experience slavery. She was too young, but her mother and her father certainly did."

"What was your maiden name?" Ned asked.

"My maiden name was Bannister. Then I married the best man in the world — Danny Moore. He was something. He was a hard, hard worker from the gitgo, and he owned his own construction company by the time he was 30. We had been married several years by then, and I had earned my college degree. That was really unusual for Blacks back then, but I just knew I could do the work, if I was given the chance," Pearly Mae reminisced.

"And you had a child named Matt Moore?" Ned scooted forward to the edge of his seat.

Matt's my first born. I have three other children, but Matt was my first. Are you asking me about my boy for a particular reason?" Miss Pearly Mae was picking up on to Ned's line of questioning.

"Maybe. Maybe I am, Miss Pearly Mae. I hope you don't mind. You see, I just discovered something about my own history that I didn't know before," Ned looked at Trudy and nodded.

"You learned something about your heritage?" Pearly Mae was suddenly interested in what Ned was saying.

"Yes. You just met my son, Kareem. I've only known about him since Thanksgiving. I wasn't aware of his his existence before then."

Pearly Mae leaned forward to hear every word.

"I learned then that I'm a father, and that Trudy is Kareem's mother," Ned stopped for a breath.

"I've known about Miss Daisy's grandson, but I haven't seen him before today. You're telling me that you, the father, didn't know about your part in this child's life until very recently?" Pearly Mae was trying to assemble the picture of this young family.

"I didn't know I had a son until Trudy decided to tell me about him," Ned answered.

"Let me interrupt here," Trudy spoke up. "Miss Pearly Mae, you need to understand, Ned is a cadet at the Air Force Academy, so when I realized we were expecting a baby I didn't want to ruin his life by forcing me and my child into his world. So, for a long time I kept Ned's identity a secret."

"I see. I can understand how you felt. It probably isn't the best answer, but I can understand it," Pearly Mae smiled at Trudy.

Ned spoke up. "When I told my folks about learning that I was a father, they were excited to hear the news, and they wanted to meet Trudy and, of course, Kareem.

"So when I brought them over to meet my folks, my mom told me this shocking story about how she had been an unmarried mother too. She and Trudy both had unexpected pregnancies!" Ned explained.

"My mom told me that my real father was a young soldier who had just completed his basic training and was on his way to some post in Germany. She didn't even know his full name, but he called himself Matt, and she remembered he mentioned that he was sometimes called 'M&M', like the candy, so she thought his last name might have begun with an 'M.' Anyway, my real father's name was Matt M. I don't suppose I'll ever know who that man is, but it is something of a coincidence that your son's name is Matt, and your last name is Moore," Ned laughed.

"Maybe it's not so much of a coincidence," Pearly Mae said. "My first boy, my Matt, couldn't be your father, because he is much too old. He was born in 1948, and, although he made the Army his profession, he wouldn't have been just coming out of basic training about the time you were conceived. On the other hand," Pearly Mae continued. "My grandson, Matt Moore, Jr. might / could very well be that man."

"Your grandson? Excuse me?" Ned asked, his interest growing quickly.

"My grandson, Matt, Jr., was in the Army for a couple of stints, but he didn't make it his career, like his daddy did. I think he was at basic training at Fort Lewis in Washington before he went overseas, and I think he came home for a couple weeks before his first assignment. There is a good possibility that your mystery has been solved," Pearly Mae announced.

"Then your grandson could be my real dad! That's amazing," Ned could hardly believe it.

"Where is he now?" Ned asked.

"He lives in Chattanooga with his family. He's been working as a plumber; he has his own business there," Pearly Mae told Ned.

"If all of this is so, then we have more family here!" Ned announced.

Pearly Mae sat back in her chair. "I think, young man, that you are right, and I'd love to get us some proof. Your child's face, his eyes, are another good reason to believe the connection."

"You know, that was the first thing I thought when Trudy was trying to find the right words to tell me about my fatherhood. She showed me a picture of Kareem, and I recognized it as a picture my mom has had sitting on her dresser all these years. I thought I was looking at the same picture. Those eyes are definitely telling," Ned smiled.

"If that is so, then I am looking at my very own great grandson!" Pearly Mae looked at the young family. Then she turned to her friend, Miss Daisy Livingston, and announced, "Miss Daisy! I think you and I are really kin!"

❊ ❊ ❊

Late on Christmas Eve afternoon the Olivers drove over to the DHR office. They were very excited about bringing Shelby Ann and Samantha Rose home for the long weekend, and they had planned certain events for their twins to see. They would take them over to the new playground everyday; they would have Christmas Day, including Santa Claus and all the trimmings; they would have music in the background all day long, and they would begin the entire time by attending the Christmas Eve service at Muddy Creek Methodist Church.

"How did you happen to choose that church?" George asked his wife.

"We don't have any roots here in a church, and Miss Winnie was so kind to me when she was here, so I thought that would be a good place for us to go," Connie explained.

* * *

Time had been flying-by for Lucy Jane. After she spoke to Pastor Allen and got the go-ahead to have the wedding after the Christmas Eve service just three days from now; she then called her boss.

"James, I have to ask you a big favor," she began.

"It's Christmas, and I'm feeling very merry, so ask away," James returned.

"I just had a most remarkable conversation with my boyfriend this afternoon, and we've decided to get married ... this week!"

"Married! This week?" James was incredulous.

"Yes, this week, and suddenly I have so much to do, I'm calling to ask if I can get time off," Lucy Jane explained excitedly.

"I should think you need it. Have you thought this through? Are you sure you two are right for each other? Come to think of it, I don't re-member you mentioning anyone special. How long have you two been going together?" James was curious.

"Oh, maybe a couple of hours!" Lucy Jane laughed. "I know this sounds quick, and it is, but we've decided this is what we want to do. You see, Tucker is the owner of the local grocery store here in Misty Falls. He's been tied to the store for a long, long time, and he hardly ever gets away, so we figure we need to marry, so we can see one another. Oh, and he's in the middle of negotiations to sell his store, so he'll probably be home more. We're really excited about the whole thing."

"I guess you are. Tell me where and when you're tying the knot, and I'll be there," James added.

Lucy explained about the Christmas Eve service and how the ending would be different this year, because she and Tucker were saying their vows then. She asked James to make a general announcement in the office, so others might come, too.

* * *

Lucy Jane spent the next morning at the West Towne Mall in Knoxville, picking up the items she knew she would be needing. Her first stop was at the jewelers. She found a set of matching wedding rings and an engagement ring with a stone she liked. She hoped that Tucker Joe's ring size hadn't changed since he bought his high school ring, because that was the size she bought.

She also found a swishy, long, Christmasy dress made of white satin embroidered with red and green poinsettias on the skirt and a long stem with a fully opened poinsettia blossom on the bodice. Lucy Jane chose a pair of heels to match the red in the dress. *It's white, but not pure white, which only makes sense since I've been married before, and for that matter, I can wear this dress again next year.*

Before she left the mall Lucy Jane stopped in the intimate apparel department at Dillard's to pick up something special for their honeymoon. *Hm. We've never mentioned going somewhere for a honeymoon, but surely we'll do something ... Anyway, I shall be prepared for whatever Tucker sees fit and is able to manage, time wise.*

"I'm sure I'm forgetting important things, but for this wedding we'll do with what we can pull together now. The decorations and the goodies that are already in place will be just fine. Oh! I really should do something about a cake. I think I remember that Miss Nina did a wedding cake for Miss Winnie. I wonder if she might be willing to help me with one now?" Lucy Jane mused.

* * *

Ned picked Trudy and Kareem up at 6:30. They had half an hour to get over to his church for the Christmas Eve worship.

"I'm excited!" Trudy admitted. "We've had so much fun this week, and I feel like you've become so very much part of my life. I don't know what to say. Ned, I love you, and I'm IN LOVE with you. You have become so dear to me these past few days. I can hardly think about you leaving, going away, again, and being gone for months," Trudy spoke with a mixture of joy and angst, "But that's completely selfish of me, and I need to ask your forgiveness. I think we've taken some good steps toward something, and I'm happy with that."

"I think you've just named what's going on for both of us. I feel the same. I'm excited yet apprehensive. These past several days have been a dream for me, and I know we've grown closer and closer. Not only is Kareem in our lives, but there's something between us that is real and beautiful. It's like some tiny creature that is alive and is growing, but it is still so young and immature that it will take kindness and careful nurturing to see it grow," Ned held up his right hand, made the fingers of his right hand close at the tips and then slowly open them, like the opening of a flower.

"That's a good picture, Ned," Trudy laughed. Yes, I think we can name this feeling, like a small living thing. I think it is love, and it is in the beginning stages of development. I think it has every hope of surviving, but we have to be careful with it."

"I hope you understand my position about us," Trudy said. We have had a magical week, and we are probably falling in love with each other, but if we look down the road a piece, we can see that your continuing on at the Academy is what is best for you, and it is ultimately best for your family. I can learn to live with that."

Ned was silent. He agreed with Trudy, but he wasn't completely comfortable about leaving things as they were. Status quo was not what he wanted for his family. He wanted to provide better for them.

❋ ❋ ❋

Christmas Eve services were packed with merry worshipers in Misty Falls, and Christmas candles could be seen lit in church windows all around town.

The Olivers arrived at Muddy Creek United Methodist Church in time to be greeted, given a bulletin, and shown to an empty pew. The whole family was present — George, Connie, Sallie, Samantha Rose, and Shelby Ann. George and Connie each held one of the babies in their lap.

The sanctuary was filled, and more people scooted into the pew next to this visiting family. "Wonder who those folks are?" Jodi Lee Barrymore elbowed her husband, Mickey Allen Barrymore and whispered to him. "I think I saw the man at the playground building, so maybe they are new," Mickey Allen whispered back.

The service began with a choral piece, and then everyone stood to sing 'O, Come, O, Come Emmanuel.' It felt very good to be standing and singing with such a group of people, each one awaiting the coming of the Christ Child into their lives.

George leaned over to Connie and said, "This feels like a good place to land. What do you think?"

Connie agreed, squeezed George's hand and hugged the daughter in her lap. "I'm so happy! I think the Christ Child has come to us this year. May He feel very welcome and stay a long, long time."

❋ ❋ ❋

As the Christmas service was about to close at St. Luke's Cumberland Presbyterian Church, Pastor Allen paused, holding his unlit candle in his hand. He would begin the final carol by lighting his candle from the Christ Candle and then starting the flame around the room so everyone would soon hold his or her own lit candle. The electric lights would be slowly dimmed, leaving the candle flames to illuminate the sanctuary as everyone sang Joy to the World, welcoming in the Yule.

"Before I light this candle and begin our traditional candle lighting, I want to invite anyone who would like to stay to remain in the sanctuary for about ten minutes longer. We have a very special celebration tonight, and all of you are invited to come.

"I'm referring to the wedding of our own Ms. Lucy Jane Smith-McPherson and Mr. Tucker Joe Tennyson. They are marrying each other tonight and would be pleased for any who desire to share this blessed moment with them to stay for the saying of the marriage vows," the pastor said.

"Joy to the World the LORD Has Come!" The hymn was sung lustily, ringing in the Christmas. Lucy Jane and Tucker Joe held hands and walked up to the center of the aisle, in the front of the sanctuary, raising their candles high, helping to shine their light in the darkness of the winter night.

A few minutes later, after they had exchanged vows and rings, Pastor Allen proclaimed them to be husband and wife and said, "Now you may kiss the bride!"

Tucker was happy to oblige and swept Lucy Jane nearly off her feet in his enthusiasm to comply with a resounding kiss.

The service ended with everyone singing, O, Come Let Us Adore Him — Venite Adoramaus!

In the back of the sanctuary, sitting next to Dr. Sedgwick, Nina Mattingly was about to leave the service and to position herself to help serve wedding cake as soon as the bridal couple had cut into the cake and taken their first bites. Nina was thoroughly enjoying watching Tucker Joe finally find what he was looking for — his 'significant other.' Suddenly, as she sat watching the wedding she felt a hand on top of her own hand. She looked up at her boss, Dr. Sedgwick. He squeezed her hand, and they smiled at one another. *"There's something about the atmosphere at a wedding that makes everyone present acutely aware of the gift of love!"* Nina thought.

✳ ✳ ✳

A very similar Christmas Eve worship service was taking place at Ebenezer Missionary Baptist Church over in nearby Kirby. Christmas Carols were sung, prayers were spoken, and Pastor Henry Wilson gave an especially heart warming message about the great event when the Christ child came to Mary and Joseph. If you listened with your heart as well as your ears, you might note how the pastor seemed to have some personal experience he was calling on as he described the child lying in the manger and later being held by his mother as his father stood watchfully beside them.

Ned sat with Trudy and Kareem and felt blessed that he was, almost, the head of his own little family. He listened to his dad's reference to Joseph's call by the angel and his obedience to the angel's message to take his family out of Bethlehem immediately because of the wicked King Herod. Joseph's response was the picture of how a father should act. He didn't question the angel; he moved quickly in the night, leading his family to safety.

After the service the worshipers shared hugs and good wishes, echoing Merry Christmas to one another, and Ned introduced Trudy and Kareem to dozens of church friends. Finally, they said good night to Ned's family, piled into the car, and began their drive back to Misty Falls.

"As beautiful as this evening has been, it still seems like we're cutting it short. Everyone else is returning to their homes for hot chocolate and goodies or to open presents, but we have to go our separate ways. That isn't quite as much fun," Ned complained to Trudy.

"Tonight was so beautiful. Your church reminds me so much of my home church, and the people at Ebenezer Church are very kind. I loved their choir. They made me think of when I used to sing with my church choir. I almost wanted to join them up there.

"Maybe we won't always be separate; maybe someday things will come together for us," Trudy suggested."

"For now we just need to be patient. Things will work out for us. You tell me how fast your time at the Academy has flown by, and I'll bet the next year and a half will speed by the same way," she added.

"Trudy ..." Ned stopped. He was trying to figure how to speak the words he needed to say. "Trudy, I think we're wrong. I think we're making a mistake, and I think we need to think a little harder. Tonight I was listening to my dad as he spoke, and I was thinking of Joseph. He wasn't really the father of Mary's child, but an angel came to him, several times, and told him what he should be doing — caring for his family, taking them where they would be safe. I think that message is for me — for us — too.

"I think I need to take that second option, you know, the one that will allow us to be together and for me to start out as enlisted. I can still finish my schooling; these days it's not that hard to do that online. We'll make that a priority and see that I finish the Bachelor of Science right away. Then I could apply for OCS and go that route to becoming commissioned. I think that would work. I KNOW that would work."

Trudy's eyes opened wider and wider as she began to take in what Ned was saying. "Are you sure? Do you really want to do that? Please don't tell me it's because you feel sorry for us! Please don't tell me that."

Ned pulled the car off the road, turned off the ignition, put the emergency flashers on, and pulled Trudy over to him. He leaned forward and kissed her. She responded to his embrace and they kissed again, deeply. "Tell me you love me, and that you'll marry me," Ned whispered in Trudy's ear.

"I will. I will, I love you so much!" Trudy spoke as tears of joy raced down her face.

"Wow! That's some Christmas present!" Ned exclaimed. He reached over to the back seat and touched his son on the shoulder. "Did you just hear that, Young Man? Your sweet mother has agreed to marry me. That means we'll be a real family very, very soon!"

∗ ∗ ∗

Christmas Eve in Chicago was wet, and crisp, so the Daniels wrapped in layers for their drive to church.

"I absolutely love Christmas Eve!" Winnie exclaimed as she snapped on her seat belt. "I love to go out late on the afternoon of the 24th for the last minute items I need — stocking stuffers or something needed for Christmas dinner. I think that late afternoon / early evening, just before the stores close on Christmas Eve, always feels somehow enchanted. Maybe it's because there are fewer shoppers, or maybe it's because snow has just fallen, dampening the sounds. Somehow it always feels unusually quiet as if the heavens are anticipating something wonderful is about to happen. Whatever it is makes me think of how very special this time of year is, remembering when God sent His Son into the world. What an incredible night it must have been!"

"This is my first Christmas, so I suppose I'm seeing the holiday with new eyes. All I used to see at Christmas time were the hoards of bustling shoppers and the stores overstuffed with goods to sell and the pervasive do-loop of holiday music. I thought <u>that</u> was what Christmas was about— obviously the biggest, most expensive holiday — but it was just like all the others: way too much stuff and food," John offered.

"Can you imagine the celebration that took place in heaven the night Jesus was born on earth?" He mused. "That's a story we have yet to hear, but when, as a person of faith, I think of the Incarnation of Christ, the meaning of Christmas suggests a completely different image.

"Tonight I'm looking forward to worshiping the God of the universe who, as St. John said, 'sent his Son to take on flesh and live among us.' I think I'm coming 'round to understanding how the church helps us believers come together and joyfully celebrate what God has done for us. I am pleased to be able to join other followers of Christ to raise our voices and sing Hallelujah, Christ is born!"

"I love your new perspective on church," Winnie assured John. "It hadn't occurred to me about how you might view Christmas differently now, but of course, you would. You are among the ranks of believers now, and we Christians take Christmas seriously and very joyfully. I'm glad to hear you mention church, too — how we come together as the People of God — to worship God, to celebrate God's good gifts, and to give thanks to our Maker. Everything else grows out of that — missions, outreach, evangelism, Christian education, all of it. I'm glad you want to join with fellow Christians to celebrate and worship the LORD. We know the church is not perfect, but we know we need one another. We can't possibly follow the LORD without each other, and holy days, like Christmas, are especially lovely.

"I'm also celebrating some good news I just heard from Misty Falls," Winnie added.

"Oh? What's that?" John was curious.

"I can't tell you names, of course, but I've just heard on email from a couple friends about some really great things that are happening for them. One family is getting back together after some serious trouble they have had; and another young couple has just committed to each other to be a family. Oh, and I can tell you about our grocer, Tucker Joe Tennyson. You remember Nina. She's the woman who made our wedding cake. She just emailed me to say me that Tucker Joe has fallen in love with a woman I knew slightly, and they are getting married tonight! They will say their vows following the Christmas Eve service tonight in her Presbyterian church! How about all that fun news!" Winnie laughed.

John pulled the car into the church parking lot and turned off the motor. He walked around the car and opened the door for Winnie and asked, "Sounds like Misty Falls is doing well. Do you miss it? Are you sorry you're not there to see those happy events?"

Winnie exited the car and the two began walking toward the church, holding hands. "If I was still in Misty Falls, I wouldn't have you, and you have changed my life in such a marvelous way! I can keep up with my friends on email and phone calls, but you and I live here now, and I wouldn't want it otherwise," Winnie hugged John's right arm.

"Win, you have made such an enormous difference for me. Think of it. Last Christmas we hadn't even been on a date yet, and now here we are in our own place and still on our honeymoon!" John put his arm around his wife and gave her a squeeze.

"It's hard to believe that so much has happened for us in just a year. Last Christmas morning I opened my email from you and discovered that you would be driving down to see me in Misty Falls. You wanted to take me out for New Year's Eve. That was so wonderful. You came all that way to take me out, and look what came of it! I think we began to fall in love that night, didn't we?" Winnie shared her memory.

"That was some evening! I also learned that you were a preacher, although you had left me enough clues to have deduced that business myself."

"Yes, and I was very glad to get that piece of deception out in the open and dealt with!" Winnie chuckled.

"For me it was our dancing that caused me to think seriously about you ... or, really, about us." John remembered. "Holding you in my arms and swirling with you around the ship's dining room floor was wonderful therapy for me. I hadn't been close to anyone in so long. You and I danced so well to the music, and we haven't stopped dancing. I love dancing with you at home. How about we put on some Christmas music and see if it is danceable when we get home tonight? I think it's worth a try!" John suggested.

"Oh, John! You <u>are</u> a romantic! Who would have known? I think I was right when I told Dr. Twingate I considered you to be a well-hidden secret!" Winnie exclaimed.

"The best secret of all shouldn't be hidden," John picked up on Winnie's thought. "The best secret is God's love for us. Even when we have fallen away and are hurting or out of sorts with ourselves, God is waiting to be included in our lives. God so wants to love us and to show us the good gifts He has for us. It sounds like your friends in Misty Falls have discovered that. I think that's what Christmas is all about — God sending his love to us, so we can truly see it."

Winnie snuggled warmly into John's outstretched arms, setting a loving kiss on his cheek. "Our Savior is about to arrive, and there is hope for us and the entire world."

THE END

Not an Option (a sermon)

Luke 17:1-4

Jesus said to his disciples, *'Occasions for stumbling are bound to come, but woe to anyone by whom they come! It would be better for you if a millstone were hung around your neck and you were thrown into the sea than for you to cause one of these little ones to stumble. Be on your guard! If another disciple sins, you must rebuke the offender, and if there is repentance, you must forgive. And if the same person sins against you seven times a day, and turns back to you seven times and says, 'I repent,' you must forgive.'*

Have you ever heard how a monkey is caught in the jungle? It seems that a trap is set for the monkey. To make the trap you must first hollow out a gourd, leaving an opening just large enough for the monkey to reach into the gourd. Place a sweet treat inside the gourd; then attach a vine to the gourd and stake the other end of the vine in the ground somewhere out of sight.

An unsuspecting monkey will smell the treat inside the gourd and reach inside to collect the sweet morsel. However, the opening, which is just large enough for the monkey's paw to pass through, is too small for the clinched fist to pass back through. The monkey cannot escape as long as he still holds the treat. It's a simple thing, then, for the poacher to take the monkey!

That's the picture I want us to remember this morning. When we clutch onto something and refuse to let it go, we may find ourselves in a very, spiritually dangerous place!

That's what's happening to us when we don't forgive someone who has done us wrong. When we are unforgiving, we, like the monkey with his hand stuck in the gourd, are not free of the thing we are grasping, and we are in a dangerous place for our souls.

Our scripture today is about forgiveness.

Jesus tells us several times in the gospels that we are to forgive others.

In Matthew's gospel we hear Peter asking Jesus about forgiving others. Peter began by pointing to the Jewish law, which dictated if someone sins against you, you must forgive up to three times, but Peter, thinking that he was catching on to Jesus' new way of thinking, asked the LORD if disciples should need to forgive as many as seven times.

Jesus surprised Peter by saying, *'It is not seven times to forgive another, but seventy-seven times!"* [You may remember this number to be seventy times seven, which is how the number was translated in the KJV.] Jesus' point is that it is a very big number of times we need to forgive.

Then Jesus told a parable to more clearly express what he meant:

The Kingdom of heaven can be compared to a king who was planning to settle his accounts with his slaves. There was one slave who owed the king a great deal of money, something like fifteen year's worth of wages. The slave was brought before the king who demanded the money. The slave could not repay the king. The king ordered that the slave be sold with his wife in payment. But the slave fell on his knees and begged, 'Have patience with me, and I will repay you everything.' The king, out of pity for the slave, released the man and completely forgave his debt.'

'But!' Jesus continued, 'that same slave went out from the king and came upon a fellow slave who owed him money —one hundred denarii, which would have been worth 100 day's wages. The man seized his fellow slave by the throat and demanded that he be paid in full right then. The fellow slave fell on his knees and pleaded with the man, 'Have patience with me, and I will pay you.' But the first slave refused. He had the man thrown into prison until his debt was paid. When the fellow slaves saw what had transpired, they saw the injustice of what had just happened, so they went to the king and told him. The king summoned the slave and said, 'You wicked slave!'

I forgave you all that debt because you pleaded with me. Should you not have had mercy on your fellow slave, as I have had mercy on you? Then the king had the man handed over to be tortured until he would pay his debt.'

Jesus added, *'So my heavenly Father will also do to anyone of you, if you do not forgive your brother or sister from your heart.'*

That story seems to say that our being forgiven is tied to our forgiving others.

Can that be right?

Does the forgiveness that Jesus offers me hinge on my forgiving others?

Remember when Jesus taught the disciples to pray he included, *'forgive us our trespasses as we forgive those who trespass against us.'*

Then, after teaching the prayer Jesus added, *'For as you forgive others their trespasses, your heavenly Father will also forgive you; but if you do not forgive others, neither will your Father forgive your trespasses.'*

Jesus calls us to forgive those who have offended us, or hurt us, or betrayed us, or built up some debt to us. If we were not forgiven ourselves, we would not have a mandate to be forgiving, but we HAVE been forgiven. The two forgivenesses are bound together. FORGIVENESS IS NOT AN OPTION!

Forgiving others seems to be one of those 'yeses' we say as Christians. That is to say, when we started following Jesus we said, 'Yes, LORD, I will follow you; I will go where you tell me to go; I will do what you want me to do.' That initial 'yes' implied other, yet unknown 'yeses' that will come upon us down the road as we walk with Jesus. Those 'yeses' may not be easy; and those 'yeses' WILL include forgiving others.

Before we get into how to forgive, I think it would be helpful to think about what forgiveness is not. Dr. Robert D. Enright suggests five things that forgiveness is not:

Forgiveness is not forgetting: Our memories are too good to be able to forget things that were bad enough to need forgiveness. Deep hurt can rarely be wiped out of our awareness. Time can fade the pain of some abuse, but the memory of it won't be forgotten completely.

When we are called to forgive, we are not expected to completely forget the event.

Forgiveness is not reconciling: Reconciliation takes two parties, both the abuser and the offended must agree to be reconciled. When we forgive another we are not expecting or requiring the offending party to be reconciled. [I'm sure it would be good if both parties would agree, but that is not the dynamic of forgiveness.

A good example is what Jesus did for us. He came to reconcile us to the Father through his sacrifice. God is willing to reconcile with us, but we have to be willing to be reconciled, or it doesn't work. Both sides have to agree for reconciliation.

Forgiveness is not condoning: We are not asked to excuse someone's bad or hurtful behavior when we forgive. The abuse still occurred, and we don't have to ignore it. We can forgive without excusing the person who hurt us.

Forgiveness is not dismissing: The evil deed still hurt and caused pain. It would be wrong to pretend it was inconsequential or insignificant. If we have been wronged, the offense should be taken seriously. The deed did take place.

Forgiveness is not pardoning: A pardon is a legal transaction that releases the offender from the consequences of an action such as a penalty. Forgiveness is a personal transaction that releases the one offended from the event. Let me reiterate: Forgiveness is a personal transaction that releases the one offended from the event.

Bishop Willimon, in North Alabama, once wrote: "The human animal is not supposed to be good at forgiveness. Forgiveness is not some innate, natural, human emotion. Vengeance, retribution, violence, these are natural, human qualities. It is natural for the human animal to defend itself, to snarl and crouch into a defensive position when attacked, to howl when wronged, to bite back when bitten. Forgiveness is not natural. It is not a universal human virtue."

What does it mean to forgive?

The dictionary tells us forgiveness means

To give up resentment or a claim to requital for

To grant relief from payment of

To cease to feel resentment against [the offender]

Forgiveness is very much part of the Christian life, and maybe it is a part of our lives every day.

I remember the time I gave my life to Jesus, many years ago. There was a period of about three weeks afterwards that I found various memories of mine that began popping up in my mind —things like anger over something; irritation at someone, grudges, all sorts of unsavory things. And I felt the nudging of the Holy Spirit to forgive the people who had hurt me, and to 'come clean,' if you would. I was carrying around a lot of stuff that needed to be let go. So I spent those few weeks ridding myself of those old, unforgiven pains.

I believe it's very important that we do that to have a healthy, Christian life. We must not let painful stuff build up that needs to be let go and forgiven.

Recently I learned something more, something you might call 'the rest of the story' about forgiveness.

This is not the first time I preached about forgiveness. I spoke this sermon to a church I was serving a couple of years ago. I was using the Matthew text, which had Jesus and Peter's conversation and the parable about the wicked slave.

But when I began working on today's sermon, I wanted to use a Lucan text, if possible, so I thought I'd see if Luke had a similar passage to Matthew's.

And there is, but there were a couple of differences. The Luke passage says that if a fellow disciple sins against you, you must rebuke him or her and if he or she repents you must forgive. Even if this happens seven times in a day!

Rebuking and repenting were added to the formula about forgiving. In other words, if/when you have been harmed you have the responsibility to the offender to inform him or her that something wrong has occurred, and you have been hurt.

I hadn't really thought about that before, and I imagine that's a place where we Christians don't go. How often have we gone to someone who has hurt us and rebuked him or her?

There was a situation that occurred to me a while ago. A woman I knew hurt me, and when the event took place I knew I would need to forgive her. And I have tried to do just that, but the thought of her words continued to plague me.

Then I read this verse, and I realized I needed to confront this woman and tell her how she had hurt me. So I wrote an email to her saying that, [rebuking her] and then I hit the 'send' button.

The next day I got an amazing response from the woman! She admitted how badly she had acted and wrote a lengthy note telling me how she had been wrong and begged my forgiveness. She even included a prayer in her writing.

There was something about that email response that cleared the entire situation clean and finished. It's really done!

Learning to forgive is something that applies to every one of us here. There is not one person in this room who has not been hurt by someone at some time.

This scripture is a reminder to us to forgive our offenders, just as Christ has forgiven us.

There is a picture I'd like us to take away from this sermon. It is the picture of our hand...opened, not closed into a fist. When we have a problem with someone

> Some bad experience

> A blowout with a colleague

> Abuse

> Betrayal

> Whatever it is

And we keep hold on it, we are continuing to be harmed by the thing. We are not allowing God to heal us from the event, and we are carrying it with us into future relationships. [I can imagine that some of us have kept such events alive by telling others of those memories and, in some way, even enjoying the attention and the sympathy we get from the telling.]

Just remember your hand gripping the thing and not letting go. You have then fallen into a trap, like the monkey who can't escape being caught, because his hand is stuck in the gourd. He's trapped. He's going to be somebody's dinner tonight.

Now imagine what we should be like, letting go of the things we're hanging on to that we need to let go of. When I mentioned this subject earlier I believe everyone here thought to him/herself about some situation, some person, with whom we're not too happy, whom we are still nursing a grudge or some kind of anger. Keep the picture in mind of opening your hand and letting go. You have no more reason to claim it, and you have no more interest in it. You have let it go! What freedom is ours! That's forgiveness!

Made in the USA
Charleston, SC
24 April 2013